SAVING REN.

SAVIOUR SERIES BOOK ONE.

LESLEY JONES

The Saviour Series

Book One: Saving Ren

Lesley Jones

Editing by Lisa Edward @ More Than Words Copyediting and Proofreading.

Cover Design by Tiffany Black @ T.E. Black Designs.

Cover Image by Wander Aguiar.

WARNING

This e-book contains scenes of domestic violence and both verbal and physical abuse. It also contains adult language which may be considered offensive to some readers. This e-book is intended for adults ONLY. Please store your files wisely, where under-aged readers cannot access them.

FOR THE BRAVE . . .

For those who left, and those who stayed. For those who died, and those who survived. You matter. We see you. We hear you. *You* matter.

A LITTLE HELP WITH THOSE ENGLISH/AUSSIE WORDS . . .

Glossary of Terms

The following is a glossary of terms that have been used throughout this book. These euphemisms and slang words form part of the United Kingdom's and Australian spoken word, which is the basis of this book's writing style.

Please remember that the words are not misspelt, they are slang terms and are part of the everyday United Kingdom and Australian lifestyle. This book has been written using UK English.

If you would like further explanation or to discuss the translation or meaning of a particular word, please do not hesitate to contact the author – contact details have been provided, for your convenience, at the end of this book.

Amazeballs: Amazing

Arvo: This afternoon

Bird: Female

Bloody Oath: Yes it is/Absolutely

Blue: Argument

Bogan: A person from an unsophisticated or uneducated background

Bonzer/Bonza: Excellent, attractive or pleasing

Bottle Shop: A place where you purchase alcohol

Bub or Bubby: Babe or baby

Cacks: Underwear

Chin Wag: Chat or gossip

Dag: Unfashionable, amusing, quirky, likeable person

Darl: A term of endearment, like love, hun or babe (abbreviated form for darling)

Doona:Duvet

Feral: Untidy, unclean, unkempt

Grog: Alcohol

Grommet: A young surfer

Huey: To vomit

Jog: Get lost

Leg Over: Sex

Loo: Toilet

Maccas: McDonalds

Pash: Kiss

Pash Rash: What you get from too much pashing (kissing)

POM: Of English descent

Pub: Bar

Pull: To seek out or pursue someone to make out with or get off with

Root: Sex

Screw Your Loaf: Think Carefully/Wisely

See Ya After: See you later

Shag: Sex

Sheila: Female

Shit-faced: Very drunk or off their face

Spa: Hot tub or Jacuzzi

Spit and Saw Dust: Rough pub where fights regularly break out

Swivel:A general dismissive term – leave me alone, or a stupid person

Thongs:Flip flops

Trackie Dacks: Tracksuit/Sweatpants/Jogging Bottoms

Tradie: Tradesman or builder

Tub: A bath or shower

Tubbed: To have bathed or showered

Unit: Small single-story apartment

Ute: Utility vehicle or truck (like a Hilux truck)

Vajazzle: To bling up your pubic area

Wharfie: Docker or dock worker

You Right? Are you mad/crazy?

PLAYLIST

SAVIOUR SERIES PLAYLIST

Saving Ren

PROLOGUE

2012.

My mobile clatters against the stone benchtop, and I hold my breath as I watch it slide along the surface, thankfully coming to a stop before reaching the edge and its possible demise.

Letting out a long sigh, tears of frustration burn my eyes, and my chest heaves with the force of my silent sob.

He promised.

It's Thursday night; we've not had dinner together once this week and just this morning, Jay promised he'd be home. It's now almost nine, and there's no sign of him. Since six this evening, he hasn't picked up the three calls I've made to him or responded to the two texts I've sent.

A lone tear finally escapes my eye. I swipe at it angrily, pissed off with myself for once again crying over a situation I've obviously not done enough to rectify.

I'm so tired. The anger I've aimed at myself for being the only one trying to save our marriage has consumed me. I know now, this is the end, and the admission of my defeat leaves me feeling exhausted.

The tension I've held inside has left me with a physical ache.

Not just in my poor broken heart, but in my head, neck, and shoulders. All of me aches.

Drawing in a deep breath, I pull myself together enough to slide back the doors leading to our deck, remove the cover from the spa, and turn it on.

While it's warming up, I head into our bedroom, take off my clothes, pull on my bathing costume, collect my kindle from my nightstand, and head back to the kitchen.

I want, no, I need a good cry. I need to curl up in a ball, alone in my bed, and sob my broken little heart out. Instead, I pull a piece of paper towel from the roll and dab at my eyes and nose. After disposing of the tissue in the bin, I take another moment, and for some reason, I start to laugh.

There's nothing funny about my situation, but while standing at the sink and washing my hands, I grin maniacally anyway. Retrieving my wine glass, I fill it with the crisp, cold New Zealand Sav I pull from the fridge. After rescuing my phone from where it sits precariously on the edge of the bench-top, I head outside.

My phone connects to the new Bluetooth speakers Jay's just had installed in the ceiling of our alfresco area. In the mood for comfort music, something I can drown my sorrows in and sing along to, I search for a playlist.

Because I'm short, Jay had our spa sunk into the ground, so rather than me having to climb into it, I step down.

Balancing my phone, wine, and kindle on the edge of the spa, I sink into the warm, bubbling water.

Reaching for my wine, I bring it to my lips and take a large gulp. Lowering myself further, I allow the jets to hit me right between my shoulder blades, which instantly, along with the wine and the voice of Adele, helps to finally ease some of the tension I'm feeling.

I close my eyes and relax back into the padded headrest. I've only just finished my wine when I hear the sliding of the door leading from the kitchen. When I open my eyes, Jason, my husband of twenty-four years, is standing in front of me. My eyes meet his, but I don't say a word.

He makes a big show of looking around while shrugging and shaking his head, so, despite the silence, I know precisely the kind of mood he's in.

"So, you've called me seventeen times to come home and eat. Where the fuck's my dinner?"

I wish I had more wine in my glass. I want to make my own show of dramatically taking a sip before dragging out my response. Instead, still without saying a word, I blankly stare at him for a long moment. I know it'll probably piss him off, invoke an angry response, but at this stage, I don't fucking care.

"Baked potatoes in the oven, steak and salad are in the fridge," I eventually state while placing down my wine glass and picking up and opening my kindle to the story of sparkling vampires, my eldest son's girlfriend insisted I '*must-read.*'

There's no warning, and I don't see it coming when my kindle is snatched from my hands and slung across the deck. Before I even get a chance to see where it lands, I'm grabbed by the messy bun my hair is in, a hand wraps tightly around my throat, and I'm pulled from the spa.

My shins hit the sides; my hands too slow to find purchase on the edge of the spa to be able to lift myself out.

"Jay, please, stop. You're hurting me. Please, please stop," I choke out. My protests go unheard as I continue to be dragged on my knees across the deck.

Unable to breathe, my eyes stream with tears of pain and absolute fear. When he finally releases my throat, I barely manage to gasp in a breath before his hand moves to the back of my neck. He keeps an agonising grip on my hair, but I instantly forget the burn in my scalp when he rams my face into our fridge door.

His hot breaths hit the side of my face, the stench of alcohol filling my nose, all while forcing my cheek against the stainless steel and holding it there.

"I'll tell you once, and once fucking only, get my dinner out of wherever you've put it, and get it on the table *now*. Right. Fucking now, Lauren," he spits into my ear.

Roughly, he pulls me back, away from the fridge.

"Open the fucking door," he demands.

I choke out a sob, my eyes and nose stream, my head pounds, and my heart bangs hard inside my chest as I pull the fridge door open. I reach for the plate with the steak I seasoned earlier on it, but it's snatched from my hand as Jay roars, "What the fuck is this? It's not even cooked. All those times you called and told me to get home, and you've not even cooked it."

He finally releases his grip on my hair, and for a few long seconds, the pain is actually worse.

“It's steak, I didn't want to ruin it, so I wasn't going to cook it till you got home.” I can barely breathe, let alone talk through my sobs.

“That's why I kept calling…” I attempt to gasp out my explanation, but he cuts me off by spinning me around with so much force, my back slams against the fridge, and the whole thing shifts.

“That's why I called,” I try again. “I just wanted to know what time you'd be home, so I didn't ruin the steak. . . I didn’t want it ruined,” I sob.

His eyes meet mine as he pins me by my throat and for an infinitesimal moment, he's there, Jay, my husband, the man I've spent over half my life loving, he's there.

And then he's gone.

He launches the plate across the kitchen; I watch as it crashes into the sink, breaking into four large pieces.

I'm not sure if it's his fist or his palm that makes contact with the side of my head, but the blow takes me off my feet, and I crash to the floor.

"Well, it's sure as fuck ruined now." Jay stands over me and sneers while I curl into the foetal position. "My steak, my night, my entire fucking life, you ruined it all. You're nothing but a fat, lazy, useless bitch."

My ears are ringing, but I hear his words and the venom and spite with which they're delivered.

The blow from his boot hits me low in the belly. While I gasp for breath, he turns and leaves while I vomit over the kitchen tiles we chose together when building our dream home.

* * *

I'M NOT sure how much later it is my tears finally stop. I'm still lying on the cold kitchen tiles. My heart rate has slowed, the pain in my scalp eased, and the echo of my blood whooshing through my ears has quietened. The bubbling of the spa and Nazareth's cover of 'Love Hurts' filter in from the alfresco. Pulling my knees to my chest, I wrap my arms around them, wincing at the pain the movement causes. My stomach cramps and I wonder for a moment if I'm going to throw up again. Rocking from side to side, I contemplate my next move.

I should leave tonight, things have become progressively worse between us over the past couple of months, but he's never been this violent towards me before.

You'd think at my age it'd be an easy decision to make. I'm forty-four, my kids are grown, but my only income is from my interior design business, and that's been a bit hit and miss of late due to a lack of effort on my part. I've become *that* woman. I lunch, I get my nails done, my brows and lashes, my hair. I'm not big on the gym, but I enjoy my weekly yoga class. I meet my friends for lunch and drinks, and we have girls' weekends away. All of this has meant I've let my business slide, but I'm good at what I do, and I'm sure I could soon pick up clients old and new if I put the word out I was looking for work.

I have friends, close friends. I have brothers, a sister, and my own two sons, who I know wouldn't hesitate to help me out. But there's not a single one of them I've told about the deterioration of my marriage over these past few months.

Given time, I thought Jay would change. But now, lying here feeling devastated by my husband's abuse, isolated by the secret I'm keeping from people, I know love and care about me, and devoid of any hope that things are likely to improve, I know I have to get out. I need to escape this marriage. I need to find the woman I used to be or at least a version of her. And to do that, I'm going to have to confide in someone and ask for help.

CHAPTER 2

Lauren

As soon as I hear Jay's key in the front door, I rush to use the heel of my hand to wipe the tears from my face and attempt to compose myself.

Deep breaths.

Relax.

Don't let him even *think* you might be awake.

It's dark, and I know. . . I know he can't see me, but the irrational part of my brain is scared he'll somehow know I'm awake. This has been the routine every night since he attacked me almost a week ago.

I contemplated sleeping in one of the spare rooms the night he attacked me, but I've done that before, and it just made things worse. Much like the way he dragged me out of the spa the other night, in the past, he's dragged me from one of the spare rooms and back to our bed, just so he could carry on the fight, and I really don't think I have any more fight left in me. Thankfully, he's stayed out late every night since then, and there's been zero communication between us.

ROLLING onto my side and into the recovery position, I settle facing away from Jay's side of the bed.

My heart rate picks up as I hear our bedroom door open.

I know exactly what to do as it closes.

I've done this so many times lately it's become my new normal. That realisation alone has me swallowing back a sob.

Now is not the time for tears. The time for sentimentality is *over.*

That time has passed.

Deep breaths.

Relax.

Don't let him even *think* you might be awake.

I keep my breathing slow and steady, not altering its pattern as he slides into bed beside me.

His hand lands heavily on my waist, and he gives it a squeeze. It takes everything in me not to freeze or attempt to back away from his touch.

I used to crave his touch, used to long for it. It's a touch that once upon a time, I couldn't live without. Never imagined I'd have to, let alone want to, but all I can think right now is how dare he. After what he did to me just days ago, without even attempting to make any kind of apology, how dare he come home here and instigate any form of intimacy.

After a minute or two, I make out to twitch, first my leg, then my arm, the way you sometimes do when you're dreaming or just about to fall asleep, this seems to do the trick. I hear him sigh and turn his back to me.

On the outside, my breaths remain steady. Inside, the sigh I let out is even more significant than his.

When my husband begins to snore, I allow my silent tears to once again fall. I allow the sense of failure to once again wash over me.

Never did I think my life would end up this way.

Never did I think our relationship would take the path it has.

Yeah, it's always been fiery, right from the beginning it's been like that. We're two very passionate people. We love hard and fight dirty. I'm a redhead and have the temper to match. My husband used to duck and then laugh when I threw something at him during the heat of an argument. Then he'd walk away until we'd both calmed down.

Our arguments never lasted long because we've never been able to keep our hands off each other. Our make-up sex was as passionate as our arguments and always meant that we'd usually kiss and make up before morning when we did fight. We'd argue, we'd fight, we'd fuck like a pair of crazy people, I'd cry, we'd both say sorry, and then we'd talk things through. It's not a pattern that'd work for everyone, a lot of couples would probably consider it unhealthy, but it worked for us.

Until it didn't.

Until it changed.

The arguments became more frequent.

The words we spat more vicious.

The apologies went unspoken.

The make-up sex replaced by violence.

For almost a year, Jay has been angry almost all of the time. His anger always directed at me, I'm left never knowing which version of my husband will be walking through the door in the evening. Each of our confrontations becoming more physical. But, instead of ending it with a passionate fucking on the kitchen table as we grind out our apologies, there are fists in my face, bruises around my throat, clumps of hair ripped from my head, but almost worse than all of that, worse than what happened the other night, are the endless days of silence between us.

I live with a permanent knot in my stomach, lump in my throat, and a sense of dread every time my husband walks through the door.

I'm permanently walking on eggshells around him. Too scared to talk in case I say something that pisses him off, and it escalates into another act of violence towards me.

I can't sleep, I've no interest in food, and my nerves are shattered. I'm lost and lonely. I thought he was my best friend, but apparently, I was wrong on that score. Who treats their best friend the way he's been treating me?

The worst part of all is the not knowing why. I have no idea what's changed, why this shift in his personality. If he's fallen out of love with me, why not just ask for a divorce, move on?

My boys have grown up and left home, so we don't need to stay together for them. Our life together has been good, almost perfect. We've always had great friends and a great social life. Jay's business has been successful to the point I only work when I want to. I'll take on a client if they seek me out, but other than that, I really have become a lady who lunches.

We've done the hard yards. Worked our arses off, raised a family, and now's the time we should be kicking back and reaping the rewards of all we've put into building this life.

Except right now, all I feel is confused, heartbroken, and shattered. My whole world has fallen down around me, and I'm clueless as to why it's happened.

NEVER DID I think I'd become a victim of domestic violence. Never did I think I'd put up with that kind of shit from my husband. But for almost a year, I've allowed Jay's actions towards me to escalate, I should've left at the first hair pull, the first squeeze of my throat, my jaw, the first grab of my wrist that left bruises, but I didn't. In the beginning, I tried to talk, to reason with him. I even attempted to fight back, but I quickly learned that would earn me a harder grab, a tighter squeeze, a more vicious pull of my hair, and now it's come to this, an all-out assault that left me bruised, bleeding, and curled in the foetal position on my kitchen floor.

I've felt crippling shame for putting up with his behaviour but now that I've *made* the decision to leave, I have a little more clarity. I'm still ashamed, I'm not sure that will ever leave me, not until I can come up with reasons as to *why* I stayed and allowed it to carry on for so long, but I am now ready to make changes and get the fuck out of Dodge.

I'll no longer allow myself to become another statistic; no longer will I be a victim. It's time to fight back, and the first return shot I need to fire will be leaving this marriage.

Victim. I hate that word only because I know that's exactly what I am. What I've allowed myself to become. I've lost sight of *me,* Lauren, and the woman I used to be.

I'll never get her back. The woman I was has gone, changed forever by events of the past months. Now it's time to find the new version of me and take back control.

Yes, I'm scared, scared *of* him, scared *for* me. Scared of what my future might look like.

But I refuse to allow my life to continue on this path of destruction. I refuse to remain a victim. I refuse to remain lost.

Whatever demons Jay's fighting, he's shut me out and refused to share with me, and I'm no longer prepared to be his punching bag while he sorts his shit out.

CHAPTER 3

Lauren

I STARE AT JEANETTE, the manager of the bank that's held our accounts ever since we moved to the area from the city, over twenty years ago. She's seen us through the setting up of our businesses, countless mortgages and loans, and watched our boys grow into men. And here she is now, witnessing the horror I must be displaying as she explains that there is no money. Our savings are currently sitting at zero balance. The last of the funds in there had to be transferred to our everyday account after Jay withdrew five hundred dollars last night, and the direct debit for our phone bills had come out this morning.

Scrutinising my reaction, I'm grateful I've waited all week before coming in and having this conversation with Jeanette. A few days ago, I'd probably be in tears again by now, but I've spent the time getting my head around the situation I've been smacked upside the head with, and I've had to come to terms with the reality of my situation.

I need to tell my friends what's going on.

I need to ask for help.

I need to leave Jay.

"Lauren?"

My head jerks back at the sound of my name. I'm looking right at Jeanette but seeing only the one million and one things I need to do to get my life into some sort of order and finding out we have no money in our savings account will make all of that a lot more complicated.

I'm not sure if I'm hot or cold. My skin burns while ice coats my insides as this latest realisation hits me.

"Were you not aware of the—"

"And the credit cards?" I ask, bracing for the answer.

"Well, here's the thing, nothing has been spent on those, not in a while."

Realisation hits as to why that is as Jeanette slides a statement towards me.

"I have his card," I explain. "I was ordering a new telly online; I always use my credit card for anything big because of the air miles. My card was in my bag, in the bedroom, Jay's card was in his wallet, which was sitting on the coffee table in front of me."

I remember it clearly because of the way he'd grabbed at my wrist when I'd reached for his wallet.

"What the fuck are you doing?" he'd snapped at me.

"I just need your card for a minute. Mine's in the bedroom."

"Ask next time," he'd said as he flicked the card in my direction.

By the time I'd processed the order and the payment, he'd gone for a shower, taking his wallet with him. I'd tucked his card into my pocket and then into my bag when I'd realised I still had it a few weeks later.

"I don't know what else I can tell you, Lauren. The business banking account is no longer held with us, so I can't tell you the state that's in, but your personal accounts, well, they aren't looking too flash right now."

"The business accounts have been moved? Since when?" I ask at this revelation; one I was unaware of.

I watch as her fingers move rapidly across the keyboard in front of her.

"Over a year ago now. Did you not know?"

"No, I didn't." Jeanette looks at me waiting for more. Not only do I not have it, but I'm also not about to spill my guts about my personal life to my bank manager.

My head spinning, I let out a long breath and begin to stand.

"Thanks, Jeanette. I'll try and find out what's going on and get some funds transferred from the business across, but they probably won't show up until Monday."

"No worries, Lauren. Hopefully, it's like you say, and Jay's just robbing Peter to pay Paul while waiting for a bill to be settled for money owing to the business."

I offer her a weak smile. Both of us knowing that probably isn't the case.

Feeling sick to my stomach, I sit in my car outside the bank and consider my options. We have a safe at home. I know it contains documents and jewellery as well as the money Jay keeps in there from cash jobs he's not declared through the business. The alarm is linked to an app on our phones, and we both get alerts when it's opened. I've had no alerts lately, so I know he hasn't been in there, but he'll get the alert if I open it.

I know my boys won't hesitate to help me out, but I don't want to drag them into this. I could ask my family, but again, I'd much rather keep them out of this until I'm away from Jay. Starting my car, I come to a decision. I know who it is that'll have my back, offer me money, a bed, and anything else I might need. I spend the drive home playing out in my head exactly how I'm going to explain everything to my girls tonight.

* * *

Despite my building nerves, I've been looking forward to this night all week. After the way things have played out over the past couple of days, a loud, raucous night of drunken girl talk, the chance to forget about everything else and the decision I've come to, is needed more than ever. I've never disclosed the violent nature of my domestic situation to any of my girlfriends. As far as they're concerned, I have a great marriage. And for over twenty years, I did. That's the gutting thing about all of this. What once was so good has become incredibly bad in such a short space of time, and I still don't know why it's happened. The sad fact now is, I don't care why. I've come to realise the past couple of days that it's gone past that point, and my mind is made up. I just hope one day, Jay wakes up and realises all that he's thrown away. I'm a good person. I've been a good wife and mother. I've given everything to those roles, but now I need to take care of me. The level of violence Jay aimed at me the other night is the worst ever. I know I should've spoken up sooner, got out earlier, fought back, whatever, but I honestly always thought I could fix things, and it breaks my heart to know that now, I don't want to.

Before I went to the bank this afternoon, I spent the morning loading my car with family photo albums and other keepsakes that Jay wouldn't notice were missing. He has a golf day with the boys tomorrow, the course over an hour's drive away. Once he leaves, I plan on packing the rest of my stuff. Then I'll remove the cash and anything else I need from the safe and be gone before he can get back home. I don't yet know where I'm going, I've not thought that far ahead. I just know before there's a repeat of what happened five nights ago, I need to get out.

* * *

As a child, I'd hated my curly red hair. It'd made me a target for bullies, and I'd had to put up with so much name-calling, it got to the point I'd sworn that as soon as I was old enough, I'd have it straightened and dye it black. But at around the age of fifteen or sixteen, I'd realised my curly red mane made me stand out from the crowd. All of my friends were blonde or brunette, and I enjoyed the sense of individuality it gave me, and I won't lie, I began to love the attention my red hair garnered.

With the help of a good quality styling product and my GHD's, tonight I'm wearing my hair in big bouncy, seventies style waves, rather than its natural loose curls.

I'd opted on jeans, tucked into long boots, and a chiffon blouse, with a short leather jacket over the top as my outfit. As I got dressed, Jay's words from Sunday night and previous times over the past few months play through my head.

'Useless fat bitch.'

'Ugly fat fuck.'

'What the fuck did I ever see in you?'

'You've let yourself go, Lauren. Look at the fucking state of you.'

For a few short moments, I'd felt delighted that everything I put on felt loose, but when I remembered the extra layer of foundation and concealer I'd had to wear to hide the bruise on my cheek and the ugly purple now black bruise covering my hip, the cost of the weight loss caused me to steady myself at the bathroom sink, and draw in a few deep breaths so I wouldn't cry and ruin my makeup.

I was fortunate to have been blessed with good genes, and with a good skincare regime, a few injections, and a lot of vanity, I'd always looked younger than my forty-four years, but staring at myself in the mirror now, for the first time in my life, I look older than my years. I'd done what I could with my makeup, but as I take in my watery gaze, the dark circles under my eyes, and the hollows under my cheeks, there's no disguising the amount of weight even I hadn't realised I'd dropped and the fact that it's aged me.

Fighting the burn of tears and the tremble of my lips, I stare down at my hands as they grip the marble counter, and I make a decision. Pursing my lips, I blow out a couple of breaths, pull off my wedding, engagement, and eternity rings, and throw them in my makeup bag.

"Fuck Him," I tell my reflection through gritted teeth.

My phone buzzes from where it sits on the edge of the sink, and I physically jump at the sound.

"Motherfucker." I laugh at my reflection while pressing my palm to my chest. My eye is instantly drawn to my bare hand. A hand that, until this week, has worn some kind of a mark of my commitment to Jason East since I was eighteen years old.

"Fuck Him," I repeat, before reading the message from Jo, letting me know she was five minutes away in the cab.

Swiping on my lipstick and giving myself another spray of perfume, I head out to the front of my house.

* * *

SLIDING into the cab next to Jo, I'm grateful for the darkness as the interior light switches off. As an accountant, Jo has an eye for details, and not much gets past her, and I'm now hyper-aware of the fact, my weight loss is apparent. After we air kiss and exchange 'how are you's', I sit as far back into the corner as possible.

"Hair looks good. It's got long. How've you been?"

A wall of every kind of emotion hits me, causing my resolve not to cry to crumble. It's the 'how are you's,' and the 'you okay's?' that get to me every time.

I swallow down the ball of emotion attempting to rise from my chest to my throat while staring out the window as views of the beach and Port Phillip Bay appear between the trees that line the foreshore.

"I've been good, and thank you. It's because I straightened it before adding the big curls, it always makes it look longer," I croak out.

I don't have to look in Jo's direction to know that her eyes are burning a path to my face.

"Okay. What's going on? What's wrong?" she snaps.

My tears spill and I use the side of my finger under each eye to catch them. I shake my head.

"Loz?" she questions softly, her concern now apparent.

"I'll explain, I promise, but I don't want to walk into the pub looking like I've been crying."

I finally turn my gaze to meet hers. "Please? Right now, I just need a drink. Then I'll talk, and believe me, you're gonna need a drink for this too."

She's nodding before I finish talking. "One drink, and then you spill," she says as we pull up outside the bar.

* * *

Jo grabs my hand, and I walk behind her as we smile at the bouncers and enter the bar. Seeing Jemma and Lou set up at a table in the corner, we head over. They have wine chilling in a bucket with glasses standing to attention and waiting to be filled. After kisses all around, I pour myself and Jo a drink, clink glasses with everyone, say "cheers", and take a very large swig before sitting on a stool at the high-top table.

"Shit, I so need this," I declare after almost draining my glass.

"You okay?" asks Jemma. "You look tired, and you've lost even *more* weight."

Jemma is my oldest friend, and like Jo, never misses a beat. Because we've known each other since I first moved to Australia from England as a moody thirteen-year-old, she knows me better than anyone and has seriously been on my case these past few months, constantly asking if everything's okay with me. I'm hit with a pang of guilt as I recall the many times I've come close to telling her everything and then backed out.

Jason and Jem's husband, Max, are pretty good mates and I know that once Jemma is made aware of what's going on, there will be no turning back. She'll tell Max, and knowing him like I do, he'll have no hesitation in confronting Jay.

"Yeah, I'm fine," I say, not wanting to dampen the mood by telling them about my woes so soon into the night. "Just had a shitty week."

I catch Jo's brows raise at my response, but choose to ignore her and look back at Jem as she asks, "Why? What's happened?"

That's when I notice Lou's gaze following our exchange with wide-eyed anticipation. This was planned. When I then look between Jo and Jemma and catch them exchanging raised brow headshakes, I'm hit with the realisation this night has been organised with the purpose of my girls finding out what's going on with me.

In that moment, I both love and dislike them very much.

Drink in hand, I take a moment to look each of them in the eye. Licking my dry lips, I draw in a deep breath and swallow.

"Okay, ladies, this is how it's gonna go. I really, really need to have some fun tonight. If you can give me a few hours of that, I promise, I will explain everything."

My heart thumps against my chest as one pair of brown eyes and two pairs of blue pin me in place

"We can give you that," Jemma says. "But before tonight is over, you are gonna tell us whatever the fuck it is that's going on."

"I will, I promise," I agree.

Lou raises her glass. "To the best friends and floors that will always hold us up," she declares our usual toast.

"To friends and floors," we join in.

* * *

We sit, we chat shit, and we catch up with what's going on in each of our lives. The girls don't question the fact I have very little to add to the conversation, and with the wine flowing, I finally begin to unwind.

Jemma and Lou both have younger children, so Jo and I both smile and nod in the right places when they share their stories about them. I had my kids young, with both my boys now in their twenties. My heart kicks against my chest, and my stomach churns at the notion of having to tell them what's gone on between me and their dad, and I make the decision right then to keep it from them for as long as possible. No matter their age, they'll always be my babies, and it'll always be my job to protect them.

At just fifteen, Jo had been even younger than me when she'd had her son, Joe, who's now thirty. Her parents were thrilled when that news broke. . . Not! Her boyfriend's even less so. They'd forbidden their son from having any contact with Jo, he then denied the baby was his. The whole family then moved interstate. With Jo's family disowning her, she would have been left to raise her son alone without us and our parents. Each of our mums had stepped up and helped Jo with a place to stay, and then with childcare after Joe was born. This enabled Jo to work while she put herself through university, eventually qualifying with degrees in accounting and commerce. She now owns her own accountancy firm, employing around six staff.

Men have come and gone over the years, but sadly—for them, not so much for Jo—none have been able to handle her strong, feisty, and fiercely independent personality.

* * *

AFTER SHARING three bottles of wine, and lots of conversation, we decide to move on to somewhere where we can dance. Not wanting to be surrounded by drunken kids falling all over the place, we head for a bar off Main Street that we know stays open late and always has a great live band and a small dance floor.

The wine, being with my friends, and listening to their easy conversation have me feeling more at ease than I have in weeks, months even. I've even found myself laughing a few times during the evening, before a flash of what my life has become and the uncertainties I'm facing hit me, and my stomach does a backflip or three.

The bar is packed, with just about everyone in the place singing along with the band's cover of Joe Jackson's 'Is She Really Going out with Him?', as we enter.

Jemma raises her fist and punches the air as she shouts, "Woohoo, it's 80's night."

"Oh no, this is gonna get messy." Lou sighs.

Jo hooks her arm through mine, pulling me towards the bar. "Let's get fucked up. When was the last time we had a big night together?"

"I can't," I lean into her ear and say, "I've got a big day tomorrow, and I need to have my head on straight for it."

We stop moving. Jo takes both my hands in hers and squeezes them. Her brown eyes fixed on mine, she stares at me for a few seconds.

"If you just wanna enjoy tonight and talk tomorrow, we can meet for breakfast. I get it if you don't wanna ruin the vibe, but we do need to talk. It's killing all of us, seeing you go through something you're not sharing when you're always the first one there for any of us."

My nose tingles as emotions clog my throat, and all I can do is nod.

"How about we just see how tonight goes, hey?"

Jo flicks her long, honey-blonde hair over her shoulder and shakes her head.

"It's 70's and 80's night, we know exactly how it's gonna go. We're all gonna drink too much, we're gonna get loud, a song will get played that makes us all emotional, one of us, either you or Lou will likely cry, and we'll all end up singing, and you'll do it badly and very out of tune."

I nudge her arm with my shoulder. "My singing's not that bad," I protest.

Lou and Jemma turn from the bar to face us, and along with Jo, say in unison, "Yeah, it is."

I shake my head before joining in the chorus and singing along with Mr Jackson as Jemma orders a round of shots.

We're just one song in, and already the music is evoking memories of my formative years. Of my life back in Barking on the outskirts of London, before my dad moved us all over to Australia when I was just thirteen.

I'd been angry at the whole world, but especially my parents when we'd first arrived in Australia. Music had been one of the things to help get me through the trauma of being 'dragged away' from my friends and everything that was familiar.

It had to be British music though. As another act of defiance aimed at my parents for ruining my life, I would only listen to songs recorded from the UK charts onto the mixtapes my friends from England would send me.

I'd lay in my room for hours, listening to bands like The Clash, The Jam, and The Specials. Sobbing my little heart out, desperate to go back to the place I loved most in the world. . . Home.

It wasn't until I had my own children, I finally came to appreciate why my parents made the move, and why they'd wanted to get us out of London. It was to give us what they hoped would be a better start, and eventually a better life for myself, my two brothers, and my sister. And it has been. I've lived a life and done and seen things my friends in Barking could only ever dream of.

Despite now being in Australia for thirty years, I still had a pretty strong Essex accent and a big Essex girl attitude. Like the saying goes, 'You can take the girl out of Essex, but you'll never take the Essex out of the girl.' And I was glad of that. That accent and attitude is part of who I am, the attitude though, is sadly part of what I've lost over these past months. I just need to dig deep and find her again, I need to find me. And that all starts with leaving my abusive husband, something I plan on doing tomorrow.

"Where did you go?" Jem asks as she shoves a shot glass in my hand.

"London," I tell her. "The eighties, right before we moved here. It's amazing the memories one song can drag up."

Jem knocks her glass against mine.

"Here's to the angry ranga kid, who rocked up to my school wearing stripy tights Doc Martens, a tiny denim skirt, a Sex Pistols t-shirt, and a really, really bad attitude."

"Here's to her," I agree, swallowing my drink down around the ever-present ball of emotion.

ORDERING ANOTHER ROUND OF SHOTS, along with a double of hard liquor for each of us, we find a table and ask the barman to bring our drinks over. This isn't the kind of establishment to sit down, we just need a table to put our drinks on so we can keep an eye on them if we dance.

We do the usual scan of the place, nod and smile at the faces we know. When our drinks arrive, we knock back the shots before I pick up my vodka, lime, soda, and turn and face the dance floor.

Knowing I have a lot to organise in the morning, I make a mental note to only have one more drink after this. I'm enjoying the buzz, the alcohol I've consumed has me feeling relaxed enough to want to dance, but with my emotions so close to the surface, I'm aware that can switch in a heartbeat, resulting in me having a major meltdown on Main Street. The instant the D chord is played by the band's opening of 'Should I Stay or Should I Go' by The Clash, I realise just how easily triggered I am. The song title's irony isn't lost on me as I knock back my vodka right along with my tears.

Fuck you, Jason East, you are not going to ruin this night the way you've ruined my life. Taking off my jacket, I grab an empty beer bottle from the table, and holding it in front of me like a mic, I begin to sing. Jemma finds her own bottle and joins me. Some random bloke from the dance floor hooks his arms over our shoulders, and we take it in turns to share our bottle/mics with him.

Random Bloke goes back to his mates when the music changes, and Jem and I climb onto a chair and serenade the crowd with our word-perfect rendition of American Pie—all six verses. It's not until I jump up on a table at the opening chords of 'Paradise by the Dashboard Light', that a barman finally comes over and confiscates our mics, threatening to throw me out if I climb on anything else, that our floor show has to end.

The barman holds out his hand, which I take, bowing, waving, and blowing kisses to my adoring audience, some of whom boo at the poor boy.

With a grin on my face and feeling so very much better than I did at the start of the night, I grab a drink from the table and take a chug.

"Hey, that's mine," Lou complains as she takes it from me. "Jo's at the bar now getting a round in."

I look towards the bar for Jo, about to head over and ask her to get me a bottle of water along with my drink, when I see that she's pressed forehead to forehead in deep conversation with someone.

"We could be waiting a while, Jo's on the prowl, and it looks like she's found tonight's victim," I announce.

"Uh oh. Jo's on the pull, lock up your sons," Jemma says from beside me.

"Naaa, she's not on the pull," Lou chimes in. "He's far too old for our Jo; he must be at least. . . thirty-five."

The three of us cackle like a coven of witches, apparently a little too loudly, I realise, when Jo and her friend both look up. I'm instantly struck silent at the most magnificent blue eyes I've ever witnessed.

CHAPTER 4

Gabe

"WHAT DO you mean they don't have the bricks in stock?" I snap at Michelle, our receptionist and office all-rounder down the phone.

"Exactly what I said. Ausbrick is waiting on a delivery. When they arrive, they'll call me back, but it probably won't be until Tuesday."

"Who did you talk to? Get hold of them, and I'll talk to them." I slam my phone down on my desk and lean back in my chair.

"Bro, chill out, stop shouting at the staff. What the fuck is wrong with you this morning?" my brother, Zac, asks.

Staring across to where he's sat behind his own desk, I shrug. If I tell him, he'll probably take the piss and tell me to go and spend the weekend getting laid.

"Did someone piss on your cornflakes this morning? You've

been an arsehole all day. You need to go out there and apologise to Michelle before she leaves."

Raking my hand through my hair, I let out a frustrated sigh.

"Ava cancelled. Her mate, Sophie, who was coming with her this weekend is sick. She's going away with her Mum and Dean next week, so now I won't get to see her until we all go away. "

"That's only two weeks away, then you'll get her for an entire week." Giving another shrug, along with a headshake, I meet his gaze head-on and admit, "Yeah, I know, but I miss my kid. I want to see more of her not less, plus I've cleared my schedule and now have no fucking clue what to do with myself."

"Dude, you're thirty-five, single, with fanny on tap. I'm sure you can come up with something."

"Believe it or not, sometimes fanny on tap gets boring."

"That'd be an 'or not' from me. Nor do I believe for a second that fanny on tap ever gets boring."

"Can you dickheads be good children and stop talking about fanny on tap?" Daniella, our sister calls from her office.

"Sorry," we both call back.

"Well, if you're up for it, me and Coop are going for a few beers down Main Street tonight, you're welcome to come with. You'd actually be doing me a massive favour. You know Coop, he only has one topic of conversation."

"Work," Dani, Zac and I all say in unison.

"I heard that, you cheeky fuckers. I do not always talk about work. I only talk about work once we've finished bitching about Gabe, which tends to take most of the night."

Cooper's lanky six-foot-four frame appears in the doorway to his office. His space is bigger and separate from mine and Zac's. Coop's our architect and also deals with contracts, planning, and all the complicated shit for our construction company. After our dad retired and we took over the running of the family business, he complained he couldn't focus when Zac and I were both in the office at the same time, so we sectioned him off and gave him his own space.

Daniella looks after our accounts and had taken over our dad's office for the same reason.

"Come and have a beer with your big brothers tonight, we'll look after you," Coop says. "Then tomorrow morning, you can come and help me and Zac gently persuade Frank Carroll to pay the money he still owes us."

As much as I like to make them think otherwise, I love my brothers. I love all of my family and like nothing better than spending time with them. Acting like it's not one of my favourite things to do, I pretend to think about it for a minute, let out a long huff, and reply, "Yeah, okay, let's do it."

* * *

AFTER GOING HOME for a quick shower and a change of clothes, I meet Zac and Coop at a sports bar along the esplanade. We then call into a few different places, having a drink in each as we make our way to Drifters, a bar that usually attracts an older crowd and has good live music.

The place is packed, and it takes a while for us to get served. Once we do, we find a spot at the end of the bar and take a look around.

Most of the faces I recognise, some I give a chin lift, others I avoid making eye contact with, mostly the women. I've been single a long time, so there have been a lot of one-night stands, and a few of them are here tonight.

I wasn't a relationship kind of bloke. It was never a conscious choice to remain single, I'd love to have what my brothers have. They're both very happily married and do not mess around on their wives, but I've had shit happen in my past that has ruined any chance of that happening for me. I don't find it easy to trust or allow anyone else in, and I've never met a woman I wanted to change all that for. My brothers are my best friends, their wives, my sister, and my daughter, the only women I can honestly say I've ever loved since the death of my mum. Casual hook ups have been my coping mechanism, and that's worked fine until recently, when weekends like this, when I don't have my daughter Ava around, make me realise just how lonely I am.

"Any of your harem in here tonight?" Coop asks as his eyes scan the room.

Turning around and resting my elbows against the top of the bar, I take a swig of my beer.

"Yeah, a couple. No one I'd like to take for a repeat run."

"You okay, bro? I know you said you were down about Ava cancelling, but you seem *really* down. Is there something else going on?" Zac asks, genuine concern apparent in his voice as both my brothers turn and position themselves beside me.

"I dunno," I admit, letting out a sigh. "I'm just fucking over it, ya know? Sick of the one and dones, over the drama queens who don't even know me but think they want more. I want something, but I don't know what."

"Mate, when you meet that person, your person. . . when *that* happens, you'll know, believe me. That first time you look at her, something will just click, and it'll be like, 'now that's what I'm talking about,' and that's when you'll be fucked," Zac says.

Cooper nudges me. "It's the best, the worst, and the most terrifying thing you'll ever experience next to becoming a father." I watch as he takes a chug from his beer bottle before turning to me and saying, "It sucks you didn't have that with Lena, there's nothing better than creating a new life with that person, *your* person."

"I don't think it'll ever happen for me. My head and my heart have been too fucked up by my past."

"No, they haven't. You just think that because you still

haven't met *the one,* when you do, nothing will stop ya. You won't let anything get in the way," Zac adds.

"You'll have no say in the fucking matter, dude. It'll be totally out of your control," Coop adds with a chuckle.

My gut clenches, terrified that I might never get to experience all of that, *terrified that I will.*

"Right, enough of the brotherly advice. Your round, dude, I'll have bourbon please, this beer is making me piss like a racehorse." Cooper places his empty bottle on the bar before disappearing in the direction of the toilets.

Pulling my wallet from my back pocket, I remove my card. Resting my elbow on the bar top, my bank card between my fingers, I attempt to make eye contact with one of the staff.

"You sure that's all that's wrong?" Zac asks from beside me.

"I'm sure," I say without looking at him.

"It's not because of Lena and the new baby?"

"Absolutely, most definitely not. I'm glad she's finally found what makes her happy. Maybe she'll stop being such a bitch now."

"I doubt that." Zac laughs from beside me, just as the barmaid approaches.

I add a shot for each of us to the order, the barmaid pouring them at the same time Cooper arrives back.

"Jo Myer just walked in. My balls are never sure if they wanna explode or shrivel up and disappear when that woman's around. If I weren't a married man, I would so go there. If you ever tell Jess I said that, I'll drown you in the fucking bay."

Zac and I laugh while shaking our heads. Comments like that usually come from me and him, not Coop. I totally get it though. Jo *is* gorgeous but fucking fierce. She owns the accountancy firm that looks after our tax affairs. She's smoking hot, but sadly for both of us, she's never fallen for my charms. Reaffirming she didn't mix business with pleasure, every single time I'd asked her out for a drink.

"Who's she with?" Zac enquires.

"No clue, a bunch of women equally as hot as she is." Coop replies. At around five-ten in her heels, Jo is pretty tall for a woman, and with her long, honey-blonde hair, when I look over Zac's shoulder, it isn't hard to spot her standing at the other end of the bar.

She's holding the hands of a little redhead, leaning in, frowning, and talking animatedly. The redhead has her back to me, but because of her lack of height, I can't get a clear view.

The two women standing at the bar in front of them turn around and say something that makes them all laugh. They knock back shots and order another round before making their way over to a table at the side of the dance floor.

"Gabe?"

"What?" I turn back to see my brothers both staring at me, along with Jack Cole, a carpenter who's done some great work for our company, and who we've attempted to talk into taking a full-time position with us, but he's decided to start developing on his own. I give Jack a chin lift and get a nod in return before he carries on his conversation with Cooper.

"What the fuck dude, are you on something tonight?" Zac asks.

"Get fucked," I snap back at my brother.

"Jack's just saying Frank Carroll owes him seven grand," Cooper turns our way and states.

"Does he now?" asks Zac. "You wanna come with us tomorrow morning and pay him a visit? He has a holiday home further down the peninsula, and we've been given the tip he'll be there this weekend."

"I'm in. What time you going?"

"Early," I reply. "We'll catch him in his jocks, make him feel vulnerable. I've had enough of his excuses. He either comes up with the cash tomorrow, or we take his fucking car."

"Is his car worth what he owes?" Jack asks.

"He drives a Maserati, so yeah, I'd say so," Cooper states.

"And if it isn't, at the very least it'll inconvenience the cunt," Zac adds.

Frank Carroll is a client we'd built a shopping complex for at the beginning of the year. He'd added a few extras to the build that weren't in the original drawings. They'd added an extra thirty-thousand dollars to the project, which we were still waiting to be paid for.

"What work did you do for him?" I ask Jack.

"I built a custom kitchen at a day care centre in Brighton for him last year."

"See, that's why you should only work for us. We always pay our trades," Coop tells him with a wink.

"Yeah, rookie mistake. I'd only been living over this side of the city a short while; I hadn't heard about his reputation."

"Well, we were born and raised here, knew all about his reputation, but because we've done work for him before, and he's always paid, we mistakenly thought we could trust him. Never again," Zac states.

"Our dad didn't work his arse off to turn his small building firm into the successful development company it is by doing things the conventional way, and that's not the way we operate either. We'll knock on his door, help him find his ATM card, escort him to a bank, and instruct him how much he needs to withdraw to cover his debt. It's either that or we take the fuckers car. You still in?" Zac asks.

Jack shrugs and nods, and while my brothers arrange a time to pick him up in the morning, I find my eyes searching out Jo and her little redheaded mate.

I've no clue what's got me so intrigued. All I've seen is her long auburn hair, I've still not been able to catch a look at her face, but as the band starts up with 'Should I Stay or Should I Go,' the redhead pulls off her jacket and starts singing into an empty beer bottle.

I have this strange sensation in my chest and wonder if the Parma I scoffed down earlier has somehow lodged there, giving me indigestion. While rubbing at it with my knuckles, I tilt my head from one side to the other in my attempt at getting a clear look at her through the crowd.

A BRUNETTE HOOKS her arms over the redhead's shoulder, but they both still have their backs to me. Some random dude moves from the dance floor and squeezes in between them, and that's when the three of them turn and face me.

Knocking back the last of my drink, I watch her as she moves the bottle in front of the dude's mouth, and he sings into it.

When the song ends, he goes back to his mates on the dance floor as they cheer, but as 'American Pie' starts to play, the whole place erupts, and the redhead jumps up on a chair, her mate follows.

The overhead downlight is shining right on her, giving me a clear view of her face. If I had to guess, I'd say she was around my age. She has the bluest of blue eyes and a tiny little upturned nose, all set in a round, smiling face.

She belts out a word perfect, all six verses rendition of the Don Mclean classic, pointing the bottle at the crowd every time they reach the chorus; she's getting more attention than the band. I find myself smiling as she again points the end of the bottle towards everyone on the dance floor and orchestrates using her other hand.

"What the fuck are you grinning at?" Zac asks from beside me.

"Who's the redhead with Jo?" I ask, not taking my eyes off her.

"No clue mate, but she's obviously got your attention. . . Oh, I can see why. You are such a tit man."

"Fuck off, I noticed her because she's fucking gorgeous," I lie. I was totally staring at her tits. They're a decent size for such a little frame and hard to miss.

"Who is?" Cooper asks, flanking my other side.

"The redhead with Jo. You know who she is?" Zac asks him.

"Nah, but you can ask Jo herself, she's on her way over here."

In practised, perfect unison, we turn away from where we were watching the girls dance and face the bar, me, making a slight adjustment in the ridiculous skinny chino things I'd been convinced by my twelve-year-old daughter to purchase.

"Dude, stop touching your dick. What the fuck is wrong with you?" Zac whisper shouts as the three of us stand in a row at the bar.

"Fuck off," is my mumbled reply.

"You caught a dose of something nasty from Alysa, or one of your harem girls?" Cooper asks.

I narrow my eyes on him before raising my brows and stare for a second.

"First off, fuck you, and fuck you." I look between my brothers.

"Second, I've not seen Alysa in months. Third, I don't have a fucking harem. Fourth, I just got tested when we had the company medicals."

"They were three weeks ago," Zac interrupts.

"If you'll let me fucking finish," I snap back. "I've not been near a bird since we had the medical, and those results state that my dick is squeaky clean because fifth, I do not dip it anywhere without wearing an overcoat. I got caught once remember, and as much as I love Ava, that will not ever be happening again."

"You're single, and haven't fucked in three weeks? Mate, that's a serious drought you got going on there."

I ignore Zac's comment.

"You don't want more kids? Dude, you're only thirty-five, way too young to make that call," Cooper advises.

"Thanks for the advice, Master Shredder, but procreating is not at the top of my list of priorities right now. Fucking, yes, making babies, definitely not, but thank you."

"Anytime, as your big brother, I feel it's my responsibility to keep you informed."

"Appreciated."

"Hey, Jo. How's it going?" Zac elbows me as he speaks to Jo, who's now standing next to him waiting to get served.

She turns our way, takes her time drinking us in, eye-fucking each of us as she does, and smiles. "Evening, boys. How are you all?"

"Good, yourself?" Zac asks.

Before she can respond, Cooper asks, "What you after, Jo? I'll get these."

"No, I'm good thanks, Coop, I'm in a round with the girls."

"That's cool, I can stretch to a drink for them too. What you having?"

She stares at Cooper for a long moment. We all watch as she tongues the inside of her cheek, exuding confidence and sex appeal, before breaking out in a smile. "That's really nice of you, Coop. I'll have a G&T, two vodka, lime, sodas, and a Jack and coke."

Cooper repeats the order, adding our drink requests to the barman. Zac gives me another small nudge before moving from between me and Jo to stand the other side of Cooper.

"Gabe, how are you?" Jo leans in and gives me a quick cuddle and a kiss on the cheek.

"I'm good. You're looking extra gorgeous tonight. What's the occasion?"

She flicks her hair over her shoulder, still giving me that all-knowing, seductive smile of hers. Jo's one of those no-bullshit kind of women. I think that's what it is about her that's always appealed to me. There's no drama, no pretence. She'll happily take you home, fuck you senseless, and expect nothing more from you in the morning. A few of my mates have been there, most always hopeful for an invite back, but have never got one. She's smart, successful, and knows exactly what she wants, and it's definitely *not* a relationship.

"No occasion, just a girls' night."

She turns and leans her back against the bar as she scans the room.

"Cool, who you with?" I ask casually.

"Lou's the tallest brunette, Jemma's the other one, and Lauren's the redhead you've been staring at since we walked in."

My head jerks back like I've been slapped. Jo slowly turns her head, knowing brown eyes land on mine.

"I'm an accountant, Gabe, it's my job to be observant and let nothing go unnoticed. We're out tonight to cheer her up."

"Why, she got shit going on? I ask.

"That, we don't know. A few more drinks and we're hoping she's going to spill."

"That's a bit slippery, Jo. Does she know that's your plan?"

"That's women, Gabe. We can be slippery in more ways than one. I thought you'd know all about that?"

I have no immediate response. I smile and shake my head, and after a few moments pause, I lean into Jo.

"Let me add a round of shots to your drinks. What dya fancy?"

"You're very kind. We'll have a round of Cowboys please."

"Can you add seven Cowboys to that round please, mate?" I ask the barman, passing Cooper a fifty to help cover the cost.

Turning back to Jo, I ask, "So, your mate, is the shit she's got going on bloke related?" Not wanting to appear desperate for information, I force my eyes to roam the bar as I talk, but they snap back to Jo when she throws her head back and laughs.

"Gabriel Wild, you want the tea on my girl, then you need to man up and go ask her yourself."

As if they'd heard what she'd said to me, the three women Jo arrived with throw their heads back and laugh.

We both study them in silence for a beat. Cooper slides a tray laden with the girls' drinks along to Jo. "You want me to carry them over for you?" I ask.

"Gabe, really? It's as if you don't know me at all. Come closer, hun, and I'll let you into a little secret." Jo crooks her pointer finger, and I move in. "Two things I've learned to handle expertly in my life, men, and alcohol. So, thank you, but I think I've got it."

Again, all I can do is shake my head, let out a sigh, and chuckle.

"You're killing me, Jo, just make sure shorty knows the shots are from me."

She picks up the tray with a smile. "I can do that for you, boo," she says with a wink.

While my brothers watch Jo's retreating arse weave its way across to the table her mates are standing around, my eyes lock with the redhead's, and something shifts inside me.

CHAPTER 5

Lauren

"Lauren," Jemma elbows me.

"What?" I snap, annoyed at her distraction. My gaze still locked on the man staring at me from across the dance floor.

"Your mouth, Lauren. Close. Your. Mouth."

"What?" I repeat.

"Your mouth, woman. Every time you answer me, you leave it hanging wide... Oh. Well damn. Who is that?"

I clamp my mouth shut. Blue eyes laughs, shakes his head, and finally looks away still smiling.

Even though he's no longer looking, I find myself smiling right back.

"Surely she didn't knock *him* back. That man is gorgeous," Lou questions as Jo moves towards us with a tray loaded with drinks.

"Do you know him?" Jemma asks.

"No, I know his face though. I've seen him around; I think they're his brothers he's with," Lou replies.

I remain silent as Jo puts the tray down on the table.

"Please tell me you didn't say no to *all* that is that?" Jemma waves her arm up and down in the general direction Jo just came from.

When *I* follow the direction of Jem's arm wave, I realise he's looking over again, so quickly steer my gaze to meet Jo's.

"Do you realise how loud you are?" Jo questions Jem.

"Sorry," Jem silently mouths.

"Despite what you might think, I don't sleep with every man that buys me a drink. And yeah, as easy on the eye as that particular man is, he's also a client. I do not fuck my clients. . . even if they do have *all that* going on."

There's a gabble of noise and questions as Lou and Jemma clamber for information. You'd never believe these are the two who are happily married out of the four of us. *Not* that my friends are aware of the demise of my marriage yet.

My head spins for a second, and my stomach churns as my reality once again hits me. My entire life is about to implode, and here I am, getting drunk and making eyes at someone probably half my age.

"So, he's a client? What does he do?" Lou asks.

I sneak another peek and feel ridiculous when he catches me and smirks. Why am I embarrassed when he's the one still blatantly staring?

"He has a construction company that he runs with his family; two brothers, one sister. Their dad, Joe, started it when he first moved over here from the UK. He retired a couple of years ago, and now the kids run it. Jay probably knows of them Lauren, Wild Construction and Development."

I'm not sure if she was asking me a question or just stating a fact. We live in a relatively small, beach-side town just outside of Melbourne. If he worked in construction, as my husband does, chances are, he would know, or at least know *of* him.

Still feeling a little out of it, I take the shot glass Jo places in my hand, realising the others are already holding theirs.

"He was very curious about you, Loz. He told me to make sure you knew this round of shots is on him."

Snapped back to my senses, I bark out aloud, "What? Me? Why?" My eyes widen as I stare at Jo.

"What the fuck, Jo? What did you say? What did you tell him?"

Nervous paranoia bubbles Inside me. I'm not sure if it's panic or anger I feel at the thought of them discussing me.

"Calm down, I didn't tell him anything. I wasn't about to break his heart and tell him you've been happily married forever."

Heat rises from my belly, spreads across my chest, and climbs my throat before settling on my cheeks. This is it. This is the moment I say the words out loud and admit to my friends the truth about what my life has become.

"To friends and floors," Lou again declares.

Choking back my emotions just long enough to knock back my shot, I slam my glass on the table, and burst into tears.

Too scared to look up, I cover my mouth with the back of my hand and stare down at the floor in an attempt at hiding my tears, but there's no controlling the movement of my shoulders as my stomach heaves out a sob.

"Lauren?" sounding panicked, Jemma says my name.

The noise from the bar drifts away, becoming just a dull collection of sounds from somewhere far away. I still don't look up.

I'm not ready.

Not ready to say the words.

Not ready for the sympathetic looks I know will come my way.

I'm the fixer, the solver of problems. I'm never the broken, the one to fall apart, and admitting that's what I've become causes physical pain in my chest and belly.

For a few seconds there's total silence. Drawing in a breath, I look up. My eyes shift from the blue, to the brown, then to the blue-eyed gazes of my friends. As a collective, they move. Lou puts her arm around my shoulders; Jo and Jemma stand either side. All of them positioned to block anyone else from witnessing my very public meltdown.

"I fucking knew it! I've thought for months something was wrong, but every time I've asked. . ."

"Jem!" Jo snaps.

"Sorry, but this is bullshit. She'd be the first to have one of us spilling our guts and the first to try and put things right." Jemma's eyes move from Jo to meet mine. "Cut the crap, Lauren, and tell us what the fuck's going on. Are you sick? What are you hiding?"

"Am I going to need a cigarette for this?" Jo asks.

My lips rattle together as I let go of a long breath. "I think *I'm* going to need a cigarette for this," I admit.

"Come on, I've got smokes," Jo says, pulling her case from the wallet hanging from her wrist.

We follow her out to the veranda, which is the designated smoking area, and all but Lou light up a cigarette.

None of us are really smokers. We dabbled when we were at school, but when Jo fell pregnant, we all stopped, only for each of us to start again at various stressful times in our lives. Now, it's mostly a social thing, when we all get together and drink too much, or right now when it's a combination of all three.

Positioning ourselves around a table in the corner furthest from the doors leading into the bar, I stand with my back to everyone but my friends, and smoke in silence.

Taking in a long sip of the drink I'd grabbed from the tray Jo had set down, I stub out my cigarette, draw in a deep breath, and speak my truth.

"I'm leaving Jay, and I'm going to need your help to do it."

My statement is met with silence, and I take a moment to study the expressions on my friend's faces as they process my news. They don't look shocked, with brows either raised or drawn together, it's more like confusion they convey.

"What?" Jemma asks with a nervous laugh.

"Why?" Lou questions quietly.

"What did he do, Lauren?" Jo's tone is cold and hard, sending a chill right through me.

I lick my lips, fold my arms across my chest, take a look around the decked area we're standing on while taking a long moment to arrange my words.

She knows how much I love my husband. My friends *all* know. My marriage was the one they each aspired to have. For the almost twenty-seven years we've been together, Jay has been my best friend. Right alongside these women, me and him have grown up together, raised our boys, and successfully run two businesses. It's been a joke amongst them all that even after all these years, we still fuck like rabbits. But now I have to explain how that all ended some months ago, that things have changed, and that idyllic life I once was living, has for me, become a living nightmare.

The hardest part though. The part that kills me to admit, is that I've let this happen. There was nothing I could do the first time he put his hands on me, but I've allowed the hair pulling, wrist grabbing, and cheek squeezing to escalate into what unfolded in my kitchen last week.

Finally returning my gaze back to where my friends huddle together waiting on my explanation, I talk.

"Things haven't been good for a while now, months, a year almost." I shrug and explain. "I don't know how, why, or when it started, but something changed. You all know what me and Jay are like, we're screaming abuse at each other one minute, ripping each other's clothes off the next."

I take another sip of my drink, expecting one of them to comment, ask a question, *something*, instead, they remain silently watching me.

I place my glass back on the table, and in an attempt to hold myself together for what comes next, I wrap my arms around my middle.

"The abuse being screamed got louder, and the ripping off of each other's clothes stopped. For a while, there was silence, nothing. We'd go for days without talking. . ." I pause while trying my best to stop the tremble of my lips and the ache in my jaw and chest as I speak.

"Then, one night, he grabbed my hair, the next, my wrist. . ."

"He put his hands on you?" Jo asks.

I shake my head. "Please just let me talk, Jo, let me get this out."

She pulls out her silver cigarette case and offers them around, even Lou takes one this time.

Lighting up, I draw the tobacco and chemical cocktail into my lungs before letting it out slowly. Despite knowing the harm it's doing, I enjoy the moment and calm down enough to continue talking without crying.

"He's rarely home lately, and when he is, he's so vicious. Not just with his words, but with his actions too. His hair pulling and the throat squeezing isn't the good kind anymore. . ."

"Loz," Jemma says my name as if she's in pain.

"Why didn't you. . ." I hold my hand up to stop her so I can say what I need to say.

"I know I should've done something. Left, or at least told you what was going on, but I thought I could fix things. . . we're Lauren and Jay." I shrug and give a knowing half-smile as I look around at my friends. "I throw things, he ducks and laughs, we fuck. . ."

I'm talking through my tears now, just wanting, needing, desperately to get the truth out there.

My legs shake as I feel my entire body vibrate. "I really thought I could save us, but then last Sunday night. . . oh, my god, last Sunday." I swipe at the tears covering my face as I heave out the words. "Sunday night he attacked me. He dragged me out of the spa by my hair. . ."

"Jesus fucking Christ," one of my friends grinds out, but I've no clue which one.

And that's it, that's all I have in me. I don't have the strength to hold anything in any longer. I let out a noise that doesn't even sound like it comes from a human, and as Jo and Jemma move in to hold me up, Lou just stands on her own, off to the side. While Jo and Jemma attempt to console me, I hear Lou speak.

"But why, Lauren? Why would he suddenly flip like that? Is there a trigger, something that sets him off?"

"Are you for fucking real?" Jemma's voice is low as she stares wide-eyed at Lou.

"Did you hear what she said he's been doing to her? Does it fucking matter what triggers him? She could fuck another man in front of him on their kitchen bench, and that still, does not, give him the right to touch her like that."

"I didn't mean that. I know that. . ." Lou's wide blue eyes meet mine, pleading for me to understand where she's coming from, but right now, I'm not really sure of anything.

"I just meant. . . you two are so good together Loz, I just thought maybe with some counselling. . ."

"He fucking hit her," Jo snaps at Lou. "What part of that are you not getting?"

Lou's shoulders physically slump, and she stares at the table. "I get all of that, I'm sorry, Lauren. I just hate this for you, I really do."

Lou has always been the sensitive one out of our group, and

I feel for her now as she attempts to process the bombshell I've just dropped.

"What can we do? What do you need?" Jo asks.

"You're not going back there tonight. You can stay at mine, or Jo's, or wherever, but you're not going back there," Jemma states before I can answer Jo.

"I'll be fine tonight. He's not been getting home till late all week, and he hasn't touched me since it happened. I'll probably be home first and just pretend I'm asleep when he gets in." I shrug. "It's what I've been doing most nights lately anyway. Besides, there are things in the safe I want to get out. He'll get an alert as soon as I open it, at least tomorrow I know it'll take him around an hour to get home once I do it, and by then, I can be long gone."

"I can't believe you haven't told us this before now."

"Says the woman who kept her pregnancy from us for seven months," I bite back at Jo.

"Oh, touché. Maybe save some of that fighting spirit for Jay next time he comes at ya."

"Jo!" Jemma snaps. "Stop being a bitch, and you," she points at me, "I still don't understand why you didn't just leave last Sunday, as soon as it happened."

Taking another sip of my drink, I consider my answer. "It's not that simple, Jem. I've spent the week getting myself organised. Tomorrow, he has a golf day with some mates. He'll be up and gone early, that'll give me a chance to pack the last of my stuff, open the safe, and be gone by the time he gets home."

I eye each of them. "That's where you ladies come in. I went to the bank today. . ." I pause a moment, swallowing back the tears that are once again threatening to spill. Shaking my head in an attempt at ridding myself of the overwhelming emotions, I take a deep breath and continue, "Our personal accounts are empty, that's why I need the cash and jewellery from the safe.

It's not just that, it's my passport, birth certificate, all of that kind of thing."

"What the fuck?" Jo questions.

"I don't know if he anticipated I'd do this and he doesn't want me to have any money, or if he's done it so I *can't* leave... I honestly have no idea what he's thinking these days, but yeah, nah, there's no money in our joint accounts, just a couple of thousand I have in my stash account I keep for lending the kids when they ask."

"That's not an issue, we'll help you out with money, with anything. Just let us know what you need," Jemma offers.

"Come to mine," Jo adds. "In the morning, I'll come to yours, help you pack, and then you can come and stay at mine until we can get you sorted out, or for as long as you like, whatever. Just don't stress about any of that side of things."

Still feeling shaky but a little less tense, I let out a long breath.

Lou, who's been mostly quiet since she got her head bitten off, asks, "You feel better now you've told us?"

"Yeah," I say, reaching for her hand. "I know you didn't mean anything earlier, don't overthink it, Lou. I know you'll always have my back."

"Always," she replies as we each move in for a hug.

"You gonna be okay, or would you rather we go home?" Jem squeezes my hand and asks.

"No," my response is instant, "I'm not okay, I don't know if I'll ever be okay again, but I'm not letting him ruin my night."

"I've got so many questions, but now's not the time," Jem adds.

"You've got questions? It's happening to me, and honestly, I don't even know where to begin." I look around at my friends and confess. "What did I do? What could I have possibly done to have caused such a massive change in..."

"Right, that's enough. You can stop with all of that crap right now. Why are you making this all about what *you've* done wrong? This isn't on you; this is all on him. There's nothing that can justify his behaviour, not a single fucking thing," Jo interrupts me.

Letting out another heavy sigh, I wipe away the tears puddling under my eyes again.

"I know, I know. I just, I don't fucking know. Should I even be here? Shouldn't I be at home trying to save my marriage?"

"Do you want to save your marriage?" Lou asks, and I instantly have to choke back a sob as I shake my head.

"I don't think I do. I love him, but I'm no longer *in* love with him. It's been fading for weeks, but after Sunday night, I'm just numb to him."

There are collective sighs and head shakes from the girls, and I hate that I'm putting such a downer on the evening.

"Let's hug it out and dance it off," Jemma orders.

"Let's also get shit-faced and forget that prick of a soon-to-be-ex of yours even exists," Jo adds. "But first, we need to get you to the bathroom and fix that cute little face of yours up. You look like you've been gagging on nine-inch dicks and they made your eyes water."

"At least if I had it would explain why my marriage has gone to shit," I respond.

"Babe, you're single now. If it's a nine-inch dick you're after, I can point you in the right direction. I'm happy to share my little black book of stats and help a sister out."

My stomach lurches at the prospect of now being single, but I bury it down somewhere deep to deal with another day.

"Thanks, Jo, but I think I'm gonna take some time and focus on me for a while, and when I'm done, I definitely won't be looking up your sloppy, or even stiff, nine-inch seconds."

Jo shrugs. "Well, the offer's there." Grabbing my hand, we follow Lou and Jemma towards the toilets so we can attempt to sort my whoreish, cock sucking but cute face out.

CHAPTER 6

Gabe

I WATCH in stunned silence as the redhead appears to burst into tears the instant she finishes the shot I sent over.

"That went well," Zac says from beside me.

"Is she crying?" Cooper asks as the three of us stand at the bar watching the scene unfolding on the other side of the room.

"Yeah," Zac chimes in again. "Apparently, the round of shots Gabe sent over tasted shit."

"Get fucked," I mumble, still watching as the group of women surround her, shielding her from everyone in the place, including me.

After a few minutes, still surrounded by her friends, I watch as she moves through the bar and out to the smoking terrace.

Taking a sip of my drink, I become aware of my brothers watching me.

"What?" I ask.

"What are you doing?" Cooper asks. "You've not taken your eyes off her and your jaw's ticking."

"No it's not," I argue.

"Kids got it bad," Zac adds.

I shake my head at the pair of them; my response is interrupted when I hear, "Hey, Gabe," from beside me.

"Oh, shit," Zac says, none too quietly.

I turn to see Kristy, a little blonde I'd hooked up with last summer.

"Hey, Kris," I respond, but quickly turn away and back towards my brothers. My gaze catches Coopers, who gives me an eye roll and a head shake. Zac points his finger at me, wagging it, and fake laughs while I mouth the word '*wankers*,' at the pair of them.

I'm not a dick, and I don't want to act like one now, but I make it clear to the women I sleep with that if we go there, it'll likely be a one-time thing. Kristy knew this when she took me home with her six months ago, but that hasn't stopped her from trying to hook up again every time we bump into each other.

I HAVE no aversion to sleeping with the same woman more than once; it's just that every time it happens, they tend to start making assumptions. No matter how many times I attempt to explain that it's only sex that I'm interested in, they play the victim when I leave after the deed is done without making any promises or plans.

NOT ALL WOMEN are like it. There are a few out there just looking to fuck with no expectations, and they're the ones I'm happy to hook up with more than once.

I'm not a man whore, just a thirty-five-year-old single bloke with a healthy sex life. My daughter stays with me every other weekend and a couple of nights during the week. During those times, she gets my undivided attention, so it's not like opportunities present themselves every minute of every day. Despite this, living in a small town does mean that I do quite often bump into someone I've slept with, which, like right now, can be awkward.

THE BAND STARTS BACK UP with a cover of 'Jack and Diane', and just as the opening guitar starts, Jo and her mates come back into the bar. With my eyes trained on the little redhead in the middle of the procession making its way towards the toilets, my knuckles again rub at my chest as the indigestion from earlier kicks back in. The burning gets worse when again I hear, "Hey, Gabe?" from beside me a few minutes later.

"BUSTED." Cooper laughs before turning his back to me, pretending to be deep in conversation with Zac.

Turning to face Kristy, I give her a small smile.

"HOW'VE YOU BEEN?" she asks, stepping in for a cuddle. I pat her back awkwardly as she stands with her arms around my neck. Pulling away, I spot the redhead making her way *back* from the bathroom conference she's just had with her girls. With the table they congregated around earlier now taken, they find another closer to where I'm standing.

"I've been good, Kris. Busy with work, you know how it is, lots going on."

I've no idea if she knows how it is because I don't really know the first thing about her.

"Too busy to return my calls?"

My head jerks back at this question because I rarely give out my number, and I definitely don't remember giving it out to Kristy.

"I'm sorry, what?"

"I called you at work, left a message with your secretary for you to call me back."

"I. . . No. I mean I didn't get your message. Why'd you call?"

I don't want to be a dick, I really don't, but for fuck's sake, how else is this conversation going to go?

"Well, it wasn't to talk about the weather," she snaps.

"Look out," I hear one of my brothers say from behind me.

"No? What was it for?"

She shakes her head.

"I wanted to talk, to catch up. . ."

"Kris, look, I'm sorry if you feel like I misled you in any way to thinking that what we had was going to be anything more than a one-time thing, but to my recollection, I'm pretty sure I made myself quite clear on that score."

"So, I'm only good enough for a fuck and run, but Alysa Hawkins gets multiple go-arounds? Why is that?"

"Because just like me, Alysa is a big fan of uncomplicated sex, Kris. She doesn't attempt to stalk me at work, and she doesn't piss me off every time I see her in the pub."

"You're a fucking root rat, Wild."

"I'm really not, and if you'd listened to a single word I'd said before you took me home to your bed, you'd know that."

OVER KRISTY'S SHOULDER, I catch the redhead watching us. My eyes meet hers, and she gives me a small smile, I give her one of my own in return.

'*THANK YOU*.' She mouths.

'*Cheers, you're welcome*.' I hold up my glass and mouth back.

"Fuck you, Gabe." Kristy's voice snaps me back just in time to dodge the contents of her wine glass she launches in my direction. Instead, the liquid covers my brother's back.

"What the fuck?" Cooper asks as he turns slowly to see Kristy's shocked expression, her hand still suspended mid-air as she holds onto the glass.

"Sorry," she snaps. "You can blame your prick of a brother for that and get him to pay for a new shirt."

"Stay the fuck away from me, Kris, stay right, the fuck, away."

She turns, retreating back to hell or wherever it was she came from.

"Unfuckingbelievable," Cooper complains. "You piss her off, but I get covered in wine? You are most definitely buying me a new shirt."

"Some of that shit hit my sleeve. You can buy me a new one too."

"Fuck off, Zac," me and Coop say in unison.

I spend the next thirty minutes or so chatting shit with my brothers while watching the redhead and her crew rocking it on the dance floor. No matter what song the band plays, she seems to know the words to every single one of them.

"Gabe?"

"What?"

Zac flicks my ear, and I mumble a '*fuck off*' as I bat his hand away.

"I swear to God, I'm gonna knock you two the fuck out before tonight's over," I threaten.

"In your dreams, little brother, you're not even man enough to go and talk to her. What the fuck is wrong with you?" Cooper questions. Before I get a chance to respond, and to my absolute horror, Zac calls Jo over.

Brows drawn down, she wears a confused, or maybe it's an amused smile on her face as she makes her way towards us.

"What's up?" She raises her chin and asks.

"Jo, put my pathetic little brother out of his misery and introduce him to your mate. It's getting painful standing here watching him drool."

I shake my head. "Ignore him. My brother's being an extra special dick tonight. I'm sorry."

Looking between her mates and me, Jo taps her pointer finger against her pouty lips.

"You want me to introduce you, I'll introduce you, but I'll tell ya now. . ." she pauses, appearing to either consider her words or decide whether she's going to actually say them, "she has a lot of shit going on right now, you make any kind of move on her tonight, and I will hunt you down."

The indigestion shifts from my chest to my gut, making it churn.

"What kind of shit?" I ask.

"Not my story to tell. I'll introduce you, but the rest is on you to find out, if, that is, she decides she wants to tell you."

Jo makes her way back to the dance floor where shorty's currently dancing to 'Everybody Wants to Rule the World'. She says something into her ear, and they both turn and look at me. I watch as she shakes her head and turns and says something to Jo, who responds by grabbing her hand and dragging her towards me.

I feel like an idiot, more like a fourteen-year-old kid at a school disco, instead of a grown man. My mouth dries as I panic at what I'm going to say to her.

"Lauren, this is Gabe. He was telling me earlier he might have a property coming up for rent soon, and I know you might be in the market. . ."

My gut cramps as my chest tightens, and I wonder if maybe

I've got a bad case of both food poisoning and heartburn or indigestion.

"Hey," she says quietly, her blue eyes darting between Jo and me as she gives this awkward little flick of her wrist.

"I. . . Hey. Lauren, yeah, sorry, sorry."

What the actual fuck is wrong with me?

Her brows raised, she watches me for a few seconds before ending my muted torture.

"Thanks for the drink, that was nice of you."

She has an accent, English, London or somewhere around it. I shake my head—no idea why, but I shake it, and I continue to shake it.

"No worries," I eventually blurt.

Catching sight of my brothers, Cooper is giving me a wanker sign, while Zac holds two fingers under his chin and pretends to shoot himself.

"So, I might be able to help you out."

She smiles, licks her lips, and gives a quick raise of her perfect brows.

"Oh, I'm sure you most definitely can. . ."

"With a place to live," I interrupt. "Or, with something else, if you need helping out with something, with other things. . ."

Fuck my life because right now, I've lost any and all ability to string a sentence together.

"Oh, that," she says before pursing her lips in an attempt not to smile. She fails, and what escapes is somewhere between sexy and suggestive. My dick twitches in my jeans and I don't feel even a little bit bad about it.

"Yeah, Jo may have jumped the gun a little bit with that. I need to sort some other. . . I'm not really in a position to commit to anything right now, but thank you."

Frowning, she narrows her eyes on Jo, who in response, turns right around and goes back to their crew on the dance floor.

"What's the problem with where you are now? Is your lease up?" Feeling proud at finally managing to form a coherent sentence, I'm as shocked as shit when her eyes shine with instant tears.

Blowing out a few short breaths, she begins fanning her face with her hand as she looks everywhere except at me.

"Sorry," she says with a nervous laugh. "Wow. Shit. This is really awkward."

Continuing to fan her face, I watch as she swallows a couple of times. Her blue eyes still shining as she attempts to smile.

I stand there, unsure of what exactly it was I said that upset her, but feeling like an absolute piece of shit for saying it anyway.

"I'm sorry. You okay? Shit, I didn't mean. . ."

"Yeah. Nah. I'm good. Just having a moment." She gives another small but obviously nervous or embarrassed laugh while still looking around the bar.

"Can I get you another drink?"

Her eyes finally meet mine, and it takes everything in me not to pull her closer and ask what or who the fuck has her so upset.

"Could I just grab a water please?"

"Water, you sure?"

"Yeah, I'm. . . no, I'm not sure of anything right now." She laughs again, this time it sounds a little more genuine. "I'll have a water, but could you also get me a vodka, lime, soda? You know what, I'll get these, you got the last round."

I watch her as she rambles. I want to argue, but not wanting to upset her any further, I nod.

"Sure, yeah. If that's what you want."

She pulls cash from the wallet attached by a strap to her wrist and hands it to me.

"Would you mind getting them?"

"Yeah, no worries."

I'm not a Neanderthal, but taking her money doesn't sit right with me, but I order our drinks and take a moment to get my shit together, at the same time, hopefully giving her time to compose herself.

I pass her the glass of ice water first, take a sip of my bourbon, before turning with her vodka in my hand. She drinks the water down in one go and places the glass back on the bar.

"I'm sorry," she says again.

"Don't be. Shall we just start again? That introduction was really fucking bad," I admit with a smile.

"It was the absolute worst," she agrees with a grin. "Hey, Gabe, I'm Lauren."

"Lauren, hey. Good to meet you. So, do you come here often?"

"Really? I give you a second chance, and that's all you've got for me? Wow," she says with a shake of her head.

Her accent is killing me. It makes everything she says sound like she's cracking a joke at my expense, which I think she actually might be. She's wearing the biggest smile as she talks before reining it in with another shake of her head.

"That was just, wow, I've literally got no words, and that's saying something. Where'd you pull that one from, the fifties?" Her head turns from side to side as she appears to be looking around the room. I silently watch her, mesmerised, transfixed. I swear, the little red-headed witch has me under some type of spell.

"What are you doing?" I finally ask.

"Sorry," she shakes her head as she speaks. "I was looking for a jukebox, the Fonz and the Cunningham's," she deadpans.

"Wow," I mimic what's apparently her favourite word. "Don't hold back. I mean, you're cutting me deep here. I'm emotionally wounded." I press a palm to my chest, feigning injury. "Fair play though, that was poor. Really poor. I'm shit at this," I admit while giving my head a shake.

"Oh, I doubt that," she says sarcastically.

"You doubt that I'm shit at small talk?"

She shrugs, sips on her drink, and looks around the bar before landing her pretty eyes back on me, shining now with mischief, not tears.

Gesturing with a nod over my shoulder, she sucks in both her lips as a voice whispers into my ear.

"Hey, stranger, where you been hiding."

"I rest my case," Lauren says, accompanied by a quick quirk of her brows.

I turn slowly to see Alysa standing there.

"Hoooooleeeeey shit!" Zac whisper shouts loud enough for me and most of the bar to hear.

"I'll leave you to it," Lauren says with a wink. "Thanks for the drink," she adds before turning and walking away.

CHAPTER 7

Lauren

"WHAT THE FUCK was that all about?" I snap at Jo when I reach where the girls are standing.

"Oh, do be quiet. I'm just helping you get back in the game."

"I don't want to be back in the game. I'm not even out of the game yet. I'm still in the game, just a different game."

"He's cute," Lou slurs. "Just use him to practise on."

"Lou!" I shake my head in horror at her suggestion. "He's someone's son. Imagine if someone talked about one of your boys like that one day?"

She shrugs.

"It's all good, Lauren, it's all good. . .tune," she shouts before bouncing on her toes and fist-pumping the air as she sings along to 'Living on a Prayer'.

"I should go home," I tell Jo and Jemma who are both watching me.

"No, you shouldn't." Jem throws her arm over my shoulder and says, "Ol' blue eyes is on his way over here, and what you're gonna do is let him buy you drinks, have a little flirt, then go home later and go to bed feeling a million times better than what you did last night."

"Sorry about that, Lauren. I meant to give you my card, just in case. . ." He trails off, shrugging awkwardly while his mouth opens and closes. I wonder if it's because I got upset earlier at the mention of finding somewhere to live, and he maybe doesn't want to bear witness to another one of my mini meltdowns.

I notice the girls slope off and join Lou on the dance floor, once again leaving me alone with this man. We stand facing each other in another awkward silence, I use the moment to take in his gorgeous face. His dark hair, brows, lashes, and stubble make the blue of his eyes pop. The dark circle around his irises highlighting the colour even more. He's tall, I mean at a little under five-two, everyone is tall to me, but he must be over six foot. Muscled, but not bulky. His limbs long and lean like an athlete. Dark chest hairs escape the T-shirt he's wearing, pooling in the divot at the base of his throat.

Those blue eyes apparently have a direct line to my clit, and I shift, embarrassed at the effect he's having on me.

Aware that I'm studying him, he smiles. It's not a big smile, just a small one. But with his head tilted to the side and the way it lights up his eyes, it's truly, heart-stoppingly magnificent.

My hand involuntarily begins to rise. I catch it, dropping the offending appendage to my side before it commits the ultimate flirting move and touches my hair. Really? This is what I've become? A horny, desperate, middle-aged woman, reacting to the slightest attention thrown my way. Could I be any more obvious?

He leans in and says huskily into my ear, "So, do you want it, Lauren?" Hot breath fans my cheek and neck setting my skin on fire. . . or that could be the alcohol or menopause. Both are possibilities.

"W-what?" I stammer.

"My card, do you want it?"

Desire is also right up there as a cause of the scorch travelling from my toes to my scalp. I haven't had sex in months. Not with an actual person at least. Since my husband stopped paying me the *right* kind of attention, I've turned more and more to battery-operated options. But there's only so much pleasure a girl can get from a kinky romance novel and a BOB. It's intimacy I crave, a kiss, a cuddle, skin on skin. I realise this is all running through my mind as I stare blankly at *him*. Gabe, Gabriel Wild, even his name oozes sex.

"Yes. Yes please. That would be great, but like I said before, I'm not in a position to be able to afford rent just yet. I have some shit going on, and I need to get back to work."

I'm rambling, unsure of why I'm explaining all of this to *him*, this man, this stranger.

"What is it you do, for work, I mean?"

"I'm an interior designer, but I've let life get in the way of work over the past few years and I need to rebuild my client base again, get my name back out there."

He nods, his eyes on mine the entire time I speak. I'm shaking inside and I'm not sure why. If my marriage wasn't falling apart, this would just be me having a polite conversation with a friend of a friend. One I'd quite possibly go home and tell my husband about, *'oh, I got chatting to Gabe Wild in the pub tonight. Do you know him? His family has a construction company too.'* But that's not how my life is anymore. I no longer have those kinds of conversations with my husband, and my brain is going off on tangents, and I'm totally overthinking all of this.

"Have you got a card? We're about to start work on a brand new shopping and apartment building at the end of Main Street, we'll be looking for someone to set up the show apartments when they're ready to sell, and we're always looking for someone to dress the show homes in our other developments, either to sell or for photos."

My heart rate picks up further at the prospect of maybe finding some work, at the same time the reality of my situation is hitting me. I need to get a job and find somewhere to live because I'm leaving my husband. Life as I know it is over. My legs feel like they're full of jelly and barely holding me up, my arms like lead weights.

What the fuck am I doing here? What am I doing? I'm forty-four years old. I can't leave Jay. I'm too old to start over. Where will I go, what will I do?

He's watching me, waiting on a response and I know I need to say something.

"I. No, I don't have a card on me, but I can get one to Jo to give to you. I'd definitely be interested in the work. My website has images and testimonials from previous clients."

"Hey, Gabe," a brunette says as she passes us by.

"Hey,' he responds, all the while not taking his eyes from me. His gaze's intensity is adding to my nerves and obviously preventing my brain from engaging with my mouth.

"That's quite the little fan club you've got going on. What do you call them? Gabriella's? No, no. I know, Gabettes?"

He rubs his palm over his stubble, lifts one dark eyebrow and smiles.

"Have you been talking to my brothers? You sound like one of them with the shit you've been giving me."

I open my mouth to speak, a little unsure if I've offended him with my comment when he laughs and shakes his head.

"Fuck me. You don't hold back, do you? Gabettes? That one's actually pretty funny."

"Thanks." I shrug and return his smile.

"That accent must let you get away with murder."

"I don't have an accent. This is how most new Australians sounded when they arrived on the First Fleet."

"Yeah, I s'pose you're right. My dad's English, from Kent."

"That's just across the Thames from where I'm from, a place called Essex."

He nods. Eyebrows raised, he tilts his head towards me.

"I've seen the show, that's where they get vajazzled and say, '*shut up, and hundred percent babe*', all the time, right?"

His impersonation of the Essex accent leaves a lot to be desired, but I'm impressed that he's seen the show.

"That's. . . that accent is nearly as bad as your chat-up line, but you've redeemed yourself by saying the word *vajazzled* and your knowledge of the spoken word from my old home county."

"I have a daughter who's about to turn thirteen. I'd probably shock the shit out of you with a lot of stuff a thirty-five-year-old single bloke shouldn't know."

Thirty-five? This is why I shouldn't be here. This is why I need to go home.

"How long have you lived in Australia?" He fills the moment's silence almost instantly, not really giving me a chance to overthink the fact he's years younger than me.

"Since I was thirteen."

"Really? Your accent. . . *non*-accent. . . is still so strong. My dad didn't move here till he was eighteen, and he sounds a lot less English than you."

"What about your mum?"

"Born here, but to Italian parents."

That explains the dark hair and skin, and now I'm aware of the fact, everything about him screams *Italian*. Tall. Dark. Chiselled cheekbones. Straight nose. Those eyes though, not what I'd assume to be typically Italian.

He's watching me watching him and somehow reads my thoughts.

"Blue eyes from my dad, hair and skin from my mum."

"It's a great combination. . ." And yep, I said that out loud.

"Glad you like it." He leans in and says against my ear, "Would you like another drink?"

My senses are invaded by the clean, citrusy smell of his aftershave combined with the unique musky smell that is all him.

He moves his head back, but he's still all up in my space as he looks down at me. We stare. It's a moment. If I press up on my toes, I could kiss him, but I don't. I won't.

"What is it exactly you think is happening here?" I ask, gesturing between us with a wave of my hand.

"I have no fucking idea. What would you like to happen here?" He mimics my gesture.

Making a split-second decision that I'm far too old and my life complicated enough for any more bull

shit, I go with total honesty.

"I'm right in the middle of what is likely to be a very messy separation from my husband."

A flicker of something passes across his eyes, but it's there and gone so quickly, I don't have any idea what it means.

"I haven't even moved out of our home yet, that's not happening till tomorrow, but even then, even once I move out, it's likely to be a very long time before I'm ready for anything. . . *any* kind of relationship with anyone else."

His thick brows are pulled down tight over those amazing blue eyes of his. He licks his lips and swallows but remains silent.

"I'm nine years older than you, my life is a shit show that is about to *implode* before it *explodes,* and as much as I would love to leave here right now with you and spend the rest of the night in your bed, it's not gonna happen. I just want you to be aware of all of that before you waste your time with me and miss out on the chance of taking one of your Gabettes home."

Scratching at his stubbled jaw, he looks around the bar before letting out a long, slow breath through his nose.

"Firstly, I don't take women back to my bed, not ever. That's my daughter's home, and I keep those two parts of my life very separate. Secondly, all I asked was if you'd like a drink. I have no expectations and no hidden agenda. Of course I'd like to take you home and fuck you senseless all night, but if that's not an option, I'm equally as happy to stand here and talk. I give zero fucks about your age, it's just a number and has fuck all to do with this." He makes another gesture, this time with his pointer finger, between us. "This—connection, or whatever the fuck it is."

I watch as he rubs between his pecs with his knuckles, something I've seen him do a few times while we've been talking.

"Connection? We met an hour ago, that makes no sense."

"Nothing about tonight is making sense. I didn't come out tonight expecting this, expecting you. I don't usually stand in a bar making small talk with a woman. If it's obvious they're interested, we leave. We go back to theirs, and we fuck. When we're done, I leave, and that's the end of our connection. I don't *ever* catch sight of a flash of red hair, and a smile from across a bar and have an overwhelming urge to get to know who all of that belongs to. That's not me, that's not who I am."

I fold my arms across my chest, unsure as to whether I should feel flattered or offended at his words.

"But I'm going with my gut right now," he continues. "And when all of that happened, when I caught sight of you earlier, something shifted inside me, and I didn't want to do *any* of the things I usually do. All I knew was that I had to know you, and that's not changed. Now that I've spoken to you, it's not likely to change. So it looks like tonight is all about doing the things we *don't* usually do, and for once in my life, I'm paying attention to the way all of *me* is reacting to all of *you*. And, not meaning to sound crass or course, instead of thinking with my dick, I'm going with my gut, and my gut is telling me something's happening here. So, would you like another drink, yes or fucking no?"

"Vodka, lime, soda," I tell him quietly, trying not to sway as my world tilts a little further on its axis.

"Don't fucking move, I'll be right back." He kisses my cheek and leaves.

Struck speechless, I can do nothing but admire the view. The band's cover of 'Sweet Dreams are Made of These', plays as I watch him move towards the bar, and I couldn't agree with those sentiments more.

"Whatchya doing?" Jemma says from beside me, and I'm so lost in my thoughts, I almost hit the ceiling in fright.

"Shit," I hiss out with my hand pressed against my chest. "I've no clue, Jem, no fucking clue. I should go. He's nine years younger than me, I've known him five minutes, I'm married, about to be separated. . ."

"Stop! You need to stop with this nonsense right now." Jem leans forward and gets all up in my face as I jerk my head back away from her.

"Stop with the overthinking. Let him hit on you, let him buy you drinks and give it all the chat. Then, at the end of the night, you go home. You go to bed remembering all the flattering bullshit that he'll doubtless come up with. You remember that this God-like man-child spent the night trying to get into your knickers. You go to sleep dreaming about all the different ways that could've played out while that bastard of a husband of yours snores next to you. Then, when you wake up, you'll pack your bags and get the fuck out of there and don't look back. No harm done, just a big fat fuck you to the man who's done nothing but shit all over the twenty-seven-years of your life that you've given him."

I let out the breath I held on to the whole time she was talking, and my head spins.

"You're my sensible friend. You're supposed to talk me out of shit like this, not encourage me."

"Exactly, I *am* your sensible friend, so trust me when I say you're doing *nothing* wrong."

She lets out a long slow breath as she looks at me, and it's the look I've been dreading getting from anyone.

"Don't, Jem, please don't feel sorry for me. Not here, not tonight."

"I just feel bad for not picking up on what was going on. I'm beyond pissed off you didn't tell any of us."

I shrug, I'm not going to apologise. It's me it was happening to, I told them when I was ready, even now, I'm not sure if it's too soon, if I maybe should've kept my mouth shut for longer and worked harder at trying to put things right with Jay.

"I'm probably gonna drink this and go. I've got a big day tomorrow and need to have my head on straight for it."

"Fair enough, but do not stand here feeling guilty about getting attention from a hot as fuck thirty-odd-year-old because of your loyalty to a man who's been putting his hands on you, in all the wrong ways, for months. Do not feel guilty about this, Lauren, not even a little bit."

"Thanks." I pull her in for a cuddle, still totally unconvinced as we stand at the side of the dance floor swaying.

"He's on his way back, I'm gonna dance. Let us know when you're ready to go."

"Will do."

I turn to see Gabe approaching as Jemma leaves. He hands me a drink with a smile.

"You didn't run away then?"

"I thought about it, but the prospect of more vodka and giving you another serve kept my feet planted right here."

"You know, if interior design doesn't take back off for you, maybe you should consider stand-up comedy." I flip him my middle finger, just as the sound of a sax or trumpet blasts out the beginning of 'Geno', and I know things are about to get messy.

"I apologise now and will totally understand if you want to disappear into the crowd and pretend we never met."

He frowns in confusion as I hand him my drink, before being grabbed from behind and pulled into a circle with my friends. Jem's arm hooks over one of my shoulders, Jo's over the other as we dance and sing along. Geno ends but *our* song, *our* anthem replaces it. It's the song we sing at the end of a drunken night together, the song we play down the phone to whichever one of us is missing from a night out. When we start singing this, our husbands know it's time to take us home. That's the way it's always been, but now, it's just the way it was.

The dynamics of our friendships will be forever changed by the fracture caused by the end of me and Jay. We take holidays together, spend Christmas, Easter, and other 'family' times together. We're godparents to each other's kids and are always there for birthday parties and special events, and all of that will be ending with the actions I plan on taking tomorrow.

When Lou and Jemma both start to cry, it hits me how much of a massive change is about to happen to my life.

Not even bothering to fight back my tears, I put one arm around Jemma's waist, wave the other in the air, and sing at the top of my lungs to 'Better be Home Soon'.

As the song ends, Jo appears in front of me. The least emotional of all of us, she places her palms on either side of my face.

"We will get you through this. Husbands come, and husbands go, but we will always have each other, and we will always have the music. I fucking love you bitches."

CHAPTER 8

Gabe

"I PRIDE myself on being comfortably in touch with my feminine side, but I swear to God I have no clue what makes women tick. I mean, seriously, what the fuck is going on right there?" Zac says into my ear as me, him, and Cooper watch Lauren and her mates cry, dance, laugh, and sing their way through at least four songs.

They squeeze each other's faces between their palms and sing to each other. There have been kisses to cheeks and to mouths, hands linked, and arms raised. They've entertained the entire bar.

"She's going through some shit, about to separate from her husband. I think she's just feeling a bit emotional and letting off steam. You know women, if one cries, they all cry."

"About to separate?" Cooper asks. "You mean she's still with him?"

"I don't know the whole back story, but the marriage is over, and she's moving out tomorrow."

"And you still wanna get involved, even with all that drama going on?" Zac asks.

My eyes on Lauren, I consider Zac's question as she sings and throws her arms about to 'Hotel California'.

She's not sloppy drunk, and now the tears seem to have stopped, it looks like she's enjoying herself. And I'm glad. I want her to have a good night. I want her to remember the night we met as a happy one, and I can't help but smile right along with her as she throws her head back and sings along to the band's cover of the Eagles classic.

"What the fuck is going on with you?"

I turn and look at Cooper, who's looking back at me wearing a frown. I scratch my head as I ponder both the questions posed by my brothers.

"I do not have a clue what's going on with me because yes, I think I do still want to get involved, even with all the drama she's got going on." I address both of them.

"I knew it. You gave Alysa Hawkins the flick earlier, so I knew you liked her." Zac nods his head towards the dance floor.

"Her name's Lauren," I inform him.

"She's gonna be a mess, Gabe. You sure you're up for that? Don't fuck the girl about if you're not."

My eyes meet Cooper's. "Don't doubt me, brother. I like her. Fucking women about is not my thing. I do everything I can to set them straight, not my fault they get their knickers in a knot when they're trying to put them back on, but this one's different. I like her. I don't know much more than that, I just know that something feels different about her. I like her, and if it's what I've gotta do, then I'll wait until she's ready."

My gaze slides to Zac as he examines his beer bottle. "What the fuck is in this stuff? I think it's got me tripping, or did Gabe just admit to liking a woman and that he's willing to wait for her to be ready?"

"Get fucked," I tell him as he throws his arm around my shoulders and pulls me into him.

"Didn't we tell you earlier that you'll know when it hits?"

"You did," I admit while trying to push Zac away. "But I don't know if this is that, or what it even is. It just is, and I'm gonna run with it and see where it takes me."

"Thanks for the drinks and everything tonight, Gabe, I'm heading off now." Lauren, flushed from her antics on the dance floor, smiles in front of me. Most of the makeup she was wearing earlier has been rubbed from her face, and I instantly notice the light blue and green bruising along her jaw.

I open my mouth to say something, but I'm not entirely sure what I should say. My gut churns, and the alcohol buzz has been replaced by something else. A strange vibration hums through me, making my fingertips tingle.

"You getting a cab? I'll walk you to the rank," I offer.

"No, that's fine, the girls are with me."

I study her smile, wondering what it's hiding. She hasn't realised her makeup has been wiped away and that her bruises are on show, and that makes me feel so fucking sad. She's cute and funny, with just the right amount of sass, and why anyone would want to hurt her, I have no idea. I don't want to point the bruises out and embarrass her, but I also can't let her leave here without knowing exactly what it is she has going on in her life.

"I'm leaving now anyway; I'll walk with you."

"Pussay," Zac coughs the word into his hand, Coop says nothing because he sees exactly what I am.

"Dude," he leans in and says into my ear.

"I know. I know, I see it." My eyes remain on the girls as they put on their coats and jackets in front of us.

As Lauren pushes her arm through the sleeve of her leather

jacket, the cuff of her blouse rides up, and that's when I see she has more bruises around her wrist.

"Man, that's just fucked up," Cooper says.

My mouth fills with saliva, and for a moment I think I'm going to vomit. Someone's obviously been putting their hands on her, and I'm pretty convinced that someone is her husband, and that would explain why she's leaving him.

My head spins as I try and work out exactly what to do with this information, especially as she's still oblivious that I know.

"I'm gonna walk with the girls to the taxi rank, then head home. I'll see you at Carroll's at six?"

After agreeing on a time for a morning meet with my brothers, I say my goodbyes and make my way outside with the girls. Without a word, I grab Lauren's hand and walk at a slower pace, so we fall behind the others.

"You got my card, right?" I ask.

"Yep, put it in my pocket."

"Use it for anything. Whatever you need, you need help with something, call me. I don't pick up, leave a message, or text me. My office number's on there as well."

"Thanks, I will," she says quietly as she walks while staring down at the pavement. I give her hand a squeeze before I stop walking and pull her against me. Head tilted back, wide blue eyes darting over my face, I look down and realise just how short she is. Why the fuck would anyone want to hurt her? Keeping my gaze pinned to hers, I focus on not letting them wander to the blue and green staining her jawline.

"Don't wait until you've got your shit together. Call me tomorrow and let me know what happens with you moving out, or if you need help with that, just, for whatever reason, call me will ya please, Lauren?"

She pulls her head back and tilts it to the side. With her perfect brows pulled down into a frown, she looks between me and her friends.

"Did Jo say something to you?"

So, Jo knows what's going on? She'll be the first person I'll be calling in the morning, maybe even tonight. I'm not sure what she must see in my face, but she pushes her hands against my chest and tries to pull away.

"I don't fucking need this. . ."

"Don't," I cut her off. "No one said anything. Your makeup has rubbed off your face."

Her hand instantly moves from where it was pushing against me to the side of her face.

"I can see the bruises, Lauren. Then when you put your jacket on, your sleeve rode up."

"Stop." Her lips tremble, and she turns her head away from me. "Just fucking stop."

I hate that I've made her cry, but I need her to know I want to help—need to help.

"Who did it, Lauren? Is your husband putting his hands on you? Is that why you're leaving him?"

"None of your . . ."

"Yeah, nah. See, that's where you're wrong," I interrupt her again. "No matter where this goes, I've seen the bruises. Whatever goes on between us, even if it goes nowhere, if he's putting his hands on you and causing those bruises, then me and him are gonna have a problem, a big fucking problem."

When she tilts her face up to meet mine, tears coat her cheeks.

My hands instinctively go to her hips. I don't pull her closer, I just hold her in place.

"I've got this. I'm getting out. I'm leaving him. Not that any of this has anything to do with you. He's not your problem, he's mine, and I've got it covered."

I turn my head, looking from one side of the street to the other while I rein in my temper and loosen my jaw.

"Don't keep telling me it's not my business. Yesterday I didn't know you, so no, it wasn't my business, it's after midnight now, a new day. Now, I know you. Now, I've seen the bruises. Now, it absolutely is my fucking business."

"You don't know me. You met me, bought me drinks, but you don't *know* me, so don't start giving it. . ."

"What about tonight? Are you gonna be safe tonight?" I cut in.

She lets out a huff, rolls her eyes, and tries to pull away but I hold her in place.

"Don't roll your eyes and behave like a brat. I'm worried, I want you safe."

"Look, thank you for being worried. . ." She licks her lips and her eyes finally meet mine as she trails off.

"I'm still not happy about you going back there. Come home with me. I have a spare room, a sofa, a huge fucking bed."

Her head's shaking before I even finish.

"I need to go home tonight, there's stuff I can't get out of the house till he's out tomorrow. I've got this." She moves her hands from her side and rests them against my pecs. I'm only wearing a long-sleeved T, and the heat from her palms feels good as it seeps through the fabric to my skin. I notice she's not wearing a wedding ring, which instantly reminds me of the bruises around her wrist and why that is.

"He has an early start tomorrow. As soon as he's out the door, I can grab what I need and be gone. I'll be all right. I wouldn't be going back there if I didn't think it was safe."

"Why can't you just go back tomorrow, once he's gone?"

"Because if I don't go home, he'll come looking for me. I don't want him banging on my mates' doors at three in the morning. Besides. . ." She shakes her head before continuing. "All of my personal documents and all of the cash that I have are in the safe. It's some state-of-the-art thing we had installed last year. It's connected to an app, and we both get alerts on our phones when the safe's opened."

"Documents are replaceable, and I can lend you money."

Looking as cute as fuck, she gives a small laugh and shakes her head.

"Gabe, seriously dude, you've known me what, all of three hours?"

"I don't fucking care, I don't want you going back there. . ."

"Lauren, move your arse," Jo calls out from the front of the taxi line.

"I've gotta go. I'll call you tomorrow once I get settled at Jo's, I promise."

I blow out a hard breath, not happy with this arrangement. Before she can pull away, I lean in and kiss her gently on the mouth. It's not the hot, passionate kind of kiss I'd like to be giving her, but I hope it conveys enough of what I'm feeling.

"Go." I smack her arse as I relinquish my hold. "Call me tomorrow, Little Ren."

With her hands buried in the pockets of her leather jacket, she turns back around and faces me. Walking backwards, she asks, "Little Ren?"

"Lau Ren. . . Wren's are birds, really little birds, you're a little Essex bird. . ." I hold my arms out to the side, palms up facing the sky, and shrug. "I don't fucking know, it made sense in my head."

Jesus, I sound like an idiot. I have no idea where I pulled that from, but my regret at having to possibly revoke my man card is short-lived when she gives me a smile and calls out, "Gabe?"

"Yeah?"

"I like it. I *really* like it. Thank you. Thank you for tonight."

The indigestion returns and I rub at my chest as I watch her turn back around and run to her mates.

"Just make sure you call me."

I stand and watch as she climbs into a cab with Jo, the remaining two women get into the ride that pulls up behind them. When they pull away, I decide to walk home along the esplanade and attempt to get my head around everything that's happened tonight.

CHAPTER 9

Lauren

Relived to see my bed is empty when I get home, I quickly head into the ensuite, remove the remnants of my makeup, clean my teeth, and climb into bed.

My entire body is vibrating, and my thoughts are a jumbled whirl.

He kissed me on the mouth. Gabe, he kissed me. And it wasn't just a little peck. He slid his hand into the back of my hair and held me in place. There were no tongues, just lips, but he held on to me like he didn't want to let me go. Another man put his mouth on me, and I allowed it. It felt good. Better than good. After so long without affection, for a very brief moment, the tender way his lips brushed mine, made me feel wanted, desirable, normal.

I've been married to the same man for twenty-four years; we've been together for almost twenty-seven. I won't claim to have never looked at another man or wondered what it would be like with someone else because I'm only human, and that would be a total lie.

Wondering is a bit different from wanting, wishing, and doing though. And tonight, all of those things happened. I wanted to go home with Gabe, I wished I'd left Jay sooner, and I did let Gabe kiss me.

If I needed any more proof that my marriage was truly over, surely tonight's actions proved it?

Despite how deliciously gorgeous Gabe is, I need to set him and everything that was said and shared between us tonight aside for the time being and focus on getting my life into some kind of order once I move out of here tomorrow.

Despite my good intentions, the memory of that kiss is the last thing I remember as I finally drift off to sleep.

* * *

I'M DRAGGED from sleep by the sensation of a hand pushing its way inside my sleep shorts. I know it's Jay before I even open my eyes. The unmistakable scent of his after-shave, shower gel, the soap powder and fabric softener I wash his clothes in, all combine to make up a smell that used to bring me comfort. A smell that meant safety, love, home. It's a smell I've spent most of my life happily bathed in. But now it's mixed with something else. There's the strong odour of alcohol that's for sure, and something else my sleepy brain can't quite pin down.

"Take your clothes off, Loz." Jay's rough whiskers scrape the tender skin of my neck as he burrows his face into the space between my ear and shoulder.

For a few long moments, I wonder if this is it. Could this be the turning point? A chance to make love, then talk things through, work out what's gone wrong, and set things right? Is this the moment where we save our marriage and everything we've spent most of our lives building together?

"Come on, Lauren, take your shorts off and open your legs. I won't take long, I promise."

And then he squeezes in exactly the spot he kicked me the other night. Exactly where he kicked me after he'd thrown me to the floor. Where he kicked me while calling me a fat lazy bitch and telling me I'd ruined his life.

A loud sob escapes me, along with the very last glimmer of hope I had of saving what we once had. It's not just the pain of him squeezing at my bruised body, it's the fact that *he's* the one who caused the bruises. *My husband,* the man who's spent so many years worshipping me. I feel utterly betrayed by his anger, the venom and rage he's aimed at me without a single explanation as to why. I hate the sad, defeated person I've become because of him, and there is absolutely no way I want his body inside mine ever again.

The self-pity and loathing I've felt for months are instantly replaced by anger and outrage.

"Take your fucking hands off me," I tell him through gritted teeth. At the same time, I push both my hands against his chest, and I'm not sure if it's because he's drunk or because he wasn't expecting it, but he falls to his back.

My ears ring with the deafening silence as I lay propped on one elbow, waiting on his reaction. I start to push myself up. Deciding in that instant that I'm going, leaving. Fuck it all. I'll worry about what's in the safe tomorrow. I don't care if I have no money, none of my personal documents, I'm done, so fucking done with him and his shit.

I expect him to grab my hair or slap my face as I start to move out of the bed. What I don't expect is for him to twist his body in such a way that he's able to use the soles of both his feet to kick me out of the bed with such force, I crash into my bedside chest of drawers.

My breath catches as my ribs smash against the edge and the whole thing tips over, taking me with it, only stopping when my head and the side of my face crack against the wall.

I'm not sure if I blackout, but the room is silent for a few moments, and stars dance in front of my eyes, and there's a shrill ringing in my ears.

"If you're not up for fucking me, then there's no need to keep you in my bed. You can sleep on the fucking floor, exactly where you belong, you useless cunt," Jay hisses from somewhere above me. There's a moment, the briefest of moments where I allow myself to hope that he's done and I attempt to sit myself up. That's when his fist connects with my cheekbone and the side of my head. I'm not sure if he kicks or pushes me, but I'm again slammed against the bedside chest of drawers I'm still laying across.

The wind is knocked out of me, and I fight to catch my breath while trying not to panic. The room is dark, and I've lost all sense of direction as I attempt to find the wall, or *anything* to lean against and right myself.

I can taste salt and blood. I try so hard to hold onto my tears and sobs, but they escape as whimpers and snorts. Too scared to move, I lay motionless as I listen to Jay climb back into bed, and within what is probably seconds, but feels like minutes, he begins to snore.

Scrambling frantically in the dark, I eventually find the wall. Pressing my palm against it, I attempt to stand. The chest of drawers tips and I fall with it, letting out a groan at the pain shooting across my ribs.

With my hand covering my mouth to quieten the sound of my heaving breaths, I take a moment for my head to stop spinning and to calm my racing thoughts. I need to get out of here and to do that, I need to stay calm. I take a few deep breaths in through my nose, with my entire body almost convulsing with how hard it shakes, I reach out a trembling hand and eventually find the wall again. Finding purchase, I leverage myself into a kneeling position, move around the drawers, collecting my phone which had been sitting on it as I go, and attempt to crawl on all fours into our walk-in wardrobe. Pain slices through my shoulder, so instead, I shuffle on my knees.

Using the light from my phone, I find my UGGs and pull them on, along with a big oversized cardigan hanging from a hook.

Standing upright, my head spins, and my stomach roils. I swipe at the blood that's pouring from my nose, has coated my chin, and is dripping onto my chest.

I blow out a few short breaths and close my eyes, again trying to get my shit together. Fuelled by pure adrenaline, I fight back the pain, ignore the blood still dripping from my nose, and now coating my ear and neck from a cut somewhere in my head. In a futile effort at holding myself together, I wrap one arm around my middle and nod. '*You can do this*,' I mouth.

Silently, I move to the opening of our walk-in, too scared to use the light on my phone to check Jay's still sleeping, I rely on his snore as an indicator. Reaching my bedroom door, I close my eyes while opening it as carefully as possible. Tiptoeing along the hallway towards the front door, I unlock it, pull it open, and step outside. Finally letting out the shaky breath I'd been holding onto, I run, leaving my home, my husband, my marriage, and the life that I thought would always be mine behind.

* * *

I RUN UNTIL I VOMIT. Scared that the sound of me throwing up and my sobs will wake someone up in our usually quiet neighbourhood, I turn down an alley and head towards the small row of shops I know are just a few blocks away.

As I walk, I dial Jo's number. My hands, legs, and insides are shaking to the point I can barely hold my phone or focus on putting one foot in front of the other. The call goes to voicemail, and I'm about to call again, when I see a set of car headlights approaching from up ahead, I can't hold back the cry of absolute fear that escapes me. Terrified it might be Jay, I duck into a driveway, my cardigan catching on something and pulling me into a bush as something sharp tears against the skin on my bare legs.

I squat in the darkness—my body heaving with the force of my tears and sobs. As the car draws level, I lose all control and wet myself.

With my hand covering my mouth to quieten the sounds I'm making, I draw in a breath through my nose before choking out heaving sighs of relief as soon as the lights and sound of the car disappear. Having no option but to keep moving, and beyond feeling ashamed, I stand, wipe the inside of the tops of my legs on my cardigan, and start moving again towards the shops.

A floodlight illuminates the small car park, so I keep close to the darkened shopfronts, dashing past the bakers—where I usually get my coffee on my morning walks—which is lit up at the back, and make my way to the alley running between an Italian deli and the barbers.

Once in the alley, I hit Jo's number again. I don't know if that was Jay's car that passed me earlier, but I remain hidden and hopefully safe from being seen from the road. It takes two more tries before Jo picks up.

"Lauren, what's wrong?"

"Jo," I sob, overwhelmed with relief at hearing her voice. "Jo, please. Please can you come and get me. Please. I've had a fight with Jay."

"Where are you?"

I can't think straight. The pain radiating through my left shoulder is now so intense, my legs buckle, and I slide down the brick wall I'm leaning against. The freezing cold of the concrete pathway permeates my piss-soaked shorts and skin.

Leaning to the side, I vomit again, all the while, Jo is firing off questions I can't quite hear.

"I'm at the shops where the bakers and deli are. I can't see the name of the street; I can't remember what. . . I don't know the name of the street, Jo, I don't know it." I'm crying and trying to catch my breath as my teeth chatter together. I do know the name of the street, but my brain refuses to function and give me the answer. Another car drives by, and I release my breaths out in short pants, terrified the occupants might hear me breathe or cry. Letting out a whimper of relief when it passes, I hear Jo calling my name down the phone.

"Lauren, listen to me. I need you to calm the fuck down and listen. I know where you are, and I'm coming there now."

"Jo, just make sure Jay's not driving about looking for me. Listen to me, Jo, make sure. . ."

"I will, I'll turn off my headlights," she cuts me off and says. "I need you to stay calm and listen. I'm just getting into my car, when I start it up the phone will cut out and the Bluetooth will kick in, but I'm still here, okay, I'm still with you. It'll just drop out for a few seconds." It takes about thirty seconds before I hear her again.

"Right, I'm back, and I'm on my way. It'll take me five minutes, tops."

There's silence for a few long seconds, and I panic that the phone has cut out.

"Jo? Jo?"

"I'm here. I'm right here. Are you hurt? Do we need to call the police or an ambulance, Lauren?"

"No. No police. I can't. I won't do that to my boys."

"I've got a feeling he might need *protecting* from your boys when they find out what he's been doing."

I can't even process an answer to that comment. The

thought of my kids finding out about all of this hurts so much more than anything Jay could physically inflict.

"I can't, I need time. I can't let them see me like this. I need time before I tell them."

"Are you hurt then? Has he marked you? Talk to me, Lauren."

"I'm fine, I'm fine. No police, no ambulance. I don't want to go to the hospital; they'll call the police. I need time, Jo, time to talk to the boys."

"Okay, okay. We'll figure it out. I'm here. My lights are off, and I'm just pulling into the car park. Where are you?"

"In the alley."

I watch as her car pulls up parallel to where I'm hiding. I'm so overwhelmed with relief that I can't move. As Jo climbs from her car and approaches, the noise that escapes me doesn't even sound human.

"It's okay. It's okay. I've got you; I've got you."

Jo squats down to my level, but I can't bring myself to meet her eyes. I don't want to see in them what she's thinking of me right now.

"Oh, Jesus. Fucking hell. Fuck. Can you walk? We need to get you to a hospital. Can you stand up? Let's get you into the car, don't even bother trying to argue with me, you need to get to the hospital."

"I can't. I pissed myself, I can't get in your car like this." I sob between almost every word. As I stand upright, I'm hit with a wall of pain but can't pinpoint the source. Everything hurts, from my head, to my heart, to my toenails and fingertips, I hurt.

"I couldn't give a fuck if you were covered from head to toe in shit, you are getting in my car, and we're going to the hospital."

CHAPTER 10

Lauren

The lie comes so easily, and once I tell the first, despite the trauma, my injuries, the alcohol I've consumed, I manage to weave an elaborate and yet believable tale of a drunken girls' night out, which results in me bouncing on the bed, losing my balance, taking a tumble and landing on the chest of drawers beside the bed. My fall resulting in bruising four ribs, dislocating my shoulder, a glued-up gash to my head, a bruised cheek and jaw, and various other bruises and contusions all over my body.

The nurse knew I was lying.

The doctor knew I was lying.

But I escaped the hospital without the police being called and am now settled in the front of Jo's car with my ribs bandaged so tight I can barely breathe, my arm temporarily in a sling, a glued together head, lumps, bumps, bruises, and scratches to the entire rest of my body while wearing a hospital gown, my UGGs, and cardigan. My pissy sleep shorts were dumped in a surgical waste bin after I convinced the nurse I'd wet myself after laughing so hard at falling off the bed.

It's eight in the morning when we pull up outside Jo's, and my phone shows forty-seven missed calls and texts from Jay.

I have nothing to say to him. I don't know that I ever will, but just in case, I've written a whole fucking speech in my head. One day I'll be able to look him in the eye and convey the fear and terror he's made me feel. But *that* day isn't *this* day, nor will it be any day soon.

Right now, I'm just grateful that his car isn't parked at Jo's with him inside waiting for my return. I'm exhausted. Mentally, physically, and emotionally drained. I feel hollow. I'd like to think I had no tears left in me to cry, but they're there, right below the surface and ready to breach the barriers of my eyelids the instant I let my guard down.

Jo cuts the engine of her car, but she speaks before I can move to open the door.

"I'm beyond pissed off at you for not getting the police involved tonight, but right now, I'm exhausted, you look like absolute shit, we both need a shower, and we both need to try and get some sleep."

I turn and meet her light brown eyes, one of those tears I was keeping prisoner escapes and rolls down my cheek.

"But at some stage, we are going to talk about this, and you are going to tell me exactly what happened tonight. There is a bed at my house for as long as you need it. I will feed you. I will clothe you. I will lend you whatever money you need, but at some point, I will expect the truth."

I nod, knowing if I even attempt to speak, the only sound that'll escape me will be yet another sob.

"Right, let's get you in and get you showered. Stay there, I'll come around and help you out."

* * *

An hour later, freshly showered, and with the blood washed from my hair—thanks to Jo's help—I'm sitting at her bench wearing one of her hoodies and a pair of hammer pants while picking at a bacon sandwich.

"Eat that, you're going to need to take some pain meds soon, and you can't do that on an empty stomach," Jo orders.

Before I can respond, my phone vibrates from where it's plugged in at the wall. Jo removes the charger and slides it to me. Jemma's name lights up the screen. I swipe to open and set it to speaker.

"What the fuck is going on? Where are you?"

"And good morning to you too, Mrs Wilson."

"Cut the crap, East! Why is your husband ringing me looking for you? What's happened?"

Jo's phone begins to vibrate. "It's Jay. Jem, we'll call you back in a few and explain everything. Love you, bye."

"Don't you dare. . ."

I cut Jem off and end my call as Jo answers hers.

"Hey, Jay. You're up bright and early. What can I do you for?" She winks at me and says before Jay even speaks.

"Morning, Jo." My eyes close at the sound of his voice, my heart stutters in my chest, and just for a moment, a very short moment, I feel something. Opening my eyes, I instantly lock it down.

"I don't suppose you've seen my wife, have you?"

"Lauren… no… not since last night. I shared a taxi with her. I don't understand. She did come home, right?"

"She did, but I got home after her, and I'd had a little too much to drink. You know how she can be? We got into a bit of a blue, and she stormed off."

My mouth drops open. Jo taps her pointer finger against her lips, telling me to shush.

"In the middle of the night?" she questions Jay.

"Yeah, I'm not exactly sure of the time."

"And you didn't go after her?"

"Like I said, I'd had too much to drink."

"We had a bit to drink ourselves. Surely she didn't drive?"

"Nah, that's the kicker, when she stormed off, I thought she'd taken her car. I'd left my car at the club last night and thought I had no way of going after her."

He's so full of shit. His car was on our drive when I left last night. He'd driven home from wherever he'd been in the state he was in. I shake my head, my mouth still hanging open. My skin tingles. I'm not sure if I'm in shock or just nervous at the sound of his voice. This entire situation is surreal. I'm listening to my husband tell blatant lies about me to one of my best friends.

"Okay. Has she got her phone with her?"

"I think so, but she's not picking up. I've called and messaged. I'm getting worried, Jo."

"She left on foot at three in the morning, and you've not heard from her since? I'm worried too. Have you tried Jemma and Lou?"

"Yeah, I've tried both of them."

"Jay, I think you need to call the police."

"I'll keep ringing around. She might've called her mum or sister to pick her up. I'll give them a try. If you hear from her, will you call me please?"

"I think that's highly unlikely. Why would she wake them up in the middle of the night when she could just come here? That doesn't make sense. I'm worried, Jay, I really think you should consider reporting this to the police." Jo rolls her eyes as she talks, knowing full well that's *not* what he's going to do.

"Yeah, I'll try her mum and sister first, then I'll do that. Call me if you hear from her. I just need to know she's safe."

"Of course, but can you do the same? I'm really worried about her."

"Yeah, me too, and I will do."

Jay ends the call. I watch Jo stare down at her phone for a moment before looking up at me.

"I can't believe the man I just spoke to is the man who did this to you." She gestures with her head towards me as she speaks, "Do you think it's a mental health thing?"

Shaking my head, I feel my lips start to tremble as my nose tingles. I really don't want to cry anymore. I'm getting on my own last nerve with all the crying.

"I honestly don't know. It's been going on for almost a year but has really escalated the last few months. I've tried talking to him, I booked weekends away for just me and him, and for his birthday, I surprised him with a golfing weekend away for him and four mates." I shrug. "I don't know Jo; I just don't know. It's not just the violence, it's the things he says, the names he calls me. It's like he hates me, despises me. But I have absolutely no idea why."

Jo's phone rattles from where she set it down on the counter and I almost fall backwards off the stool. Holding the palm of my hand against my chest, I attempt to calm my erratically beating heart.

"Hey," Jo aims a raised brow smile my way as she answers. "Yep, she's right here."

I attempt to screw up my face in confusion as she hands me the phone, but it hurts so I take it from her. My battered heart that I'd managed to settle does the opposite when I see the name displayed on the screen.

"Shit," I whisper-hiss before answering.

"Hey," I narrow my gaze on Jo, and shake my head as I speak.

The bitch winks at me.

"Hey. You okay?" Gabe's voice sounds down the phone with a worried edge to it.

Again—and not because the sound of his voice does things to me—I forget about my injuries and frown, which hurts my puffy eye, making me wince instead.

"Yeah. . . Why wouldn't I be okay?" I question. Panicking for a moment that Jo might have called him and told him what happened when I got home last night.

"What's he want?" Jo whispers from beside me. "Put him on speaker, I want to hear." I give her my middle finger and turn my back.

"You at Jo's already?" Gabe asks, ignoring my question.

"Yeah," is my short reply. I'm probably sounding like an absolute bitch, but I just don't have a conversation in me right now. Nor am I ready to admit that I was wrong and everyone else was right and I shouldn't have gone home last night.

"So, you got it all done and moved out okay?" There's a short pause as he waits for my answer, but I'm unsure of what to say, and he continues before I can get my brain into gear.

"Look, I know it's none of my business, and I don't know what it is exactly that you've got going on, and I get we don't know each other, but I meant what I said, if there's anything you need help with, just shout, and I'm there."

"I'm good, but thanks." I let out a long slow breath and give my head a shake as I inwardly cringe at my response. "Sorry, didn't mean to sound snappy, I'm just tired."

Jo moves into my line of sight, clicks her finger, raises her brows, holds her palms up, and shrugs, waiting on my response to her earlier demands.

'Fuck off,' I mouth.

"Ohhhh. Interesting. You don't want me listening?" This time she doesn't bother to whisper.

Ignoring both my apology and Jo's comment, he continues, "Listen, I got everything done I needed to this morning, and if you're all set at Jo's, I wondered if you'd like to come and have a look at this unit we've got coming up for rent. . . If you're still looking?"

I remain silent as I try to think of an excuse, but my exhausted, battle-weary brain has nothing.

"I. . . yeah. I'm still looking, but I'm sorry, I'm not going to be able to make it work today."

"Tomorrow then? I can text you the address and meet you there around. . ."

"Gabe, look. This is really good of you, but right now, I can't. I need to find work and just generally get my shit together before I can even consider taking on a rental."

A menagerie of birds, bats, and butterflies all flapping their wings at once replaces the hollowness in my chest and belly as I start to panic at how much I really do need to organise.

"Look, you need somewhere to live. We can work something out with the rent, it's honestly not a problem."

Overwhelmed and exhausted, I'm done with the back and forth and let out a long sigh before responding.

"Again, thanks, but I'm not looking for a handout or any other kind of charity. When I've got my life in some kind of order, I'll be in touch, but that's not likely to be any time soon," I bite out.

Leaning forward, I rest my forehead on Jo's granite bench-top, and almost bang it against the surface before remembering it's broken and glued together.

I don't know why I'm being so horrible to him. Even as I'm saying the words and using the tone I'm using I know it's arse-holish of me. He's been nothing but nice, and here I am being a total bitch.

"Okay. Well, no worries then, Lauren. . ."

I'm knocked sideways and again nearly come off my stool as Jo snatches the phone from my hand.

"Gabe? It's Jo again, can I call you back? Lauren is definitely interested in the place you have for rent, and we'll be looking at it soon. Call you back, bye."

I'm in pain, and can barely keep my eyes open, my mouth on the other hand just hangs there gapping.

"What?" Jo asks but doesn't wait for an answer. "*You* need somewhere to live, *he* has a place to rent, he's obviously into you, and who wouldn't want *him* as a landlord? I'll go and have a look at the unit for you if you don't want to go."

I let out a loud sigh. "I need to sleep, Jo, and to be able to do that, I need some more drugs. When I've done that, then I'll argue with you about this, but I don't have one more battle left in me right now."

Even before I finish talking, she gets up, pours me a glass of water, and hands it to me with the pain meds we picked up on the way home from the hospital.

"Take them and go, I'm gonna try and get a couple of hours myself."

"I love you," I tell her. "Thank you for everything."

"Stop talking, you know you'll only end up crying. Go." She waves me away with a flick of her wrist.

I slide off the stool and take my battered heart, mind, and body to Jo's guest room.

CHAPTER 11

Gabe

I HAVE zero idea as to what the fuck I'm doing, but apparently, it's not the right thing. Never in my life have I pursued a woman, and it's pretty fucking obvious after just sounding like the world's biggest pussy on the phone to Lauren and getting totally shot down for it.

I'm not sure what it is I'm so attracted to. I like my life drama free, and this woman is literally draped in one giant red flag, but there's just something about her that has me hooked.

I make my way back into the Italian place where I'm having breakfast with my brothers and Jack.

Sitting back down at the table, Zac doesn't miss the stench of failure that must be oozing from my pores.

"Who pissed in your Weet Bix?" he asks before my arse even hits the chair.

I give him a blank stare which I hope conveys the '*fuck right off'* I'm thinking.

"Did you call? She get away okay?" Cooper asks. Like me, he'd seen Lauren's bruises last night and assumed, also like me, they were the reason she was leaving her husband. I'd also shared with him earlier that I was going to show her a unit we've just renovated and were about to rent out. He's not stupid and knew exactly who I was calling when I stepped outside with my phone in my hand.

"Yeah, she's at Jo's already."

"She gonna look at the place on Gardener Street?"

I avoid making eye contact with my brother by looking up at the waitress and thanking her as she puts my eggs beni down in front of me. I shake my head while busying myself with the salt and pepper and asking for the hot sauce.

"Why not?" Cooper asks as I finally look up and meet his eyes, aware that both Zac and Jack are watching us.

"She needs to sort her head out, find a job, whatever," I offer with a shrug.

"And you're gonna just leave it at that? I thought you liked this chick?"

"Who?" Zac and Jack ask in unison.

"Lauren..."

"The redhead from last night?" Zac questions. I nod, proceeding to fork food into my mouth so I don't have to answer any more questions.

"The short one who was with the blonde you were talking to at the bar?" Jack asks, my eyes instantly narrowing on him as a little tug of jealousy pulls at my gut.

"Oh shit, looks like you've got competition, Gabe," Zac chimes in.

I take a sip of my coffee and study Jack for a moment. He's a couple of years younger than me, but I know he has a kid a bit younger than Ava. I thought I was young at twenty-three, and becoming a father, but Jack must've only been nineteen or twenty. He's recently moved down here from the North Coast of New South Wales but already has a bit of a celebrity status in the area because of his brother's fame as an MMA fighter. It might also have something to do with the fact he's a good-looking rooster. My sister's telling me constantly that with his pouty lips, hair that he's constantly pushing back off his face, and his green eyes, he could easily be a model.

Can a stare be violent? I hope so because that's how I feel about Jack having any interest in Lauren, and I want him to know it. He doesn't back down from the look I'm serving him from across the table, he just smiles and shakes his head.

"Good luck with that redhead voodoo, their magic is pretty potent stuff," he says through a mouthful of bacon.

"You talking from experience?" I ask.

"Yep. . ." He finishes chewing his food and appears to be considering his next words as he does.

"You know there's always that one girl, the one you just feel different about? You just feel that thing, that pull. Right from the very start, you just know she's got something special?"

My mouth feels instantly dry, and I take a gulp of my coffee as he talks.

"I married mine," Zac says. "Straight up, I still feel that thing every time I look at Sam."

"Same," Cooper adds. "It's what I was talking to you about last night. It's not something that makes sense or that you can even put into words, it just is. It's there, and there's nothing you can do to change it."

I watch them nod, feeling like they've been inside my head all night.

"Nope," I admit, loudly popping my lips on the p sound. "It's never happened for me. There have been women I've wanted to see again, but if I don't," I shrug, "then, no drama. It's no big deal."

I watch a look pass between the three men I'm sitting with.

"What?" I question.

"Until last night?" Coop asks.

I let out a groan. "I don't fucking know. Something happened last night. As soon as I looked at her, I don't know. . ." I shrug again, rubbing at my chest with my knuckles. The indigestion from last night obviously returning. "It was like something shifted inside me."

My audience throw their heads back in unison and laugh.

"Until last night," Coop repeats. Only this time it's not a question.

"So what happened with you?" Cooper then asks Jack.

He scratches the back of his neck, pushes his floppy fringe my sister has a thing for, back off his face, and lets out a long slow breath.

"We were new, been seeing each other a couple of months. Man, I'm not embarrassed to admit, I was falling hard and fucking fast. I'd just turned twenty-one, had finally ended the toxic relationship I'd been in since school a few weeks before we met, and she was everything the last one wasn't."

My brothers are both holding forks laden with food mid-air as they listen to Jack. He puts his cutlery down and rubs both palms over his jaw and cheeks.

"She was heading off to Uni after the summer, so I went into it thinking it was just gonna be a casual, summer thing. I knew pretty much straight away I was wrong, that it was gonna be more. She was a couple of years younger than me, not much experience, so we took it slow." He leans forward, resting his elbows on the table, and my chest actually feels tight watching the way talking about this girl is affecting him.

"Finally, ya know, spent the best night ever together. I left her in bed the morning after, working out plans in my head on how to make the long-distance thing work once she went off to Uni when my ex calls to tell me she's pregnant."

"Ohhh," Zac says, putting down his fork and leaning back in

his chair.

"That sucks," Coop adds.

"Is this your kid's mum?" I ask.

"Yeah," he responds. "That phone call literally knocked me on my arse, took me a few days to get my shit together and decide what I was gonna do. Biggest fuck up I've ever made wasn't getting Eden pregnant, I love my kid and will never regret him, but Blue, I fucked up big time with her."

"Why, what happened?" Zac asks the question we all want the answer to.

"I spent the day thinking I should just let her go. She was eighteen, about to start a whole new life in Sydney. She didn't need to be dealing with my shit. So, I did what I thought was the right thing and stayed away. No contact."

He shrugs again, and again pushes back his fringe.

"I'd fucked her for the first time. . . no, that's not the right term. Man, how do I say it without sounding like a pussy? It was more than that."

He scratches at the back of his head and gives us all a grin before shaking his head.

"It was though, it was so much more, but then I stood her up that night, thinking a clean break was for the best, and didn't make any contact with her for the next couple of days. When I did finally get my head on straight, she didn't answer my calls or reply to my texts, so I went to her house. Her older brother opened the door and basically threatened to end my life if I didn't fuck off and leave her alone, so I did exactly that. A few days later I was like, yeah, fuck that, I went back to her house, and it was too late, she'd gone. Packed up her life and moved to Sydney a few weeks earlier than planned."

Jack wipes his hands on a paper napkin, screws it up, and drops it onto his plate.

"I shouldn't have waited, shouldn't have hesitated. We lived in a small beach town where everyone knows everybody else's business, bit like this place but smaller, much smaller. As soon as I got that call, I should've gone back and told her what was going on. The biggest regret of my life is that, instead, I acted like the world's biggest dick and left her hanging. I let her down, and she didn't deserve that. She was a good girl, the best. She'd obviously heard about the baby through the town's gossip network at some stage, packed up her bags, and left. I've never seen or heard from her since."

We're all quiet for a long moment. I don't think I've ever had such an intense conversation, about a girl, with a bunch of blokes sat around a table in my life. My jaw is clenched so hard I have a sharp pain in my temple.

"And she was a redhead?" Zac asks.

"Yep. Red hair, blue eyes, short, curvy. That's why I noticed *your* little redhead last night. I had to look twice just to make sure."

"She's not *my* little redhead," I snap.

"Fuck off," Jack says. "You looked like you wanted to reach across the table and rip my nuts out through my throat when I mentioned her earlier."

"He's got a point there, mate. You totally looked at him like that's what you wanted to do," Zac feels the need to voice his opinion.

"Who asked you, fuck face?" I ball my napkin and throw it across the table at him.

"Calm ya fucking farm. Far out, this bird really has got you all tied up in knots." I have no response to Zac this time. Instead, I fold my arms across my chest and sit back in my chair.

Cooper, who's sitting next to me, slides his arm across my back, slaps my shoulder, and asks, "Well, in light of all that, what would your advice to our young Gabriel be?"

"Mate, if you've got it this bad after only meeting her last night, then I'd say pursue things."

"She only left her husband this morning. He's playing golf,

chances are, he don't even know she's gone yet."

"Fucking hell," Jack adds a whistle to his response. "That's, yeah, nah. I don't honestly know what to say then."

Coop squeezes my shoulder where his hand still rests. He knows there's more to Lauren's story, but it's not my place to be saying anything to the boys about it.

"Did you say she's staying at Jo's?" Zac asks.

Still not wanting to speak to the mouthy fucker, I nod.

"Why don't you go around there later and drop off the key to Gardener Street and tell her to look at it whenever she's ready?"

"Because she's already told me she can't afford it till she gets a job."

"What sort of job does she want? Weren't you looking for someone to run your office for you?" Cooper asks me, then questions Jack.

"My sister's moved down. She's looking after Finn and helping me out with ordering and accounts and shit while she finishes college."

"Lauren's an interior designer, I said we might have some work for her at the new apartment block, but that won't help her out right now," I explain.

"Dude, that is fucking spooky. My redhead is an interior designer too... at least that's what she wanted to do after Uni."

"Yeah? Well, don't go getting any ideas..."

"Not interested, mate," he cuts me off. "I've got enough on my plate with work and keeping up with my kid." Jack holds his hands up in surrender as he responds to my comment.

"Yeah, I've got all of that shit happening too. That's why I should be staying the fuck away, not chasing after her."

Jack shrugs and chews on his bottom lip. "You need to work out what's gonna hurt more, dealing with the drama she comes with or the regret of not having tried?"

"Where does Jo live again?" I ask Cooper without even a moment's hesitation.

* * *

I DECIDE to give Lauren the day to unpack her stuff and get settled at Jo's before rocking up unannounced.

The weather's dark and gloomy, the surf too lumpy to take my board out, so after a quick chat with Ava on the phone, I'd spent the afternoon just lying on my sofa wondering what the actual fuck I was doing with my life.

Jo hasn't called me back like she'd said she would on the phone earlier, and although I'd pulled both hers and Lauren's numbers up on my screen, I hadn't had the balls to actually call either of them and say that I'd be dropping a key over.

Hoping not to come across as too desperate, I stop off at the bottle shop and pick up a decent bottle of Prosecco as a gift for the girls to celebrate their temporary living situation with.

Jo lives in a gorgeous single-story place off the esplanade that we'd done a complete reno job on for her a couple of years ago. Turning off the beach road and onto a dirt track, I notice a Land Cruiser parked on the in and out drive and assume it must be Lauren's.

I pull my truck up behind the cruiser, rehearsing in my head what I'm going to say to explain my uninvited appearance. Wiping my palms on my jeans, I grab the bottle of drink, climb out the cab, and make my way to the front door.

Stepping back so the entryway camera can pick me up and I don't freak the girls out, I press the doorbell. It takes a few moments, but Jo eventually pulls the door open.

"Gabe?" She wears a frown on her face as she says my name like a question. For a split second, I regret coming here, but I brush it aside, lean one shoulder against the door frame, and give Jo my best smile.

"Hey, Jo. Was wondering if I could have a quick word with Lauren?"

"Huh! Okay. I'm not sure. . ." She pauses, studying me for a moment. "Talk to me, Gabe. What's going on here? Why the interest in my girl? With the greatest respect to you and your past conquests, but she is not your usual one and done type."

I consider bullshitting her with the key and Prosecco story, instead, I respect Jo's blunt approach and respond with my own.

"I really fucking like her, Jo. I haven't stopped thinking about her since last night. You heard her on the phone, she doesn't want a bar of me but I. . ."

"She does, she likes you, she's just got a lot going on, Gabe, like seriously. A. Lot."

"I saw the bruises, I worked that out for myself."

"You saw the bruises?" she asks, her arms folding across her chest, as she moves to the middle of the door to block my entry.

"Last night. Her makeup rubbed off when you were dancing. I noticed bruises along her jaw, then on her wrist when she was pulling her jacket on. I want to help her out, Jo. . ." I step back from the door and hold my arms out to the side. "I don't fucking know, I've no idea what I'm doing. I just know I want to see her again."

Raking her fingers through her long hair, she tosses it over one shoulder and gathers it over the other. When her brown eyes meet mine, I know she's made her decision.

"I'm going to let you in, and we're going to talk, I'm gonna set you straight about a few things, and if you don't like what I'm gonna tell you, you can leave and it'll stay just between us. Lauren will never know you were here."

"So, she's not here?"

"Yeah, she's sleeping, probably will be for a while yet."

I offer the bottle of Prosecco, accompanied by my best smile. Jo takes the Prosecco from me and steps aside.

"Save your smile for Lauren, I'm immune to your charms, Wild."

Shaking my head, I follow her inside.

CHAPTER 12

Lauren

WITHOUT EVEN BEING FULLY AWAKE, I sense the presence and then feel the body's heat pressed against me from behind.

A hand slides across my hip, as a stubbled jaw brushes against my shoulder, before burying itself in the curve of my neck.

My skin ignites as goosebumps erupt across its surface. As his unique scent fills my nose, I know who it is before he even lays a hand on me. Hot breath spreads across my ear and against my head as a hard dick presses against my arse.

"You shouldn't be here," I croak in my sleep-affected voice.

"I couldn't stay away," he replies before leaving a trail of wet kisses along my jaw.

"You need to leave."

His hand slides under the singlet I'm wearing, and my head spins at the sensation of his skin against mine. His hand slides from the curve of my waist to rest at the top of my ribs, right below my boobs. Everything clenches tightly inside me, and I shudder.

There's no way he didn't feel that. No way he doesn't know the effect he's having on me.

"Is that really what you want?"

His hand slides higher, his thumb brushes across my hard nipple, and I pant out a short, sharp breath when he again grinds against me.

"Didn't think so."

I can feel his smile against my cheek as he talks.

I'm lying on my side, legs pressed together as tightly as I can get them, everything inside me tensed.

His fingertips trail a path from the centre of my chest, down past my belly, before sliding inside my sleep shorts.

"Gabe," I whisper.

"I've got you. I've got. . ."

Jo's laugh interrupts my vivid dream and drags me back to consciousness. I force my eyes to open. One of them not quite as wide as the other. I'm instantly hit with a pounding headache and the realisation that my hand is inside my shorts.

"Seriously. What the fuck is wrong with you? Now is not the time," I whisper out loud to myself.

I assumed Jo was on the phone, but when I hear the low rumble of a second voice, I slide carefully up and sit on the side of the bed.

There's a bottle of water and my next round of pain meds sitting on the bedside table next to me, I take them before I even attempt to move, and chug down the entire contents of the bottle. I regret that the instant I stand; nausea hits my stomach, and not only does my head spin, but it pounds with a dull thump. The pain in my shoulder has eased, and I lean into the bed with both hands and wait for the dizziness to pass, hoping I don't throw up all over it.

Making my way to the ensuite, I use the toilet before washing my hands and splashing water on my face. Staring down into the sink, I have to take a few moments to prepare before I look at my reflection in the mirror.

"Far out." I shake my head at the strangely familiar woman looking back at me before taking all of her in. It's me, but not me. It's a version of me.

I pant out my breath in short gasps as I fight the burn at the back of my eyes and the tingle in my nose. My jaw trembles, but not a single tear falls.

"I fucking hate you, Jason East, you will not beat me," I tell my reflection through gritted teeth.

My lip is split and swollen at the bottom right corner and swollen in the middle at the top. The bruises along my jawline are yellowing, but fresh purple and blue covers my cheek and eye, which is almost swollen completely closed.

My hair's natural curl has won the battle with the straightened version I wore last night after the steam from my shower earlier made it damp. It's piled on top of my head in a messy bun, and I attempt to apply some order by tipping my head forward and combing it through with my fingers. This hurts my ribs and I have to hold my breath as I do it. Even holding my arms above my head to put my scrunchy back in has to be done slowly.

I want to cry again. Not because I'm in so much pain, but because I'm angry and frustrated. Right now, I hate my husband.

I don't get it. I'll never get it. He's my husband. Even if he's fallen out of love with me, why this?

I take a few more moments, gently tracing the cuts and bruises with my fingertips.

When I get my emotions in check, I freshen myself up.

There's a new toothbrush, tube of toothpaste, moisturiser, face wipes, and deodorant sitting next to the sink, and I use them all.

Still looking as rough as fuck but feeling marginally better I go out to the bedroom and carefully pull on the trackie pants and hoodie Jo had lent me earlier. My breath catches, and I let out a groan as I slowly raise my arms. The pain in my ribs feeling even worse now than it was a few minutes ago. I've obviously slept past the time my meds were due, making almost every move I now make painful.

Sitting back on the edge of the bed, I struggle to push my feet into my UGGs without bending over and pulling them on. How the fuck I managed to do it last night, I'll never know.

Looking at my phone, I'm shocked to see it's just after seven, meaning I've slept around eight hours. I also note another thirty-seven missed calls from Jay, along with twenty-two text messages, two of which are from my boys.

I don't have it in me to talk to my kids right now, but Jay has apparently spoken to them. Not wanting them to worry, I fire off a text.

Me: **I'm safe. I love you and will call tomorrow and explain everything. Please don't worry xoxo**

Keeping my phone on silent, I slide it into the pocket at the front of the hoodie and head to Jo's kitchen.

CHAPTER 13

G abe

FOLLOWING Jo along the hallway of her home into the open plan, kitchen, meals, and dining area, I'm greeted with a cautious half-smile from the brunette who was out with her and Lauren last night.

"Jem, you remember Gabe from last night?"

"Hey." I smile and offer a chin lift, receiving a nod, chin lift, and a lip twitch in response. I watch her eyes slide to Jo as she slowly shakes her head.

"What?" Jo questions.

"This is not what she'd want. If she wakes up and finds him here, she's gonna be so pissed off with you."

"He brought Prosecco," Jo announces, holding the bottle up in response.

"Is that what got you past the barricade?" Her dark blue eyes land back on mine.

I shrug. "That and my charm and good looks," I respond with a wink.

"She's too easy to bribe. A cheap bottle of grog and a few words from a dude with a face like yours are all it ever takes to get Jo to say yes."

"Fuck you, Wilson, it's Brown Brothers King Valley, my favourite. I wouldn't have let him in if it was any old bottle." Turning to me, Jo bats her lashes. "Ignore her, Gabe. Now, can I get you a drink? I think you're gonna need it for what I'm about to tell you."

Curious at her words, I nod slowly. "Sure. . . have you got a bourbon?" I ask while making myself comfortable on a stool at Jo's bench next to Jemma.

"Of course. You want that over ice?" Jo asks while pulling a bottle of Makers Mark from a cupboard.

"Yeah, please. Why am I going to need a drink?" I question while watching her fill the glass with ice from the fridge's dispenser. She slides the glass and the bottle in front of me.

"Gabe noticed bruises on Lauren's jaw and wrist last night." Jo ignores my question and instead addresses Jemma, who tilts her head to the side and studies me while topping up her glass with wine. I break eye contact and fill up my own.

"Like Jemma said, you being here isn't what she'd want, but if you're determined to pursue things with Lauren, there are a few things you need to know."

Jo's still talking when I hear the double doors behind her open. I tilt my head to look around her, my brain taking a moment to process what I'm seeing, my skin reacts with a prickling sensation rushing across it before my brain can catch on.

I should stand up. I should go to her.

"Lauren," Jemma whispers from beside me. A glass is knocked over, red wine spills, and the legs of a stool scrape across the tiled floor, but I don't move. I stare, but I don't move.

Looking slowly from Jemma to Jo to me, Lauren shakes her head as her lips tremble.

"Why?" she asks, sounding croaky. Clearing her throat, I watch as tears fill both her eyes. Her left eye is red and bloodshot, a purple bruise surrounds her right eye which barely opens. A tear escapes and rolls down her cheek, the knot in my belly tightens, and I instinctively stand but hold back from moving towards her.

"Why is he here? Why would you do that to me?"

The room remains silent, and I think I must've been holding my breath from the moment she appeared in the doorway because when a "What the fuck?" escapes me in a whispered rush of air, I feel like I can barely breathe like I've been punched in the gut and left winded.

Jemma moves around me and towards Lauren, who holds up a hand to stop her.

"Lauren," she whispers on a sob. "I'm so sorry. We should've insisted, as your friends, we shouldn't have let you go back there. . ."

"He did this to you? Your husband? I fucking told you, I asked you not to go back there last night. Where is he now? Did you have him arrested for this?" The instant the words are out, I feel like a total dick.

"Will you both sit the fuck down and shut up. This is not what she needs to hear right now," Jo snaps.

Lauren stands in the middle of the room looking small, battered, bruised and beaten, and for a few long moments, my head spins as I fight to control the anger brewing inside me. I grip the edge of the benchtop as I watch her wrap her arms around her middle in what I assume is an attempt at holding herself together.

"I'm sorry," Jemma repeats. We've both ignored Jo's order for us to sit down. Lacing my fingers together at the back of my head, I take in a few deep breaths as Jemma moves towards Lauren while she talks.

"Not just that this has happened, but that it's been happening for so long. You're always there for all of us, Loz, and we weren't there for you. We weren't there and I'm so fucking sorry."

I watch as Jemma gently touches Lauren's hair and face while she stands there with her eyes closed.

"What's his name?" I ask. "Your husband, what's his fucking name?"

Lauren opens her eyes, steps around Jemma, and moves to stand on the other side of the benchtop next to Jo, all without answering my question or looking at me.

"Have you had him charged?"

Leaning forward, I watch as she picks up the wine glass that's lying on its side and drinks what's left of the contents.

"Loz, I don't think that's a good idea, not with those pain killers. . ." Jo says.

"You don't think that's a good idea, but inviting him here to see me like this is? Fuck you, Jo. Why would you do that? Why would you do that to me?"

"I didn't invite him."

"She didn't invite me." Jo and I reply at the same time.

"Then why are you here?" Lauren asks through a swollen top and split bottom lip.

Unsure of what to say, I play her at her own game and ignore the question, and instead, repeat my own.

"What's his name?" I ask again.

"Who?" she questions.

"Don't fuck around, Ren, you know who, the prick who put his hands on you?"

"Gabe, that's not going to help. . ." Jo interjects. I cut her off.

"His name, Lauren? I'll find it out somehow, so you might as well just. . ."

"Jason," Jemma says from beside me. "Jason East."

My eyes widen as I turn to look first at Jemma, then back to Lauren.

"Jason East? Jay from JME Developments? You're married to Jay? He did this to you?" My voice rises with every question. I know the bloke, only because we're both in the building game and operate in the same area, but I've met him, spoken to him.

"I thought I told you last night you probably know him?" Jo questions.

"No, I had no fucking idea," I reply. My eyes still on Lauren.

"What does it matter?" Lauren asks. "It's done, I'm fine. I've left him, and I'm fine." She pours more wine into the glass and chugs it down.

"Seriously, that's enough." Jo snatches the empty glass from her hand. Turning around, Lauren grabs the bottle of wine Jo's been pouring from and drinks straight from it.

"What the fuck," Jo shouts as she pulls it from her mouth, red wine spilling down her chin and chest. "What the fuck is wrong with you?"

Lauren winces and presses the back of her hand against her split lip, eyeing Jo the whole time.

"What the fuck is wrong with me? Where would you like me to start? Oh, I know. Why. Is. He. Here?" She jabs her finger in my direction as she speaks.

"I came to see you," I explain.

Pulling the house key from my back pocket, I hold it out as both women turn and look at me.

"Jo didn't invite me. I knocked on the off chance I'd get to see you and give you this." I hold up the key.

"But I already told you. . ."

"I know," I interrupt while leaning across the bench to get closer to her.

"I know what you fucking told me, but I didn't know about

any of this. I didn't know. . ." I raise my hand and wave it in her general direction before letting it fall back to my side.

My entire body vibrating with rage, I straighten, take a step back, then another forward.

"I needed an excuse to see you again, for fucks sake." I shrug. "That's it. I wanted to see you and the key and Prosecco were the best I could come up with."

Burying my hands in my pockets because I don't know what else to do with them, we stare at each other in silence for a few seconds. I use that time to consider all the ways I'm going to break Jason East's bones.

"Well, here I am. You've seen me now, in all my fucking glory," Lauren shouts, gestures with her arms out wide, before wincing and letting them fall back to her sides.

"Did you all have a good chin wag before I walked in? Discuss the state of my marriage, the fact my husband's been beating me these past few months, and the absolute shit show that *is* my life?"

Her chest heaves and her breathing shudders when she stops talking. Her eyes slide to where Jo has placed the wine bottle back down, but Jo reacts at the same time Lauren makes her move.

"Don't even fucking think about it," Jo says, snatching the bottle back up.

"Well, I need something to blur the vision of you lot sitting here giving me your sympathetic sad eyes. Don't feel sorry for me, just don't. I appreciate your help, but I don't need your sympathy," her eyes slice to me, "a pissing contest with my husband, or your charity. I don't need looking after."

She pauses, her face bruised, lips trembling, chest heaving as she fights to compose herself. It's possibly the most heart-breaking scene I've ever witnessed, and I feel absolutely fucking helpless.

"It's happened," she continues. "I should've listened to all of you last night and I didn't. I fucked up, and I went home. I thought. . ." she trails off again, her tongue darts out, the tip flicks over the cut on her lip before she huffs out a breath. "I thought the beating he gave me last week was the end of it, I didn't think for a minute he'd do something like this, otherwise I wouldn't have gone there."

She steps back and leans against the sink for support and again wraps her arms around her middle. It's heart-breaking to watch, and all I want to do is go to her, but I know that's not what she needs right now. She needs to vent, to get all of this off her chest. I can't even begin to imagine how she's feeling, but I know I have to give her this moment to let her say what she needs to say.

Nodding, she stares down at the timber floor.

"I gave him the benefit of the doubt, and these are the consequences." She holds her arms out to the side again. "I fucked up. But now it's done. I just want to heal my heart and my body, and then I want

. . . no, I need to start patching my life back together. What I don't need is sympathy. What I don't need is retaliation. I hate him for what he's done." She waves her hand up and down her body.

"Not just this, not just the violence, but what he's done to our lives, how this is going to impact our kids' lives. I need your support, but please, please don't give me your sympathy. That'll just make me feel like a victim, and I'm not a victim, I refuse to be."

She looks up, and in turn makes eye contact with each of us as she wipes her nose across the back of her hand and shakes her head.

"I will not let him win," she almost whispers.

Absolute silence fills the room. I watch her lips and jaw tremble as she breathes in through her nose.

Folding her arms across her chest, she tilts her chin and

looks in my direction. "I'm sorry, Gabe, that you had to witness all of this, and maybe in another life, we could've given things a try, but right now, in this life, it ain't happening."

Grinding my teeth together, I debate on walking away, hunting down her cock of a husband, and kicking the living fucking daylights out of him, but then Jack's words from earlier hit me. . .

'What's gonna hurt more, dealing with the drama she comes with, or the regret of not having tried?'

I lean with both elbows on the benchtop. My head spins slightly as my heart rate slows, and my legs feel like jelly after the adrenaline-fuelled last few minutes begin to calm.

"I don't see you as a victim," I tell her quietly. "When I look at you, that's not sympathy you're seeing written on my face. That's me struggling to contain the anger I'm feeling right down to my very marrow."

I again lean towards her as I try to get my point across without raising my voice.

"I can't even begin to put into words how fucking pissed off I am every single time I look at you and find another bruise, see the damage he's done. . ."

Lauren holds her pointer finger up in the air. "Sorry, but I think I'm gonna. . ."

Before she can finish what she's saying, she spins around and throws up in Jo's sink.

CHAPTER 14

Lauren

The bile I'm heaving up burns my throat and I barely have a chance to catch my breath before my stomach cramps again and repeats the action.

I heave so hard I think I've wet myself just a little bit. Twice in less than twenty-four hours, my bladder has reminded me of my age. When my stomach finally settles, I cross my arms over the edge of the sink and rest my forehead on them. A hand gently rubs at my back, but I've no idea who it belongs to, and I'm too embarrassed to turn around and find out. Not because I've never felt so humiliated in my life, but because of my irrational behaviour. I saw Gabe sitting at Jo's bench when I walked into the room and turned into a crazy woman.

"Take a swig of this, just rinse your mouth if you think it's gonna make you throw up again," Jo says as she passes me a bottle of water.

"Thank you," I mumble, still staring into the sink rather than look her in the eye. I swirl the water around my mouth and spit. Jo must've turned on the tap at some stage, and I watch as everything disappears down the plughole. I stare for a moment, contemplating the apology I know I need to make while wondering if the fact my pelvic floor isn't what it once was is now apparent to everyone else in the room. Hopefully, the fact the trackies I'm wearing are a little big will mean there isn't an obvious wet patch, and I'm the only person who knows I need to take another shower.

Taking my time to stand upright, I turn and face the room. Gabe is leaning against the opposite side of the bench, Jemma, next to him is sweeping glass into a dustpan. Jo is to my left, leaning her hip into the benchtop, arms folded across her chest.

"Sorry," slicing my gaze between each of them, I make my apology. "I've no idea what the fuck just happened; concussion maybe?" I shrug and give a small smile, then wince as the action tugs apart the split in my lip.

"You're a fucking lunatic," Jemma states, moving around the bench and emptying glass from the dustpan into the bin hiding in the drawer next to me. Tapping my leg for me to move, I step aside allowing her to dispose of the dustpan and brush in the cupboard under the sink.

Standing up, she leans against the bench beside me, folds her arms, and raises her brows. I feel like a naughty kid having to explain my behaviour.

"This is very true. I blame it on the meds and the blood loss from my head injury," I attempt to joke.

"Head injury?" Gabe and Jemma question in unison.

I wave my hand in an *'it's nothing'* gesture.

"It's fine, bled a bit, but it's all glued back together now. Essex girl remember." I raise my arm and pointlessly tense my non-existent muscle that's hidden beneath the sleeve of the hoodie I'm wearing.

I'm rambling, highly aware of Gabe's striking blue eyes watching me from beneath dark brows and lashes. His lips twitch as if he's attempting to hold back a smile, and despite everything that's happened to me over the past eighteen or so hours, he still manages to stir something inside me.

"You sound very. . . Essex when you're behaving like a lunatic," he says. The smile he was fighting to contain finally escaping as he speaks.

I shrug. "What can I say? There's a bit of a lunatic hiding in most Essex girls."

"Or a bit of an Essex girl hiding in most lunatics," Jem quips.

"Well, yours wasn't hiding tonight, darl, she was front, centre, and on full fucking show," Jo adds while pouring herself a glass of wine from the bottle I'd previously chugged from.

"And you can take your eyes off that bottle," Jem says as she pulls my pain meds from the bag sitting on the bench, reading the label before holding them up. "These contain codeine, they shouldn't be taken on an empty stomach, and they definitely shouldn't be taken with alcohol, in fact, I'd highly suggest you avoid it until at least two or three days after you finish taking these. Codeine hangs around in the system and will end up making you vomit again."

She pulls the other box out. "Antibiotics, so you shouldn't be drinking anyway. Did they give you a tetanus shot?"

I nod. Jem can be a bit scary when she's in nurse mode. A job she still manages to fit in between raising her two boys.

"Good. No alcohol, and please, eat something, will you?"

I nod again as a phone rings.

"It's yours," Gabe says, handing Jem the phone sitting next to him on the bench.

"Hey," she says after swiping to answer. "Yep." Her eyes come to me before she moves them to Jo, then Gabe. "Don't stress, we'll be fine," she says into the phone before looking at me. "Go get your shit. Jay's been to mine looking for you. Max says he was raging and is on his way here. Max is about fifteen minutes away and is right behind him in the car, but it might be better if you're not here when they arrive."

My skin tingles, so many thoughts rush through my mind, I don't think I even breathe for a few seconds.

"Yep, see you soon." Jem ends the call.

"Can she go to yours?" Jo asks, and it takes me a beat to realise she's talking to Gabe.

"What? No," I protest.

"Of course she can, but I'm more than happy to wait here for that prick to arrive," Gabe responds.

"No!" Jem snaps. "Max is on his way, and he has my boys in the car with him. I don't want any trouble in front of them. I'll happily call the police if he starts anything, but I really don't want any trouble in front of my boys."

"Get your stuff," Gabe orders.

"No, I'll go to a hotel, I'm not going to yours."

"If you think I'm gonna drop you at a hotel while your psycho husband is riding around looking for you, you're fucking deluded. Get your stuff. You can stay at mine tonight, and we'll sort something out long-term tomorrow."

"Please, Loz, you know you have a bed here anytime, but right now, I need you to be safe, and unless you want the police involved and Jay locked up, it's better that you're somewhere he'll never think to look," Jo pleads.

She looks drained, and a pang of guilt fights with everything else I'm feeling right now to make itself known.

"Get your stuff," Gabe orders again.

"I only have my phone and the cardigan I was wearing last night. I don't have any other *things*," I explain.

"Your cardigan's in the laundry, it's caked in blood," Jo tells me.

"I'll wash it at Gabe's, That and my UGGs are all I've got." Saying that out loud has my eyes filling with tears again. It's the truth, all I have in the world is a blood-stained cardigan, my UGGs and my phone, but now's not the time to be getting sentimental over what I've left behind. I've caused my friends enough trouble, and as much as I don't really like the idea, staying at Gabe's tonight is the sensible option.

Jo disappears then reappears with my cardi in a black plastic sack and hands it to me. Gabe, who's now at my side, takes the bag from me, sliding his free hand to the small of my back and steering me towards Jo's front door.

"Please don't look so terrified, you're safe with me, I promise."

He's so close I can smell him. When I tilt my head to meet his gaze, all I see is a concerned frown.

"I'm so sorry you've been dragged into all of this. I'm. . . this is. . ."

"Seriously?" He interrupts me, which is probably a good thing because I'm all out of words right now. "You're standing there, looking like you do, with everything you own in this fucking bag." He holds the black sack up. "And you're the one apologising?"

He draws in a deep breath and lets it out with a huff. "We need to go because if your husband gets here before we've left, I will break his fucking face."

"That's really *not* what she needs to hear right now. Don't you think there's been enough violence? Just take her to yours, Gabe, and make sure you look after her, otherwise I'll be breaking your face," Jo threatens.

She's not prone to displays of emotion, she'll tell you that she's about to kill you with the same reserve she'll ask you if you'd like a drink, but I actually saw her cry at the hospital this morning when they were patching me up. She remained silent, but the sound her tears made as they spilled onto her cheeks deafened me and were an indicator as to how bad I must look.

Stepping forward, I wrap my good arm around her. The arm that was dislocated is throbbing and I daren't even try lifting it.

"Thank you for being there for me. I'll never forget what you did this morning," I say into her chest.

"I'm not going anywhere. I'll always be here for you any time, you know that. It's just that right now, I can't keep you safe, he can, and just so you know, I'd never send you with him if I didn't trust him one hundred percent."

"I know that, I know."

Jo kisses my cheek, and I step away in time to see Jemma hand Gabe the bag with my pain meds in, right before she wraps her arms around me.

"I'll never forgive myself for not knowing what he was doing to you. I don't know how I'm going to hold my temper if he turns up here, and just so you know, if he plays up, I'm calling the police, and I won't hesitate in telling them everything. I love you and respect that you want to talk to the boys first, but I think you're wrong, and I think your boys would rather have you safe than their feelings hurt."

I nod.

"Don't be ridiculous, it's my fault for keeping it a secret for so long. You have my total support if you choose not to hold on to your temper. Feel free to really go for it and kick him in the nuts as hard as you can for me, then you can call the police."

"Go. Text us when you get to Saint Gabe the Saviour's place."

"Wasn't Gabriel an angel?" I question Jem.

"Maybe. He looks more like a devil to me, which is probably more fun than an angel, who needs a good boy when you could have a dirty, filthy. . . but yeah, whatever, you lucky but also unlucky bitch. I love you, go."

I allow the good side of my lips to pull into a smile, grateful for my friends' attempts at lightening the shitty situation, and turn towards the front door, my path instantly blocked by Gabe.

"I can hear every word ya know?"

"Yeah, well, you already know Jo, it can't really come as any surprise what the people she chooses to be friends with would be like."

He turns, then pauses in his strides towards the front door and looks at me. I think he's going to say something, instead, he shakes his head before moving on.

* * *

GABE HELPS me into his truck by holding onto my hips and lifting me. I wince in pain, grateful that my back is to him.

"Which way is he likely to come in?" he asks as soon as he slides into the driver's seat, with a lot more grace and ease than I displayed climbing into the passenger side.

"What?" I question.

"Your husband. If he's coming from Jemma's, is he likely to turn on to this street from the esplanade or the highway?"

"Highway."

"Too easy."

Despite the car being fitted with a reverse camera, he stretches one arm along the back of my seat, twists his head and body around so he can see out of the back window, and reverses out of Jo's drive onto the dirt road it sits on, steering with one hand in a really blokey way.

I take in his profile, with views of both one side and then the other as he turns and straightens in his seat. The stubble on his chin and along his jawline has spread to his cheeks since last night, highlighting his sharp cheekbones. Like last night, the hairs at the base of his throat stick out from the round-necked T-shirt he's wearing. I know the fashion right now is for men to shave or wax their chests, but I'm old school and like a man with a bit of body hair, not too much, but a bit of chest hair and hairy legs are fine with me. His jaw isn't overly square but still perfectly masculine, especially covered in so much stubble, his lips are full and plump, and the memory of how soft they felt when he crushed them against mine last night forces itself to the front of my brain and demands to be replayed. I'm in the process of letting out a little sigh when we must hit a pothole, and it instead comes out as a grunt when some degree of pain shoots through every part of me. I instantly feel sick and open the window to let in some air as we turn out onto the esplanade.

"You doing okay?" he asks.

I take a moment to consider my answer. "To be perfectly honest, I've no fucking idea how I'm doing."

He shrugs, my eyes back on him, his on the road.

"Understandable. I know you said last night you were planning on leaving him, but you obviously weren't expecting all of this." He points his finger, moving it up and down in my general direction as he talks.

"I honestly wasn't expecting anything about the way my life has gone this past year. Believe it or not, I've usually got my shit together. I'm just a normal, boring Peninsula housewife. My life has never before been such an unmitigated disaster. . . or, to put it bluntly, such a shit show."

"I don't think that under any circumstances you could be described as normal or boring."

"That's very nice of you to say, but I can assure you, that's exactly what I am."

We're both quiet for a minute or two. The bay on one side of us, houses set high amongst the cliffs on the other. Supertramp's 'Breakfast in America' plays in the background. It's an old song, one of my dad's favourites that I haven't heard in years. I'm instantly reminded of the first man I ever loved and wonder what his reaction would be to what's happened to me when, in the moment of relative quiet, I become aware of the fact I'm shaking so badly, my entire body feels like it's vibrating.

I lower my window further, but the cool air does nothing to clear my fuzzy head or ease my churning stomach.

"I think. . . I'm sorry, can you pull over?"

Gabe swings the car to the opposite side of the road, and I have the door open before he comes to a stop. Forgetting how high up I am, I collapse in a heap of pain onto the tarmac. Not having time to right myself before I heave, I remain on my knees as I lean forward and vomit.

I'm empty, so there's really not much to bring up. After a few more dry heaves, I'm done. Both my eyes and nose are streaming from the effort, and I swipe at them quickly before taking the bottle of water Gabe is offering me.

He's already removed the lid, which I appreciate, so I rinse my mouth and spit a couple of times before taking a few small sips, all without making eye contact with him.

He crouches down beside me, putting us at eye level, and giving me no option but to meet his gaze. I'm still shaking, my teeth chatter together as I attempt to offer him a smile.

"Like I said, just normal and boring. Nothing to see here."

Sliding his hands under my armpits, he gently helps me to stand. My head spins, and I sway. Gabe pulls me into him and wraps his arms across my back.

"Fucking hell, Lauren, you're shaking. I think this might be a little bit of shock setting in. Let's get you home and into bed."

"I need a shower," I protest.

"You can do that too, shower or bath, whatever helps. Let's just get you home."

He practically lifts me back into the car, and it's only two or three minutes later that we're facing a set of electric gates in the process of sliding back.

As the truck slows, I take in the circular driveway. It goes past the front of the house and back around, so you come in and go out of the same set of gates. In the middle are a pool and a small building I can't make out in the dark. The house is double storey and set back from the edge of the driveway, about halfway around it.

"Wait there, I don't want you adding any more bruises," he orders.

"I thought my last exit was pretty spectacular." All I get in response are raised brows and a head shake.

We enter through a set of double timber doors into a wide entryway. There's a rattan chair in the corner, a piece of art on the wall, and a surfboard leaning next to it.

Taking these things in helps slow down my breathing and gets the shaking under control. Interior design is my thing, observing and taking mental stock of his home and contents are what calm me, it's not a method I've ever used before, but right now, I'm realising it works.

There's a long hallway to the left of a set of stairs, and if his house is anything like what's typical of those by the beach, the living areas will all be upstairs to take in the views of the bay.

"You okay to get up the stairs?" His question confirms my thoughts.

"Yeah, it's my soul and self-respect that are broken, not my legs."

He flips on a couple of lights, illuminating the stairs. When I reach the top, Gabe flips on another light somewhere behind me, revealing a large open plan, kitchen, dining, and living area. There are floor-to-ceiling timber bi-fold doors at the front of the space, which, I assume, lead out to the deck running the length of the house, I saw on the way in.

"You want a drink of anything?"

I turn to him with raised brows and wide eyes.

"Drink?" I question.

"I meant a hot drink, tea, coffee, Milo, definitely *not* alcohol."

"Oh," I say quietly before shaking my head.

"I'm good, thanks. I'd really appreciate a quick shower and some clean clothes if you have something I could borrow though?"

His arms are folded across his chest as he watches me for a

moment, and I wonder what he must see, what he must be thinking.

"What?" I decide to ask.

"I'm tempted to go back to Jo's while you shower and beat the fuck out of your husband for this."

"Gabe. . ." I start to protest, but he keeps talking.

"I can't comprehend any man doing this to a woman, let alone a husband to his wife. I just can't," he says with a shrug. "I really wish you'd go to the police. . ."

He must see my shoulders slump and hear the defeated sigh I release because he steps towards me with his arm held out before stopping and dropping it back at his side.

"I'm sorry, I shouldn't have said that, it's just. . ."

"It's my boys. He'll lose everything, and I can't do that to my boys. Ryder, my youngest, works for him, and if Sonny ever comes back to Australia, he probably will too. I can't do that to them, not when they don't even know what's been going on."

He nods. "Fair enough, but don't be surprised if they're pissed off when you tell them the reasons *why* you didn't have him arrested. If my dad ever did anything like this to my mum, I'd fucking kill him."

"I get that, and I fully expect them to be pissed off with me, but until I've spoken to them, that's the way it's going to be."

Brushing his palm over his jaw, I can see the debate going on in his head as to whether to say any more, reflected in the way he's looking at me. Instead, he changes the subject.

"Bathroom's this way. I'll put you in my bed tonight, and I'll take the sofa. . ."

"No, that's not fair, I'll take the sofa."

"It's not up for debate, Lauren. I've got three spare bedrooms downstairs, I could sleep in any one of them or put you down there and sleep in my own bed if I wanted." I open my mouth to ask why we don't just do one of those things, but he puts his hand up in a halt gesture.

"I want you close. You're in a strange house with a lunatic running around looking for you. If shit goes down, I want you close. That's it, no arguing."

I shrug and nod. I'm exhausted and have no more debate left in me.

"It's this way."

I follow him through an opening into a hallway off the dining area. There's a set of double doors towards the front of the house, a single door towards the back.

"Bedroom." He points to the doors towards the front. "My office." He points to the back.

We enter his bedroom, and when he flips on the light, it's not at all what I'm expecting to find. A huge mango wood and rattan headboard sits at the top of his timber-framed bed. There are matching side tables, a low but long six-drawer unit on the wall opposite his bed, with a large flat-screen telly mounted on the wall above it. The walls are all painted in what I know because of my job, is Dulux, White Beach Quarter. The floor-to-ceiling timber doors at the end of the room have off-white shears hanging from a chunky gunmetal rod in front of them. They've been dyed to match the paintwork exactly.

"Ensuite's through here, walk-in is behind the bed." I follow the direction he points. "I'll find you something to put on, then leave you to shower. Sal, my cleaner, put clean sheets on the bed yesterday. I did sleep in it last night so I'll change them if you'd. . ."

"No, no. It's fine. Honestly."

He pushes his hands into the back pockets of his jeans and rocks back on his heels. The action makes him appear so young and boyish. I inwardly cringe at the mess I must look.

"I'll, just erm. . ." I point towards the ensuite.

"Yeah, right. Sure. I'll find you something to put on."

I head into the bathroom, which is as gorgeous as the bedroom. Mango wood cabinetry, white tiles, gunmetal tapwear. I need to find out who did the interiors for him because I love their work.

"Lauren?"

"Yeah?" Gabe's head appears around the door. "There's a clean T-shirt, jocks, a hoodie, and a pair of trackies on the bed, clean towels are on the shelf. You okay using my stuff? I can go down to Ava's bathroom and get you some girlie shit if you'd prefer?"

"Your stuff is fine, thanks."

"Right, I'll leave you to it then."

He gives me a strange little wave and leaves. Despite having very little to smile about, for some reason, I stand there grinning like a lunatic.

CHAPTER 15

Gabe

I DON'T KNOW what that fucking wave was all about. I internally groan and shake my head as I walk out of my bedroom and head towards the kitchen.

I'm starving, and after throwing up so many times, I'm pretty sure Lauren must be too. I knock up some eggs and scramble them in a pan while toasting some bread. I just get it all dished up when she walks back into the room.

Her hair is wet and piled into a curly mess on top of her head, and she's wearing clothes that you could probably fit another three of her in, but she finally has some colour in her cheeks and looks gorgeous standing there rolling up the sleeves on my hoodie.

I move towards her, and without asking, help her with the sleeves.

"I cleaned my teeth with my finger, I couldn't find a spare toothbrush, but anything was better than nothing."

I'm close enough to be able to smell the mix of my shower gel, shampoo, and toothpaste on her.

"Should've just used mine," I tell her.

"I barely know you; I don't make a habit of sticking things that belong to strangers in my mouth." She closes her eyes, realising instantly how what she said sounded. I take a step closer but hold back from wrapping her in my arms like I want to.

"There are so many things I could say in response to that, most of them inappropriate, but now's not the time," I tell her.

"I walked right into that one, didn't I?"

"You made it so fucking easy," I lean in and say against her ear.

"I'm usually better than this, quicker comebacks. When I'm on form, I'm actually quite funny."

"I can well believe it. Right now though, I have something else for you to stick in your mouth. How'd you like your eggs?"

"Fertilised," she whispers. Quickly following it up with, "scrambled are also good."

"Jesus woman," I groan before reluctantly stepping away and steering her towards the benchtop and the unfertilised eggs on toast that await us.

"Tea or coffee?" I ask as I flip the kettle back on to boil.

"Tea please. No sugar, dash of milk, leave the teabag in."

"Builders' tea," I stupidly reply.

"Yeah, it's..." She gives a half-smile and shrugs.

"Sorry, didn't think."

"Don't be sorry. It is what it is, no need to tiptoe around the subject. I think I've had all the meltdowns I'm gonna have for one day."

I place her tea down next to her plate as she scrapes the eggs off the toast before biting into the corner.

"Have all the meltdowns you want; I think you've earned the right. Do you not like the eggs?"

"Essex girl, remember." She points at herself as I sit down beside her and start eating. "Be careful what you wish for because I can meltdown to a professional standard." She takes another bite of her toast, wincing then taping her finger on the split on her lip and checking it for blood. "And the eggs are perfect, I just didn't want them to make the toast soggy, but maybe that was a bad idea, it might be easier to eat if it's soft."

She clears her plate, except for one slice of toast, which she folds in half and dunks into her tea before eating it.

"That's. . . that is pretty gross."

"It's better with jam on," she says, wiping the tea that dripped off the toast from her chin.

"I'll take your word for it," I tell her with a smile while reaching for my coffee.

We eat in silence for a while, and because I don't want her to feel awkward, or maybe it's more to reassure her, I clear my throat and speak. "I know this. . . I don't want this to be awkward Lauren, you can stay as long as you like. I'm actually going away in a couple of weeks so you'll have the place to yourself. I'll use one of the bathrooms downstairs, so you'll have that one to yourself." She watches me as she chews her soggy toast but remains silent.

"You're safe here, the gates are key coded, the front door's locked and bolted, and I'm gonna sleep out here on the sofa just in case, but I just want you to know that your safe."

"Thank you. I really do appreciate it."

I nod.

"Leaving Jo's with a bloke you barely know after what you've just been through can't have been easy. . . I won't even pretend to have even half an idea, but I just want you to know you're safe here, you can trust me."

I watch as she struggles with her emotions, her eyes well

with tears and she swallows a few times before blowing out a long slow breath.

We both remain silent.

When she's finished eating, she slides off her stool and makes her way around the bench. I watch and enjoy the moment she has to roll the waistband of the trackies of mine she's wearing over a couple of times to keep them from falling down. Despite the shitty situation, I like that she's here in my home, the way she looks in my clothes, and the fact that I'm able to offer her a place to stay and be the one to keep her safe.

"Pass your plate," she orders from where she stands at the sink.

"Leave them, I'll put them in the dishwasher."

"I'm right here, the dishwasher is right there, it'll literally take me seconds. Pass your plate."

I do as she orders, instantly regretting it the moment I see her wince when she leans down to load the plates into the dishwasher.

"Just leave them and come and sit down. I've left your pain meds in the truck. Sit on the sofa, and I'll go down and get them."

"Anyone ever tell you you're bossy?" She dries her hands on a towel as she speaks, hanging it over the edge of the sink before she moves around the benchtop and towards the sofa.

"I'm not bossy, you just seem to have an issue following orders."

"Then stop dishing them out. I'm not a child, I can make my own decisions about what my capabilities are." She folds her arms across her chest and winces again. The colour she had on her cheeks after her shower has faded, the bruises now a stark contrast on her pale English rose complexion. I find my teeth once again grinding together, something that happens each time I fully acknowledge exactly what this woman has been through over the past twenty-four hours.

"I'm sure you're more than capable of anything you set your mind to, but just because you can, it doesn't mean you should. Now sit your arse down while I get your medication. The remotes are on the coffee table if you want to put something on the telly." When she walks past and has her back to me, I grab my phone from the benchtop and head downstairs to my car.

As soon as I'm outside, I call Jo.

"Hey," she answers on the second ring.

"All good?" I question.

"Yeah. He turned up ranting and raving that we know where she is, Max was right behind him, so he didn't pull any shit, then he. . . he kinda broke down. I think he's genuinely worried, but that doesn't excuse what he's done."

"No, it doesn't. How was it left?" I lean against my truck as I talk.

"He just asked that we contact him if we hear from her. Even if she's not coming back, he just needs to know she's okay."

"Yeah, his concern is very touching."

"Hmm. Something's off with him, he's not the Jay I've known for over twenty years. Anyway, he left believing we know nothing, so Lauren's welcome to come back here tomorrow if that's what she'd like to do. How is the patient?"

"Difficult."

"Need me to talk to her?"

"Nah. I've got a preteen daughter who's full of attitude; I think I can handle a mouthy little Essex bird."

"I wouldn't count on it. Don't be deceived by her lack of height. When she's pissed off, Lauren could take on a bear and I'd worry for its welfare. If her sharp tongue don't take you down, her fist will."

"Duly noted."

"Seriously though, she's been through a lot, is she doing okay?"

"She had a bit of a wobble on the drive here, I think shock

set in, but she's had a shower, has some clean clothes on, and has had something to eat."

"Go you, quite the little Florence Nightingale."

"Who?"

"No one, I'm just showing my age."

I smile as I unlock my car, knowing full well who Florence is; my mum was a nurse after all.

The black sack Jo put Lauren's clothes in has emptied its contents over my back seat, and when I start stuffing Lauren's cardigans back into it, I see just how bloodstained it is.

"Hey, would you do me a favour in the morning?"

"Go for it. Whadya need?"

"It's not for me, it's for Ren. Would you pop into Target and get her some basics? I'm gonna dump the cardigan she had on last night. She doesn't need to be seeing that."

"Gabe, anyone ever tell you you're a sweetheart? Why haven't you been snapped up and married before now? And Ren? That is seriously cute."

I pull the bag of meds from the car, leave everything else of Lauren's inside and close the door. Pausing at my front door, I allow a flash of a memory from a life that now feels like it wasn't actually mine to hit.

"I was married, remember? All be it briefly, but I was married." I deflect by ignoring the Ren remark and make Jo feel bad by reminding her of my failed marriage.

"Shit, yeah. Sorry, I forgot all about that."

"I try to."

"Sorry."

"Honestly, not a problem. Listen, I'm gonna sort Lauren out with some pain meds. If you could grab her some clothes tomorrow, that'd be great."

"No worries."

I end the call, head back into the house and up the stairs to find a sleeping Lauren curled into the corner of my sofa.

* * *

AFTER A DEBATE with myself as to whether I should just leave her to sleep where she is, I eventually carry her to my room. Despite lifting her as carefully as I can, she half wakes up, mumbles something about a 'suntannedie surfie sex God' before curling back up on her side and snoring quietly.

I watch her for a minute, wondering what the fuck it is I think I'm doing with this woman in my bed. This isn't me; this isn't what my life has been about for the last however many years, and now look at me. Falling all over myself to look after a woman I've only known for twenty-four hours.

Zac's words from last night resonate through my head. . . *'Mate, when you meet that person,* your *person. . . when that happens, you'll know, believe me. That first time you look at her, something will just click, and it'll be like,* 'now that's what I'm talking about,' *and that's when you'll be truly fucked.'*

And right now, that's what I am. Just minutes after Zac had said all that, it happened. I laid eyes on Lauren, and something happened that I would describe as more of a shift than a click. A shift from only having a vague indifference to most of the women I chat to in the pub on a Friday night to really wanting to talk to her, wanting to know about her.

Feeling like a perv standing over her while she's so defenceless, I resist the urge to lay a kiss on her cheek. Instead, I rub my palm over my stubble and head back out to lie on my sofa.

I flip the telly on, but can't get into anything, so turn it off after about ten minutes. I sneak into my bathroom, clean my teeth, and grab a pillow from next to where Lauren is now snoring. Flipping on the lamp on the opposite side of the bed, I turn the rest of the lights out, and head back to the sofa.

It's been a long fucking day, and despite staring up at the ceiling for what feels like forever, I must eventually go off to sleep.

* * *

ROLLING onto the floor and landing on my knees, I instinctively know to put my hand out to steady myself on the coffee table. I've no idea how long I've been asleep, and I'm not sure what woke me.

Tapping my phone, it lights up to display three-twenty am. Just as I sit my arse back on my sofa, I hear it, Lauren's talking in her sleep.

Standing up, I make my way to the bedroom. When I walk into the room, she's still lying curled on her side, hands tucked under her chin, but has hooked one leg out of the bed.

She's facing away from the lamp I left on, so I can barely make out her face in the dim light, but there's no mistaking the whimper, followed by a loud sob coming from her.

Moving to the edge of the bed, I crouch down beside her. She continues to whimper and mumble, so I lay the palm of one hand on her shoulder, and with my other, I brush her hair from her face. She mumbles something about angels and seems to settle. When her breathing evens out, I move my hand away.

Still feeling awkward being so close as she sleeps, I back my creepy arse towards the door, but before I reach it, Lauren turns on to her back, arms and legs flailing, before curling into the foetal position on her side and shouting a loud, "No," followed by more whimpering and mumbling. I go back to the sofa and collect my pillow before returning to the bedroom and climbing into bed. Curling myself in behind her, it's only when I rest my hand on her hip, the whimpering and mumbling stops.

Her breathing once again evens out as she begins to snore. . . not so quietly.

I should probably feel at least a small shred of guilt for climbing into bed with a practically unconscious woman, but I don't. As long as Lauren gets the sleep she obviously needs, I'll deal with the consequences of our sleeping arrangements when she wakes up later.

I don't remember the last time I went to sleep with a woman next to me. I've never brought one back to my home, and I usually only hang around after sex for any length of time to be polite, and that varies according to the situation. Sometimes I'll leave a woman sleeping, other times we might have an awkward conversation before I head off. Very occasionally, I'll hook up with someone with zero expectations, and we'll end our time together with a 'Thanks, I'll see you around.' Those kinds of nights are so few and far between that lately, it's been simpler to rely on my right hand.

The fact I like my relationships drama free and to last just the one night has me again wondering what the actual fuck I'm doing, feeling so fucking happy to be in my bed, wrapped around a woman I barely know, who's wearing my clothes, and smelling of my shampoo and body wash.

After gently kissing her temple, I lay my head next to hers and only have what feels like a few moments to debate with myself if this is really what I want or need in my life before finally drifting back off to sleep.

CHAPTER 16

Lauren

As I DRAG myself back to consciousness, I fight to open my eyes and remind myself exactly where I went to sleep last night. My brain takes a very long moment to catch up as I process that I'm way too hot, and nothing smells familiar. The fabric softener the pillow has been washed in isn't what I use, my own body doesn't smell of me, and what the fuck am I wearing?

Blinking a few times, a bare-chested Gabriel Wild finally comes into all its glorious focus. When *my* eyes travel up his throat, over his darkly stubbled jaw, perfectly straight nose, and sharp cheekbones, they meet *his*, looking down at me. I quickly close mine again, hoping that by blocking the beautiful distraction in the bed beside me, it will prompt my brain into remembering how exactly we ended up here. Together. In his bed.

I come up with nothing.

Slowly reopening my eyes, I'm drawn first to the smirk he's wearing, then back to his eyes looking down at me.

"Hey," he says quietly.

"Hey," I croak in response. Clearing my throat, I lick my lips before gesturing with my hand between us. "What. . . how did. . ?"

"You were dreaming, sobbing, crying, talking. The only way I could stop you was by resting my hand on you."

I'm lying on my side as he sits with his back to the headboard, looking up, I focus on his bare chest for a moment, but that just makes my mind blank out, so instead, my gaze traces the path of his happy trail to where it disappears beneath the doona. Lifting it, I nod in confirmation, or maybe it's admiration, of the fact he's wearing a pair of jocks, and nothing else.

"And you obviously needed to be nearly naked to do that?" I question.

He shrugs.

"Would you believe me if I told you I didn't plan it that way?"

This time I shrug. Before I get a chance to ask for an explanation, he gives me one.

"I went down to get your meds from the car, when I came back up you were asleep on the sofa. I debated leaving you there but thought you might be uncomfortable, so I carried you to bed. I got out of my jeans and T, set myself up on the sofa, and was sleeping out there until you woke me up around three-thirty this morning talking and crying in your sleep."

I remain curled on my side, looking up at him as he talks.

"What was I saying?" I ask while trying to recall any dreams I might've had.

"Something about an angel, and a suntannedie sex God, other than that, nothing I could make sense of."

. . .

I CLOSE my eyes for a long moment as I inwardly groan. I'd like to bury my head under the doona and hide my face from him, but he's virtually naked under there, and the sight could possibly induce a hot flush, which is something I definitely don't need right now.

"What's a suntannedie sex God?" he asks. I can hear the smile in his voice but refuse to look up and witness it.

"No idea, Thor, maybe? After he's been on holiday and comes back all brown?"

"Right," he says quietly.

Slowly and carefully, I sit myself up and push my back against the headboard next to him.

"What were you dreaming about?" his voice still quiet and low.

"I honestly don't know. I don't even remember falling asleep. I remember sitting on your sofa thinking that you were taking a long time down at your car. . ."

"I was talking to Jo on the phone. She said your husband turned up, had a bit of a rant about everyone knowing where you are and keeping it from him, and then he left."

I turn my head enough to watch him puff out his cheeks and exhale a long, slow breath, but still don't meet his eyes. I expect him to say something, instead he scratches at his stubbly jaw.

"WHAT?" I question.

"Don't go back to Jo's."

"What?" I screw my nose up in confusion.

"Jo's going to come around here this morning sometime, I think she's expecting you to go back to hers with her, don't go."

Muted sunlight shines through the sheers at the windows, illuminating the room enough for me to be able to vaguely make out our reflections in the screen of the television mounted on the wall opposite the bed.

I'm grateful not to be able to see my image in any kind of detail. I can only imagine the mess I must look, especially compared to Mr Wild in all his perfection.

I'm still wearing the trackies and hoodie Gabe gave me last night, and after what he just said, I am way, way, too warm.

These thoughts run parallel through my head, right alongside his words. My brain is trying to process all of this while attempting to formulate an answer.

"Why?" Is all I come up with.

I watch his eyes dart all over my face and wait for his response.

"Can I be frank?"

I shrug. "You can be whoever you want. I can call you Princes or Philomena if it'll make you happy?" I suggest.

He rolls his eyes, I grin. Who knew I could be this hilarious first thing in the morning?

"That's, that was terrible. Like the female equivalent of a dad joke."

"Come on, it wasn't that bad."

"Yeah, it really was, but anyway, what I mean is, can I be blunt?"

"Go for it," I tell him with a definite nod.

"Jo has no gates at the front of her place, I do. Your husband is likely to go back there until he finds out where you are. What if you're there on your own?"

I open my mouth to tell him I'll hide, that I won't open the door, but he continues.

"Right now, he doesn't know about me, so there's absolutely no reason for him to come here... and if he does..."

"You've got gates," I interrupt him, all the while replaying *'right now, he doesn't know about me.'*

"I've got gates, yes, but that's not what I..."

"Then get to the point, Gabe."

"I want you safe." He shifts slightly while looking around the room. His eyes finally settling on mine.

"It matters to me that you're safe, that you're somewhere he likely won't find you."

My stomach has twisted itself into knots so tight, it hurts.

"*Why* does it matter to you?" I ask.

"Aside from the fact that no man should ever do that to a woman, I don't *know* why it matters but it does."

He scratches his fingernails over his whiskers, the rasping sound filling the room.

"I've been thinking about it, and I'd be happier if you took my room, and I'll sleep in the guest room downstairs, that way, I'm closer to the front door if. . ."

"But why?" I cut him off. "I don't get it. I'm not understanding what this. . ." I pause, letting out a frustrated sigh. I've had months of my husband telling me I've let myself go, that I'm fat, and I'm useless and I've allowed it in. Like an ear worm, Jay's words have gotten into my head and buried themselves deep. I don't want to come across as insecure but. . .

"Gabe, I'm forty-four. I have two grown-up sons, a psycho soon-to-be ex. No doubt a messy divorce to make the ex an official title is going to be a big part of my life in the coming months. I have boobs that are starting to droop, a belly that is not only absolutely, most definitely drooping, but it also wobbles and is covered in stretch marks. Then there's this," I air circle my face with my pointer finger. "Split lip, bruised cheek, black eye, dried blood in my hair, a glued together head, bruised ribs and hip, and a shoulder still sore from being dislocated. Add to that, *all* of the issues *all* of that combined has left me with, I'm a mess. Mentally, physically, all the 'ally's' you can think of. Each and every one of them points to me being a big fat fucking mess."

I have to look away from that penetrating gaze of his as I talk. His eyes display so much emotion, he has me forgetting how to use my words. It's like *he feels* everything I say, every emotion I hope to convey, he gets them, then reflects them right back at me, and it's too much, so I look away. I stare at his bare chest feeling exactly like the insecure woman I really don't want to be, but know I've become.

"Did I not tell you Friday night how fucking hot I find wobbly bellies and stretch marks? Split lips, glued heads, and black eyes are definitely not my thing, but ya know what, they're gonna fade. In a couple of weeks, the bruises will be gone, the scar on your head will fade. When you do notice it's there, it'll just be a reminder of your story, like your stretch marks and wobbly belly are reminders of the babies you carried. They're all just a small part of what makes up your life story. They don't define it, but they'll always be a part of it, you can't change that. What you can change is how you let all of that impact the way you feel about yourself, and the way you live the rest of your life."

This man isn't real. In real life, blokes like him don't exist. I'm either dreaming or delusional right now. Concussed maybe?

Closing my eyes, I draw in a deep breath, then slowly open them as I let it out. In all his dark-haired, blue-eyed glory, he's still there. Right beside me, in his bed, as real as you like, looking at me that way that he does. It overwhelms me. With everything else I have going on, I don't have the brain capacity to deal with the way he looks at me, *or* his words. They're wise and honest, and I know they come from a good place, but I'm not sure that I'm ready to hear them, and I'm certainly not at a place where I believe them.

"I can't. . . I don't want to be living my story right now. I don't even want to be living someone else's, even if theirs is a fairy tale. I want a break. I *need* a break."

I raise my palms to my head, pressing them against my temples as I try to articulate what I'm thinking and feeling.

"It's too much. I just need to go somewhere and just *be*. I'm still struggling to process what's happened to my marriage, my husband's behaviour, and now there's you, and it's too much."

I can't think of any other way to explain how I feel so I pause, watching as he pulls his knees up, rests his elbows on them, and laces his fingers together.

"There's *me*?" he questions.

That's all he took from that?

"Yeah, you, and all. . ." I trail off, waving my hand in his general direction.

"You've got all what you've got going on, so why exactly are *you* interested in *me*? I saw the girls you were talking to on Friday, young, blonde, you obviously have a type, and it's definitely not *me*."

"Don't tell me what my type is. If I don't even know that, then you definitely don't, so don't make assumptions."

"Then what is it? What is it about me that after less than forty-eight hours you want to move me into your house?"

"You want blunt?"

"I want total honesty, that's what I want."

"Total honesty? I have no fucking idea. Physically, I don't know if you're my type because, like I said, I don't know what my type is, but that does *not* mean you *aren't* my type. I like my life drama-free, so emotionally, mentally, that would be a big fat *no* too. My head is telling me that everything about you right now is one giant red flag and will mean nothing *but* drama, but ya know what? I don't fucking care. I went out for a drink with my brother's Friday, and the last thing I was looking for or expecting was you, but there you were, and now, here we are."

"This doesn't make sense. *We* don't make sense," I say quietly, without making eye contact with him.

"Not even a little bit. Does that matter?"

My head feels like it's underwater, my chest feels like someone's sitting on it, and my stomach? My stomach chooses that moment to rumble really loudly.

I wince and turn my head to look at him through just one eye. He's grinning, and I'm hit with so many thoughts and feelings, my head spins.

"Answer that later. Let me feed you while you think about it." It's an order, not a question, but before I can let him do that, I feel I need to clarify something.

"Gabe, total honesty? I've been with one man since I was eighteen, I've never cheated on him, or even considered an affair, so please don't think that this," I again gesture between us, "that me waking up in another man's bed is normal behaviour for me."

He reaches out and tucks a wayward strand of hair behind my ear. The gesture should feel nice, really nice. Instead, it makes my stomach churn with nerves.

"Ren, if I thought for one second that waking up with anyone other than your husband was your normal MO, I would've fucked you in an alley Friday night and forgotten your name by Saturday morning."

That comment leaves me wondering if that's how he usually spends his Friday nights.

Out of nowhere, what was mentally too much, hits me physically. My skin prickles and panic bubbles inside me.

"I'm not ready for this. I need time," I pant out, my voice creeping higher. "I can't jump out of a twenty-four-year marriage straight into your bed. I need to talk to my boys; I need to process what's happened. He hit me. When I was already down on the floor. . ." My legs and hands feel numb, and my breathing doesn't seem to have any kind of rhythm.

"Twenty-six years we've been together, married for twenty-four. We've been a team, inseparable. He's been my world, then out of nowhere, he did this." I randomly gesture with my hands towards my face and body. "And the worst part is, I don't know why. I don't know what I've done wrong. . ." My breath catches at the pain in my ribs as Gabe pulls me into his lap, wraps his arms around me, and holds me against him. While rocking me like a baby, he lets me cry.

* * *

IN THE BRIGHT WINTER SUNSHINE, I sit out on Gabe's balcony and drink my coffee. After I finally stopped crying and pulled myself together, he insisted that I eat, but after a close inspection of the contents of his fridge, he realised there was little in there to create breakfast or any other kind of meal with. He's now at the supermarket rectifying that.

Gabe's house is set on a hill above the beach. It sits high enough that the traffic noise from the cars passing along the esplanade doesn't drown out the sound of the waves, which calm me enough to make the call I've been dreading.

With one hand wrapped around my coffee cup, the other presses my phone to my ear while I wait for my husband to pick up.

"Where the fuck are you?" Is how he greets me.

"Doesn't matter where I am, I just need you to know that I won't be coming home. I also need. . . no, I *want* you to stop calling me. There is nothing for us to discuss. All future correspondence should be made through our solicitors. You'll be hearing from mine sometime next week."

"Stop talking shit, tell me where you are, and I'll come pick you up."

Jay's voice sounds raspy, the way it does when he hasn't had enough sleep, for a split second, I worry about him. I put it down to habit, and *not* because I actually give a fuck about how he's sleeping.

"Jay, you really need to listen to me, what you did to me Friday night. . . what you've *been* doing to me for. . ." I'm pulled up short of delivering what I want to say by the tears that are once again threatening to fall. I've given this man enough of me,

I gave him almost everything, and the very small piece I've managed to hold on to will not be spilled in tears that he gets to hear.

"It's over, Jay. We're done."

"You don't mean that, Lauren. You're pissed, I get it. Just come home and we'll talk."

"I don't want to talk, Jay, I don't want. . ."

"For fucks sake, why has it always got to be like this with you? You pitch a bitch fit at the slightest thing, then turn it all around and blame me. Then you wonder why I lose my shit."

I don't know why I'm shocked at the way he's flipped so easily, but I am.

"I'm going now."

"I'll fucking find you."

"You ever come near me again, and I'll press charges, Jay. The only reason I haven't done it yet is because of our boys." An alarm sounds somewhere in the house, and I watch as Gabe's gate slides open; a few seconds later his black truck turns onto the drive.

"And what exactly do you plan on telling the boys? Ryder knows you've not been home all weekend. I called him, looking for you."

I stand and lean against the balcony as Gabe climbs from his truck looking up at me. Leaning over, I hold my phone against my chest and my finger against my lips hoping he'll understand I need him to be quiet. I get a chin lift, followed by a quick nod as he pulls a couple of bags from inside the car.

"I'll tell the boys the truth. I'm not covering for you anymore."

"You'd do that? You'd do that to *me*, to the *boys*?"

"You think that's worse than the shit you've done to me?"

"Oh, here we go, so what if you broke a fucking fingernail. . . wah, wah, wah."

"You broke more than my fucking nail, you broke my heart,

you very nearly broke my spirit, but not anymore. I'm done. I won't be back, so you'd better get your head around it."

"You're so full of shit. You give it all that mouthy little Essex girl front on the phone, but I've seen how tough you really are when you're laying on the floor begging me not to hurt you anymore, snivelling and fucking crying. Who the fuck wants that anyway? You used to have a bit of fight in you, Lauren, now you're just a fat mess with no getup and go."

I turn to see Gabe coming through the sliding timber doors. I switch my phone to speaker and place it down on the outdoor table. "Jay," I mouth to Gabe.

"Come home, don't come home, I don't fucking care. Maybe stay away for a few weeks and work on yourself, lose some weight, and learn how not to be a mouthy little cunt."

Eyes on mine, Gabe leans in silently, ends the call, then pulls me into him. With my face buried in his chest, I breathe in all that is him. Fresh clean air, citrus and sunshine, his unique scent already familiar.

"Why the fuck are you listening to that prick? The man's obviously having some kind of mental breakdown now that he's realised what he's done and how badly he's fucked up. I don't understand why you're putting yourself through listening to his bullshit when you don't have to." He speaks with his mouth pressed up against my ear. Despite slipping into bed beside me as I slept, this is the first attempt he's made at getting close to me, and even though my head is still trying to catch up with events going on in my life, I'm only human. My skin erupts in goosebumps, my stomach clenches, and I physically shudder at his proximity and the sensation of his hot breath on me.

Hoping to disguise my body's reaction to his, I let out a slow exhale.

"You're right, I don't. Putting up with his abuse has become a habit. I called to tell him to stop calling *me*. He was all over the place. Do you think that's really what's wrong with him, that he's having some kind of breakdown? One second he's telling me to come home so we can talk, the next, he's coming out with all the shit you just heard."

"No fucking idea, and I can't say I really give a fuck about his mental state either."

I feel a little pang of. . . something. . . in my chest. I shouldn't care about what Gabe's just said, I shouldn't worry about Jay, but I've spent my entire adult life with him, and all of my old thoughts, feelings, and habits are going to take a while to move on from that.

"I understand why you do though, he's still your husband, you're not going to be able to switch all that off in just a matter of hours."

I look up and meet his eyes looking down at me. He slides his palm up my arm and over my shoulder, his fingers brush across the curve of my neck until they finally meet bare skin at my jaw. His thumb gently strokes across my bruised cheek.

"You've spent most of your life loving him, you're entitled. . . expected, to feel torn, but me? I have no affiliation, and as far as I'm concerned, he's a coward who put his hands on you, and I'd like nothing more than to be given a chance to return the favour. Mark him, the way he's marked you."

I hold my breath the whole time he talks, letting it out slowly when he finishes.

"What do you need from me? What can I do to make this shit show a little better for you?"

I'm shaking so hard I feel like I'm vibrating, but talking to Jay was, surprisingly, easier than I thought it would be.

"You've done more than enough, and I think I'm actually doing all right."

His lips twitch before eventually forming a smile.

"What?" I ask.

"All right? Yeah, I'm all right, you all right?"

"What are you doing? What is that?" I question, knowing full well he's attempting to mimic my accent.

"Shut up. Hundred percent babe, you all right?"

"You need to stop. I don't know what you're attempting, but it's so bad, you're making all my bruises hurt at once." I attempt to wriggle out of his arms but wince at the pain in my ribs and shoulder as he holds me in place.

His brows raise, and the smile is instantly wiped from his face, making me feel a pang of guilt. "Shit, sorry, did I hurt you? You didn't take your painkillers last night. Have you had any this morning?"

"Nah, mate," I reply in my best Australian accent. "I don't like the way they make me feel. The pain's okay anyway, at least it was, till you started talking like Bert The Chimney Sweep."

"My Essex is better than your Aussie any day."

I roll my eyes in response as he stares down at me. His eyes scan my face, focusing mostly on my mouth, and I wonder, right before he finally meets my gaze, if he's going to kiss me. His breaths come heavier, faster as he watches me, but he just stares, making no attempt to instigate anything physical between us, not even a kiss. I'm not disappointed, I'm not ready for that yet, but I am curious. I got to experience the gentle press of his lips against mine on Friday night, but right now, with my body pulled flush against his, I *am* wondering how a real kiss from him would feel. Mouths open, tongues tangling.

"I really wanna kiss you right now."

"Get out of my head," I say out loud.

His eyebrows shoot up, and he gives me a sexy smirk.

"You want me to kiss you?"

I shrug. I do, but I shouldn't. I don't want to complicate my life further or blur the lines of what might or might not be happening between us.

"I'm. . . curious? I know it's too soon; I know I'm not ready, but I won't lie, I *am* curious."

"Total honesty," he says quietly. I'm not sure if that's a request or him voicing his understanding of what I'm trying to say.

"Always. It's my one. . ." I consider the word I want to use. "Demand."

"Oh, you're making demands already?"

"I am," I answer with a small nod. "I need that from you, if you're not going to give me that. . ."

"Whatever you want. I already told you that. Whatever you need, whatever it takes, that's what you'll get from me."

With his unwavering gaze fixed on mine, I believe him. There's something there, here, happening between us. If it was just about sex, he wouldn't be putting up with all the extra bullshit I bring to the table. He's already told me I come draped in a red flag wearing a crown with the word DRAMA flashing front and centre of it, and despite all of this, for some reason, he still wants to pursue something with me. Right now though, I'm not sure I'm brave or reckless enough.

"Total honesty, Ren. Despite you telling me it's too soon and you're not ready, I think you're wrong. I think the moment's perfect, and I still, really, really wanna kiss you."

His hands slide down to my arse as he gently pulls me against him, his very obvious erection presses against my belly.

"I think you might want to do more than kiss me."

"With my dick. You didn't let me finish. I really wanna kiss you with my dick."

I lick my lips. Despite everything inside me pulling tight, I shake my head with a smile.

"Not happening," I tell him quietly.

"*I* can wait," he says against my ear. His lips brush along my jaw before resting on the corner of my mouth for a long moment. "Just let me know when *you* can't."

With that, he pulls away and heads back inside.

"Come back," I say in a tiny quiet voice. "But not really. But not really not really."

I sit back down in my chair and let out a huff. "Far out, that man does things to my brain," I say to no one in particular while picking up my phone and calling my youngest child.

* * *

"MUM, WHAT THE FUCK?"

"Language, Ryde," I respond to the way my youngest answers my call.

"Language? Are you kidding me right now? Where are you? Dad's going out of his mind, and Sonny's about to book a flight home."

"You done?"

"Not even a little bit. Talk to me, mother, what's going on?"

Brushing the tip of my tongue over the split in my lip, I attempt not to cry as I'm hit with a tsunami of emotions. I thought I had this, but admitting to my kid that my marriage to his dad is over makes my throat feel tight and causes an ache in my chest.

Lifting my gaze, I look to the door, seeking out Gabe for reassurance. Instead, all I get is my own reflection bouncing back at me. It's an image I barely recognise. A woman with a messy bun, wearing oversized sweatpants and a hoodie, sits curled in a chair. I keep forgetting that one side of my face is still swollen and bruised, my eye barely open. Raising my hand, I brush the tips of my fingers over my face and lips, reminding myself exactly why I'm in this state and needing to make this call.

As much as it kills me to do it, my boys deserve honesty. They're both grown men, but as their mum, the need to protect them will forever be present in me.

Taking a deep breath in through my nose, I let it out slowly and organise the words in my head before speaking them out loud.

"I had to get out, Ryde. Things have been bad for months, but this past week. . ." I take in a mouthful of air, hoping I can gulp it down with my threatening tears.

"I ended up in the hospital Friday night. . ."

"What? Why? The fuck, Mum?"

"He just lost it. It's not the first time, you know what he's like, but every week lately, it's just getting worse and worse."

"He hit you? He's been hitting you?"

"I thought things would get better, I thought I could handle him."

"Handle him? Mum, he's your husband. You shouldn't have to handle him. Far out. He fucking lied to me. He told me you stormed off after he got home late. He's been a nightmare at work, losing his temper over shit all the time, but I thought that was just at work."

He's quiet for a moment, and I allow the silence to continue, to give my son the time he needs to process what I've just told him.

"Where are you now? Are you somewhere safe?" he asks quietly. While I consider my answer, he continues.

"Are you okay, Mum? I can't believe you didn't say anything, that you didn't tell us what was going on."

"I'm sorry. I didn't tell anyone," I respond.

"I'm gonna kill him, I'm gonna fucking kill him."

"No, you're not. I got away, Ryde, I'm okay. Honestly, I'm fine. You can be angry with him, but you have to work with him. Don't let what goes on between me and him, mess things up for you at work. I don't want that. This isn't just about me, it's about you and your brother and the business. . ."

"Mum, he's been putting his hands on you. You really think I want to keep working for him?"

My lips rattle together as I let out a long breath, and I

instantly wince at the pain that action causes. I'm pissed off with myself for forgetting about the split in my bottom lip while feeling sick with guilt at what this is going to mean for my kids. This is not how I ever imagined my life would go. I'm sitting on an almost stranger's balcony, wearing an almost stranger's clothes, hiding from my husband as I tell my kid I've left his dad.

"What about your job?"

"He should be more worried about *his* job. He rarely turns up these days, Mum. It's not an issue, I've got everything under control at the office, and I've promoted Spencer. We've taken on two new site managers and Spencer is now project managing all our jobs while I run the office."

"Why didn't you tell me any of this?"

"Because I assumed you knew. I thought he was just slowing down, spending more time at home with you. That's why I couldn't work out why he's been so pissed off on the rare occasions he does show up. If anything, I expected him to be more chill."

"He's not been spending his time with me, I assumed he was at work, and when he has been home, he barely says a word. He didn't even tell me he'd moved the business account to a different bank."

"Did he tell you I've bought the townhouse?"

"What? No, he hasn't mentioned it. That was in both our names. How was he able to do that?"

Ryder lives in an investment property I jointly own with Jay. He pays minimal rent, but it covers the small mortgage we have on it and gives him somewhere to live.

"I'm not sure. There's been a few things that have gone on that have had me confused lately. I offered to buy the townhouse because Dad said you guys were struggling. The business hasn't been doing great, but since I put Spencer in charge, things have picked up."

"I'm so sorry you've been dealing with all of this. I had no idea. What did he charge you to buy the house? Was there any profit made?"

"Mum, you purchased that place off-plan and only paid a couple of hundred thousand for it. It was mostly paid for. I paid five-hundred thousand for it and all of the profit Dad put back into the business to make up for what he's been drawing out. Before he even knew it was in the account, I paid all the trades we owed money to, as well as all the suppliers. What was left, I've moved to an account he doesn't have access to."

My head is spinning from all of this information. I feel like I don't know my husband or the life he's been living, at all.

"My mind is blown, Ryde. I've no clue what's going on with him, but as long as you've got the business under control, I'm happy."

"I've got things covered, Mum, it's you we need to worry about. What are you going to do? Where will you live?"

"I don't know, I've got a lot to think about. I'm staying with a friend Dad doesn't know until he calms down, then I'll probably go to Jo's and stay with her until I get back on my feet."

"Is there anything you need? You need money?"

"I'm okay right now, I'm just gonna lay low, but I might need some help in the week."

"Just let me know, anything you need I'll get it sorted out before I go away next week."

There's a moments pause before he asks, "You will be all right if I go away right? I can cancel if you need me here."

Ryder has a two week holiday in Thailand booked. I knew it was coming up, but wasn't sure of the exact date.

"I'll be fine. What about work though?"

"Work will be okay. I've got it covered. Just let me know what you need."

"Thanks, mate. I love you. Try not to worry about me, I'll be okay, and please don't fight with your dad over all this."

"Yeah, I can't promise any of that. Love you, Mum, call me if you need anything, I mean it, and call Sonny, he needs to know what's going on."

"I will, promise. Love you."

I end the call, stand, lean against the balcony rail, and look out at the view across the bay. The door slides open and closed behind me, but I don't turn. Gabe presses against my side and hands me a coffee.

"Black, half a sugar, right?"

"How'd you know?" I take the mug from him and question while still looking out at the water.

"Didn't want to interrupt your call, so I messaged Jo. She's on her way here."

I nod slowly and take a sip from the steaming mug but don't respond with words.

"You talk to your kids?"

"Just Ryder. It's a bit late to be calling Sonny, he lives in England."

I feel him shift beside me, but I don't turn to look at him as I speak.

"He's a professional rugby player, his girlfriend's a paediatrician, or about to qualify as one. They both have British parents, so applied for UK passports, and decided to live over there for a bit before they come back here and eventually settle down."

"You miss him?"

"Of course. Ryder only lives up the road, and I still miss him not being at home. I love being a Mum."

He's quiet for a moment. I hear him sip at his own drink as we both take in the view.

"I've got some shit for you inside," he breaks the silence and says, and I finally turn my head and make eye contact.

"You got some shit for me inside?"

"Yeah." He nods, sips from his cup, and turns his eyes back towards the bay.

"What kind of shit?"

"Girlie shit."

I smile, even silently laugh a little, as something warm begins to kindle in my chest at his thoughtfulness.

"What kind of girlie shit?" I question through my smile.

"You know, the shit girls can't live without, face cream, those makeup wipe things, deodorant, shampoo, conditioner, lotion shit that you rub in, shower wash shit."

"That's a lot of shit," I remark through an even bigger smile. Gabe still refuses to look at me. He shrugs.

"Yeah, like I said, I just got all the shit I know my sister and my daughter don't seem to be able to live without. Got you a toothbrush too."

I turn and place my mug on the table, then I take Gabe's mug from him and place it next to mine. Forcing my way between him and the railing, I wrap my arms around his waist and look up at him.

"Thank you for my girlie shit, that was really kind and considerate of you."

I kiss his jaw, then his chin, then the other side of his jaw. His eyes still don't meet mine. Sliding his arms around my waist and under my hoodie, his palms rest on the bare skin of my lower back while my lips rest at the corner of his mouth.

After a silent pause, he releases his hold on me with one hand and moves it to brush his fingertips up and down my spine, and all of the things I've tried to convince myself I'm not ready for since meeting him, I'm now very desperate to happen, or, at least, willing to discuss.

"Don't stop," he says quietly, his mouth moving against my lips.

This is a moment. Even knowing it's far too soon, I still want to do it. Despite the implications, I want this to happen.

Standing up on my tiptoes so I can reach, I place a gentle kiss on his right cheek, then on his left. Gabe's eyes close and then open slowly. His hands slide down and under the waistband of the trackies I'm wearing, resting them on my bare arse before gently pulling me against him tighter.

Eyes locked on mine, he repeats, "Don't stop."

Slow and careful, I raise my arms. Ignoring the burn to my ribs, I slide my fingers into his hair, I tilt his head down, stand back up on my tiptoes, and kiss his nose.

Keeping my fingers laced through his hair, I stand back down flat on my feet. He gives my arse a gentle squeeze before moving his hands to my waist. He's wearing jeans, but even through the denim I can feel he's hard. I watch his throat move as he swallows before the tip of his tongue flicks out again, I lick my lips, and I swear he gives the slightest of headshakes.

"Ren," he whispers, closing then opening his eyes slowly.

"Gabe," I reply before tugging at his hair and tilting his head back. With his throat exposed, I kiss from the base, up to the underside of his jaw to his chin, pausing again, right below his bottom lip. This time, he moves, tilting his head to look down at me, his eyes dance across my face.

"Don't stop," he whispers so quietly, I can barely hear over the sound of the waves out on the bay.

His gaze settles on my mouth for a long moment before returning to meet mine. I know exactly what his eyes are trying to convey, he's making it very clear what he wants, but do I really want to go there?

I know he's already kissed me once, but that came out of nowhere. It was him kissing me and took me totally by surprise. This is different. This is *me* making a conscious decision to kiss *him*. This is *him* asking me to kiss *him*.

I know if I do this, it'll change things.

It'll move things along, altering our relationship from a flirtatious friendship to something else, something different.

Do I want that? I'm not sure.

Am I ready for that? Definitely not.

Should I back the fuck away, right this very second? Absolutely.

Do I do that? Fuck no.

Pulling him closer, I stand back up on my toes and find his mouth with mine.

This kiss is entirely different to the one we shared on Friday night. It's still gentle, but this time Gabe wastes no time in exploring my mouth with his tongue. *His* mouth is open and covers mine, his tongue pushes inside, tangling with mine. His breaths come heavy, tasting of coffee, and they mix with mine.

He slides his mouth to my ear and says against it, "Fuck I want you."

"Too many clothes between us, Ren. I want you naked. Pressed against me just like this, but without the clothes. You want that?"

I nod.

"Use your words, Ren, tell me you want this."

"I want this," I say into his mouth, which is now back on mine.

Still under my hoodie, his hands push up my back until they reach my hair. He keeps them moving down my back, around to my ribs."

"Tell me if I hurt you and I'll stop," he says against my ear. I nod.

"Words, Ren."

"I'll tell you," I tell him quietly.

He slides his hands back to my arse and rests them there.

"I want to touch you everywhere, but I don't want to hurt you," he says against my ear.

"This is good," I respond.

"Yeah? Like this?"

Sliding his hand to my outer thigh, he lifts my leg, wrapping it around his, and grinds into me. I groan out a sound that makes it blatantly obvious, without words, just how very good that does feel.

Turning me around, he walks me backwards until we reach the outside table. Moving the chairs away with his feet, and helps me shuffle up to sit on it. Nudging my legs apart with his knee, he moves to stand between my parted thighs. Sliding me to the edge of the table, he buries his face in my neck and grinds against me. I hook my legs around his thighs and hold him there. The moment I do the gate alarm sounds.

Tilting his head up to the sky, Gabe stops moving. I press my forehead against his chest and close my eyes while trying to catch my breath.

"Fuck, your mate has the worst timing."

I look up, but Gabe's face is still aimed skyward. He gives my thighs a gentle squeeze and I take that as my cue to unhook them. Wrapping his arms across my shoulders and back, he keeps me in place held against him. I slide my arms around his waist, and with the side of my face pressed against his chest, we stand perfectly still and attempt to compose ourselves.

His hand eventually moves to my face, and with the knuckle of his finger under my chin, he tilts it towards him. Eyes once again doing their dance across my features, he leans in and gently kisses me on the mouth.

"I shouldn't have lifted you up here like that. I didn't hurt you, did I?"

The jolts of pain in my ribs and shoulder were absolutely worth the jolts of pleasure I felt in other parts of me, so I shake my head just as the intercom buzzes to let us know someone's downstairs. I hadn't even noticed the sound of Jo's car pulling up or her door slam shut.

"I stupidly gave her the gate code earlier so she could let herself in."

After another quick peck on my mouth, he steps away.

"I'm not done with you; we're picking this straight back up as soon as Jo leaves."

I watch his fine arse turn and head down the stairs to the front door, feeling both grateful and disappointed at Jo's interruption.

CHAPTER 17

Gabe

WITH MY LAPTOP tucked under my arm and my keys swinging around my finger, I head out my office door and through our reception area.

"See ya, Dan," I call out to my sister.

"See ya. Have a good . . ."

"You not coming to the pub?" Zac cuts off Daniella's response.

"No, I'm going home."

I watch as Cooper joins Zac in Coop's office doorway. I didn't realise they were both still here and thought I'd managed to avoid an interrogation.

"What are your plans for the weekend? You wanna catch up Saturday night or something?" My eldest brother asks.

I give my keys another go around my finger as I formulate an answer.

"I'm not sure what I'm doing yet. Can I let you know in the morning?" I ask.

"Am I invited?" Dani asks from behind her desk.

"No," Zac responds. "Grown-ups only, you don't qualify."

"Suck my dick," Dani flips Zac her middle finger as she replies.

"Children, you are all more than welcome. Dad and Jackie are coming over, so I thought. . ."

"Ah shit, just remembered, I've got something on," I tell my brother.

I watch as he lets out a long breath before leaning into the door frame and folding his arms across his chest and crossing his long legs at the ankle.

"I'm sorry, mate, he's coming down here to play golf tomorrow and wanted to catch up. I had no choice," my brother apologises.

"I understand, it is what it is, and it's not your fault," I tell him honestly.

"You and Dad fallen out?" Dani asks. "Or has *she* done something to piss you off?"

"Nope, just busy," I lie.

"Got plans with the non-girlfriend?" Zac asks. I know he's asked in order to deflect Dani's enquiry, but his new favourite phrase he's taken to using to describe Lauren is beginning to piss me off.

"You still sleeping in the guest bedroom?" Cooper joins with a question of his own.

"None of your fucking business," I tell them both. "I'm done. Enjoy your weekend, everyone."

As I reach the door that'll lead me out of the building and the refuge of my truck, Zac calls my name, and I turn.

"You'll be needing a wheelbarrow to carry your balls in here Monday, they're gonna be so blue."

I flip him my middle finger and keep walking towards the door.

"He doesn't have any balls. He handed them straight to Lauren the second he laid eyes on her in the pub last week." Ignoring the pair of stand-up comedians I'm related to, I make my way to my truck.

Once I hit the highway towards home, I call Ren.

"Ello, my lover," she answers with an accent sounding something like the farmer's wife in the 'Babe' movie. I both shudder and smile at the same time.

"Chance'd be a fine fucking thing."

Two weeks! Tonight will mark fourteen nights Lauren has been staying with me. Apart from a couple of times I've climbed into bed beside her when she's been having another one of her nightmares, it's been fourteen nights she's slept in my bed while I've laid downstairs in the guest bedroom, *not* sleeping.

"Well, play your cards right, Mr Wild, and you just might get lucky."

"Really? And I thought coming home to you every night for the past few weeks already made me the luckiest bloke on the Peninsula."

I hear someone making a gagging sound in the background.

"Which member of the coven can I look forward to the company of this evening?" I ask.

"You're on speaker, Wild. I heard that," Jo calls out.

After Jo's son and his girlfriend arrived home from their overseas travels unexpectedly the Sunday after Lauren was attacked, I managed to convince her to stay with me rather than go back with Jo to her now full house. Jo agreed with me, Lauren conceded, and I'd gotten to keep her close. The downside of this is one of her girl posse is here almost every day or evening. I'm glad she's had the company, but the endless talking blows my mind a little.

Lauren can spend an hour on the phone, either messaging or

talking shit with her girls, and still find things to talk nonstop about when they come over. Despite having a daughter of my own, and being very aware of how much girls can talk, I swear these women not only have it off to an Olympic standard, they do it talking in some kind of code.

Jemma was over last night, and they spent an entire hour discussing the best filling for a European pillow if you want to chop it. Then they went off to my bedroom so Lauren could show Jem an example of a 'quality duck down filled Euro.'

A day later, and despite apparently owning one, I'm still unsure of what exactly a chopped European pillow even is.

"Jo's invited herself to dinner. You fancy Chinese?"

"As long as there's zero talk about Euro chopping pillows or thread counts, I fancy whatever it is you're going to actually eat, and not just pick at."

I'd had a battle the couple of weeks Lauren's been with me, getting her to eat more than just a few mouthfuls of whatever we'd had for dinner each night. She'd also refused to leave the house. I'm not sure if this is because of her bruises or if she's scared of bumping into her prick of an ex.

"I told you you'd lost more weight. Has she not been eating, Gabe?" Jo questions.

"She eats, just not enough."

"I am here you know, listening to every word. Sorry that I've not been hungry, a good hiding from your husband, homelessness, and an imminent divorce don't exactly encourage much of an appetite."

"You're not homeless," I tell her quietly. "And it pisses me the fuck off that you keep saying you are."

There's silence for a few beats.

"Sorry, I didn't mean it like that."

"Forgiven," I tell her, instantly feeling guilty.

"Besides," she adds. "I've got this hot as fuck boy toy I need to stay slim and sylphlike for."

"Is that right?" I question. "Well, I have it on excellent authority, your hot as fuck boy toy likes the curves his new woman has, and he'd much prefer she keep them."

"Well, my options here are limited. There's barely any food in your fridge, except the humus the girls have bought over when they've come to visit, and there's only so much chipping and dipping a girl can do."

Again, another pang of guilt hits me square in the chest. She's right. My fridge and pantry are both usually pretty empty except when Ava's coming. She cancelled her last weekend with me and has been away for the past week visiting her grandparents interstate.

I get to see her at the end of this week, but I'll pick her up from her mum's and head straight to the airport for a week's holiday up in Cairns with the rest of my family.

Lauren has messaged me daily with a list of things to pick up so she could make dinner, and she's used stuff she'd found in my freezer and pantry, but I haven't done a big shop and filled my fridge and pantry. And now I feel bad that I've been leaving Lauren at home with nothing to eat.

"Babe, order whatever you like from the Chinese. I'll pick it up and grab a couple of bottles of wine on my way through. We'll go out and do a grocery shop tomorrow; that way, you'll have plenty of options and zero excuses next week."

I hear her let out a sigh, followed by a too-long moment of silence.

"Shall I order from Wok?" she eventually asks.

"Of course." Despite living in a popular tourist destination, surrounded by Michelin starred restaurants, there's only one Chinese the locals use.

"What would you like?"

"Salt and pepper prawns, and Singapore noodles extra spicy, please. What wine would you like?"

"Far out," I hear her whisper.

"What?" I ask, confused.

"That's too cute. You two order the same thing from Wok," Jo calls out.

"See, made for each other," I respond. "This is the exact reason you should be letting me sleep in your bed."

"Technically, it's your bed, and I don't tend to sleep with someone just because they order the same dish as me from the local Chinese. If I did, I'd need a bigger bed."

"So what does it take?" I question.

I've put no pressure on her in the time she's been with me. I've flirted, that's just the way I am, and in all fairness, she's flirted right back, but despite the blue ball's situation, I'm not a dick and can totally appreciate she's not in the right headspace to move things forward with us yet.

We've kissed, and there's been a lot of grinding against each other, but one or the other of us, usually her, has pulled back before taking things too far.

I'm hoping some time apart will make her realise that we're good together, and as much as I don't want to leave her here alone, I think maybe she needs that time to do some healing both mentally and physically.

I've tried to give her space, working till late, or going to the gym straight from work, but I then worry that she's spending too much time on her own. Her girls call in and out almost daily at different times, but the fact she's still refusing to leave the house is worrying me.

"It's been so long, I've forgotten," Lauren's quiet voice interrupts my thoughts.

"Well, I'll be right here waiting patiently until you remember."

"You sure?"

"Absolutely. Sleeping in the guest room while imagining you upstairs in my bed is my absolute most favourite thing in the world, right next to sleeping next to you with all our clothes on."

"Wow," she responds with her favourite word. "I detect a note of sarcasm in your tone, Mr Wild. Did no one ever tell you it's the lowest form of wit?"

"If they did, I don't remember. Just order the food, Lauren. I'm nearly home and don't want to have to hang around waiting for it."

"Laters taters," she says before ending the call. I've noticed she says it at the end of every one of our telephone conversations, and like a few things she says, I still have no idea what it means.

* * *

I ARRIVE HOME to the sound of Chaka Khan singing and Lauren laughing. Everything about this situation is as foreign to me as it is to her.

Apart from the few months my marriage lasted, I've never shared my home with anyone other than my daughter, and I've been mostly happy with it that way. I grew up in a noisy house. Working with my brothers and sister means that our office is never quiet, and when I'm out on site, my workplace is even less so. My home has always been my escape from all of that, but I won't lie, I've loved coming home every night knowing Lauren is here waiting for me, opening the front door to the sound of music playing and the smell of food cooking.

There've been a few awkward moments, but it's mostly been easy having her in my space. I definitely like it more than hate it, because I like Lauren. I like her a lot, and the more time I spend with her, the more I find to like.

I've no clue where we're going with what we've got. I've no clue what it is we even have; I just know we've got something that I've never felt before.

Lauren's still sleeping most mornings when I leave, but in the evenings, once her friends go home, we talk nonstop. Through dinner, and until she falls asleep on top of me, as we lay on the sofa, we talk shit about anything and everything, and that's something I've never had with a woman.

Despite all the talking we do in the evening, I still find myself calling her while I'm at work to ask about her day, or maybe it's just to hear her voice, I've no fucking idea. I'm fumbling my way through this and shit scared that at some stage, I'm going to fuck it up and lose all of the trust I keep assuring her she can have in me.

"Hey." Lauren's blue eyes meet mine as soon as I hit the top of the stairs.

I place the bag containing the Chinese takeaway, the two bottles of wine, and my laptop down on the dining table where Lauren's sitting.

"Little bird," I greet her before my mouth brushes gently across hers. Then I tell her what I tell her every night when I get home, "You look better today."

"Thanks," she smiles up at me, "I think I'm finally working the beaten housewife look."

"Not funny, Ren," I shake my head and tell her, getting an eye-roll in return.

"How's your day been?"

She's washed her hair and has left it loose, hanging down her back in curls. My eyes scan her face, noting that the swelling around her eye is finally going down, and her bruises are fading to light greens and yellows. The split in her lip has almost healed, and she seems to have almost full range of motion in her shoulder.

"Oh, you know, caught a few waves first thing this morning, then went to the gym, run home from there, took a shower, made a Croquembouche. . ."

She stares up at me, smiling, blinking, and attempting to look innocent.

"What was it you were saying about sarcasm being the lowest form of wit? And what the fuck is a croquet bush?"

"Croquembouche, it's like a pointy cake made from lots of little profiteroles stuck together."

"Sounds good, now tell me what you *really* did?"

"I did the washing, put the hoover round, worked on my website, and Jo washed and dried my hair for me."

"You mean you did laundry and vacuumed?"

"That's exactly what I said," she says with a grin.

"Put her down." I'm still leaning into Lauren, my hand cupping her jaw, as my thumb gently brushes across her cheek when Jo appears from the direction of my bathroom.

"I don't think she wants me to," I reply. "It's been what, all of eleven hours since she had her fix."

Lauren pushes against me and attempts to escape as Jo shifts my laptop off the table and unpacks the takeaway containers.

"You think very highly of yourself, Mr Wild."

"Just working every angle, Mrs. . ." I stop the words leaving my mouth but know that I've already fucked up when Lauren winces.

"Fuck." I press my lips against her forehead.

"Day," she whispers. Her hands slide from my neck and wrap around my waist. "It's Ms, not Mrs, and it's Day, Lauren Day," she says with a squeeze, making me feel just a little better.

"Foods up," Jo calls.

Taking a step back, I ask, "We good?"

She nods and gives me a small smile. "It was close there for a minute, but we're good."

CHAPTER 18

Lauren

IT'S BEEN over two weeks.

Over two weeks since I left my house in the middle of the night after my husband beat me.

Tonight, will be the eighteenth night I've slept in the bed of a man I barely know—Gabe's bed.

Although I've gone to bed alone each night that I've been here, there've been a couple of mornings I've woken with Gabe pressed in tight behind me. His explanation for his presence in my/his bed is that I'm having nightmares, and the only way to calm me down, is for him to hold me.

Sometimes I remember having the nightmare. Sometimes I don't. What I'm sure of is, it's the same scene that plays out every time, and it involves Jason dragging me from my bed and away from Gabe. I've even had the same dream during the day when I've fallen asleep on the sofa.

Each morning, after Gabe leaves for work, I've cried. I've cried great, heaving, body-wracking sobs of hurt, and silent tears of anger. It's been cathartic. I'm not sure what stage of the process I'm at, but after spending the past weeks mourning for my marriage and the loss of the life I once had, I think I'm finally coming to terms with things, or I could be delusional and it hasn't even really hit me yet I'm not an expert on these things so I can't really say with any authority, I just know that I've felt similar to the way I felt in the first few weeks after losing my dad.

His death was sudden and unexpected. At first I was in shock, then denial, then I lost track of the order. I think it was anger for a while.

I don't even know if the same rules apply to death as they do for the end of a relationship, but mourning is the only word to describe how it's left me feeling.

I'm still not okay with it. I'm not over it. I don't know that I ever will be either, especially while I'm still so confused as to why it ended the way it did. Despite all that's happened, I still have a tight knot of guilt lodged firmly in my chest at being here with Gabe and how easy it is being with him. How comfortable I've become in his company, living in his home, in such a short space of time.

There's been no sex, but there has been kissing. The kissing started out sweet and gentle. I think Gabe is being mindful of my injuries *and* my mental state, but as each day passes, the more time I spend with him, the longer, hotter, wetter, and more passionate our kisses have become. They're now also backed up by the grinding of hips and thumbs brushing nipples. All of which is making it hard! Hard for me to control myself, to pull away and put the brakes on things, and hard for Gabe in the dick department. I know this because it's absolutely impossible not to know this when I'm lying on top or straddling him.

I don't know what all of this means; whether we actually

have any kind of a future together, or if it's my husband's rejection, my need to feel wanted, or our forced confinement that's making me feel so attracted to him.

It's a mess, a complete and utter shit show. My situation, us being here together, the timing of everything. Almost every night since I've been here, I've laid spread out on top of him on his sofa, and we've talked and talked and talked, and it feels right. It feels good. It feels like I'm exactly where I'm supposed to be, but in the morning, the guilt, self-doubt, and humiliation creep in, and I wallow in the misery they cause me.

Jo keeps telling me I'm overthinking everything and that my guilt is unwarranted but understandable.

She'd run me a bath down in Gabe's guest bathroom earlier, and, using a jug she'd found in a kitchen cupboard, she'd washed my hair.

"So, you going to fill me in on what's going on between the two of you? And don't say 'nothing' because if there was nothing there, you wouldn't still be here, you'd have gone to Ryder's or your mum's, aaaaand, I've been around the pair of you, and the way he looks at you, I don't know how you haven't combusted. Seriously, Lauren, I nearly combusted."

Sitting with my knees pulled up to my chest, my face tilted up to the ceiling, I take a moment to enjoy the warmth of the water Jo pours over me. The sensation relaxing my tight muscles, easing some of the tension in my body in what feels like the first time in forever.

"You can tell me, you know. There'll be no judgement from me, ever."

Jo is very much a live for the moment type of girl, something I've always admired about her. She has a man's attitude to sex, something you don't often find in women our age. We're from a generation who were encouraged to be good girls, to save ourselves for 'the one.' We were raised to believe it's okay to slut-shame, that to be a promiscuous woman is so very wrong.

But Jo, she'll sleep with who she wants, when she wants, and she doesn't give a fuck what others think. And that's okay with me because that's what works for her. That's what makes her happy. Maybe if I'm single long enough, I can let go of some of my own preconceived ideas about women and their sexuality I was raised to believe were true.

"I know you wouldn't judge; it's just that I don't really have an answer for you. I honestly don't know myself what's going on between us."

I let out a deep sigh as she massages shampoo into my scalp, avoiding the area that's glued together.

"I like him. He's been so good, letting me stay here when he barely knows me. He hasn't pushed anything to happen, hasn't put me under any kind of pressure. I mean, we've kissed, a lot, and there have been hands. . . on bare skin a few times, but we've gone no further than that. I think he knows I'm not ready. . ."

"You're a stronger woman than me then. There's no way I could be holding back from all that's Gabriel Wild grinding up against me."

I open my eyes and send an eye roll in her direction, accompanied by a head shake.

"What? Have you seen that man, and I don't just mean the way he looks, I mean, have you actually seen him? He's been so worried about you, he's called me almost daily to ask if I've heard from Jay, he's called and asked what wine you like, what food you like. He wants to make you happy, Loz. He wants you safe and he wants you happy."

"I know. I'm aware of all of that. It's just me. I'm not sure I'm ready. I'm worried that it's too soon."

"Is it you who thinks it's too soon, or are you worried that other people will think it's too soon?"

I shrug because I'm not entirely sure.

"Fuck other people, their thoughts are exactly that, theirs, and they have no bearing on your life, the way you live it, or the decisions you make. If you want it and it feels right, then go for it. He's obviously into you, so don't hold back just because you're worried about what others will think. Seize the day, Lauren. What's the worst that could happen? If it doesn't work out, move on. At least you'll do it knowing you gave it a go, and if the rumours are true, at least you'll have the memories to get you through the dry times."

"I have the pool bloke coming in the morning. He's gonna test the spa and pool for me and get them up and running so you can use them while I'm away if you want," Gabe says, interrupting my contemplative silence as I recalled what Jo had said to me earlier.

I'm lying on top of Gabe on his sofa. I listen to his heartbeat and his voice echoing through his chest, with my ear pressed against it. His fingers draw lazy circles on the bare skin of my back, making me feel loose-limbed and relaxed.

"I thought the spa might be good for getting some of these knots out of your back and shoulders, and swimming might tire you out enough that you don't have nightmares while I'm away."

"I don't have any bathers," I say without looking at him.

His hands slide down inside the pyjama bottoms I'm wearing, and he gives the bare skin of each of my arse cheeks a squeeze.

"Works for me," he says with a kiss to the top of my head.

I lace my fingers across his chest, rest my chin on them and look up at him, letting out a long slow breath as I do.

Out of curiosity, I ask, "What happened to the unit I was supposed to look at? The one you said would be. . ."

His hands release their grip on my arse, and his entire body tenses beneath me as he cuts me off.

"You said you couldn't afford a place of your own yet. You had shit to sort out."

He stares down his perfectly straight nose at me as he speaks.

"You said we could come to some arrangement over the rent?"

His head tilts to the side, brows drawn down over those expressive blue eyes of his. "You don't want to be here?"

I swallow and lick my lips as Jo's words rattle around in my head. *'Seize the day, Lauren!'*

"Do you not think this is all a little bit ridiculous?" Yeah, my brain obviously chose to ignore Jo's words and say these words instead.

Gabe pulls his head back and stares at me wide-eyed for a few seconds.

"Ridiculous? What the fuck, babe?" He swings his legs out from under me, planting his feet on the floor, and sits up, shifting me to sit beside him.

"Explain to me exactly what it is that you think is ridiculous? Us? You being here?"

My mouth dries as I watch how pissed off what I've said has made him. I open it to speak, but he cuts me off again.

"Ya know what? I like you. I wanted you safe, and yeah, I've liked having you near, I know we're just getting to know each other, and this hasn't been the ideal way to start a relationship, but that's what I thought we were doing, starting something. Am I wrong on that score?"

I stare at him for a few seconds, my own anger now bubbling in my belly.

He stands, rakes his fingers through his hair, and paces in front of me.

"I don't do this." I watch as he waves his hand between us. "I don't do relationships, so excuse my fucking ignorance if I'm reading this all wrong, but what is it exactly you think is happening here, between you and me, I mean?"

"You gonna listen to my answers before you fire off any

more questions?" I ask. He stops pacing and looks at me. I stare or may be glare at him for a few seconds. His hands bury themselves inside his pockets as he lets out a sigh and his shoulders relax a fraction.

"Sorry," he mumbles. "It's just that. . ."

"Ugh!" I put my finger up, he narrows his eyes on me. "My turn," I tell him. That earns me a scowl.

"Woman. . ."

"Don't woman me either, Wild."

Without another word, he sits on the edge of the coffee table in front of me.

"I like it when you're bossy," he says with a wink followed by a lick of his lips.

'Stop trying to distract me."

"Wouldn't dream of it," he says quietly, knowing full well that's exactly what he's doing.

I launch right in.

"We've just met, and I'm already living in your house. I'm eating your food, sleeping in your bed. We don't really know each other, and yet, right now, I feel like I'm *totally* dependent on you. That's what I meant about the whole situation being ridiculous. Us, this." I make my own hand gesture between us. "The way we've been thrown together, I mean seriously, you couldn't make this shit up. That's what I meant by this situation being ridiculous."

I pull a cushion onto my lap, raise my knees and squash it against my chest as I sit back into the corner of Gabe's big leather sofa. His hands go to his hips as he watches me.

"Do you want to be here?"

Seize the fucking day, Lauren.

"No," I tell him honestly. I actually hear the rapid expulsion of air that escapes him at my response. His mouth opens to say something, but I continue talking. "What I want is to be in my own place, for me and you to be taking our time, going out on dates, getting to know each other like normal couples do. What I want is for there to be no pressure on us to make this work. What I want is *not* to be wondering if I still need to be worrying about whether my crazy ex is still trying to hunt me down."

"You want to go out on dates? I asked you the other night if you wanted to go for dinner. I want to take you on dates."

I let out a sigh. "That's all you got from what I just said? That's your response?"

"You're here, Lauren. The situation is what it is. All relationships start with a couple *not* knowing each other. We're just doing the *getting* to know each other part while living in the same house. That just means we'll get to know each other quicker. I don't think either of us are stupid people, so I reckon, we'd both know by now if there was no chance of what we've got going anywhere, don't you?"

He's up and pacing in front of me again. His hands moving between his hair, the back of his neck, to his hip, or animatedly gesturing towards me. He stops pacing at the end of each sentence but starts moving again before I can respond.

"There's no more pressure on *us* to make this work than there is on any other relationship out there, and the fact that you're worried about your fuckwit of an ex still wanting to hunt you down, is why, amongst a few other reasons, I want you *here,* where I know you're safe."

He stops his pacing, sits back down on the coffee table, and leans towards me. "Now," he says softly. "You wanna go on a fucking date with me or what?"

Looking across at him, I chew on my bottom lip and shrug while fighting not to smile.

"Well, seeing as you asked so nicely, how could I possibly say no? But not till you're back from your holiday, when my bruises have faded a bit more."

He aims a small smile my way that warms my insides, mostly

the inside of my vagina, but I think I manage to hide that reaction from him.

"I did ask nicely, didn't I? Of course you couldn't say no."

"You have a seriously high opinion of yourself, Wild."

"Don't pretend you don't like it, Day."

I choose to ignore that comment because I do like it. It's one of the many things I like about him, and one of the reasons I'm glad that he's going away in the morning.

A little bit of space, some distance between us will be good. I need it.

I thought about using his holiday as an excuse to move out, but if I do that, I'll have to go and stay at either Jo's or Ryder's and there's a chance Jay might turn up. Plus, if I stay here, I could have over a week all to myself.

I've never lived on my own. I moved from my parents' house straight in with Jason, and right now, I really like the idea of some alone time.

"I'll book us somewhere nice for the weekend after I get back," Gabe says as he moves towards the kitchen. Pausing, he turns back and looks at me. "We good?" he asks.

"We're good," I tell him with a smile.

"You wanna beer?" he asks. I shake my head and watch his fine arse as he walks towards the kitchen.

* * *

LIKE EVERY MORNING since I've been here, it takes a few heartbeats till I get my bearings, then I'm hit with a flood of every kind of emotion. This morning though is different because I've woken with my head resting just below Gabe's bare chest.

Last night's dream was the most vivid and terrifying I've had so far and the only one I've remembered from beginning to end. Jay, kicking in the front door as I sleep next to Gabe, grabbing me by the hair, and pulling me from the bed as I scream at Gabe to help me. But he doesn't wake up. I kick, and I fight, I reach out my hands, but Gabe continues sleeping while Jay drags me further towards the door, further away from Gabe.

The recollection of the fear, the absolute terror of knowing what's going to happen, what Jay's going to do if he gets me through that door has my eyes burning with tears. Remembering how I felt when I woke up, the way I cried as I clung on to Gabe. The way he held me, told me he wouldn't leave, that I was safe.

I close my eyes, listening to the sound of the waves out on the bay. I attempt to slow my racing heart and drift back off to sleep, but I'm too wired and too warm.

Opening my eyes, I take in my view. Gabe's flat stomach, my arm, slung across his hips, the trail of hair leading from his chest, disappearing under the sheet that's covering us.

He has one arm curled around me, the other raised above his head. I'm hot, not just because of the hot body pressed against me, but also, very much because of the *hot* body pressed against me.

I'm a little bit uncomfortable, but Gabe has a long day today, he's picking up his daughter late this morning, before they catch their flight up to Queensland with the rest of his family, so I don't want to wake him. . . or move away from him. Without thinking it through, I turn my head slightly and kiss his belly. When he sighs and tilts his hips towards me, I freeze.

When he settles, my eyes travel lower. I'm sure he's not naked but decide to double-check.

Lifting it slowly and as carefully as I can, I take a peep beneath the sheet.

My stomach churns. I wish I were more like Jo, and brave enough to do more than take just a peep. I wish I had the confidence to reach across and take what I really want.

Confidence, or lack of it, is the key. I've always been an outgoing, confident person, but months of put-downs and insults from my husband have rattled the foundations of that confidence, and it's going to take a bit more than a younger man being interested in me to get it back.

I hold my breath as Gabe shifts. Moving the arm tucked behind his head, he slides his hand inside his boxers. Still holding up the sheet, I watch as he gets comfortable and just leaves his hand *there*. Tucked down his jocks. Cupping his dick. And for some unknown reason, I'm hit with an uncontrollable fit of the giggles.

I manage to keep quiet but can't stop my shoulders shaking up and down or the tears rolling down my cheeks.

"Something funny down there?"

"No," I snort out.

"I'm up here getting a complex about the way you're down there, laughing at my dick, babe. Just sayin'."

"I'm not laughing at your dick. I'm sure it's a magnificent dick, with nothing to laugh at about it. It was just the way you slid your hands inside your jocks, and. . . and. . ." I struggle to come up with a word. . . or to even look at him.

"Readjusted?" he offers. "It's a bloke thing."

"Not having a dick, I wouldn't know this."

"Good to know that you know nothing about having a dick, babe. Just putting it out there, I consider myself pretty open-minded, and love is love, wherever you might find it, but dicks, and specifically birds with dicks, as far as I know, are not my thing."

"Good. Glad we got that sorted. You wanna coffee?" I ask, still not looking at him but wanting, very much, to get off the subject of dicks.

"Glad we got it sorted too, but before you make coffee, I wanna know what last night was all about?"

I enjoy the sensation of his thumb brushing against the bare skin of my lower black, beneath the T of his I went to bed wearing last night. Finally looking up at him, I shrug.

"You don't know, or don't wanna talk about it?"

Scooting up the bed, I sit with my back against the headboard, putting me slightly higher than him. I look down to where his eyes are on me.

"It was just another nightmare, but more vivid than the others. I actually remember this one."

His eyes dart rapidly over my face before meeting back up with mine.

"Was he in it?" I know exactly who 'he' is, and I nod.

"Did he hurt you? You tried to fight me when I held on to you," he says quietly.

My eyes close, and my gut clenches at the thought of lashing out at Gabe.

"I'm so sorry," I choke out.

"No. No, no, no. Don't be sorry. You didn't hurt me, and it wouldn't matter if you did. I just hate that it's happening."

Gabe sits up, puts his arm around my shoulders, and pulls me against his chest.

"I hate that you're still reliving what that fucker did to you. I hate that he's still got the power to do that."

He kisses the top of my head. I slide my hand across his belly, leaving it to rest on his hip, and tilt my face up to meet his. His mouth is closer than I expected, and our lips brush.

It's like an explosion.

An instant reaction to all the emotion, hurt, anger, sexual attraction, and tension that's been bubbling between and inside us for the past weeks.

It ignites so fast that my head spins with the speed. His mouth is on mine, his tongue pushing inside, tasting me. In seconds I'm on my back, my legs spread wide, Gabe's hips grinding against mine. My T-shirt comes off, and I'm hyper-aware of his chest hair on my nipples as my hips buck, and I wrap my legs around him. His teeth rake across my jaw and down my neck. My fingers claw at his hair and dig into his scalp. His hand finds my breast, pushing it up to meet his mouth, his tongue, his teeth, and I let out a groan at the exact same time the gate alarm sounds.

My groan dissolves into a whimper, but I continue to grind against him.

"Fuck," he says against my neck, his thumb still brushing back and forth across my nipple. "It's Jimmy, the pool bloke. Fuck."

"Ignore it. I'm happy to swim in a dirty pool or sit in a dirty spa. . . or just not use them at all. We can just go down to the beach if we wanna swim."

He adjusts his position above me. Looking down, he gives me a lop-sided sexy smile.

"You could, but you'd probably freeze your tits off, and I'd prefer to come home and find them still attached to the rest of you."

Opening my eyes and mouth as wide as I can, I stare up at him. "You only want me for my rack?"

He instantly pushes up on his elbows, cups both of my boobs in his hands, and pushes them up and together. Lowering his head, he kisses each of my nipples before looking up at me.

"It's a pretty spectacular rack," he tells me with a wink and a smile that sends a pulse to so many parts of me. "Besides, when I get back, I'd like to be able to use the pool and spa with you, without freezing my dick off."

"Yeah, I get that. From what I can feel, you have a pretty spectacular dick, but I like you for a lot more than the six inches you have tucked in. . ."

"Six inches?" Now it's his turn to stare at me wide-eyed. "Woman, even on a cold day, it's at least seven and a half."

"And you know this because?"

He shrugs. That sexy smile of his spreads across his stubble-covered face, along with a quick quirk of his brows.

"It's a bloke thing."

A knock sounds at the front door. Gabe leans in, brushes his mouth against mine, and climbs off me.

"Fuck. My. Life," he says while pulling on his trackies and the T I was wearing earlier. I grin as I watch the muscles in his back work when he raises his arms and pulls on the T-shirt.

* * *

I SPEND the rest of the morning helping Gabe pack while reassuring him I would be okay on my own.

"Jo's coming tonight, and Jem and Lou are both staying Friday and Saturday night. We're going to pretend we're in our own little resort. I'll be fine."

"What about next week, is Jo staying then?" he asks as he looks down at me.

We're at the front door. His case is on the back seat of his truck, and he should've left ten minutes ago. Instead, he's standing here stressing over me.

"I wish your son wasn't away. I'd be much happier if he was around in case there's an emergency."

"What kind of emergency is there likely to be? I've heard nothing from Jay. We're done and he knows it."

He lets out a huff and looks everywhere except at me.

"Go, have fun, be with your daughter. Don't have too much fun though, or go banging some leggy, Queensland beach babe."

It strikes me then, we haven't had that conversation yet. We haven't even had a conversation about what we are to each other, so we definitely haven't had one about exclusivity.

He lets out another sigh, or this one could even be construed as a huff. Before he can say any more, I pull away, hold my arm out towards his truck and say, "Go. I'm going in now, and if you don't leave, you're going to be late."

Before I can turn towards the front door, he steps back towards me, wraps his arm around my waist, and pulls me towards him. I open my mouth, but don't get a sound out before his lips are on mine.

Moving his hands to either side of my jaw, he kisses me long, deep, and wet. It's the kind of kiss that speaks to you, and if I were a wiser woman, I would understand what he was trying to convey, but as he steps away and into his truck, I'm just left feeling confused.

CHAPTER 19

Gabe

Because Lena's pregnant, I go to the front door and knock when I arrive to collect Ava. I know my daughter, we might only be going away for nine nights, but she will have packed for two-hundred and seventy-nine, and I don't want either of them struggling with her cases.

"Hey," I say to my ex when she opens the door. "She ready?"

Lena looks past me and over my shoulder to my truck.

"You on your own?" she answers with a question of her own. Despite knowing the answer to this, I still look behind me to my truck.

"Yeah, we're meeting everyone else at the airport. Why's that?"

"Including your new girlfriend?"

What the fuck?

"My new girlfriend?" I question. That earns me a roll of her pale blue eyes. Funny how it amuses me when Lauren does it but pisses me the fuck off when it's Lena.

"My new girlfriend is just that," I get in before Lena can say any more. "We're new. You really think I'd bring her on holiday with me when Ava's never even met her?"

With one hand on her hip, Lena brings the other around to rest on her very pregnant belly. She looks well, I note. Lena's naturally very slim, to the point where she can sometimes look frail and gaunt, so the weight she gains during her pregnancies always looks good on her. . . at least I think so. Not that she'd give a fuck what I thought.

"I don't know, Gabe. It's out of character for you to have a girlfriend, so I wasn't sure what to think or expect, especially since Ava said she's moved in with you."

My daughter has a big mouth, not that I'd ever encourage her to keep secrets from her mother.

"We had an argument, and she couldn't wait to ram that bit of information down my throat," Lena enlightens me.

Not wanting to get involved in whatever's going on between Ava and Lena, I ignore the comment.

"This her case?" I ask, pointing to the bright orange suitcase sitting in the hallway. Not waiting for an answer, I reach around Lena, extend the handle, and drag it to my car. As expected, it weighs a ton and will no doubt mean an excess baggage fee when we get to the airport.

I launch it into the back of my truck, and when I turn around, Ava is standing next to me and the front door's closed.

I swear, being around my kid brings on a physical change to my body. My heartbeat slows, my blood pressure lowers, and my jaw and shoulders relax. Without a word, I pull her into me and note instantly that she's grown in the almost four weeks since I last saw her.

"Is there anything you haven't packed?" I ask.

"I left a couple of pairs of thongs out, and my yellow bikini, my boobs have grown, and they don't fit in the top anymore."

She stands up on her toes and gives me a kiss on the cheek before moving around my truck and climbing into the passenger side.

I don't want to even consider my twelve-year-old daughter having boobs, but I'm grateful that she chose to leave the yellow bikini at home. I'll ask her to bring it to my place next time she visits so I can burn it in the fire pit.

"It's okay though, I brought three new ones, and they all have padding. Sophie said I look hot in them and that they give amazing cleavage."

"Did I not tell you?" I ask as I reverse out of the drive. "The resort has a modesty policy, one-piece bathers only. I'll pick something out for you at the airport. It'll be plain, navy blue or black, long-sleeved and will come with matching boardies that must be worn at all times. There'll also be zero padding involved."

"Great bantz, Dad. You're hilarious."

The kid thinks I'm joking. The three new bikinis will be getting burnt right along with the yellow one.

"How's Lauren?" she asks after we've caught up on what's happening in her life. We talk and text almost daily, but there are always things she forgets to mention until she sees me.

"She's good," I say with a nod. "What were you arguing with your mum about to make you tell her about Lauren?" I ask.

"Jesus, she didn't waste time telling you, did she?"

"You know your mother, any excuse to get into it with me. She thought I'd be bringing Lauren away with us."

"You should have. Then I could've gotten to know her. Why didn't you?"

I don't want to tell my kid that if we had time, I'd turn

around right now and go get her. Instead, I say, "I've not seen you in almost a month, this holiday is about you and me time. Lauren knows that, and she's happy for me, for us, but she can't wait to meet you in a couple of weeks when you come stay."

"I can't wait to meet her. You're different since you met her, Dad."

I laugh at that. "Different how?"

"I don't know, you just sound different on the phone, especially when you talk about her. You sound happier, like. . ." I turn and take a quick look at my daughter as she struggles to find the right word.

"Like you have more life in you."

I look back to the freeway. In an attempt at ignoring the tightness in my chest and throat, I concentrate on the traffic as we take the exit for the airport.

She's right. My daughter is absolutely spot on. Having Lauren in my life, has given me the kind of purpose I only usually have on the weeks and weekends Ava comes to stay.

"You've only had *me* for so long, since forever, so I'm glad. Happy that you've found someone, now I won't have to move in and look after you when you get old, Lauren can do it."

"Thanks, I'm glad that makes you happy."

"You can talk about her you know. You're probably going to miss her while we're away, so if you wanna talk about her, I'm okay with that."

"Again, thanks. That's good to know, but when did you grow up and become a psychologist?"

That earns me an eye roll. What is it with women and their eye rolls?

Ava reaches across the centre console and takes the hand I don't have on the wheel. "It's okay, Dad, you can open up to me, tell me anything. It's okay to miss Lauren. It's good to be in touch with your emotions. Women love a man who's comfortable enough with their masculinity to show their vulnerable side. We find it hot."

"Jesus," I choke out, almost missing the off-ramp to the airport car park.

CHAPTER 20

Lauren

I HOLD my wine glass against my chest and sit in contemplative silence while staring into the glowing fire pit.

"So, it's agreed, once he gets home Friday night, you're gonna jump his bones?" Lou asks.

"Yep, we're gonna take her to get all her bits waxed in the week so she's silky smooth and ready to. . ."

"I'm not getting anything waxed, and I'm not jumping Gabe's bones as soon as he gets home Friday," I cut Jemma off.

"Why not?" Jo asks.

"I don't need waxing. You've seen how little I've got going on down there."

"I meant why are you not gonna jump Gabe's bones?"

I look across the fire pit to where she sits wrapped in a blanket and let out a long heavy sigh.

It's Saturday night, Gabe's been gone since Wednesday, Jo

arrived after work that night, the girls got here Friday afternoon. The alone time I've been looking forward to hasn't really happened, but Gabe not being in the equation has at least given me some breathing space.

I've had time to think clearly about my situation, to consider my feelings for him, Gabe. I definitely want to see where what we've got will go, but I'd like to do it from a distance and at a slower pace.

"I'm not ready," I tell Jo.

"Not ready, or not ready to admit you *are* ready?" she questions.

Candie Staton sings about young hearts running free in the background, and without even looking, I know that Jemma and Lou are watching me.

"Why are you so determined to have me fuck Gabe? What difference does it make to your life?"

"I just want to see you happy."

"And I need to fuck Gabe to achieve that? I'm not you, Jo. I've been having sex with the same man for almost twenty-seven years. I don't know how to have sex without there being an emotional connection to the person I'm having sex with." I let out a long breath when I finish what I'm saying.

"You telling me there's no connection there with Gabe? Coz if that *is* what you're saying, I call bullshit. I've been around the pair of you, that connection's so strong, it sizzles."

"Yeah, and if I have sex with him it'll be even stronger, and then what happens when he changes his mind? When he decides I'm not for him, that an older woman isn't what he was looking for after all? My heart's already in pieces, if I hand those pieces over to him and he leaves, they'll be ground to dust." I'm so fucking angry with myself for crying as I talk, I want to throw my glass. I don't. I empty it. I don't know where all of that came from. I didn't realise until I said out loud that's how I was feeling, and I'm pissed off with that too.

"Loz," Lou whispers my name as her hand reaches out for mine. I take it, the contact calming me somewhat.

"Why wouldn't he want you, Lauren? Look at you. You have a beautiful heart. . ."

"Don't think it's my beautiful heart Gabe would be interested in fucking, Jem." I manage to pull a laugh from somewhere as I talk, even if it is meant with sarcasm. "I've seen his past conquests, young, slim. . ."

"And did he move any of them in here the night after he met them? The fuck he did. You need to pull your head out of your arse, Lauren. I've seen the way he looks at you. He's moved you in here, and for three weeks he hasn't touched you."

"That's not entirely true," Jemma interrupts Jo. "She said there's been kissing and grinding."

"And she got her tits out for him the morning before he left," Lou adds.

Meanwhile, I sit silently with a million thoughts churning inside my brain.

"Look," Jo continues as if nobody else has spoken. "I'm not telling you to rush into anything until you're ready, I'm just saying, don't deny yourself what you really want."

"If the situation were different, if you'd met and just started dating, do you think you would've slept with him by now? Or would you have stayed away from men for a while?" Lou asks.

"I don't know the answer to that, Lou. I don't think this is about him or me, it's more the circumstances. I haven't come out of my marriage fearing all men and scared that what happened with Jay could happen again. I've been surrounded by good men all my life and know better than that. I just feel that, now my physical injuries are mostly healed, my heart needs time to catch up."

"Well, I say, go at your own pace. Ignore what that greedy cock gobbling bitch over there says, she forgets we don't all crave the D the way she does."

"Fuck you, Wilson," Jo responds to Jemma's comment with the flip of her middle finger.

"You'd like to, Myer," Jem responds with a flip of her own.

"I agree with Jem. You do you boo, and forget what everyone else thinks, it's none of their business. Now, let's all go up and get in the spa, I'm freezing," Lou suggests.

* * *

It's Thursday evening, and after eight whole days and nights without Gabe, my brain has done a complete one-eighty, and I'm now planning on doing exactly what Jo suggested and attacking Gabe the minute he walks through the door.

She had a conference in the city on Tuesday and Wednesday, and after spending hours convincing her I didn't need one of the other girls to come babysit me, I've had two nights, and three glorious days where I've been completely alone.

When Jason stopped coming home from work till late and started spending all of his weekends on the golf course, I felt lonelier and more isolated than I did when my parents brought me to Australia as a thirteen-year-old.

But these past days here on my own have been good for my soul. I've swum, I've cooked—Gabe had contacted Jo and made sure I was left with a full fridge and pantry—I've been on the treadmill I found in the garage every morning, I've worked on my website, I've read an entire book, and I've watched every old film and television show I could fit in. I've not had one single nightmare since Gabe has been gone. I've slept so well, I can't even remember dreaming.

For the first time in my life, I think I've learned how to be alone without being lonely. I've also done a lot of soul searching and thinking, and I've come to the conclusion, that I'm ready. Ready to take a chance and move on.

I think.

No doubt, the minute Gabe walks up those stairs later, I'll once again be full of self-doubt and indecision, but for now, the plan is to hit him with a kiss, then take it from there.

I've had multiple texts and daily phone calls from Gabe while he's been away. The calls have been short, sweet, check-ins, the texts shift from caring to flirtatious, and if he's had a few drinks in the evening, a little sentimental.

The last text I got from him last night was:

Gabe: **This time tomorrow, I'll be back home with you. I've missed everything about you, Little Bird, but especially your three S's.**

Me: **???**

Gabe: **Your smile, your scent, and your sass.**

Me: **Nawww. You're too sweet. What about my snoring, and cheery morning disposition?**

Gabe: **Fuck no!**

This morning he woke me with:

Gabe: **You still in bed?**

Me: **Nope. Just done 5k on the treadmill, now gonna shower.**

Gabe: **Wanna film it and send to me?**

Me: **Nope!**

Me: **You're no fun**

An hour later...

Gabe: **You eaten yet?**

Me: **Nope!**

Gabe: **Wanna suck on this?**

He sends a photo of a choc ice, so I pull a banana off the bunch hanging on the bench, remove the skin, then take a photo of me deep throating it and send it to him with the caption:

Me: **No thanks. I'm full! ;)**

Gabe: **You don't play fair! X**

His last message was an hour or so ago, telling me their flight was delayed and wouldn't be getting in till eight this evening. By the time he drops Ava home, it'll be around eleven when he gets here.

I'm showered, wearing nothing but Gabe's T-shirt and a pair of his boxers, and am now seriously worried that I've peaked too early. Expecting him home around eight, I opened a bottle of Prosecco at six. It's now nine-thirty, and I'm on my second bottle and struggling to stay awake.

At ten, unable to keep my eyes open, I crawl into bed and pass out.

* * *

I WAKE TO A HARD, hot body pressed in behind me, and a finger trailing over the dip of my waist. His scent invades my senses before I've even opened my eyes.

Turning to look over my shoulder, I find Gabriel Wild, in all his dark-haired, blue-eyed, stubble-covered-jaw-perfection, looking back at me.

"Hey," I croak out while trying not to breathe my morning breath over him.

His eyes trail a path all over my face before coming back to land on mine.

He smiles.

And something lights up inside me.

"You're looking better today. I've missed you so fucking much," he shakes his head and tells me. "Coming home has *never*, not *ever* felt so good, Ren."

"I missed you too, but right now, I really need the bathroom."

All of my plans to go in for a kiss have now gone out of the window, right along with my Prosecco-induced bravado. The timing's all wrong. I need to use the bathroom and I need to clean my teeth. Meanwhile, Gabe's still shaking his head.

"That's it? That's all you've got for me?"

"I'll have more for you once I've had a wee and cleaned my

teeth," I promise while attempting to slide out from where I'm wedged up against him.

He shifts, and I slide out of bed and walk to the bathroom on unsteady legs, acutely aware that he's watching me.

I do what I need to do, and when I walk back out to the bedroom, Gabe's sitting with his back to the headboard holding up his phone to me. I hadn't even noticed earlier that he was shirtless, but I do now.

"Jimmy's on his way, he needs to check the levels on the pool."

"He was only here last week. Why's he need to check them again?" I ask as I move back towards the bed, his eyes looking me up and down as I approach him.

"He always comes back the week after he first sets it up, then he switches to just once a month. Stay there," he orders with barely a pause.

I stop moving.

"You forget to do laundry while I was away?" Gabe asks while obviously *not* trying too hard to fight a grin.

I suddenly feel stupid and self-conscious. I've pyjamas and knickers that Jo bought me the day after I got here that I could've worn, but last night I thought it a good idea to be wearing his clothes when he got home.

I shrug one shoulder and look away from him.

"No, I just. . ."

"You look good in my jocks, Ren. Fucking gorgeous."

My hands go to my hips and my eyes go to his. He rakes his top teeth over the corner of his bottom lip, and I feel them, those teeth. On me.

"C'mere." He holds out his hand.

I shake my head.

"No?" he questions.

"No," I whisper before pulling his T-shirt over my head and throwing it to the floor.

He releases a rush of air, followed by, "Fuck me, fucking hell, Ren."

And that's when the bloody alarm sounds to let us know Jimmy's arrived.

"You have got to be fucking kidding me?" Gabe almost snarls out the words. "Stay there. I'm gonna go down and drown Jimmy, it shouldn't take long."

I watch as he moves from the bed and stalks towards the door. Feeling self-conscious, I retrieve the T-shirt from the floor and pull it back on.

"What time is it?" I call after him.

"Just after nine."

"Are we still going on our date tonight?" He stops in his tracks and turns back to me.

"No, the restaurant I wanna take you to is full tonight, I've got us a booking for a couple of weeks' time, but we're on the waitlist for next Saturday."

I feel relieved at this news. The white of my eye is still a little red and bloodshot, and I have some faint yellow bruising right in the corner. I also have nothing to wear, and if he's taking me somewhere with a waitlist, it's likely upmarket, and I *do not* want to go wearing leggings and my UGGs.

"You okay with that?" Gabe asks from where he's still standing at the bedroom door.

"Yeah, I've got nothing to wear anyway. I really need to talk to Jay about collecting my stuff."

I thought I mumbled the last part under my breath, but apparently not.

"Yeah, no way in the fuck is that happening. Did you not go out with the girls at all while I was away?"

I shake my head. Not wanting to admit I'm not yet ready to face the world outside. Gabe's eyes roam the room, and I know when they land on mine, he's made a decision about something.

I like that I know that about him already. I'm nervous as to what that decision might be, but I like that I already know his tells. It gives me the warm and fuzzies inside.

When you're young and naive, you assume that goes, the ability to feel the way I'm feeling now. If you'd have asked eighteen-year-old me about dating in your forties, I probably would have made a gagging sound and used the word *gross*. But it's no different. Whatever age you are when girl meets boy, the racing heart and back flipping belly still happen, and if anything, the fanny flutters are even better. I know about sex now. Know what I like, and how *good* sex can make me feel.

That thought has me crossing my legs.

"Get dressed, Ren," Gabe's low rumble interrupts my thoughts.

"Get dressed?" I question. Not trying even a little bit to hide the disappointment in my voice.

"Get dressed, we're going shopping."

Wait. What?

He turns and heads out the door.

"I can't leave the house. I still have a black eye," I call out, acutely aware of how whiney I sound.

"You're full of shit, you can barely even notice the bruising, and anyway, I don't give a fuck. You're not hiding in here any longer. You need something nice to wear on our date. Get dressed."

I throw myself down on the bed, really not wanting or feeling ready to go out and face the world but still grinning at the fact every inch of my skin is tingling, feeling more alive than I have in a very long time.

* * *

AFTER PILING my hair up in the tidiest, messy bun I can, I pull on the leggings and hoodie Jo brought for me. The only shoes I have here are my UGGs, so I have no choice but to pair my outfit with them. Thankfully, she also bought me a BB cream and brush to apply it, and I use this to help cover the yellowing around my eye.

When I pick my phone up from where I left it on the chest of drawers beside the bed last night, I notice it says 'No Service' at the top of the screen. Making my way out to the kitchen, I call Gabe's number, only to hear a 'your call cannot be connected' recording.

I'd been expecting this. My phone is under contract through Jay's business, and I knew he'd have it disconnected at some stage, but it still hits me.

I move from the kitchen out to the deck and look down on Gabe as he stands outside talking to the pool bloke while again contemplating what the actual fuck I'm doing with my life.

It's only a phone, but it's something else Jay has taken from me. Something else I'm now going to have to rely on someone else to sort out for me.

Drawing in deep breaths through my nose, I attempt not to feel overwhelmed with the anger, frustration, and hopelessness I'm feeling at having literally nothing to my name.

And then my eyes land on Gabe. Face tilted to me, he gives me the five-minute sign, smiles, and winks. And fuck it all to kingdom come. I have no clue what the actual fuck I'm doing with my life. I'm angry, frustrated, and literally have just a pair of UGGs and the clothes Jo bought me to my name, but I have him.

I have no idea how this will play out, how it's going to go, where it will lead me or leave me, but for right now, it's right here, with him. It's crazy, insane, ridiculous, and however many other synonyms there are out there to describe how potentially fucked up our relationship is, but he's into me, I'm into him, so I'm going to try very hard to let go of at least some of my insecurities and give this relationship a chance.

"You ready, babe?"

I jump at the sound of Gabe's voice behind me. Lost inside my own head, I hadn't even realised he'd left Jimmy downstairs sorting out the pool while he'd come up, changed into jeans and a hoodie, and was now looking good to go—exceptionally good!

"He's had my phone cut off," I blurt.

Straightening the hood at the back of his neck, Gabe steps out onto the deck towards me.

"Jay? You on his contract?"

I nod.

"Fuck him, I'll get you added to mine," he says with a shrug. "You ready to go?"

And that's it. Without missing a beat, the problem's solved. After only a month of knowing me, just like that, he's willing to add me to his phone plan.

"You'd do that?" I question as I move towards him.

"You need a phone. Of course I'll do that." He shrugs again, brows pulled down into a frown, totally not getting what this means to me.

When I get to where he's standing, I stand up on my tiptoes, wrap my arms around his neck, and kiss him gently on the mouth.

"Thank you," I tell him. "I promise as soon as I get myself straight. . ."

He starts shaking his head.

"Ren, let's just go get you a phone, some clothes, some groceries, and whatever the fuck else we need and worry about payback later."

His dark blue eyes dance across my face for a few moments before meeting mine. He's probably expecting an argument. Instead, I nod.

"Okay," I tell him quietly.

CHAPTER 21

Gabe

"Which milk?" Lauren asks from the open fridge doorway in the supermarket.

"Babe, it's milk."

"Full fat? Semi-skimmed?"

"Babe, seriously, just grab some fucking milk."

I don't mean to snap, but I'm rapidly losing the will to fucking live right now. The trip to get Lauren a new phone was quick and painless. The hunt for new clothes, an outfit for our date next week, and now the grocery shop, not so much.

I only really stock up before Ava's weekends. I know what she likes. I know what I like. I throw it in the trolley, go through the checkout, and I'm done in fifteen minutes tops.

Lauren reads the label on everything, checks the price per kilo, the cost per litre. We've been in here for at least nine-hundred and seventy-eight hours already, and we're not even halfway around.

The clothes shopping was no better. Two-hundred and thirty shops. She tried on ninety-seven outfits for our date, bought nothing. Picked up a couple of pairs of jeans, a couple of tops, a pair of ankle boots, some bras and knickers, a couple of pairs of pyjamas, and bought the lot without trying on any of them. How does that work?

She gives me a look over the cartons of milk she's holding up. It's the same look she gave me when I told her she looked fine in one of the many, many, many outfits she tried on earlier. She could seriously rock up in a black plastic sack and look fucking gorgeous. I don't care what she wears. As long as I get to take her out, give her a good time, and take her home at the end of the night, I don't care about the rest of it.

"Full fat," she declares without waiting for my answer and placing the milk in the trolley I'm pushing. The only upside of this trip is that I've walked behind her the whole way around the supermarket and have been able to watch her arse move in the leggings she's wearing. Despite the exceptional view, I'd much rather be back at home, peeling her out of those leggings and picking up where we left off this morning than comparing the calorific content of different brands of cheese.

It feels like three days later when we finally get home, all of the shopping's put away, and I'm able to crack open a beer and pour Lauren a glass of wine. It's late afternoon, and I'm starving after leaving the house without eating breakfast this morning.

"You want something quick for a late lunch, or shall we just have an early dinner?" I call out to Lauren, who's taken her bags to the bedroom. She appears back in the kitchen, grinning.

Seeing that smile on her face hits me in the chest. I've missed her like fuck while I've been away, and even though all I really want to do is wrap myself around her, I take a moment to just take her in. Even with all the shit she's dealing with right now, she's standing there smiling, looking cute, happy, and totally fuckable.

"Hark at you. You make us sound like an old married couple." She also sounds very Essex.

I know she wasn't comfortable walking around the shops. Even though you can barely see them now, she's still paranoid about her bruises, as well as the clothes she's wearing. I'm pretty certain when she said she didn't want to stop for food because she wasn't hungry, she was lying. And looking at her face all lit up right now, at something as simple as me asking her a question about lunch, I feel like a complete dick for complaining about the time she took trying things on and selecting groceries earlier. I can't even begin to imagine how it'd feel to have your world turned upside down like hers has. To have everything you own ripped away, and be left with literally nothing and left to rely on other people to help you out.

I let out a heavy sigh as I feel the weight of all what she's going through hit me.

"C'mere," I tell her.

Her hands go to her hips, and her smile falters a little.

"What?" she questions quietly with a shrug, her brows pulling down into a frown, eyes darting over my shoulder before landing back on mine.

"Get your arse over here."

She moves to stand in front of me. At six-two, I'm not overly tall, but I feel it as I look down at Lauren. Her hands disappear inside the sleeves of her hoodie, and I watch as her fingers grip the cuffs.

"Did I do something?"

When my eyes meet hers again, it hits me how wide they are, and a wave of nausea churns my gut as I realise I've made her nervous. Reaching out, I wrap my arms around her back and pull her into me.

"Of course not. Far out, Ren. Don't look at me like that. Seriously, don't ever look at me like that."

Moving my hands up to hold on to each side of her face, I tilt it up towards mine.

"I just wanted my mouth on yours. I've missed you, and you're standing there in your UGGs, looking cute and smiley, and I just wanted to do this."

I kiss her gently on the mouth, slide my hands around to cup her arse before moving my mouth to brush along her jaw, then kiss just below her ear. Pulling her against me, I move my mouth back to hers, but this time I'm all in. Mouth open, I push my tongue inside and tangle it with hers. Moving my hands to the backs of her thighs, I lift her and set her down on the benchtop and stand between her open legs.

Pulling my mouth from hers, I take in the flush of colour painting her cheeks, and her wide blue eyes.

"Babe, you need to listen when I say this. I'm not him. I would never, not ever, lay a hand on you. I'm not saying we'll never blue because shit'll happen. I'll piss you off, you'll piss me off, we'll have words, maybe even shout and scream, but I will never, not ever, lay a hand on you. You get that?"

She nods.

"Words Lauren, use your words."

"I know, I know you wouldn't, you just seemed pissed off at the shops, and I thought. . ." She shrugs as she trails off, and again I feel like a dick. "I don't know what I thought, but I know you wouldn't hurt me. I wouldn't be here If I thought for a second you would. It's a bad habit I've gotten into, always thinking I've done something wrong, that I'm gonna be in trouble, and that's on me. It's something I need to work on."

She lets out a sigh, and I kiss her nose. I want to kiss more than her nose, kiss her in other places, but right now, I want her to chill out and relax.

"You want a quick lunch, and then we'll get in the spa. Was it warm enough when you used it with the girls?"

"It was perfect, but I don't have anything to wear in the spa."

"What did you wear when you went in with the girls?" I question. Trying not to think of four naked women bouncing about in my spa.

"Just a crop top and a pair of your jocks."

My dick twitches and I have to physically shake my head to clear the image of Lauren in a wet crop top. I saw her naked tits this morning, which was fucking amazing, but the thought of them in wet clothing is making me hard.

"That'll work, or naked's fine. No one can see us."

"I'm not getting in the spa naked. *You'll* see me, even if the neighbours can't." Her voice rises, and she pushes against my chest. I hold her tighter.

"I'm not seeing a problem here, Ren. You've been sleeping in my bed. You were practically naked in front of me this morning. I had your tits in my hands, and in my mouth the morning before I left. What's the problem if you get naked in the spa?"

"That's different. We were... I wasn't."

"You're gorgeous. I want you naked in my spa, in my bed, in my house, anywhere I can have you naked, that's the way I want you."

"Seriously, Gabe. No one needs to see that. You obviously have never dated an older woman."

My mouth opens and closes because I'm unsure how to respond to that assumption.

"We really gonna go over this again?" I finally question.

"YES! Because I'm old and insecure," she snaps, still trying to fight her way out of my arms. "I'm forty-four. I've carried and given birth to two children, and my body shows all of that. Stretch marks, wobbly bits. I'm not tight and toned. I don't have flawless skin like one of your twenty-five-year-old Gabettes from the pub."

"Did I go home with any of those women from the pub? Did I have anything more than a two-minute conversation with them?"

Once again, holding her face up towards mine, I give her no choice but to meet my eyes as I look down at her. I'm pissed off with the assumptions she's made about me. The kind of assumptions everyone makes about me.

"No, I fucking didn't. I gave *them* the flick and spent the night talking to *you*. I walked *you* to the taxi rank, and I went to Jo's the next night to see *you*, Ren. I didn't call one of them, didn't hook up with one of them. I went to Jo's because I wanted to see *you*."

She licks her lips, sighs, and closes her eyes for a long moment. I give her that moment to take in what I've just said. Then, I keep talking, this time quieter.

"I chose you. Despite seeing the bruises, despite you telling me you had a husband you were about to leave, despite you telling me you had a lot going on, I chose you. You're here, somewhere none of those women have ever, ever been. So, can we please just stop with all this bullshit about your age and the condition of your body?"

I pause, but she says nothing, just staring up at me while breathing heavily instead.

"Do you really think so little of me, think that I'm that fucking shallow?"

"No, I didn't think…"

I step away from her. She's pushed my buttons, and now I'm triggered. Needing to work off some of my anger and disappointment at her words, I move to the other side of the kitchen island.

"No, you didn't fucking think. Is there anything I've done to make you think I only brought you here to fuck you? That I'm only interested in the way you look? I brought you home here when you were beaten black and blue. If I cared that much about your appearance, would I have done that?"

She shakes her head as I pace and rant. I need to say what I have to say, then if she wants to stick around to have her say, she can do that, or she can leave.

Okay, not leave. That's definitely not what I want her to do.

"I wanted you safe, Ren. I wanted you with me, where I knew I could keep you that way. After spending just one night talking to you in the pub, I wanted that. I've known you a little over a month, and I still want that. But please, don't make fucking assumptions about what you think *I* want, based on *your* insecurities."

Folding her arms across her chest, she leans back against the benchtop on the other side of my kitchen and stares at the floor.

I keep my voice low. As much as what she's said has pissed me off, the last thing I want to do is scare her. Her eyes finally blaze a path across the kitchen to meet mine.

"I'm sorry. Like I said earlier, they're my issues, and I know I need to work on them but give me a break here. It's been four weeks. I've spent months, almost a year, being told that I'm fat, ugly, and useless. It's going to take a little while for me not to believe all of that. And I know you've been nothing but nice to me but look at you, Gabe. Just look at you, and all that you are, all that you're offering me, all that you're bringing to this relationship." She waves her hand in my direction, and I can see that she's getting upset, but we need to get this shit sorted.

"Then look at me. I'm an emotional and physical mess. I've got nothing. All I have to offer are red flags, and baggage."

"And have I let any of that put me off? No, because it's you I fucking care about, not the drama you come with, your age, or the stretch marks you may or may not have."

"You haven't seen them yet."

"Fuck. Me. Dead. Woman!" That time I did raise my voice,

and I stand with my face tilted to the ceiling, drawing in deep breaths as I attempt to compose myself.

"You've been in my bed for a month, have I put you under any kind of pressure to take things further? Have I made you feel uncomfortable at any time?"

She swallows and shakes her head.

"No. But please, do not think for a second that I haven't wanted to. I don't know how I've managed to keep my hands mostly to myself. But I've done it. I've missed you like fuck this week. I love my kid, love spending time with her, but I spent every day and every fucking night missing you, wishing you were there. And now I'm home," I shake my head, struggling to keep my voice low. The last thing I want to do is scare her and the Italian parts of my blood tend to make me loud and animated when I feel passionately about something.

"And I don't know, Ren. I've got all this shit going on in my head that I don't know how to deal with. I've spent the past ten years living like a wombat. I haven't had a meaningful relationship with a woman, other than my daughter, my mother, and my sister in my entire life, then I walk into the pub, and there's you." Now it's my turn to wave my hand about.

"With your fucking hair, your arse, your tits, and your blue fucking eyes. You've rocked my fucking world, Ren, don't you get that? You've flipped my world on its fucking head."

Her lips twitch, and I think, I *hope,* I'm finally getting through to her.

"Wombat?" she questions.

"Yes, Wombat. Eats, roots, and leaves." Our eyes meet. She rolls her lips together, but I can see she's fighting a smile.

"Do you realise how many times you just said fuck or fucking?"

"No, and I don't care. A lot, probably. You frustrate the fuck out of me. I just wish you could see yourself through my eyes. You're gorgeous. I've kept you safe from your husband. I've saved you from him. That was the easy part. The hard part is going to be saving you from yourself."

"I warned you I have issues,' she says with a shrug.

"And you weren't fucking lying, but we'll work through them, we'll get you there, but you've gotta let me help you. You've gotta believe what I say. Now get your sexy arse over here and kiss me."

I watch as her top teeth chew on her bottom lip for a second, brows pulled down into a frown as she looks right back at me.

"You put me up here, you gonna help get me down? She questions. I move towards her open arms and legs in and instant.

After a quick kiss and make-up session, we eat a sandwich. As soon as Lauren's done, she heads towards the deck. Reaching the doors, she turns and looks at me.

"Bring my wine out to the spa," she orders. Grabbing my beer off the counter, I pick up the glass of wine I poured her earlier, along with the rest of the bottle, and follow her outside.

* * *

SETTING everything down on the table next to the spa, I remove the cover as Lauren stands off to the side and watches me.

I'd had the deck around the top floor of my house custom built to house the spa in a way that you step down into it, rather than having to climb over the side.

Leaning the cover against the side of the house, I watch as Lauren bends. I do the same. We both lean in at the same time and test the water. The daylight's fading, the sky rapidly turning grey and gloomy, but it's not overly cold. I'd asked Jimmy to set the temperature to thirty-seven, and I'd adjust it to whatever suited Lauren.

"That's perfect," she declares, moving her hand through the water.

"You want some music?" I ask.

"Sure." She shrugs at the same time she aims a small smile in my direction.

"Don't move," I order before going back inside and collecting my phone. Hooking it up to the new Bluetooth speaker system I'd had installed last summer, I choose a playlist, and Bruno Mars, 'Just The Way You Are,' is first up as I head back outside.

"Fuck me," I declare and come to a stop when I see Lauren standing next to the spa, totally naked.

From her toes, up to where her fingertips rub against each other in a repeated nervous action at her sides, I take her in. Allowing my eyes to settle for a while on her full, perfectly round tits, noting the way her chest is rising and falling rapidly. When I shift my gaze to her face, her mouth is partly open, blue eyes wide, brows drawn together, and I realise she looks terrified.

Unconsciously, I shake my head.

"You are so fucking gorgeous," I tell her.

"Don't," she shakes her head and murmurs, "I just. . . you just need to see. . ." She trails off when without moving any closer, I take off all of my clothes. With just the sound of Bruno's voice, accompanied by the bubbles from the spa jets, we stare for a few long moments before I shift our drinks from the table to the cup holders built into the side of the spa.

I step in, then hold my hand out to help Lauren.

"Get your tits, arse, and wobbly bits in here, woman, before I fuck you on the deck for the whole peninsula to see."

Because of how my house is built into the side of a hill, and the positioning of the established trees surrounding it, most of the upper deck is hidden from my neighbours, anyone on the beach, or passing by on the road in front.

Despite the seclusion, I watch Lauren's eyes dart over my shoulder, then to each end of my deck, before taking my hand.

Once in, I pull her flush against me, and she presses her forehead against my chest.

"No one can see us up here, Ren." Wrapping one arm around her waist and brushing my fingers up and down her spine with my other hand, I kiss the top of her head.

"You sure? I don't want my wobbly bits and bruises to cause a car crash on the esplanade or someone to drown out on the bay."

Her forehead still pressed against my chest, she says all of this to the water bubbling around our legs.

"How about I turn you around. That way, if anyone does happen to have the ability to see through trees, they'll only get an eyeful of *my* arse and nothing of yours."

Holding her shoulders, I turn her around but keep her held flush against me. Like it has been all day, her hair is still piled up on top of her head, exposing her neck and shoulders to me. Brushing my palms as gently as I can from her hips to beneath her tits, I kiss from behind her ear to her shoulder. Following the same path back to her ear, I use my teeth.

Her back arches slightly, and she tilts her head to rest on my pec. I take this opportunity to drag my fingers from just below her belly button, up her torso, between her tits, all the way to her exposed throat. Cupping her jaw in my hand, I turn her head so my mouth can meet hers. Kissing her wet and deep, I roll my hips, letting her know exactly what effect she's having on me.

Both my hands find her tits, my thumbs brushing across her nipples before I squeeze and pull at them.

"Gabe," the sound of my name on a breathy sigh shoots straight to my dick, and it twitches against her. Trailing the fingers of one hand down to between her legs, I drag my teeth along the curve of her neck and whisper against her ear.

"Open up, Ren, lift your leg onto the seat. I want inside you."

Her body jerks before going rigid against me, and panic hits that I've hurt her somehow.

"What? What is it?" I ask, remaining as still as she is.

The only sound is from the spa jets and the bubbles they're creating around our legs. A car engine revs out on the esplanade, Michael Hutchins sings about needing someone tonight, and I'm right there with him.

Lauren doesn't say a word.

Moving my hands to her shoulders, I turn her back around to face me. Her hip brushes the tip of my dick as she moves, and I fight not to grind against her.

"Ren?" Using my index finger, I left her chin till her eyes meet mine in the fading afternoon light.

Despite standing naked in warm, knee-deep water, I hadn't noticed the air temperature until Lauren's erect nipples brush against me, and I feel the goosebumps that have risen on her skin.

Pulling her closer, I keep my eyes on hers. "Tell me what's wrong?"

"I didn't shower this morning," she slides her gaze to the side and replies.

"What?"

"You told me to hurry up and get ready after Jimmy turned up this morning. I didn't have time to shower."

"Babe, you're gonna have to help me out here coz I'm a little bit confused as to what the fuck that has got to do with anything right now."

She lets out a huff, her eyes locked on something to my right.

"Eyes on me, Ren," I order.

She gives another huff, looks back at me, and rolls her eyes.

"You want to touch me. . . I haven't showered today." She throws her arms out to the side, palms raised to the sky. From her actions and her tone, I'm guessing this should mean something to me.

I scratch my head, then the stubble on my jaw. "I'm trying here but still not following."

"Are you gonna fuck me tonight?"

My head pulls back at her bluntness.

"Well, yeah, if that's what you want. Is it what you want?"

Another eye roll.

"Not appreciating the eye action, babe."

Another huff.

Fuck me.

"Well, I wish I'd had a chance to freshen up, that's all."

"Freshen up?"

"Yeah, my fanny Gabe"

She pulls away and points downwards between us.

"Your pussy?" I can't help the laugh that escapes me as I work out what it is worrying her.

"You seriously think I'm bothered that you haven't showered today? I've been desperate to get inside you for a month. I don't give a single fuck that you haven't showered, Not one. I still wanna fuck you, taste you. And we're standing in a spa for fucks sake. Sit down and give it a quick rinse if you're that worried, but babe, believe me when I tell ya, *I'm not.*"

I step back, sit down on the seat running around the edge of the spa, and pull her down to straddle my lap.

Her tits bounce in the water, my dick throbs, and I can't wipe the smile off my face as I watch her frown.

"You feel that?" I ask while grinding against her. "That feel like I give a fuck when you last showered?"

She shrugs, then shakes her head. Her eyes sparkling as she gives me a smile, and I'm fucking done. My hands slide into her hair, and I pull out the scrunchie. Wrapping her hair around my hand, I move her mouth towards mine.

"Gonna kiss you now, Ren. I'm gonna kiss you. Then I'm gonna slide inside and fuck you. You good with that?"

She nods.

"I need your words, baby; tell me you want that."

"I want that. I want you inside me."

Against the chill of the late afternoon air, her mouth feels hot against mine. Our tongues tangle and taste. Her hands find my jaw, her fingernails scrape at the stubble covering it, before moving to my scalp as my hands, mouth, tongue, and teeth find her tits, and my hips buck up in search of the heat between her legs.

With her legs spread, thighs either side of mine, knees on the seat my arse is on, I lift her by her hips but am as shocked as shit when Lauren takes over by wrapping her hand around my cock and working it against her clit a few times before lining us up and sliding her pussy over me.

Warm and wet, she feels fucking perfect.

I'm thirty-five years old, and despite being married very briefly, I've never experienced a connection to a woman like I do to Ren. Not just right now, but since I very first laid eyes on her. I wish I was good with words, articulate enough to let her know how I feel, that I *get* what a big step it is we've just taken. Nothing I can come up with seems adequate. Instead, with my dick buried inside her, I wrap her in my arms and hold her against me. Her tits press against my bare chest, her head rests on my shoulder, as her hair spreads all around us, and I hope that it's enough.

CHAPTER 22

Lauren

IT FEELS RIGHT.

The weight of his body on mine is different, but not wrong.

His taste, his scent, they're different too, but not wrong.

The way he pushed inside me, the way he feels now, after such a long time with the same man, of course it feels different, but it doesn't feel wrong.

It feels right.

My marriage is over. I refuse to feel guilty. I just want to lose myself to the pleasure, and to wipe out the memories of my last experience in a spa. It was that thought that led to my little moment of insanity, in which I decided taking off all my clothes out on Gabe's deck was a good idea.

I just wanted the getting naked part of out of the way. I hate each and every one of my hang-ups and insecurities and decided to just face them head-on, get naked, and let Gabe decide if he still wanted to go there with me.

I knew what I was doing, knew what getting naked would likely lead to, but with the way things have been going, we were going to end up there at some stage anyway.

And now it was done, I'd taken that final step. Yes, it was fast, no, I wasn't ready, and yes, I absolutely still needed time to heal from my husband's betrayal, but right now, I'm exactly where I want to be, with a man who, *for now*, is exactly who and what I need.

Gabe holds me against him, his cock buried deep, warm water bubbling all around us, and as the sky darkens, I take a moment.

My head's spinning, skin tingling, body vibrating. I'm unsure if I'm hot or I'm cold, if my senses are heightened, or if I'm tripping on the edge of reality.

Gabe's hands slide up my back, over my arms, into my hair, and around to my jaw. Dragging my eyes from the stars beginning to make themselves known in the darkening sky, I lock them with his blues. He holds me in place as his mouth once again finds mine, and what starts as gentle soon becomes a frantic tangle of lips and tongues. He bites on my bottom lip, and I claw at his scalp and shoulder. His hands move to cup my arse cheeks, helping me rise on my knees before sliding back down on him.

With me wrapped around him, Gabe stands and turns us around. Setting me down on the edge of the spa, he slides back inside me. Locking my legs around the back of his thighs and my arms around his neck, I lean back against the deck and bring him down with me.

We move, our pace slow as we enjoy the sensation of our bodies gliding and grinding together. Bending my knee up towards my shoulder, he angles deeper.

"Tell me if I hurt you," he whispers in my ear, his hot breath making me shudder as it dances across my skin.

Holding his weight off me with his elbows, he looks down to where his body meets mine, and for a moment, I fight the panic I feel at what he might see. My tits are bouncing, my belly no doubt wobbling with each drive of his hips, but all doubt leaves my overthinking brain when he slides my arse to the edge of the spa. My legs hang over the side; still in the water, my feet land on the seat that runs around the edge, the position giving me the traction I need to push back against Gabe as he stands, eyes still fixed to where he's moving in and out of me, we both watch as he brings his fingers to my clit, he applies just the right pressure and begins to circle them.

It's too much, he's too far away, and I have to grip at my own hair because Gabe's is out of reach. I watch as his eyes travel up my body, focusing on my tits as they bounce. His fingers continue to work at my clit, and I let out a groan as my back arches. His eyes finally meet mine, and he begins to shake his head slowly.

"Fuck me, you're gorgeous. You are *so* fucking gorgeous, Ren."

My head falls back, my stomach and every internal muscle below my waist clench tight as my orgasm begins to roll through me.

My legs and my insides feel weak, and my head feels light, but before I'm ready to relinquish the last of my high, Gabe's grip on my hips tightens as he picks up his pace, and I switch my attention from all that I'm feeling, to focus on him.

His eyes close for long moments but find mine each time they open. Brows drawn down, lips slightly parted, I don't think I've ever seen anything more beautiful than Gabriel Wild as he comes.

"Ren." I barely hear the sigh of my name as he leans forward and buries his face into the side of my neck.

Eyes closed; I breathe in the scent I've been surrounded with for the past week. It's all that is Gabe, his home, his sheets, shampoo, and shower gel. The clothes of his I've been wearing. It's the smell of safety and hope.

I expect his hips to stop moving. They don't. He again stands upright, continuing to move in and out of me and with slow, luxurious strokes, he stares down and watches.

With one hand cupping the side of my face, he uses the fingers of the other to again trail a path from my throat, through my cleavage, down my belly to the landing strip of hair above where we remain connected.

The timer on the jets runs out, the bubbles stop, and all I can hear is the voice of Adele.

21 has been my album of choice these past months, and hearing her tonight is like having a friend whisper in my ear, giving me confidence, reassuring me that what I've just done, what I'm doing, is the right thing.

I shiver, the cool night air hitting me now that it's only my feet dangling in the warm water of the spa.

As if finally realising I'm there, Gabe looks up at me.

"You good?" he asks quietly.

I nod. "Yeah. You?"

Until that moment, he'd looked intense. Jaw set, brows pulled down and together, but as his eyes dart over my face, he visibly relaxes. His mouth quirks up into a small smile that makes his eyes shine.

"I don't think I've ever been better, Ren," he says with a wink. Before I can even think about stopping it, my heart trips over itself, my belly does a backflip, and my pussy squeezes so tight it causes his dick to twitch in response.

We stare, both of us with stupid grins on our faces, at our bodies' reactions, but we still don't move to break apart.

"As much as I'd like to stay buried balls deep inside you, I don't want you catching pneumonia. I'm gonna go inside, grab a couple of towels, and another beer. You good with that?"

I nod.

He leans in and gently brushes his mouth against mine before pulling out of me, stepping out of the spa, and heading towards where the timber bi-folds open. Obviously, I watch his bare, sexy arse until he disappears inside.

Sitting up, I lift my glass of wine from the side of the spa, press the button to set the jets back in motion, and slide beneath the heat of the bubbling water.

Sipping my wine, I stare up at the sky and attempt to gather my thoughts.

The Australian night sky has always fascinated me. I was born and lived in London until I was thirteen and was not impressed with my parents' decision to move here, dragging me away from all my friends and a life that I truly loved. I had defied them at every opportunity in the first few months we lived here, and after every argument we had, I would sneak out of the house, lay in the garden, and look up at the stars. They were my constant, the thing that I still had in common with the friends I had to leave behind. The moon and the stars were the same ones my mates back in London would see.

I would lay there, my thirteen-year-old brain plotting revenge on my parents for ruining my life, planning my escape back to England as soon as I could get the money together for my airfare. All the while, I was fascinated by the fact you could see the Milky Way with the naked eye, which was something that wasn't possible with all the light pollution in London.

Seeing my first ever shooting star only a few nights after getting here was a memory I'd treasure forever. For some reason, I took great comfort from it, imagining it was a sign, the universe telling me everything was going to be all right.

Letting out a sigh, I cast my gaze to Gabe as he reappears on the deck. A towel wrapped low on his hips, another in his hand, beer raised to his lips, eyes on me as he moves.

I fight not to smile as The Corrs 'Breathless' plays as he makes his approach.

Inwardly I groan as I decide not to dwell on what needs to be said and instead go straight into the conversation we should've had before we fucked.

"We didn't use a condom," I say as Gabe drops the towel from his hips before stepping back down into the water.

Without a word, he leans towards the spa's control panel and presses a button. LED's light up beneath the water and the area surrounding us.

I sip my wine; Gabe takes a long swig on his beer.

"Are you not on the pill?" he asks with a shake of his head.

"No, I have an IUD, a coil... the coil, whatever. I'm not worried about getting pregnant. I think those days are behind me."

He nods but says no more.

"I've been sleeping with the same man for almost twenty-seven years. Before him, I'd only ever slept with one other. You're my third."

He rubs at the back of his neck, takes another swig from his bottle before setting it down.

"That's my number, three. I'm assuming. . ." I trail off with a nervous laugh, not sure how to word my question without offending him.

"I reckon your number's a lot higher than mine?"

"You'd reckon right."

He reaches for his bottle, and despite there only being a dribble in the bottom, he knocks it back, giving me my first indicator that he's pissed off with my line of questioning.

"So, does that mean. . ."

"Gonna stop you right the fuck there, Ren."

I raise my brows at his tone. That being the second indicator he was *not* happy.

"When I was twenty-two, I got drunk at a party. I ended up in a bedroom with a girl. We fucked on top of a pile of coats before falling asleep. I woke in the middle of the night to her sucking my cock. I'd used the only condom I had with me earlier. So, when she climbed on top of me, telling me she was on the pill, that she was safe, she was clean, I believed her. That was the night Ava was conceived. I've never been inside a woman without protection since."

I nod. My mouth feels dry, my stomach queasy at the vision of him fucking on a pile of coats. I thought or assumed the woman he'd married was the mother of his daughter, but perhaps I'd got it wrong. I sip at my wine as I contemplate this —an ex as well as a Baby Mumma.

Great.

"What about your wife?" I decide to put myself out of my misery and ask.

"What about her?"

"Well, surely you didn't use a condom while you were married?"

He gives a small laugh and shakes his head.

"I didn't fuck my wife while we were married. I only fucked her twice ever. First time I used a condom, second time without, and Ava was conceived."

"So, Ava's Mum *is* the woman you married?"

"Yeah. Fuck me, Ren. How many women do you think I've actually had in my life?"

I open my mouth to answer, but he interrupts me as he steps back out of the spa.

"Ya know what, don't answer that. I'm probably gonna need another beer first."

He doesn't even bother with the towel, instead walking his fine arse back into the house totally naked. Again, I watch him until he disappears inside. I just finish topping up my glass when I watch him in all of his naked glory walk back to join me, this time carrying four beers.

"I need to get a beer fridge for this end of the deck," he says as he steps back down into the water.

"The kitchen's only just there."

"I'm aware. I've nearly frozen my nuts off four times, walking backwards and forwards tonight. A beer fridge will solve that."

We're both quiet for a minute as he opens one of the beers and swigs from the bottle.

Eyes on me, he shrugs.

"This is gonna make me sound like an absolute prick, but Lena should've remained just a one-night stand. One of the biggest regrets of my life is marrying her."

"Why did you?"

"She was still sleeping when I left the party. I was a dick. She was drunk, and I just left her there. If a bloke ever did that to my daughter, I'd fucking kill them."

He takes a moment as if he's actually considering the scene.

"She called a few times in the weeks after, tried to hook up again, but I wasn't interested. Then she started showing up at the places I usually drank, so, me being twenty-two and an absolute dick, I started hooking up with different girls in front of her. I'm not proud of anything about my relationship with Lena, except that it produced Ava, and honestly, at the time, I thought it was better to be cruel to be kind. She wouldn't take the hint with the knockbacks, so I thought I'd *show* her."

The jets time out, and I slide lower down in the water rather than turning them back on. Chris Martin sings about a cold December, and I give an involuntary shiver.

"You getting cold?" Gabe asks.

"Nope, carry on," I reply instantly.

"Long story short. She turns up at the place I was living in

Elwood, tells me she's pregnant and that the baby's mine. I didn't believe her at first, but she had paperwork. Positive pregnancy test from her doctor, her first ultrasound images with all the dates on, then she invites me to go with her to the next ultrasound."

"Did you go?"

"Yep. I was fucking clueless, knew nothing about babies or pregnancy, so had this weird idea in my head that I'd just know by looking at the ultrasound whether the baby was mine. Plus, I wanted to get the dates verified. The weird thing is, even though the ultrasound image looked very little like a baby, as soon as I heard her heart beating, saw the image on the monitor, I knew. I just knew she was mine."

"So, you got married."

"No, not right away. I moved Lena into the spare room at my place, promised to support her, but told her straight, other than sharing a baby, there would be *no* relationship between us. There was just nothing there for me, and I wanted her to have more than that. She deserved to be with someone who loved her."

He pauses again, but I have no questions, so he keeps on going.

"Out of nowhere, when she was about six-months pregnant, Lena tells me she has feelings for me, and if I'm not prepared to fully commit, she's moving to Perth to be closer to her parents and the rest of her family."

He stares at me for a long few moments in silence, but I'm not sure if he's looking at or through me.

"I've fucked up a lot in my life, Ren. Done a lot of shit I'm not proud of, but there was no way I was going to fuck up being a parent to my little girl, so I panicked and did what I thought was the right thing. I married Lena a week before Ava was born.

"I didn't love her. I'm not even sure I liked her much, and there was absolutely no physical attraction, on my part at least.

This wasn't a problem while she was pregnant or for the first month after Ava was born, but as time went on and it became apparent that *for me* our marriage was in name only, Lena became more and more pissed off and repeatedly made threats about taking my daughter away from me.

"When Ava was two months old, I came home from work to pick up some drawings that I'd left behind that morning and caught her in bed with a bloke. I'd moved her into my room once Ava was born because it was bigger, I moved to the spare room, and that's where they were fucking. While my daughter slept in her crib downstairs, Lena fucked some random in the bed I slept in."

"Why? Although, I s'pose really, nowhere was a good place."

"I think I fucked with her head. . . I don't know. She needed some attention. Something she wasn't getting from me, so she got it where she could."

"What did you do?"

"I threw the fucker out."

"Lena?" My voice rises in shock that he would do that.

"No, the bloke. I was pissed off with Lena, though. Not because she was fucking someone else, but that she did it in our house while our daughter was present. At least I was discreet." My mouth drops open at that comment, but he keeps on talking.

"I felt like the whole thing had been a waste of everyone's time and energy. I just didn't get why she wanted to be with me, knowing I didn't love or find her attractive. So, I moved out and left her in the flat. We eventually talked, came to a joint custody arrangement, and got divorced just over a year later."

"So *you* were unfaithful?"

He frowns in confusion, and I wonder if I misheard him. "You said you were discreet. . ."

He drains the contents of his bottle, sets it down, and opens another.

"I wasn't faithful, no. But I never fucked anyone in the home we shared, and never with anyone she knew."

My stomach churns, and what feels like acid burns in my chest at his admission. I set my glass down, not wanting any more wine.

"I was twenty-two, twenty-three when Ava was born, and like I said, I was a dick. I'm not proud of how I handled things, Ren, and I'm not making excuses, but I think me and Lena both went about things badly."

I don't have a response to what he's just confessed. My brain feels overloaded with information. Instead, I reach for the towel he set beside me earlier.

"I'm getting cold. I think I'm gonna go in and get showered."

"Don't do that, Ren. Don't walk away after I just spilled my guts."

Pulling the towel around me, I stand on shaky legs, unsure if it's the result of my orgasm, the wine, or his confession.

"I need some time, Gabe. You've just told me you cheated on your wife, the mother of your child. I need some time to process that."

"No, I'm not giving you that. I know it was all kinds of fucked up, but that was then, that was my relationship with Lena, this is now, and it's definitely *not* my relationship with you, or how it will ever be with us."

He stands, and totally naked, helps me step out of the spa. When he turns to pick his towel up from the floor, I turn to head inside without him.

CHAPTER 23

Gabe

STARK BOLLOCK NAKED, I stand on my deck and watch Lauren walk away.

"Fuck me," I turn my head towards the bay, my words carried away on the breeze.

"This conversation isn't over, Ren. You asked for total honesty, and that's what I'll always give you, whether it's what you want to hear or not," I turn back towards her and call out.

She pulls open the door and pauses to look at me. Her damp auburn hair is a mass of curls and waves around her face and hanging over her shoulders. The light from inside the house illuminates the water droplets on her bare skin. She looks gorgeous as she stands there holding the towel around her. Gorgeous but sad, and it's like a punch to the gut that I've probably fucked this whole thing up by telling her about my shit show of a marriage.

Too soon, Wild. Too fucking soon, I think to myself while wrapping the towel around my hips before moving towards her. I expect her to put distance between us and head inside, but she stands and watches my approach.

Powderfinger play through the speakers, and I'm not sure if I want to turn Bernard Fanning's voice off or up the volume as he sings about how *we should be together now.*

When I get to where she's standing, I don't hesitate in reaching out to touch the side of her face. Cupping her jaw, I move her head until her eyes meet mine.

"I've no clue what I'm fucking doing here, Ren. This is all new to me. Outside of my family, relationships are a whole new concept. Now I've explained the way my marriage went, you'll hopefully *get* why I'm so shit at this."

She closes her eyes for a few long seconds, and I watch her chest move as she takes a deep breath in before releasing it slowly. She leans her face into my palm, and I take that as a positive and keep talking.

"I've spent a lot of my life fucking things up, getting them wrong. There are gonna be times I fuck this. . . what we have. . . up, and times I get this wrong, but you can trust me, Ren. I promise you, you *can* trust me."

She nods slowly and licks her lips before speaking.

"I. . . it's just been a big. . . it's a lot. What we just did, what you told me afterwards, it's just been a lot, and I'm feeling a little overwhelmed."

Her hand comes up to cover mine at the side of her face, and she gives me a small smile.

"I just had sex with a man who's not my husband. My head was still spinning, *is* still spinning from that, and then you dropped all of that on me about your wife. I'm sorry if I overreacted but like I said, what happened between us is a big deal to me, Gabe, a really big fucking deal."

"And you think it meant nothing to me? You think I don't appreciate you letting me in? Giving that to me?"

Her mouth opens, her eyes close, and she drops her forehead against my chest as she takes in and lets out another long breath, or maybe it's a sigh, I'm not sure.

"I don't know. Like I said, it's a lot, and my head's still spinning."

Sliding her arms around me, I pull her close. Her skin's cold and covered in goosebumps.

"Yeah, my head's still spinning after our shopping expedition."

"What?" she questions without looking up.

"Babe, it's bread and milk, none of this sourdough, rye, light rye, dark rye, soy, kefir, lactose-free. . ."

"*That* made your head spin, but what we did in the spa didn't?"

She lifts her head and looks back up at me. Brows raised, mouth hanging open even though she's finished talking.

"Ren, what we did in the spa blew my fucking mind."

She rolls her top and bottom lips between her teeth before releasing them to smile up at me. At the same time, I can feel her twisting from side to side like a kid.

"Really?"

"Babe, you seriously gotta ask me. . ."

"Even with all this?" She steps back, grips her towel in one hand, and gestures with her other up and down her body.

I'm not sure if the look on my face clearly expresses the fucking horror I feel as I work out the meaning of her words, but I sure as shit hope so.

"What the actual fuck, Lauren?"

"You don't have to make out, I get you like me, but I know I'm punching above my weight. I've *seen* you in all your naked perfection now, but even before, with your clothes on, just your face, without all of that. I get that I'm not up to your usual standard. . ."

This time she gestures towards me, but I'm done listening to this bullshit. Grabbing her hand, I head inside and towards my bedroom.

"Gabe!" Her voice sounds high-pitched as I pull her behind me, but I don't slow my pace.

Pulling her through my bedroom and into my bathroom, I ignore her protests and flip on the light. Without letting go of her hand, I turn on the shower before turning to face her.

"What the fuck is wrong with you?" Her eyes narrowed on me as she struggles and attempts to pull away. Letting go of her wrist, I pull her towel away from her body, turn her around to face the mirror above the sink, and press myself against her from behind.

"You've lost the fucking plot," she grits out, still trying to wriggle away from me.

With one arm around her waist, the other at her jaw, I hold her in place until her eyes finally meet mine in the mirror.

"Calm the fuck down and look at yourself."

"Fuck off. You're hurting me."

I adjust my stance and twist myself around her body to look directly into her eyes, not at her reflection.

"Stop being such a drama queen. I'm not hurting you. I'd never hurt you, and you fucking know it."

Her eyes dart back to her reflection and then back at me before staring at nothing over my shoulder.

"Look at yourself, Ren."

"How about you fuck off, *Gabe*." Her Essex accent comes through loud and strong when she's pissed off, and I fight not to smile at the attitude she gives, but not the hard-on she's giving me. Instead, I push my hips forward and introduce my dick to the crack of her arse. Her eyes widen as they dart to mine in the mirror and her mouth drops open.

"Feel that?" I question. "That's what you do to me. I've just had you, but I'm already hard. In a minute, we're gonna get in that shower, and I'm gonna fuck you again."

I get a huff and an eye roll. Releasing her jaw, I move both my hands to her hips.

"I'm hard because of all of this." With one hand, I gesture up and down her naked body like she did mine earlier.

Splaying my palms across her belly, I move my mouth to her ear.

"I'm hard because I fucking love this." I squeeze at the loose skin beneath my hands.

"Gabe," she whispers my name as she blinks rapidly at our reflection. My dick twitches and I nip at her shoulder.

"And I fucking love these." Using just the tips of my fingers, I trail them over the faint silver lines and indentations on her belly and hips.

"You earned them, Ren. You grew two babies inside you. You should wear these like a badge of honour and be proud. Not every woman gets the opportunity to do that, so you should wear your Mummy Marks with fucking pride."

"Gabe," she whispers out my name again, but this time it's said with a trembling jaw and accompanied by a small sob. I don't want to make her cry, but I *do* want her to listen and hear what I'm saying.

"And these. . ." I shift my hands to cup each of her tits, bringing them up and together. "Babe, these are fucking perfect. But it's not just about these." I kiss along the curve of her neck to her shoulder and enjoy the sensation of her shuddering against me as my mouth moves over her skin.

"It's about what's in here." I press my palm against her chest, over her heart. "And all that you've got going on up here." I tap my index finger against her temple.

"All of that together, it tells me a story, your story. It's a story

I like a fucking lot, one I wanna be part of. *That's* what makes me hard for you, Ren."

Wrapping both my arms around her from behind, I bury my face in her neck, brushing my lips over her skin as I talk.

"So please, don't ever question what you've got going on. Because, Babe. . ."

Kiss.

"Tight bits."

Kiss.

"Loose bits."

Kiss.

"Baggy bits."

Kiss.

"Stretch mark covered bits."

Kiss.

"They're part of you, and by default, that makes them fucking gorgeous."

A tear drops from her chin onto the back of my hand, where it rests on her heaving chest.

"Don't cry. I don't wanna make you cry, Little Bird. I just want you to hear me."

Turning her in my arms, I hold her against me before lifting her to sit beside the sink on the stone bench. I slide her to the edge and stand between her legs. Using my thumbs, I brush the tears from her face.

"I need you to stop with the tears because I need to fuck you again, and I'm not gonna do that while you're crying."

I lean in and kiss her forehead. She wraps her arms and legs around me and rests her face against my chest.

"You say all the things and do all things and I'm just a bitch and don't even deserve you," she says without pausing for breath.

Her shoulders shake as she breathes in and out on a shudder.

"And now I've got snot in your chest hair. . ."

That sets off another round of tears, and I fight not to laugh at what's set her off this time. Instead, I slide my hands under her arse and carry her into the shower.

Setting her down on the built-in tiled bench, I drop to my knees in front of her and bury my face in her sweet pussy. With the hot water from the showerhead and body jets hitting us from all angles, I use my mouth and my fingers to fuck her until she comes. After washing each other clean, I carry her to my bed and fuck her until she passes out. Then, like the sad individual that I am, I watch her sleep, wondering where the fuck I'm going with this.

A month ago, I met a woman in a bar. She's been living in my house, sleeping in my bed, and has taken up permanent residence in my head and my heart ever since.

I've no idea if what we have has legs or how long it might last, but just the thought of her moving out and me going back to coming home to an empty house every night makes my gut and my chest physically hurt.

Next to the first time I held my daughter in my arms, I've never been more scared in my life.

CHAPTER 24

Lauren

I'm warm, but not too warm as there's a slight breeze brushing across my bare skin. Dragging my eyes open, the sun streams through the glass and timber bi-fold doors, and I have to blink a few times until they adjust.

The sheer curtains that hang there billow into the room with each gust, and I focus on the tiny dust motes being blown on the breeze. Captured in the sun's rays, they look like tiny dancers under a spotlight on a stage, enjoying their big moment.

What was my big moment in life I wonder? Have I had it or is it still to come?

Becoming a mother has been at the top of my list for over twenty years - as a woman, is there any greater achievement? A successful career? Maybe. But is a successful career greater than growing another human being inside you? Then raising that human to be a happy, well-adjusted person? I can imagine feminists and career go-getting women across the world screaming abuse at me for thinking that way.

I knew first-hand it *was* possible to do both, to successfully juggle raising a family and a career, I'd done it. Being born at the very end of the sixties and leaving school and college in the eighties, my generation was probably one of the first where it was considered normal to return to work after having a baby. But, despite my career as an interior designer being successful, I still considered my kids my greatest achievement, and as grown up and independent as they now are, I really hope the breakdown of my marriage, and whatever it is I've started here with Gabe, doesn't impact them too greatly.

On a tangent, I then wonder if there's something wrong with me. I'm waking up after a night of the most mind-blowing sex of my life. I should be happy, ecstatic even. Instead, I'm feeling scared and a little sad.

Scared of what the future holds, sad for what I've left behind.

I need to find a job; I need an income. I genuinely believe Gabe when he says he's happy to support me until I get my shit sorted, but I need to get that shit sorted sooner, not later. I can't keep living on somebody else's handouts, especially a man I've just met.

The fact that I've only just met him raises all sorts of other questions, the first being, what the fuck am I doing? Right now, I don't have a definitive answer. We've been landed with a situation that we're both trying to figure out and make the most of. The thing for me is, despite everything, Jason, my kids, my financial situation, my issues, despite *all* of that, I like him. I like him a lot, and as sure as I know to never eat yellow snow, I already know Gabriel Wild has the ability to break my bruised, battered, and very fragile heart into a million tiny pieces, and it terrifies me.

Then there's the end of my marriage to deal with. There's no going back for me. I know that with absolute certainty, but still, the thought of what I once had, what Jay and I built together and worked so hard for, is over, done, and a divorce looming still makes me sad.

I don't want him back. There will never be any kind of reconciliation. Right now, I'm happy never to see or speak to him again, and that in itself is sad. After almost twenty-seven years together, twenty-four of them married, just like that, it's over, and I'm waking up in bed with another man after a night of wild sex. Wild sex, despite my sadness, I manage a little chuckle, which leads to a snort at my own joke.

Gabriel shifts. I'm lying in the recovery position, and he's pressed in tight behind me—one of his legs over and between mine, his arm over me, his palm cupping my boob.

He'd fucked me into oblivion last night. After spa, shower, and bed sex I'd slept soundly the entire night. No dreams, good or bad, and despite the constant whir of emotions churning inside me, I actually feel rested.

I'm desperately in need of the bathroom but unsure if I'm yet ready to leave the warmth of the bed and the sensation of Gabe's naked body pressed against mine.

Right on cue, his thumb brushes across my nipple before his hand moves slowly down my body. As he reaches my belly, I instinctively breathe in, hoping to make it flatter. Screwing my face up and squeezing my eyes tightly together, I cringe and hope that he didn't notice, while feeling grateful that I'm lying mostly on my front, not my side.

His hand stills just below my belly button, his palm settling there as he takes in a deep breath while rubbing his nose into my hair.

I shift slightly, my eyes meeting his over my shoulder, and damn, he is so fucking pretty. Closing my eyes for a few seconds, I allow the swoon I'm hit with to wash over me and just enjoy the dizziness it causes. I blink a couple of times before focusing on the blue eyes focused on mine, and smile.

"Good morning." His scratchy morning voice hits me right in the chest. A warmth moves through me. An appreciation of how lucky I am to be here, experiencing this. That after everything, I have this, I have him.

"You smell delicious," he adds, his nose again brushing against my hair, his breath on my ear and neck. That sends warmth to other parts of me, and I smile through the urge to close my legs and squeeze everything between them tight.

"Good morning," I respond. "I smell of you."

The arm that's not over me slides under me. He pulls my back into his front, and buries his face in the side of my neck.

"Yeah? Well, I like the smell of you smelling of me." He gives me a squeeze as he talks, and I can hear the smile in his voice.

I get a rush of something inside me. It leaves me with that Christmas morning feeling. The one you only get for a few years, in those years when you truly believe. My parents always told us if we didn't go to sleep, we might see Father Christmas, and he'd know and wouldn't leave us any presents. I used to squeeze my eyes so tightly shut Christmas Eve night that I'd end up with a headache. I'm one of four kids, and we'd all come down the stairs and approach the closed living room door nudging each other and whisper asking, *'did you look?' 'Did you go to sleep in time?' 'Did you see him?'*

Just to add to the tension, my dad would always pause at the door, turn and look at each of us and say, *'Hmm, not sure if he's been. Are you sure you've all been good?'*

Of course, there were always presents when we walked into the front room, way too many usually.

I've spent almost a year living every day feeling like I did before my dad opened that door. Sick with nerves, wondering if I'd been good enough for Jay to come home and *not* want to grab hold of me or hurl insults.

But that feeling, the way I would vibrate with excitement and anticipation when I saw all of the presents. My head feeling dizzy as I wondered what was inside them and which one I should open first. That's what I've been experiencing since Gabe showed up at Jo's, then brought me home with him.

"Ren?"

I'm so lost in my thoughts, despite being hyper-aware of his presence, I jump at the sound of Gabe's voice.

"What?"

"Give it up."

"What?" I turn my head fully towards him and ask in confusion. Moving me to my back, he rolls on top of me. Supporting his weight on his elbows, he uses his thumbs to brush my hair from my face, making me aware of what a mess it must be after spa, shower, bed sex, and finally sleep, all with wet hair.

"The overthinking; give it up. We did what we did, there's no going back now."

Not being able to resist the dark stubble covering his jaw, I raise my hand and scrape my fingernails over it.

"I don't want to go back. My brain's just trying to process and catch up."

His eyes dart over my entire face as he studies me, probably searching for the truth in my words.

"I'm doing okay, I promise. I've just had so many seeds of doubt planted over the past year, it's probably going to take a while to harvest those crops and for my brain to be left fallow."

"Good. I've no idea what you just said, but it sounds good."

"Arable farming. It's something I was taught in geography right before we left England. A fallow field is one the farmer harvests, then ploughs and leaves to rest for a year or two so it can recover. The analogy..."

"Is a pretty good one for so early on a Sunday morning."

"Right? I think so too. No idea where I plucked it from, but maybe I should consider a career as a poet or creative writer if no one wants my interior design services?"

He screws up his face and gives his head a small shake.

"I'm thinking not. Just brush up on your interior design skills and put yourself back out there."

"Fair enough, but right now, I need to put myself in the loo before I wet the bed."

"You know a full bladder is supposed to make a woman's orgasm much more intense? If you let me plough your field. . ."

"SERIOUSLY? My field has been thoroughly ploughed. Ploughed to the point that I'm not even sure I'm going to be able to walk to the toilet."

He waggles his brows at me and talks through a grin that lights up his entire face.

"You fucking loved it and didn't complain once that I was hurting you."

"I did love it. You'll get no complaints from me, Mr Sex God Surfie Dude, but that does not negate the fact, I'm still not sure if I can walk."

My stomach chooses that moment to growl really loudly.

"We didn't eat much yesterday," I whisper.

"I ate you," Gabe says with a wink which brings on an onslaught of fanny flutters. Having no other response, I smile and shake my head.

Gabe rolls off me, taking the sheet with him. The harsh morning sun glares down on my exposed body, and I fight every insecure atom of my being not to react.

"Hurry up and go to the toilet, Ren. If you don't, I'm coming back over there, then I'm gonna fuck you."

I turn my head to look at where he's now lying on his back staring up at the ceiling.

"Thank you," I whisper quietly.

"For what?" He turns to meet my gaze and asks.

"It's going to take a while till all of those seeds of self-doubt are harvested, and all of my old insecurities stop rearing their ugly heads. I knew I was a mess. . ."

"Only because he got in your head and made you that way," he interrupts me and says.

Rolling onto his side, he reaches out his hand and rests his palm on the side of my face.

"He did, I know that, and I know I need to stop overthinking every thought that goes through my head. I used to have so much confidence, and I know if I dig deep, I can find that part of me again, and you're helping me do that, you're making me want to do that, to be that person again, and all of that is making me wonder, what was I thinking? Why did I stay and let him fuck with my mind like that? Why didn't I get out sooner?"

His thumb brushes back and forth over my cheek, his tongue darts out and swipes at first his bottom lip, then his top. He leans in, kisses me oh so gently on each of my cheeks, then my nose, and finally my mouth.

"Because you've been waiting for me."

His words are almost a whisper, as gentle as his kiss, but he says them with absolute conviction. He says them in a way that I wonder why it's not blatantly obvious. Like it's a fact, and my whole life has brought me to him; has led me across the world and through a marriage, all so I could find him.

I fight not to drown in the ocean of his blue eyes as tears burn at my own.

"How are you still single?" I ask around the lump in my throat.

"Because I've been waiting for you."

That might just be the most beautiful thing anyone has ever said to me. He's truly just made my day - my life even.

"You're too much, you know that, right? Too gorgeous, too perfect, too. . ."

He cuts me off with a shake of his head.

"I think we established last night that I'm not perfect, Ren.

Like I said, there will be times I fuck this up, but always try and remember that I'm *not him*. I know this is hard for you, but what you've come to accept as normal really isn't. It's going to take time, I get that, but please, have a little faith in me. I want this to work. I've *never* wanted that, didn't think it was something I needed in my life, and then there was you, and now I feel the way I do, and I want you in my life. I don't know what else to say, how to explain myself better."

"You don't have to. I get what you're saying," I tell him.

"Do you? Because I can't even begin to imagine what's going on in your head right now, but just know this, while you're sorting through the shit you've got to sort through, I'll be right here. I've got you, Lauren. You don't have to deal with any of that shit on your own."

He leans in and kisses my nose again.

"Now go use the bathroom. I'm gonna go sort us out some breakfast."

CHAPTER 25

Gabe

WHEN I HEAD BACK into the kitchen after breakfast and a shower, Lauren isn't on her stool at the bench where I left her adding numbers and setting up her new phone.

After checking out on the deck and not finding her, my gut tightens as I begin to wonder if she's left, and my eyes dart to the dining table and benchtop for a note.

"Gabe, can you come down here," she calls from downstairs, and I move my bottom jaw from side to side to loosen it before I start moving.

I find her in the doorway of Ava's bedroom leaning against the frame.

"What are you doing?" I ask, coming to a stop beside her.

"I wasn't being nosey; I brought some towels down to do some washing, and the door was open."

I move to stand and wrap my arms around her waist from behind. Pulling her against me, I rest my chin on her shoulder.

"Ren, you live here, you can open any door you like. This one is usually closed because I can't stand to look at the mess she leaves it in most of the time."

She doesn't respond to my comment but turns her head to look at me after a few seconds of silence.

"How long have you lived here?"

"Just under a year."

"And how old's Ava?"

"Twelve, she'll turn thirteen in September."

"Did you let her decorate this room?" She turns back to take in the space, and I cast my own eyes over it. Her walls are painted in the standard builders white the rest of the downstairs of the house is painted. Three sliding doors cover the built-in robe along one wall, a pink, metal framed single bed sits against the other, a bedside table with a lamp on it beside the bed. There are a couple of posters on the wall, a pile of clothes on the bed, shoes scattered under it.

It's a big room, and as I stand here and take in what I imagine Lauren is seeing, I realise it's a bit lacking.

"I just sent Dani out shopping for girlie stuff and told Ava she could do what she likes with the walls, but, as you can see. . ." I shrug and trail off.

"Dani?" She questions.

"Daniella, my sister."

Her head moves next to mine as she nods. Tilting her head, she aims her eyes and a small smile my way.

"Tell me about her?"

"Ava?"

"No, the woman walking her dog on the beach out there."

Despite her sarcastic tone and knowing full well I can't even see the beach from here, I still look out the window before slicing my narrowed eyes back to Lauren. She rolls hers before shaking her head.

"Did anyone ever tell you. . ."

"That sarcasm is the lowest form of wit? Yes, but I'm funny in other ways so I can get away with it."

We stare at each other in silence for a few seconds. I consider kissing her smart mouth, but we're standing in the doorway of my daughter's bedroom, and kissing will likely lead to other things I don't want to be doing, or even thinking about, anywhere near my daughter's bedroom.

"Yes," Lauren finally says. "Tell me about Ava."

"Despite everything, for Ava's sake, me and Lena try and keep things civil. We mostly achieve this by having as little to do with each other as possible, and when we do have any kind of direct communication, she makes it blatantly obvious, she hates my fucking guts."

"Wow," she huffs out what I have learned is her go-to response for varying situations.

"Yeah, look, I was a dick. I was twenty-three and clueless, but I've always wondered why she wanted more from me, why she agreed to get married. But anyway. . . Ava." I move from behind Lauren into the bedroom, shift the pile of clothes and soft toys out of the way, and sit on my daughter's bed.

"Ava has never known life any other way, so she's grown up spending every other weekend and half her school holidays with me. She's a good kid, doing great at school, loves anything and everything One Direction, and is growing up way too fast for my liking."

"Who does she look like?"

It hits me then, I still haven't found frames for all the photos Dani had printed off for me, so Lauren wouldn't yet have seen an image of Ava.

"She's a mix of both of us—my olive skin and blue eyes, Lena's blonde hair. We're both fairly tall, so she gets her height from both of us. She's a lot more outgoing than her mum, which, believe me, is a good thing. She's sharp, funny, probably a lot like my sister."

I notice Lauren smiling at me at the same time she rubs at her chest with her palm as she watches me talk.

"You okay?" I ask.

"Missing my kids, but love seeing the way you light up when you talk about yours," she says with a shrug, completely throwing me off what I was saying.

"Carry on," she orders.

I clear my throat.

"Right now, I think the hormones are kicking in as she's clashing with her mum a lot. She can't go anywhere without Sophie, her sidekick, and I've noticed she's started wearing a little bit of makeup."

"Is Lena married or with anyone else?"

"Yeah, she remarried around five years ago. She has a three-year-old and another one on the way."

"Did you never want more kids?"

I spin a pink and purple octopus around in my hands as I think about my answer to that question.

"If I'd have been in the right relationship, found the right girl, then yeah, I would've liked more kids. But it didn't happen. I've never really put myself out there enough to let it happen. I've never been in love. . ."

"Never?" She questions.

"Nope," I answer with a headshake.

"I lost my mum when I was eleven. It broke my heart, probably to the point it'll always be that way and I just never wanted to experience that kind of pain, or loss again. Maybe that makes me a coward." I shrug and shake my head as I speak. "I dunno? If it does, I'll take it on the chin. I was at a point where I accepted that it would always just be me and Ava, but then you happened, and now look at me. Falling all over myself to spill my guts, keep you close, and breaking all the rules I've lived by over the years. And guess what?"

I meet her eyes from across the room, where she's still leaning against the door frame.

"What?" she asks quietly.

"It doesn't feel terrible."

She smiles, and I fucking love the way it lights up her entire face, but it's gone almost instantly.

"I'm sorry you lost your mum. It's shit at any age, but at eleven when you're going through so many changes already. . ."

She trails off with a headshake.

"Like I said, it's a hurt that'll never heal."

She moves towards me and asks, "What happened?" I watch as she leans her back against the wardrobe door opposite me and slides her arse to the floor.

"Cancer. She was diagnosed the same week she found out she was pregnant with Dani, refused any kind of treatment, and by the time my sister was born it was too late. It started with a lump in her breast, but it metastasised to her bones and lungs. She died before Dani turned one."

"Jesus, Gabe."

"Yeah, it messed me up for a lot of years. Led to me making a lot of bad choices, fucking things up, but, I got Ava."

Her arms are wrapped around her knees which are pulled up to her chest, she watches me over the top of them, and we just stare at each other in silence for a while. I want to ask about her, her life, her family, but think maybe now's not the time. I've done a lot of sharing over the past twenty-four hours, and she probably needs to process all of that before we go there with her life.

"I want to do something for you," she says quietly. "I don't have the money to pay for what I want to do, but if you pay for the materials, I'll do all the work."

"Babe, I can think of a million and one things I'd like you to do for me, none of them requiring materials. You wanna be a little more specific?"

That earns me a little half-smile that makes my dick twitch. But, I'm sitting on my daughter's bed so I rein that in.

"When do you next have Ava here?"

"In two weeks, I'll pick her up Friday and drop her at school Monday."

"That'll work. Would you let me fix her room up, make it a little more. . ." She trails off and looks around. "A little more like somewhere an almost teenage girl would want to spend time?"

"I would absolutely love for you to do that, just tell me what you need."

"Do you know her favourite colours?"

"I think she's on a purple kick at the moment. It was orange a few weeks ago when she found out it was Harry Styles' favourite, before that, dark red because it's Louis'."

"They her favourites in the band?"

I nod.

"Your girl's got taste, they're my favourites too."

"Seriously? You have favourite members of One Direction?"

"Hell, yeah. I might have knickers older than those boys, but Louis and Harry, I still would."

She's keeping a straight face as she talks, but I'm not entirely sure she's serious. Also, I now want to punch the heads in of two boy band members. Something I haven't even felt while listening to my daughter swoon over them. I decide to move the conversation along.

"So, you wanna go shopping and buy what you need to fix this room up?" I ask as I stand.

"Actually, I text Ryder earlier and asked him to meet me at my old house, and was wondering if I could borrow your car so I can. . ."

"Not happening, Ren." I interrupt. Her head jerks back as if I've slapped her.

"I can't borrow your car?" I'm not sure if it's shock or hurt I hear in her voice.

"You don't need to borrow my car, I'll take you to your old place, but you're not going there without me."

"Jay's not there, he's in Tassie on a golfing trip. He's not due home till later tonight."

I hold out my hand and she takes it. I pull her up to stand in front of me.

"I don't give a fuck. You're not going back there on your own."

She folds her arms across her chest, tilts her chin up towards me, and narrows her eyes. I brace myself for her argument.

"How do I explain who you are to my son?"

Well, fuck me. That cut a little deeper than it should.

"He's a big boy, how about you tell him the truth?"

She lets out a huff.

"And how would you like me to introduce you exactly?"

"Sex God will do. Master also works," I reply.

She chews on her bottom lip, head again shaking as she fights not to smile.

"I'm thinking Dick Head might be the best option right now."

"We can go with that too. What exactly is it you need to do at your old place anyway?"

"I need my things, Gabe. My clothes, my hairdryer and straighteners. I just need some of my own stuff around me."

"You best get your arse into gear then. If you want to do all of that, and get paint and furniture for in here, we need to get going."

I move my hand to the back of her neck and pull her against me.

"Before we do any of that though, you need to give me a kiss."

"I reckon I can manage that."

Wrapping her arms around my neck and pulling herself up on her tiptoes, she does.

* * *

LESS THAN TEN MINUTES LATER, we're driving towards Lauren's in my truck. Her old home is just five minutes from mine, and I instantly recognise her son, who's standing at the front door when we pull up.

I don't know him, but I've seen his face around over the years. I decide it's pointless to fuck around with who and what I am to Lauren and climb straight out and walk towards him with my hand out.

"Gabe," I tell him with a chin lift. "Your mum's staying at my place."

He looks a lot like his dad with his dark hair, brows, and eyes, which are narrowed on me right now.

I hear the door of my truck slam shut behind me and realise too late I should've helped Lauren out. His eyes slice from me to look over my shoulder before he takes my hand and shakes.

"Ryder East," he says, giving his own chin lift. "Thanks for looking after her," he drops my hand and says as he moves past me.

"Not a problem," I reply, watching him move to the front of my truck.

"You doing okay?" he asks his mum, wrapping his arms around her and holding her against him.

"This is bullshit, mum. You should've told us what was going on."

Lauren eventually pulls away, takes a small step back, and looks up at her son as she cups the side of his face.

"I know, and I'm sorry. I thought I was doing the right thing, keeping it from you."

Her jaw trembles as she talks, her eyes and cheeks are wet

with tears, and she looks defeated as she looks up at Ryder and shrugs.

Fuck it. I know it'll probably get me in all kinds of trouble, but I can't just stand here when she's looking so broken all over again. Hooking my arm around her neck, I pull her against me and kiss the side of her head. I feel her stiffen but have zero fucks to give right now.

"You okay to go in there on your own, or you want me to come in with you?" I ask, looking down at her.

"Am I missing something here?" Ryder asks, and before Lauren can, *I* respond.

"Yeah, mate. Look, sorry to be introducing myself like this, but we're actually together. We literally just met as all this happened between your mum and dad, but things escalated quickly and your mum's living with me, and, yeah, we're together."

Ryder takes a step back, his eyes darting between us.

"It's only been a few fucking weeks, Mum. What the fuck?"

"Dude, seriously, don't talk to your mum like that. She's got enough going on right now."

Lauren's palm presses against my gut, and she steps in front of me.

"Ryde, don't start. It's as complicated or as straightforward as you wanna make it. I've left your dad, and now I'm with Gabe. It's all new. We have no idea where it's going, but right now, it's going good."

With one hand on his hip, the other raking through his hair, his eyes continue to move between us.

"He looking after you?"

"Like a Queen," Lauren replies, and fuck me, I really want to smile.

"Wild, right?" he questions, obviously knowing who I am.

"Yeah. Your dad's crew have worked on a couple of our developments."

He folds his arms across his chest and nods.

"You fixed up that old seventies place on the esplanade. Is that where you're living?"

I feel Lauren nod from beside me, and I do the same.

"You can move into my place, Mum, you know that, right? Don't go rushing into something just out of convenience."

I don't think I tense, but I definitely pull myself up a little straighter at his words.

"I know that," Lauren replies. "It's not like that. He genuinely offered me somewhere to stay just to help me out, but things changed. . ." She trails off, then lets out a long sigh. "You really want me to go into details and explain all what's gone on between us, Ryder?"

"Fuck no. But I do want to know you're safe, that you're not gonna be used or fucked around." His eyes land square on me, he even gestures with his head in my direction, just to clarify who his comments are aimed at.

The kid's got balls, I'll give him that. I like that Lauren has that though, that her kid is protective and looking out for his mum.

"I know who you are, know your reputation, couldn't give a fuck about any of it as long as you look after my mum. You don't, I *will* give a fuck, and me and you *will* have a problem," he states. Before I get a chance to reply, Lauren moves away from me and steps towards the front door.

"Right, now that the pissing contest is out of the way, can I get my stuff and get out of here?"

With Ryder's eyes still burning a hole in the side of my head, I follow Lauren into the house.

* * *

BEFORE THE NIGHT Lauren left her home, she'd loaded some of her stuff into her car. We found everything she'd packed on the floor of her garage and the car gone. Ryder helped me load all of that onto my truck while Lauren went through the house and threw the rest of her stuff into the black bin bags we'd brought with us.

I didn't go inside. If she'd needed me to, for her, I would've done it, but she didn't ask, and I didn't need to look inside the home she'd shared with another man.

It takes around an hour until most of what she owns is piled under the tray cover on the back of my truck.

I wouldn't say Ryder and I have bonded during this exercise, but I think he gets that I'm into his mum and not going to fuck her around. If he doesn't, then that's for him to work through, I could *not* give a fuck.

I get a chin lift from him as Lauren climbs into the passenger seat and he closes the door behind her. I've told him he's welcome at our place whenever, so only time will tell whether he takes up that offer.

"Where to now?" I ask as we pull out of the drive.

"Was that really necessary?"

I know that she's pissed off with me for laying it out there to her son about our relationship, so I don't even bother acting like I don't.

"I just thought I'd get in before you introduced me as Dick Head."

"You could've given me a chance to explain things though, you didn't have to give it all, 'mate, I'm banging your mum, get over it'. You could've. . ."

"Mate, I'm banging your mum?" I question, trying not to laugh at Lauren's shit impersonation of my voice and accent.

She turns her head from the passenger door window and glares at me.

"Well, whatever you said. I don't know, can't remember because I was too busy trying to dig a hole to bury myself in."

"I said we were together, that's all, Ren. Like I said earlier, he's a grown man, I'm pretty sure he gets it."

"Maybe I didn't want him to *get it*. Maybe I wanted him to get used to the idea of his parents separating before I told him I was shacking-up with someone else."

"And maybe I wanted him to know you're living with me and you're safe."

My phone rings over the car's Bluetooth system, and for a moment, I consider driving across the beach and straight into the bay when I see Alysa's name on the dashboard screen.

Ignoring it, I remain silent until it rings off. A second later, it rings again.

"Best get that, she obviously needs to talk to you," Lauren snaps.

Using the controls on the steering wheel, I answer.

"Lyss?"

"Mr Wild, you avoiding me?"

"Just answered your call, so apparently not."

"First time in weeks. What you up to?"

"Just heading out."

"Fancy calling into mine on the way back from wherever you're going?"

"Calling into mine? Is that what it's called now? Or did she mean '*coming*' into mine?" Lauren hisses out from beside me. I ignore her.

"Nope," I reply to Alysa, making the P sound pop.

"No? You sure?"

"Positive, Lyss."

"So, the rumours are true?"

Fuck me. I knew at that moment driving into the bay was a better idea than answering this call.

"Depends on the rumours."

"Someone's busted through that wall that Wild built and got in there."

"Then yep, those rumours would be true."

Lauren lets out a loud huff, and I'm not sure if I want to

laugh or drive into the next tree we pass.

"She there with you now?"

"Yep."

"Yeah, I'm here bitch," Lauren adds.

"Sorry, Gabe. You gonna be in trouble for this?"

"He sure fucking is," Lauren gets in before I can reply.

I know if I laugh, I'll be in even more trouble, but I still have to fight to control it.

"I was in trouble before you called, this probably won't help redeem me in any way," I smile in Lauren's direction and say. Luckily, she's gone back to staring out of the passenger window.

"Fuck. Sorry again, Gabe."

"Shit happens, Lyss."

"Right? Listen, I'll let you go. You know where to find me when you work out you're the same as me and not cut out for anything other than casual hook ups."

I open my mouth to protest that things have changed. *I've* changed, and *won't* be getting in touch, but Lauren spins in her seat, taps the dash screen, and ends the call.

The cab of my truck fills with the voice of Florence Welch, as she tells us, 'You've Got the Love'. Without even looking at Lauren, I pull over and into one of the beach car parks. Turning the music down low, I twist in the driver's seat and face her, but she keeps her eyes forward, staring out across the beach to the bay.

"I'm sorry. You didn't need to hear all that, but, in all fairness, you did tell me to answer."

"It's fine. I'm fine. Are we going to look for furniture and paint, or are we gonna sit here and watch the waves?"

"You're not fine, you're pissed off. Will you look at me, Ren?"

To my surprise, she turns. Her face perfectly blank, her eyes conveying nothing.

"I thought you only did one and dones?" She questions.

"Alysa's probably the only exception," I tell her honestly.

"Great." She nods while raking her top teeth over the corner of her bottom lip. "Good to know."

"The reason for that is, she doesn't want more. She's happy for a hook up and nothing else."

"So glad you've got that in common. Happy for you."

"You gonna stop being a child about this so we can enjoy the rest of our day?"

"Probably not."

"Great. Fucking perfect."

I start the truck and drive towards the retail park on the edge of town. I keep the music low, the silence between us almost deafening.

"Is she good? I mean, if she's got you going back more than once, there has to be more there than just the fact she apparently doesn't want more. . . which, incidentally, I call bullshit on. She wants more, she wants more so fucking bad that she's willing to wait around for whatever you're prepared to give her."

"Think what you like, that's not how it is with me and her."

"Whatever. Answer the question."

"Which was?" I know what the question was, but I'm buying time because I do *not* want to answer it.

"Is she good, Gabe?"

"It's sex, Ren."

"And that's your answer?"

"I don't know what else you want me to say. I apologised that you had to hear the conversation, but I won't apologise for having sex with someone before I even met you. You heard me tell her we won't be hooking up again, you heard me tell her I'm with you now. What more exactly do you want?"

I hate shopping at the best of times, and as I pull into a parking spot outside a furniture store, I know for a fact I'd rather be anywhere else on this planet right now.

"I'm sorry," Lauren says quietly.

Cutting the engine, I turn to look at her as she stares out the windscreen, arms still folded across her chest.

"I'm sorry, I'm behaving like a brat. It was hard, ya know?" She pulls her shoulders up to her ears and holds them there as she turns and looks at me, letting out a long breath.

"I get you've got a past, I'd rather it wasn't in my face like that, but, like you said, shit happens. But it's not that. . . going back *there* to what *was* my house, my home, it was hard. Then *her* calling, it was just the icing on the cake of my shitty morning."

"Babe, why are you doing this to yourself? You didn't have to go back there today, you didn't have to tell me to answer that call, you didn't have to question me about the sex I've had in the past. It's like you're deliberately trying to punish yourself and sabotaging what *we* have at the same time."

She lets out a long shaky breath and nods slowly.

"You're right. Self-sabotage, that's exactly what I'm doing." Turning to look at me, her jaw trembles and tears fill her eyes as she talks.

"I don't feel worthy, Gabe. I don't feel like I deserve you, or this second chance at possible happiness. I just caused an argument for no reason. . ."

"Babe, get the fuck over here," I interrupt. Shifting my seat as far back as it will go, I lean across the centre console, slide my hands under her armpits and pull her into my lap. Holding her against me, I breathe in her scent, loving the fact she smells like me and our home.

"I think I might need some professional help," she sniffs out against my neck.

"Totally understandable considering the shit you've been through. If that's the case, and you think it'll help, then we'll get it for you, but please, let's not argue over things we can't change. I promised you total honesty, Ren, so when you ask me questions about my past, I won't lie to you. I'll always give you that honesty, but it's a two-way thing. When we pulled away from your old house, you should've told me that you were struggling, we could've gone home, camped out on the sofa and watched the shitty reality shows on the telly you love so much. We could've done anything you wanted, all you had to do was let me know."

She brushes under her eyes with the palms of her hands and looks down at me. She's makeup-free with her hair piled on top of her head. A few wispy curls have escaped, and I tuck them behind her ears.

"No, I want to get the stuff for Ava's room. Working on that will give me something to do during the week, keep me from overthinking."

"You can redecorate every room in the house if that's what it's going to achieve." I lean in and kiss her nose, which leads to a kiss on the mouth, her hand sliding into my hair, our tongues tasting. A car door slams, reminding us we're in a public place, and we pull apart.

"C'mon," I tell her. "Let's go buy my daughter a new bedroom."

CHAPTER 26

Lauren

AFTER PAYING for the furniture I'd chosen for Ava's bedroom, we headed across to the other side of the retail park for bedding, sheer window coverings, a rug, and some throw cushions. While I was in my element, Gabe was mostly silent, and it has my paranoia kicking in.

After my tantrum earlier, no one could blame him if he was finally sick of me, done with my drama and meltdowns.

As I stand with two cushions in my hands, holding them up to a print I've just spotted, I sense Gabe's presence to the side and slightly behind me. I smell his aftershave and everything else that makes up his unique scent before he leans in.

"You're good at this. Watching you work is making my dick hard," he says into my ear.

I feel heat creep up my chest, neck, and cheeks. Tilting my head to the side, I turn and look at him.

"Really? I thought you were over me and keeping quiet while considering whether you were going to dump me somewhere on the highway or take pity and return me to Jo's."

He takes both the cushions from my hands and throws them in the trolley along with the sheet sets and doona covers I've already added.

Putting his hands on either side of my hips, he turns me around to face him.

"I'm pissed off that pricks' words have stayed with you, I'm pissed off that they're still affecting you, and I'm pissed off you don't always share how you're feeling with me, but I'm not pissed off *with* you. The only place you'll be getting dumped is back into our bed later."

The words *'our bed'* have me wrapping my arms around his neck and smiling up at him.

"I have no words for you sometimes. You say things that leave everything inside my head scattered and scrambled, and I can't think of a single response."

"An Essex Girl without a comeback? I don't believe that for a minute, and if it's true, perhaps it's time to finally hand back your membership and declare yourself full-on Aussie." The sexy smirk he's wearing as he talks is doing all kinds of things to my insides, and before I can recover and come up with a comeback, I see a woman staring at us from across the store.

"Fuck," I say against Gabe's chest.

"Lauren? I thought that was you," she calls out as she moves towards us.

Julie fucking jug ears, the wife of one of Jay's foreman is now standing next to where Gabe still has a hold of my hips. My hands have dropped to my sides, and as I step away and turn to face her, Gabe grabs hold of one.

I can't stand this woman. She's a gossip. There's barely a thing that happens on the entire peninsula that she doesn't know about. Her eldest son went to school with Ryder, and she was all over whatever went on there too. Whenever we held work functions or dinner parties at our home, I always made sure to seat her as far away from me as possible.

"Julie," I greet her quietly. Giving a chin lift, I turn and add the print I was admiring to our trolley.

She doesn't take the hint that I have nothing to say and continues standing there.

"How have you been? I'm assuming by that little PDA, the rumours are true, you and Jay have split?" Holding her hand out to Gabe, she adds, "Hey, I'm Julie. My husband is Lauren's *husband's* head foreman."

I give an eye roll as Gabe takes her hand and shakes it. I watch on as he gives it a gentle squeeze and brushes his thumb across the back.

"Hey, Jules," he says huskily. "I'm Gabe," I can't help but roll my eyes when he adds a wink.

She nods. Still holding his hand, she continues to nod.

"Gabe... that's... Gabe, right. So, you're..?"

"Who I moved in with after Jay kicked seven kinds of shit out of me, and who I'm now fucking," I tell her in my sweetest voice.

Still under Gabe's spell, it takes her a beat to catch up and turn her wide eyes back to meet mine.

"He was beating you?"

I nod and something shifts in her eyes, her face, her entire demeanour changes.

"Oh, Lauren, really? I didn't. Oh, Lauren..." Finally letting go of Gabe's hand, she reaches for mine.

"I'm sorry. Really sorry, Lauren. I had no idea." She finally takes a step back, her eyes darting between me and Gabe, and I'm more than a little surprised at the sincerity in her voice.

"I honestly didn't know."

"Why would you?" I shrug. "Not exactly something he'd go to work and broadcast."

"No, you're right, it wouldn't be. Well, I'm glad you managed to get away from that situation. I wish you happiness with. . ." She gestures with her head. "With Gabe. Both of you, I wish you both happiness."

She actually looks sad as she talks and a niggly little thought worms its way into my head, and I can't *not* say something.

"Thanks, Julie. Listen, I have a new mobile. Would you like to take my number, you know, just in case you might ever want to catch up for a coffee?"

I watch as she swallows, and I wonder for a moment if she's going to cry.

"You know what, yeah, I will take your number. Thanks, Lauren."

"No worries," I tell her before reeling off my number as she taps it into her phone.

"Goes without saying, I'd rather you didn't share that with anyone else at this stage."

Julie pulls her phone in and holds it against her chest.

"Of course. It's safe with me, I promise, I won't even mention to. . . anyone, that I've seen you."

"Thanks, that'd really be appreciated."

We say our goodbyes and Gabe and I stand silently as we watch Julie head straight for the doors and leave the store.

"Well, that took a one-eighty," Gabe says just loud enough for me to hear.

"Graham, her husband is a dick, and I'll be totally honest, she's a gossip, has an opinion on everything and everyone, and I can't stand her, but. . ."

"He's putting his hands on her."

"You get that vibe too?" I ask him.

"Fucking oath I did. I thought she was gonna throw up when you told her what happened to you."

Throwing his arm over my shoulder, he pulls me against him.

"She's probably the way she is because she's so unhappy with her own life. That was a really nice thing you just did, reaching out to her like that," he says into the top of my head.

"Don't, coz I'll cry," I say into his chest. "I had no one I was comfortable telling. If he is doing that shit to *her*, I don't want her to feel as alone with it as *I* did."

"Yeah, I get that. I've been there, Lauren, believe me, I've fucking been there."

I look up at him, frowning in confusion. "You've been there? Someone was hitting you?"

His eyes aren't on me, they're staring out across the store.

"Not hitting, but I had some other shit going on and didn't know who I could turn to and ask for help."

Without even knowing what it was, my heart hurts for him.

"Gabe?" I reach up and touch my hand to the side of his face, and he lets out a deep sigh.

"Fuck me." His lips and warm breath brush against my ear. "This isn't the place, but we'll talk about it soon, just not right now. Let's get this lot paid for, we can come out again one night in the week for anything we've forgotten, but we need to go get paint now, then I need to get you home and get inside you."

So, we do exactly that.

* * *

It's been almost a week since our shopping trip. My clothes are in Gabe's wardrobe, my GHD's on his bathroom bench, photos of my boys sit on the bedside table, and my arse is in his bed every night.

It's all the little things that have helped make this week better. Having my perfume so I smell like me, seeing my things around the place, so it starts to feel more like home. All of this has helped me adjust and feel more settled. I've also been busy, giving me no time to overthink.

I've spent the week painting a feature wall in Ava's bedroom, washing and drying the new bedding we bought for her and hanging the prints on the wall.

Shopping online, I used my business credentials to purchase a makeup station and *Hollywood*-style mirror, some photo frames, and a cool lava lamp from a company that is usually supplied to trade only.

Now we just have to wait for the furniture to be delivered next week, and the room will be finished. Gabe has encouraged me to record the makeover and has spent a couple of nights this week helping me make the final updates to my website, including adding my new number, which I'd totally forgotten to do.

It's now Saturday. Gabe was up and out for a surf early this morning, something I would absolutely love to see him do if only he didn't do it at the arse crack of dawn when normal people are still sleeping. He's back home now; after hearing the shower running in the downstairs bathroom, I can hear him moving about in the kitchen. I debate with myself on whether I should get up but decide to wait and see if he brings me coffee instead. As I lie here, my thoughts turn to the path my life has taken the last few weeks.

I think Gabe and I are now an 'official couple' but I'm not entirely sure. My kids know about us, we've been seen in public together, and tonight is the night of our first official date. I've no idea where he's taking me, I'm just glad I have the contents of most of my old wardrobe here and won't have to go out wearing a hoodie, leggings, and UGGs for it.

It's been a good week. I've mostly kept a lid on my emotional meltdowns. I'm not over the end of my marriage, having never experienced something like that, I'm not sure if it's something you ever do. It's hard to explain, especially with the speed it all ended, although, if I look at it realistically, it ended the first time my husband put his hands on me.

That was when what we'd once had, came to an end. I didn't stay on after that because I had to, Jay was never the controlling type. I worked, had my own money, own car, he never dictated what I wore or told me who I could hang out with. He just decided one day that it was okay to grab hold of my wrist and things escalated from there.

I could've left sooner, should've left sooner, but I chose to stay because I was one hundred percent convinced things would eventually get better.

My biggest mistake was not leaving after he dragged me out of the spa. I think I spent most of that week in shock and was trying to formulate a plan. I put too much emphasis on getting my documents and cash out of the safe, and here we are, over a month later and I've not needed either for anything so far.

There's been a few times, late at night when I can't sleep, or during the day when I get lost inside my own head when I wonder if I deliberately dragged things out. Hung about for as long as possible, hoping that we could still turn things around. And even now, after everything, I can't give an honest answer to that because I don't know.

It's now six weeks later and I have a new life, with a new man. Despite my emotional meltdowns, insecurities, and general whininess, Gabe wants me around, and I want to be here. It's not just that the physical side of things works so well, but because of the way we've been thrown together, the amount of time we spend in each other's company, talking, laughing, sharing stories and finding out about each other, it feels like we've been together longer than the time we have. There are moments where I forget I had another life before him, that I was living in a different house, with a different man, and when it hits, it just all feels so surreal.

I both love and hate it.

Mostly I'm terrified.

WHENEVER GABE TALKS ABOUT US, he talks like this *is it,* now I'm moved in, I won't ever be moving out, not without him, but he's not actually said it. Neither of us have said the words that would best describe the status of our relationship.

Right now, I have no doubts that he's into me, but I worry about the future. How will he feel when I turn fifty and he's only forty? Will my age be a problem for him then? What about when my kids start having kids, making me a Grandma?

I hold on to that thought as the bedroom door opens and Gabe walks in, bare-chested, trackie pants low on his hips, a tray loaded with coffee and toast in his hands.

I lick my lips, smile, and sit up.

"You like?" he asks with a wiggle of his brows and a smirk on his face.

I adjust my pillows and lean back against the headboard as Gabe flips out the legs on the tray and sets it down in the middle of the bed.

"Hell yeah, who doesn't like coffee and toast brought to them in bed?" I respond to his question, knowing that's probably not what he meant when he asked.

Climbing carefully into bed beside me, he passes me my coffee and a plate with two slices of buttery toast on it.

"Babe, I meant all this," he rubs his fingers over the bumps and ridges of his abs while giving me a nod and a cocky smirk.

Folding one slice of toast in half, I put the plate back down on the tray and dunk the toast into my coffee.

"That's truly disgusting," he states.

"Oh, I don't know, disgusting's a bit harsh, I think you scrub up pretty decent."

He shakes his head, then nods slowly.

"I'm talking about your dunking habit, not me. I'm as fit as fuck, and you know it."

"Dude, you have a seriously high opinion of yourself this morning."

"Dude? Dude? Lauren, Dude is not the term you use when talking to, or referring to your man."

"I wasn't, I was talking to you."

He takes a sip of his coffee, eyes on me over the top of his mug.

"And am I not your man?"

The smile has gone from both of our faces, and I decide to just put it out there and be done with the not knowing.

"You tell me?" I ask.

"Is your arse not in this bed, your clothes not in that walk-in, your girlie shit in the shower?"

I take note of the way he called it *this* bed and not *his* bed and nod slowly.

"All of those things are in all of those places, yes."

With a flick of his wrist, what's left of his slice of toast lands on the tray, but he doesn't take his eyes off me.

"My dick not inside you at least once a day?"

"It is."

"Do we not stay up half the night talking shit once we've done fucking?"

"We do."

"Are we not lying on sheets you washed? Do I not come home from work every evening to a dinner you cook?"

"We are and you mostly do, yes."

"Despite the fact you're still married, are *we* not together?" He uses air quotes when he says the word 'together.'

"We are," I agree without hesitation.

"Tell me then, what part of all of that says that I am anything, *anyfuckingthing* other than *your* man, Ren?"

I've never known his voice so quiet and intense. His dark

brows are drawn down low making the blue of his eyes pop more than usual.

"You've never said it though, you've never told me what. . ."

"You need a label?" he interrupts. His voice rising in pitch.

"Not a label as such. Reassurance, maybe?"

"You don't *know*? You don't *already* know?"

I shake my head. "I'm insecure and needy, remember?"

Setting his mug down on the tray, he takes mine out of my hand and does the same, then moves the tray to the floor.

I'm taken totally by surprise when he turns, grabs my ankles, and pulls me across the bed towards him.

He's on top of me in a second. My legs do what they have a habit of doing when in his presence, and they spread. . . wide! His hips grind against mine, his hard dick presses into me.

"You need me to spell it out, put into words what you mean to me? What I hope we are to each other? Because if you do, Little Bird, then I need to hear it right back. I need you to use *your* words and tell me exactly what I am and what I mean to you."

He looks down at me, his elbows bent at the side of my head, taking the weight of his body, except his hips, which are expertly driving me insane as he moves them against me.

Using his thumbs, he brushes soothing strokes across my cheeks as his scent invades my senses.

"You gonna show me, Ren, or you gonna tell me first?"

I consider telling him I'm gonna combust because that's what it feels like I'm going to do. I'm not sure if it's arousal or menopause, but I am so fucking hot right now.

"I'm hot," I whisper.

"That is not news to me, Ren."

That earns him a chuckle.

"I mean I'm overheating menopausal kind of hot," I tell him through my laugh.

"It's got fuck all to do with the menopause and everything to do with me and the effect I have on women," he says with a wink. I narrow my eyes on him, and that earns *me* a chuckle.

Rolling us over, I end up on top of him.

"Take your singlet off," he orders.

I consider the consequences if I were to do this for a few seconds. Although it's almost eight in the morning and the sun's up, the day is dark and cloudy, so at least there's no harsh sunlight blazing through the sheers at the window to highlight my many flaws and imperfections.

"I wanna look at you, Ren. Take it off."

Feeling brave, I straddle him and without hesitation, pull my top over my head and toss it on the floor.

I watch him watching me. Raising his hand, with a featherlight touch, his fingertips settle at my throat, then, very gently, very slowly, trail their usual path down and over my chest, between my breasts. He doesn't hesitate when he hits the rolls at my belly and just keeps going until they're pushed inside the waist of my sleep shorts and his middle finger settles on my clit. I rock into it, rubbing myself against it, gaining the friction I need.

His other hand comes up to tweak and pull at my nipple, and I watch him watch what he's doing to me.

His hips buck up, in turn moving his fingers against me harder.

"Take what you need. Make yourself come," he orders.

I want to. I want to so fucking badly, but this is about *me* showing *him* what he means to me, so instead, I pull his hand from my shorts, slide down his body, and slide his trackies over his hips as I go. He's wearing no underwear and his cock springs free.

Gabe uses his feet to get his trackies all the way off, and as soon as he stills, I set to work.

Blow jobs have never been my favourite thing in the world to give, but I'm almost desperate to give this to him. To show him what he already means to me. Tonight, after a few wines, I might even get brave enough to tell him.

I stroke him a couple of times before flicking my tongue over the slit. This earns me a shaky hiss, giving me enough of a boost to take all of him that I can into my mouth.

I stroke with my hand, flick with my tongue, and suck with my mouth.

Gabe grips at my hair and bucks with his hips. Sometimes he controls the pace as he face fucks me, others he lets me take charge. When his bucking and groaning are almost out of control, he slides his hands to my pits, lifts me, spins me around, sits my pussy on his face, and pushes into the middle of my back until I fall forward and take him back in my mouth again.

This time, Gabe's in charge of everything. While his tongue flicks and rolls over my clit, his fingers push deep inside me, his hand pushes down between my shoulders, his hips buck up and down, and he fucks my mouth.

When my orgasm hits, it's almost too intense, I try to outrun it by lifting off him and slowing its pace, but he moves his hand from my back to wrap around my hips and hold me in place. My knees press into the mattress and against the side of his head as my entire body convulses. When I moan against his dick, it's his turn to explode, and he fills my mouth.

Without giving either of us a chance to recover, he flips me to my back, spins his own body around, and is once again looking down at me.

Dark blue eyes shining, his look is still intense.

"Are we clear now?"

I nod.

"Use ya fucking words, Ren. Tell me, we together? You mine?"

"I'm yours," I tell him.

"And who the fuck am I, what am I, to you?"

"You're Gabe, my Gabe. Mine."

"And that's all we need. Right now, *for* now, that's all we need. I know it's quick, I get everything's happened fast, but that just means there's been no fucking about. We just know, we've both known from the beginning that if we went there, we'd be in deep, and that's exactly what's happened."

He lets out a long slow breath, the heat from it brushes my cheeks, right along with the gentle sweep of his eyes.

"I'll get you an appointment with our family lawyer next week. You can talk to him about getting your divorce sorted. Unless the laws have changed, I think it takes around a year. Once that happens, *then* we'll talk about changing things and maybe adding some labels."

I say nothing to that because I'm not entirely sure what he means or whether I will ever be ready for anything more than what we already have.

I spend the rest of the day taking my time getting ready for our date. Gabe takes me to an Italian restaurant in Sorrento, down at the end of the peninsula. We eat good food, we drink far too much good wine, we talk nonstop. Everything about the night is *normal*. It's drama-free. It's exactly what we need—what I need—to make us feel like a *real* couple.

I pass out in the taxi on the way home, I don't remember getting back to the house or Gabe putting me to bed. I can't remember if I told Gabe exactly what he means to me or if I even needed to after showing him this morning.

* * *

I WAKE on Sunday morning to a banging headache, the sound of Gabe singing along to Coldplay, and the smell of bacon.

It's a beautiful, bright, sunny morning, and as I lay there, smiling up at the ceiling, listening to Gabe sing, I realise that for the first time in a long time, that's exactly the way I would describe how I'm feeling: Bright and sunny.

Gabe's voice is actually pretty good. I'd noticed a couple of acoustic guitars in one of the guestrooms downstairs, and I'd been meaning to ask him if he played.

I decide to take a quick shower in an attempt to help ease my alcohol-induced headache. Showering and moisturising, I wrap myself in my robe and head quietly out to the kitchen, where Gabe's now singing along to an Alex Clare song.

He has his back to me as he stands at the cooktop. At the same time he moves something around in the pan, he moves his hips and arse to the music.

He's wearing boardies, his top half naked, hair still wet from his shower.

He looks delicious.

Mesmerised, I watch the muscles beneath the tanned skin of his back and shoulders work as he moves. He's so fucking gorgeous it causes a tangible ache in my chest and belly to think that for right now, this man is mine.

The way he's looked out for me, said and done all the right things to reassure me that what we've got is real and not just a quick fling all adds to that ache.

Even if we don't last forever, right now, this is what I need. Not someone *like* him, but him. Just him.

I'm not a religious person, but with a name like Gabriel, I could almost believe he's a gift sent from heaven, an angel sent to guide and help me through some of the worst weeks of my life.

"Ahhh, here she is. Awake are you, princess?"

I jolt at his voice, wondering if I am in fact awake because the man of my dreams is standing in front of me, half-naked and cooking me breakfast.

I stare mindlessly. The only thing registering is the trail of dark hair leading down inside the shorts that are sitting indecently low on his hips.

"You sleep okay? You snored well."

My head jerks up, and my eyes meet his as my mouth drops open to protest, but it's pointless. I know I snore. I wake myself up doing it sometimes, and I know it's worse when I've had a drink.

"Shit, did I? I'm sorry."

Far out, how embarrassing!

"No worries, you didn't wake me. I set my alarm so I could go for a surf as soon as the sun came up, that's the only reason I heard you."

I return the smile he offers, thinking what a perfect combination of cute and sexy he looks standing there, bare-chested with a spatula in his hand.

"Don't look so worried, I've gotten used to it over the past month. Compared to some nights, you were pretty quiet this morning."

It's at that moment I consider just throwing myself off his deck.

"I much prefer you sleeping deep and soundly enough you snore, than waking and having nightmares. You hungry?"

I let out a long breath and move towards the centre Island.

"Ren?" My eyes meet his. "You okay, you hungry?"

"Um, yeah, thanks."

I need to find my phone and google cures for snoring, maybe go to the chemist and see if I can get something for it. Gabe doesn't come across as too fazed, but I'm wondering what he really thinks. "Go sit down outside, I'll bring your brekkie out."

I wander out onto the deck, visions of me wearing one of those face masks attached to a breathing machine in the coming years running though my head. Staring at the glass of orange juice on the table, I hope that maybe there's some Prosecco mixed with it. It might make my headache worse, but if I drink enough, at least I won't give a flying fuck about the snoring.

Taking a sip, I'm disappointed to find it's plain OJ, and I just need to woman up and *own* the fact that I snore, like a boss.

Gabe appears, carrying plates loaded with scrambled eggs, bacon, mushrooms, and toast, I watch and wonder if he's the sexiest waiter ever to have existed.

Despite the sunshine, it can't be above fifteen degrees right now, and Gabe's perfectly erect nipples display that he must be feeling that.

"You not cold?" I ask.

"Nah," is all I get in response as he shoves a forkful of eggs into his mouth.

"Why, are you? I can put the heater on. . ."

"No, no." I smile at how quickly he offers to accommodate me. "It's just not that warm, and you're not wearing a shirt."

"Does all this distract you?" He waves his open palm over his chest and abs, brows raised, lips pulled up into a smile as he waits for my answer.

"Hmm. All that skin on show, those bumpy things on your belly, that V thing you've got going on, it is kinda putting me off my breakfast a bit."

"You are so full of shit, woman," he says, eyes narrowed on me as he shakes his head.

The sound of a car engine running at the gates has us both turning that way. Due to the sun glare, I can't see anything.

"You know anyone with a Golf?" Gabe asks.

"Yeah, Ryder." I stand up as I answer, my son's car now visible.

"Shit," I say as I head back inside. "I need to put some clothes on. Let him in will you and put a bloody shirt on," I call over my shoulder.

Ryder has checked in with me regularly since I've been here, but it's been twice a day since meeting Gabe and finding out we're in a relationship. He'd obviously got straight on the phone to Sonny, my eldest son, after we'd been at the house last Sunday because he's called me a couple of times this week too, questioning me about what was going on.

"Far out, my mother's a Cougar," had basically been his reaction.

I don't know if word has gotten back to Jay yet, or if he even knows I was at the house collecting my stuff. I assume he would've noticed the empty space in the wardrobe and bathroom, but who knows what's going on with that man right now?

I pull on a pair of leggings, an oversized long-sleeved T, and my UGGs before heading back out to the family room, only to find Ryder sitting at the table on the deck next to Gabe, tucking into my breakfast as the pair of them chat.

I watch for a minute, my brain and my heart competing to work out how I feel about this, resulting in making me feel a little sick and lightheaded—or that could be the hangover, I'm not entirely sure.

"Hey," I say to my kid as I step outside. "Everything okay?"

"Hey, Mum. Yeah, all good. Just thought I'd come and check my new dad's looking after you right."

I sit down in the chair next to him as I attempt to come up with a response. I look towards Gabe, expecting him to be wearing a look of horror, instead, he's smiling while shaking his head at my son.

"New Dad, seriously? I'm what, ten years older than you?"

"Thirteen," I blurt. "I've done the maths," I add a little quieter. The men at the table both staring at me. I stare at Gabe's chest, noting that it's still bare. I'm about to remind him to put a shirt on when Ryder speaks.

"Thirteen, it happens. I know a kid who knocked some woman up at that age and became a dad. She was older though, his parents pushed to have her arrested because she was over eighteen, twenty-odd, I think. She ended up on the sex offenders register and everything."

"That's. . . that's something else entirely. He was a minor," I mumble. Feeling judged as I reach across for my orange juice.

My eyes meet Gabe's and my stomach churns again with the way he's looking at me.

"That's not what we are," he shakes his head and murmurs so quietly, I can barely make out the words.

"Great eggs," Ryder continues. "You cook these?" he asks Gabe. "Mum's a great cook, but her eggs aren't this good."

"Cheers, brat," I reply to my child. "You just tuck into my breakfast while insulting my culinary skills. What are you doing here anyway?"

Putting the fork down, Ryder takes the glass I'm holding from me and drains the contents.

"Dad's gone away," he announces.

My head snaps back at the sudden mention of Jay.

"Gone away where?" I ask.

"He didn't say. He messaged Monday saying he wouldn't be coming into work for a couple of days. . ."

"Does he know I was at the house?" I interrupt him and ask.

"He didn't say. He just said he had a few things to sort out and wouldn't be in, then he messaged Wednesday and said he needed a bit of time away, he'd been drinking too much lately and was gonna book himself in somewhere, get himself straight, and then when he gets back, he's gonna work on sorting everything out with you."

"What?" I ask, my voice high-pitched with incredulity.

"That's what he said?" Gabe asks. "You don't know where he's gone?" he continues without giving Ryder a chance to answer.

"Yeah, and no, he didn't say."

"I've spoken to you since Wednesday. Why didn't you say anything?" I ask.

I know my kid, and the long sigh and the look he gives me with brown eyes so much like his father's, I know that there's more to this.

"Mum. . . "

"Just tell me, Ryde."

Ryder looks from me to Gabe, his knee bounces under the table as his fingers tap on top of it.

"I know shit's happened between you two, but he's still my dad, and I'm worried. I've not. . ."

"You don't ever have to take sides, Ryde, I'd never make you choose, not ever," I tell my son. My voice sounding thick as it clogs with tears.

Ryder studies me for a moment, his own eyes shining.

"I've not heard from him since Wednesday and I'm worried," he says quietly.

The queasiness I felt earlier is nothing compared to how I feel now. My insides churn and my skin prickles with what I've learned lately is fear.

I may no longer want to remain married to Jason East, I don't like or respect the man, and my brain may have stopped loving him, but he's still the father of my children and the man I've spent almost twenty-seven years of my life with, and my heart hasn't caught up with all of that yet.

"He wouldn't do anything stupid," I attempt to reassure my son. "How did he sound?"

"Yeah, he did sound a bit down. He said he knew he'd fucked things up between you, but he needed to do some work on himself before trying to sort things out."

I so want that not to affect me, for it not to hurt my heart or have my eyes brimming with tears. For just a few minutes, I want to be a cold-hearted bitch who feels nothing. But I'm not, and so it hurts like a mother fucker!

"If he's booked himself in somewhere, they've probably taken his phone off him," Gabe adds. "Even the places you go to voluntarily make you do that."

I wonder for a moment how he knows this before refocusing my attention back on Ryder.

"Gabe's right, but ya know what, Ryde, if you're that

worried, if it'd make you feel better, call into the police station and tell them what you've told us." I reach across the table and take hold of my boy's hand as I speak, and he gives mine a squeeze.

"Yeah, wouldn't hurt I suppose," Ryder replies.

A phone rings from inside the house, and I know from the ring tone, it's Gabe's. He makes his excuses and heads inside. I sit in silence, staring out at the bay as my son sits beside me.

"You okay, Mum, I mean really okay?"

Chewing at the skin on the corner of my thumb for a few seconds, I continue watching the waves lap at the sand before shifting my gaze to my kid.

"I really am," I tell him. "The first few weeks were awful. I felt like I was in mourning, but the last couple of weeks have been better, I feel calmer."

"And he's looking after you?"

"Like you wouldn't believe," I say with an emphatic nod.

"The blokes at work are talking. They know you've split, but I've not said anything about the reason why."

"Just let them think I'm the baddie, that I've left him for Gabe. At least for now, while he sorts his shit out."

"Thanks, Mum. I don't support him in any way, but I also don't wanna lose clients over his behaviour."

"I get it, Ryde; I totally get it. The reason I never went to the police in the first place was to protect you and Sonny, as well as the business."

"That's different. If you'd have told us while it was happening, we would've told you to report it, but you're away from him now. You've got Gabe, and you're safe."

We're both quiet for another moment before I speak. "It's mental, how much has changed."

"It's insane," Ryder agrees. "Can I ask you something, Mum?"

"Go for it."

"Were you and Gabe having an affair? Is that what started all this?"

I consider lying for a moment. Just so that my son doesn't think so badly of his dad, I contemplate taking the blame with a lie, then Gabe walks back out onto the deck. He's pulled on a long-sleeved T and is talking on the phone, and I shake my head.

"I met Gabe at the pub the night before I was going to leave your dad. Jo introduced us, there was some flirting, but nothing happened. . . that's a lie," I correct myself. "He walked me to my taxi with the girls. After seeing some week-old bruises on my jaw and wrist, he offered me somewhere safe to stay and gave me his card, along with a quick kiss. If I hadn't been planning on leaving your father the next day, I wouldn't have let things go that far. As it turns out, when your dad came in that night, he beat me so badly, Jo had to take me to the hospital. If we'd been having an affair, and I'd just gone home with him, that might never have happened."

I've been staring out at the water as I talk, but now allow my eyes to rest on my child as I attempt to gauge his reaction to all of that. He nods but says nothing for a while.

"It's gotta be the drink, he's always had a temper, but something's changed in him these past few months, and the drink is all I can think of that's different."

I agree with my own nod.

"I just hope he gets the help he needs."

"I don't expect you to get back together. Even if he really is getting help right now, I don't expect you to go back to him after what he's done to you."

"That's not ever going to happen," I state. "Maybe if he'd sought help sooner, if he'd let me in, allowed me to help him, but after the things he's said and done to me, nah. There's no going back for me, and that has nothing to do with what's going on between me and Gabe."

I look up as I say his name and see that he's leaning against the wooden rail that runs around the deck, phone to his ear, eyes on me. The sun chooses that moment to peek out from behind a cloud. Its rays bounce off the water out on the bay, creating an ethereal glow behind Gabe.

He winks and gives me a smile, I cross my legs beneath the table and mentally re-christen him Orgasmos, the Mighty God of Orgasms.

"Anyway, I've got shit to do. Just thought I'd pop in and give you the heads up. . ." My son interrupts my inappropriate thoughts.

"And to check that Gabe's looking after me," I add as if I've been listening to anything he's said the last couple of minutes.

"That as well," he says as he stands.

Giving a chin lift to Gabe as his goodbye, I walk my kid down to his car, enjoy a long cuddle, and tell him to keep me posted on news of his dad. I hate that he's worried, but also kind of proud that I raised him right, and despite everything, he still is.

When I head back up and out to the deck, Gabe has ended his call and is looking out towards the bay. I lean against the rail next to him.

"You think he'd off himself?" he questions almost instantly.

My brows raise at his bluntness as I consider my answer. "I don't know, but I honestly can't say that I know *anything* about the man who's been using me as his punching bag for almost a year, so who knows."

"Do you care?" Gabe turns towards me and asks.

I don't hesitate with my answer. "Of course I care. I don't want my kids to lose a parent to suicide. Would you want that for Ava?" I'm a little taken aback by his question and stare at him with my mouth open even when I finish my response.

"Of course not. I'm just trying to gauge where your head's at with this news, that's all. We've had a good week, I don't wanna see you disappear inside your own head again and lose yourself."

He reaches out, hooks his arm around my neck, and pulls me into him.

"I like having you around, plus I've just spent the last fifteen minutes telling my daughter all about you."

He shifts us so my back is against the railing and traps me there with his body pressed against mine.

"How'd that go?" I ask.

"She's cool with it, can't wait to meet you. Maybe a little disappointed I'm not actually gay like she's been convinced I am the past year or so because apparently, that'd be way cooler. But having a hot dad is nearly as cool as having a gay dad, so she's not too disappointed."

"She seriously thought you were gay?" I ask.

"Yep. My dad's asked me before too."

"Really?"

"Really."

"Would it have been a problem if you were?" I ask. Wondering what kind of man Gabe's father is.

"My old man?"

"Yeah."

"Fuck no. He's lost too many people in his life to give a fuck about that kind of thing. Love is love is the way we were raised."

"As it should be. So why then, what made them think that? Have they never met any of your other girlfriends?"

"Little Bird, have you not listened to what I've been telling you the past few weeks? There have been no girlfriends. Until you, there's been no one I've ever wanted a relationship with, and I'd only ever introduce someone I was in a relationship with to Ava, I'd never expose her to a conveyor belt of one-night stands. That's why I'd never bring anyone back here. It's her home. . ."

He shrugs and trails off.

"Do you never go on dates the weekends she stays here?"

His arms are wrapped around me. The fingertips of one of his hands are massaging my scalp, the others are under my T, tracing the bumps along my spine.

"Never. When she's here, she gets all of me. She started getting bored with that a couple of years ago, and now, Sophie, her best mate comes with her a lot of the time. Other times, Dani, my sister, will come over and stay. To be honest, I think she's been worried I'd always be on my own and sounded relieved that I've finally met someone."

"Is her mate coming with her this time?"

"Yeah."

"Great," I mumble.

He steps back and looks down at me with a frown, obviously taking my comment the wrong way.

"Two tweenies judging me, I can't wait." This time I make my sarcasm apparent.

"You'll be fine. They're just kids. You've raised two of your own. What are you worried about?"

I say nothing, mainly because I don't want him to know that the nearly thirteen-year-old girls I've come across in my time are far from kids. Who am I to shatter his illusions regarding his baby girl?

"Boys are very different to girls, Gabe, especially at that age."

He kisses the top of my head. "Ren?"

"What?"

"She's gonna love her bedroom, she's gonna love that you did that for her, you're gonna be good."

Before I can say any more, my phone rings from inside the house, and he releases me to go and answer it.

It rings off but rings again instantly. I answer without even looking at the caller ID.

"Hello."

"Hey, Lauren. It's Karen McAlister. How are you?"

My stomach does a backflip, and my heart rate picks up as I close my eyes and hope that this call is *everything* I hope it is.

"I'm good. How can I help you?"

"Sorry for calling you on a Sunday, but I only had your old number, and it's taken me a few days to find this new one on your website."

"No worries," I tell her.

"So, we've just purchased a place up at Red Hill, and I was wondering how you were fixed to work your magic and fix up the interior for us?"

I fist pump the air. Karen's an old client I've worked for on a number of projects. Home's her and her husband purchased in Toorak and Brighton, and a couple of apartments in the city.

"How soon do you need the work carried out?" I ask, pretending I'm going to have to consider the job.

"We'd love to be able to host Christmas there this year. Sounds a long time, but the place needs a lot of work. It's not been touched since the seventies."

"How many rooms?"

"Six bedrooms, all with ensuites, kitchen, butler's pantry, laundry, dining, four living, a couple of powder rooms, entryway, plus games, and a separate cinema room. We'd like you to design for all of them."

"I can do that. When can I take a look?"

"I can send you the link to have a look through online, and I can meet you up there tomorrow afternoon if you're free?"

"Let me just check my diary." I cringe as I lie through my teeth. I don't want to ask Gabe for a lift while she's on the phone, but I also don't want to assume he'll be free to take me. Fuck it, I'll hire a car if I have to.

Switching back to bullshit mode, I lick my lips and straighten my back.

"I can do two o'clock?"

"That'll be perfect. I'll text you the address along with the link."

"Too easy," I reply.

"Look forward to seeing you, Lauren. Thanks, and sorry again."

"See you tomorrow, Karen."

After dancing around the kitchen for a few seconds. I hook my phone's Bluetooth up to Gabe's speakers and hit play on my music.

Grabbing a bottle of wine from the fridge and two glasses from the cupboard, I dance my way out to the deck.

I haven't had time to sort my music into separate playlists since I got my new phone, and it's not until I step outside that I realise the first song up is White Christmas.

"Bing fucking Crosby?" Gabe turns and laughs at me.

"Oi, leave my taste in music alone. I like White Christmas; it reminds me of England." I pout my bottom lip before deciding I'm too happy and switch it to a grin.

"What?" Gabe questions.

"I got a job," I announce.

"A design job?" he asks, taking the wine glasses out of my hands. I fill each one before putting the bottle on the table.

"No, a pole-dancing job at Kitties in the city. They've taken me on for their new Thursday night special feature 'Forty and Flabulous'," I tell him with an eye roll. His eyes narrow on me, he gives a head shake and laughs.

"Yes, darling. A design job. An old client has bought a big new place up at Red Hill, wants it ready to host Christmas there this year."

"Well done, excellent news."

"Only snag is, she wants me to do a walk-through with her tomorrow at two. Any chance I could borrow your car or get a lift?"

He holds his glass up to mine and we knock them together.

"Depends," he says.

"On what?" I don't mean to let my smile falter, but I panic that he's got other plans and I should've checked with him first.

"On whether you're going to let me take you out for a late lunch today to celebrate."

"I think I can manage that."

"Then we're all set. Well done, you clever girl, I'm proud of you." Reaching out, he laces his fingers through mine and pulls me in for a kiss.

"How long is it gonna take you to get ready?"

"Not long. I only washed my hair last night, and I've already showered this morning."

"Good. That means we have time to fuck before we leave," he says with his mouth pressed to mine.

"That means I'll need another shower."

"I'll fuck you in the shower then. Problem solved."

"Problem solved," I agree.

CHAPTER 27

Gabe

I'M STRUGGLING to keep my eyes on the road as Lauren gasps for air, tears rolling down her cheeks as she almost chokes with laughter in the passenger seat next to me.

"We've literally gone from Carole King to Eminem, to Neil Diamond, to Tinie Tempah, to Luther Vandross, and now The Clash. Your taste is… I can't even think of a word," I tell her.

Finally managing to compose herself, she draws in a few deep breaths and grins at me.

"Eclectic?" she offers.

I smile back at her, not just because that word pretty much sums up everything about Lauren, not just her taste in music, but because it's the first time I've ever seen her this chilled, relaxed, and apparently happy. I know the bottle of wine we shared over lunch, along with the Espresso Martini she chose instead of dessert has loosened her up a little, but I'm not lying when I say I hope I've played a part in making her laugh and smile the way she is right now.

We're driving back home on a sunny Sunday afternoon, and she's hooked her phone up to my car's Bluetooth system and has been playing her music through it.

"Isn't that the point of creating a playlist? It's uniquely yours, you can add every single one of your favourites, whatever the era or genre."

Still dazzling me with her smile, she shrugs. "I like what I like."

"That include me?" I slice my gaze from the road to her, then back to the road again.

"You know it does," she replies quietly. Reaching out, she rests her hand palm up on the centre console and I take it in mine and give it a squeeze.

It hits me then how comfortable being with her is. Despite the situation, all the reasons behind us being here together, it feels right. And even though nothing about it *has* been, it feels easy. Being with her feels easy like it's exactly where I'm supposed to be, and everything my brothers have told me over the years about meeting *'The One,'* I'm now finally getting it.

I can't explain the attraction. Probably couldn't if my life depended on it, but it's there. I like having her in my bed every night, being able to text her every day, knowing that she'll be there when I get home from work.

It's been just over a month that I've had her in my life, and she has pretty much flipped it on its head.

Her lack of confidence in herself, her self-doubts and insecurities frustrate the fuck out of me. Her quick wit, sense of humour, smart mouth and sass have me shaking my head and chuckling simultaneously, and her smile makes my day brighter. All of that, combined with her sexy little body has my dick constantly hard, but nothing so far has had my gut twisting the way it is right now.

"Thanks for today. Not just today, the whole weekend, the past six weeks. Everything," she says from where she sits beside me.

I can feel her eyes burning into the side of my head and face, but I keep staring straight ahead, giving her hand a squeeze and a small nod to acknowledge that I've heard what she's saying.

"When everything was going on, when Jay was at his worst, I never thought I'd have this again. I didn't think I'd want it. I've never thought all men are the same, but I just thought I'd be done, have nothing left. . ." She trails off, and I finally look at her, but she's now staring straight ahead.

"Am I making sense?" Her eyes finally meet mine as she asks. I raise both our hands to my mouth and kiss the back of hers.

"Kinda," I tell her honestly. "My circumstances were. . . are, a lot different to yours, but I've spent most of my adult life thinking I'd never have something like this, and until you, it didn't matter. I didn't get what I was missing out on."

"What happened to make you think that?"

"That's not a story to tell you while I'm driving," I reply without looking at her. Grateful for the song change as an excuse for a subject change, I use the controls on my steering wheel to turn up the volume on Life House as they start to sing about the First Time. Smiling, I gesture with my head towards my truck's sound system just as I slow and pull off the road and wait for the gates to open at the front of our drive.

Instead of pulling up to the house, I remain stationary and turn to look at her.

"I'm taking a big fucking chance, letting you inside," she says, letting me know that she gets the song lyrics and why I turned them up.

"Total honesty, Ren. I've no clue what I'm doing, and I'm scared to fucking death," I respond.

"Total honesty, Gabe. Neither have I."

"You think we'll work it out?"

She shakes her head, making my heart freefall into my stomach.

"I honestly don't know. A year ago, I thought I had my life worked out. Two months ago, I celebrated twenty-four years of marriage dodging a glass of bourbon that had been thrown at me and having my arm twisted so far up my back, I thought it was going to snap, but even then, right in the midst of all that, I never could've imagined or predicted what was to come, and never, *not ever*, did I foresee you."

She blinks, and the tears she's fiercely been holding on to finally escape down her cheeks.

"At no time ever did I plan on you, and yet here we are. Never will I assume or expect anything again," she adds.

Without letting go of her hand, I move the car onto the drive and park outside the house.

Turning off the engine, we sit in silence for a few seconds before Ren speaks.

"I want to know." I know exactly what she's talking about, but I'm not sure she's ready for the answer.

"I want to know what happened to you that made you think you wouldn't ever have this. You know all about me and why I'm so fucked up, but I feel like I'm missing something with you."

"I don't think you're ready," I tell her, kissing the back of her hand to ease the blow of my words. "I know I promised total honesty, and you will get that from me, but I think right now is too soon."

I watch as she undoes her seatbelt and turns in her seat to face me.

"You've seen me at my worst. Beaten black and blue and at my most vulnerable. You've witnessed me throwing up in a sink and held my hair when I did it on the side of the road. You've held me tight when I've cried in the middle of the night, even when I've tried to fight you off after the nightmares I've had about my husband coming back to finish what he started. And after all of that, you don't think I'm ready to know *your* story?"

I know by her tone that I've pissed her off. Taking off my seatbelt, I let out a long sigh.

"What happened to you *happened to you*. My story's different. You were helpless to stop what your husband did. . . I. . . fuck." I don't know how to explain this to her *without* explaining it to her, without telling her everything.

"You don't know me well enough yet. When you know me better. . ."

"So you can know all of my humiliating, dirty little secrets, let me sleep in your bed, bury your tongue inside me, but I can't know? Ya know what? It's fine. Total honesty you said, so how's this for some total honesty? You're full of shit."

Before I can respond, she pushes the passenger door open, slides out of my truck, then uses two hands to slam the door shut.

"Fuck!" I tilt my head towards the interior roof and shout while squeezing my eyes shut. When I open them and turn towards the front door, I expect to see Lauren standing there waiting for me to let her in. She's not.

When I look around, I find her inside the pool fence, the pool cover winding back while Lauren's pulling off her clothes.

"What the fuck?" I question as I climb out of my truck. "What the fuck are you doing?" I shout again as I approach her. Without a word, she steps off the side and straight under the water wearing just her underwear.

Despite the sunny skies, it's after four in the afternoon in mid-July. It's mid-winter, and Melbourne's coldest time of year. Thankfully, since having the pool cleaned, I've had the solar kicking over, but we've had barely any sun this week, so the water will be freezing.

Reaching the edge, I stare down at where Lauren jumped in,

but she comes up in the middle of the pool and takes in a loud gulp of air.

"It's fucking freezing in there. What the fuck is wrong with you?"

"Fuck off," she shouts before going back under. Coming up this time at the other end of the pool, about the farthest part away from me.

"Get. The. Fuck. Out of there, Ren," I shout as I march around to where she is. Still gasping for breath, she goes back under before I can reach her, this time, coming up treading water right in the middle of the pool.

"Frustrated much?" she shouts. "Sucks big fat hairy balls when something's out of your control, doesn't it? When someone won't do as you ask and there's nothing you can do to make them? Well, suck it up, buttercup, and welcome to my fucking world."

"Ya know what? You wanna act like a child, stay there. Freeze. I don't give a fuck." Sounding a lot calmer than I feel, I shout out to her as I walk back towards the pool fence gate.

"I'm the child? You can't have a discussion about events in your life that have made you the way you are, but I'm the fucking child? I think it's you that needs to grow the fuck up, Gabe. This is how adult relationships work. It's called communication, and guess what? It's a two-way thing."

She throws my own words back at me from a week ago, and on the inside, I lose my shit.

Reaching the outdoor furniture that sits in front of my pool house, rage and frustration hit me like it hasn't done in years. I kick the first chair I come to, sending it crashing into the fence. I pick the next one up and throw it. It bounces off the table I aim it at before hitting the tiled floor.

I walk to the edge of the pool and snarl down at where Lauren now stands in the shallow end. "You want total. . ." I'm stopped dead in my tracks as she flinches and steps away from me. I take in her wide eyes, the way her chest moves up and down and her mouth hangs open as she draws in breaths.

"Ren," I say quietly, reaching out with my hand. The water splashes as she ducks and backs further away from me.

"No," I straighten and call after her. "No, no, no. Baby, please. I would never. . ."

She pulls herself up the steps and out of the pool, arms wrapped around her as she moves to the sun lounger where she left her clothes.

"Babe, listen to me. . ." I stop both talking and moving towards her when she holds up her hand to me.

"Stay—Stay over there," she pants out.

I want to believe she's cold and that's what's making her body shake and her jaw tremble, but I know, I fucking know what I've done.

"Shit," I hiss, but stay back, watching on helplessly as she fights to pull the blouse, she'd looked so gorgeous in as we laughed our way through lunch earlier, over her wet body. Sticking to her skin, it rolls and bunches at her back. She senses the movement as I instinctively step forward to help her.

She lets out a small sob that guts me as she cowers and steps away from me. I shake my head.

"Let me help you. I'd never hurt you, not ever. You know that, Ren, you fucking know that."

Holding her phone, jeans, and ankle boots against her, she turns to look at me. Her brows are raised, eyes still wide and I can see her entire body physically shake.

"Please, just let me in the house to get my stuff, and I'll leave. I just need to get some—some things." She sobs out the last two words.

"I'm sorry. I'm so fucking sorry," I tell her as I follow her to the front door. She doesn't reply, instead, she steps to the side, giving me a wide birth so I can open it for her.

Pushing at the door, I move out of the way.

"I'll go," I tell her. "You stay here. Go up and shower. Warm yourself up. I'm gonna go. I'll stay at my brother's tonight. You stay here, and we'll talk tomorrow."

When I give her the space to move past me, she's shaking her head but doesn't say anything.

"You've nowhere to go, Ren. Please. . . Look. . ." I take my house key off my keyring and throw it into the hallway. "I won't come back tonight, I promise. I'll call you tomorrow, and we'll talk, but please, please don't leave."

I watch as she walks inside, bends and picks up the key, gripping it in her hand as she holds it to her chest.

"Please, Ren. Please don't go," I repeat. She stands there, hair and body dripping wet and vibrating with fear as she gives me a small nod.

"I'm so sorry," I repeat before climbing back into my truck, pulling out of my drive and onto the esplanade.

* * *

PALMS PRESSED against the frame surrounding Cooper's door, I wait for someone to open it. When it finally swings back, it's Jess I come face to face with. She smiles, opens her mouth to say something then closes it when her eyes meet mine. Once she's done a top-to-toe scan and sees that I'm not physically hurt, she steps aside.

"What happened?" she asks quietly.

I don't move from the doorway.

"Coop," she calls before stepping closer to me. "What happened, Gabe?"

"I fucked up," I squeeze out around the ball of guilt and self-loathing lodged in my chest and throat.

Staring down at the floor, I feel too ashamed to look Jess in the eye and admit what I did. Her hand brushes the side of my face, her warm palm remains there, and that's when I feel the tears burn the backs of my eyes.

"Dude, what happened? You okay?" I hear my brother ask. I swallow a couple of times, then let out a long-held breath before looking up and meeting both their eyes.

Instead of talking, I shake my head.

"Get in here," Cooper orders as he hooks his arm over my shoulder and pulls me into the house. Steering me towards his den, I hear Jess call out, "Is this a beer or bourbon kind of fuck up?"

"He can't even talk, Jess. I'm guessing bourbon."

Jess is already behind the bar pouring our drinks when I sit down on a stool in front of her. Cooper sits down next to me.

My sister-in-law pushes a half-filled glass towards each of us and leaves the bottle on the bar as she starts to walk away.

"Stay?" I request. "I don't know how I'm gonna fix this, I'm gonna need all the help I can get."

"Sure."

With her lips pressed together tightly, she gives a small smile and a quick nod. Moving back around the bar, I watch as she pours herself a glass of wine.

"Fuck me, what did you do, little brother?"

I knock back the entire contents of my glass without even bothering to add ice. The warmth hits my belly, and I savour it for a few long moments before meeting my brother's concerned brown eyes.

"I lost my shit and threw a chair," I admit.

"What?" Jess and Cooper ask in unison.

"I scared the fucking life out of her."

"You did this in front of Lauren," Jess asks. "The woman who's just left her violent husband?"

The hot sting of shameful tears hits the back of my eyes again as I nod.

"Where the fuck is she now? What did she do?" Jess continues to question.

"At my place. She wanted to leave, but I told her to stay and I left."

"You left her on her own?" Jess snaps out.

I nod, remorse causing the bourbon in my belly to bubble like acid.

"Mate," my brother says with a headshake. "What the fuck? Why'd you kick the chair?"

I snort out a laugh.

"We were talking about how good things are between us, how blown away we both are at finding what we have."

Jess adds ice to my glass before topping it up. This time adding only half the amount she did earlier.

"It's good, ya know?" I admit. "Like what you said in the pub the night I met her, you don't know why, you don't know what it is, but it's there. It's not going away, and there's nothing you can do about it."

"You said all that?" Jess asks Coop with a soft smile.

"Babe, like you don't know how it is," my brother responds.

"Carry on," Jess orders, still grinning at my brother.

My eyes dart between the two of them, and I want to punch myself in the head knowing how badly I've fucked up my chance of ever having something like this with Lauren.

"She asked me why I've never let anyone in before," I explain with a shrug. "I refused to go into details, and she cracked it when I wouldn't tell her."

"She cracked it, or she was hurt?" Jess asks.

"Hurt?" I question.

"Hurt, Gabe." Looking from me to Coop, she continues, "Didn't you tell me he saw her straight after her husband hit her when she was still beat black and blue?"

"I did," I answer for him. "I saw her the very next night, that's when I took her back to mine."

"So you've seen her at her worst, at her most vulnerable, and you couldn't share with her why you're the way you are, what you've been through? So yeah, she was hurt. I thought you really liked this woman?"

"I do, a lot. And what happened with me is different."

"It's not what happened *with* you, Gabe, it's what happened *to* you. Why do you still not accept this?"

I rake my fingers through my hair and close my eyes.

"I fucked up," I mumble.

"Damn straight you did. You held back like you always do, refused to share with her, then you behave just like her ex, get angry and start throwing furniture about, terrifying the poor girl, and just to make sure the jobs well done, you fuck off and leave her on her own," Jess doesn't hold back as she lists my fuck ups.

"You definitely fucked up," my brother agrees.

"You think I should've stayed? She was pissed off and scared, I thought it'd be better if I left. I didn't want her going somewhere her husband might find her."

"Yes, you should've stayed. You should've stayed and shared with her exactly what's gone on in your life to make you so closed off to the idea of a relationship," Jess tells me.

"It's too soon. What if it changed her mind about me? What if she thought it was my fault or that I instigated it? She already thinks I'm a dog. She saw girls coming up to me in the bar when we first met, then Alysa called while we were in the car the other day and asked to hook up."

I watch Cooper close his eyes and give a head shake of his own.

"Gabe, you have never, not once, turned up at our door asking for relationship advice, so the fact that you've done that today, tells me you like this woman, right?"

"I think that's blatantly fucking obvious, Jess," I bite back.

"Mate, watch yourself. Don't talk to her like that coz you've fucked up. Now settle down and listen to me." I grind my teeth together, waiting for the lecture I'm about to receive from my eldest brother.

"Relationships are about putting yourself out there. They're about taking a chance on someone else. Handing over your heart, and saying, there ya go, that's yours now, look after it. It sounds to me like she's giving you all of that. I know it's early days and you've kinda been thrown together, but I also know *you*, probably better than anyone. I've never seen you so turned inside out by a woman."

He pauses and we stare at each other. I feel a nerve tick in my jaw because I'm tensing it so hard. Breathing heavily out of my nose, I stand and start to pace while waiting for him to continue.

"It's a two-way thing. You can't take all that from her and expect her to put all her faith in you if you're not gonna give her anything back, even if it does mean risking everything."

"But what if I fucking lose her? Once it's out there, there's no taking it back," I throw my arms out to the side and shout.

"But what if you fucking don't?" Cooper shouts in response.

With my hands to my hips, I stand and stare at my brother. His long legs stretched out in front of him, crossed at the ankles, arms folded over his chest as he rests his arse on a stool and stares right back at me.

"What if telling her is the start of the best thing that's ever happened to you?"

"What if it's not? I don't know that I'm ready to risk losing her," I admit quietly.

"Then you don't deserve to keep her. It's gonna come out, Gabe, she'll find out, and she'll be devastated that you didn't tell her."

"You got your phone with you?" Jess asks.

"Yeah?" I reply, confused.

"Text and ask her if she's okay. Apologise, then ask if she's comfortable with you going back there and talking. If she says yes, I'll run you home."

I finish my drink, use Coop's bathroom, then I text Lauren.

I'm so sorry Ren. You doing ok? X

I wait. Fifteen minutes later I get a reply.

Trunk

I'm still staring at my phone, trying to work out what she means, when the next text comes through.

DURNK

Then the next.

FFS

Followed by:

Drunk

"Great," I announce to my brother and sister-in-law. "I'm here pouring my guts out, and she's at home getting pissed."

"Good girl," Jess says with a smile. "You better let me get you home and sort this shit. She sounds like my kind of girl, I wanna be able to get drunk with her one of these days."

I want that. I want my family to know her, for her to know them, and as much as it scares the shit out of me, I know what I need to do to make that happen.

"You'll love her," I tell Jess, not caring even a little bit that my brother is hearing all of this. "She's as funny as fuck, can't sing to save her life, dunks her toast in her coffee, has the best comebacks, and is miserable in the mornings. . ."

"But instead of crying over today's events, she got drunk. My kind of girl," Jess says.

"She probably cried *and* got drunk."

"Still my kinda girl."

* * *

COOPER DRIVES my car back to my place; Jess follows behind in hers. Luckily, she has a spare key to my place on her car keys because I get no response when I knock at the door. When I make my way upstairs, I find an empty wine bottle on the kitchen bench, a half-empty bottle of vodka on the bedside table, and a passed-out Lauren in my bed.

She's makeup-free, damp hair piled on her head and already in her pyjamas. Even with her eyes closed, I can see she's been crying. The pile of tissues on the bed next to her add another twist to the knot of guilt in my gut.

Sitting beside her, the adrenaline rush that had been with me since I left, finally fades and a wave of tiredness hits me.

I have a site meeting in the city at seven tomorrow, then brunch with a client. I promised Lauren I'd be back here in time to give her a lift to Red Hill for her 2 o'clock client walk-through. It's doable, but it's not going to give us any time to talk until tomorrow evening.

I'd rather we get our shit sorted now, but, knowing that's not going to happen, I take a quick shower and climb into bed beside Lauren.

I stare at the ceiling unable to sleep with the day's events replaying on a loop through my head.

My brother and Jess are right, if I want to keep her, I need to take a chance, put myself out there, and tell her my truths.

Feeling absolutely terrified for what's to come, I finally fall asleep.

When my alarm wakes me in the morning, it's still dark outside, and Lauren is still sleeping. The only good thing about the last part of yesterday, is that as soon as I climbed into bed, she wrapped herself around me, and before I can climb out of it this morning, I have to gently untangle her arms and legs from over me.

CHAPTER 28

Lauren

Keeping my eyes closed, I listen to Gabe move around the bedroom. I didn't hear him come home last night, but I woke a couple of times and felt his presence.

After a mostly great day, yesterday ended spectacularly badly. I behaved like a brat. Gabe, in turn, behaved like an absolute dick and scared the crap out of me. I know it wasn't intentional, and I still truly believe he would never hurt me, but right at that moment, his level of anger freaked me out, and I just needed to get away from him. I'm not sure how I feel about all of that. Our argument seems petty in the cold light of day, and yet, he still lost his shit to a level that he was throwing furniture around.

For my part, I behaved the way that I did out of pure frustration. Wine followed by an Espresso Martini also egged me on from the side lines. Neither of them is any excuse for my behaviour, but I'm so over Gabe constantly banging on about how I frustrate him when he just wasn't getting how he made *me* feel yesterday.

I appreciate it's still early days between us, but he already knows so much about me. He's explained the circumstances surrounding his marriage. Still, I've always felt there's something else, some kind of trauma or event that happened in his past. Whenever I get close to asking him to share, he steers the conversation away and onto a different subject, usually switching it all back to being about me.

I smell the clean, fresh scent of him before I feel his body sit gently on the bed next to me. Keeping my eyes closed, I enjoy the soothing sensation of his fingers brushing my hair from my face. After my shower, I'd piled it on top of my head, and after drinking myself into oblivion, climbed into bed with it wet last night. His touch feels good but does nothing to ease the pounding headache I've woken up with.

He leans in and kisses my temple, and I open my eyes to meet the dark blue of his looking right at me.

His hand stills, his eyes trail a cautious path over my face before settling back on mine.

"I'm sorry," he whispers.

"I know. I'm sorry too." I reach out and wrap my arms around his neck and pull him into me. He exhales slowly. I can feel the tension leave his body right along with his breath. I hold him against me and breathe him in.

"I'm creasing your shirt," I finally say as I try to pull away.

"I don't care, I've got twenty others, but I have to get going."

He kisses my temple, then the top of my head.

"I'll be home around one to take you to your meeting. We need to talk, but it'll have to wait until after you get done with that."

I nod.

"Sometime this weekend, we need to go car shopping. If you're going to be working, then you're gonna need a car. . ."

"Gabe. . ." I start to sit up. After what happened yesterday, I don't want to start the day with another argument. He moves, allowing me to position my back against the headboard. My headache kicks up a notch and my stomach churns.

"Before you start throwing attitude, our cars and trucks are all loaned and leased through the business. We can claim some of it as a tax write-off. Jess and Sam both have cars purchased this way, and so will you. No arguments."

I narrow my eyes at him and shake my head. He ignores me.

"How's your head?" he asks instead.

"Banging," I admit.

"Not surprised, you smell like a brewery."

"Shit," I hiss, my hands instantly flying up to cup my mouth, and I attempt to breathe in my own breath through my nose.

"It's seeping through your pores, babe,' he says with a chuckle. "There's a bottle of water and a couple of pain killers there." He gestures to the bedside table with a lift of his chin. "Try and sleep it off. I'll give you a call a bit later whenever I get a chance."

He stands up, but then leans back in and gives me a quick peck on the lips.

"Drink your water, take your pills, and go back to sleep," he orders before turning and heading towards the door. He's wearing light grey suit trousers, which define his fine arse and long legs perfectly, and a pale blue shirt that stretches across his chest, arms, and back.

"You have the best arse," I call out.

He pauses in the doorway.

"Don't make me come back there and fuck the hangover out of you."

"I can think of worse cures."

"Fuck me, Ren, take your bloody pills, drink your water, and go back to sleep."

He leaves without looking back.

* * *

AFTER SLEEPING off the worst of my hangover, I use Gabe's computer to create a file for a virtual mood board and email it to myself, making sure that I can open it from my phone. I've not had time to order in or go and collect swatches and samples, but I want to have some way of showing Karen what my thoughts are so far.

I've only viewed the property online, so until I walk through and get a feel for the place, I don't want to pull too much together in case I'm way off with my thinking.

Making sure my phone is fully charged and I have my notepad and a couple of pens and pencils with me, I head downstairs and wait at the front door.

Gabe called earlier to say he was stuck in traffic and running late, and although my phone's telling me the property is only twenty minutes away, it's now one-thirty, and I'm worried I'm going to be late.

As much as I don't want to appear desperate—but let's face it, I've probably never been in a more desperate situation in my life—I need this job.

Not just for the money.

I need this job for me.

To get back to being the *me* I used to be, I need to work.

My nose tingles with the tears that are now close to the surface, and I draw in deep breaths in an attempt at calming myself down.

"You've got this," I say out loud while pacing at Gabe's front door.

The gate slides back, and relief washes over me as Gabe's

black truck pulls on to the drive. He pulls to a stop in front of where I'm standing, and I jump in.

"Hey," I greet Gabe with a smile and lean in and give him a kiss.

"Hey. You look gorgeous."

I look down at my outfit. I've gone smart casual and worn a loose-fitting cream coloured, cheesecloth maxi dress and paired it with a denim jacket and my brown cowboy boots. Rather than fight with my hair, I've plaited it across the back of my head, so it curves around my neck and hangs over my shoulder. It's kind of a boho meets mountain girl look and was inspired by the ideas I'm having for the property: Beachy Boho meets Colorado Log Cabin. It's not an official 'style' but one I think could work for this property, in this location.

"Thank you." I grin big and strap myself in. "You don't think it's too casual?"

"Nope, you can keep those boots on for me later," he says with a wink.

I shake my head, change my mind and nod. "I can do that. . . *after* we talk."

"After we talk," he agrees with a mumble. "What's the address?" As usual, he moves the subject along. Now's not the time to be getting into any of that with him, so I reel off the address, he types it into his Sat Nav, and we head off.

* * *

I ASK him how his meetings went this morning, but other than that, I'm quiet for most of the journey. Despite the painkillers and copious amount of water I've consumed today, I still have a dull headache and feel a little sick, although I could put that down to nerves. Gabe obviously assumes that's the reason for my lack of conversation.

"You've got this, Ren. No need to look so nervous," Gabe says as we approach the road the house sits on.

"Thanks, I'm not nervous, but I sort of am." I look at him and shrug as I speak.

He pulls into the sweeping in and out drive, and as soon as the property comes into view, my gut instantly tells me I was absolutely right with my concepts. My skin prickles with anticipation at seeing the inside, and it feels so good to be back doing the job that I love so very much.

"Can you stop the car please? I want to walk up and take it in."

Gabe pulls to a stop, and when I turn to look at him to say bye, his eyes are darting all over my face as he smiles.

The Cure's 'Just Like Heaven' plays quietly in the background, and when he doesn't say anything, I start to get paranoid.

"What?" I ask quietly. "Do I have lipstick on my teeth?" I flip the visor down and check in the mirror. Gabe reaches out and takes my hand.

"There's no lipstick anywhere it shouldn't be, you look beautiful. I just love watching you when you switch into design mode. You change, Ren. Honestly, it's like you become a different person, and I fucking love watching it."

He kisses the back of my hand, then he leans in and kisses my nose, and finally my lips.

"Go work your magic, baby, I have every faith this is the beginning of bigger and better things."

"Don't make me cry," I order as I slide out the cab.

"Call or text when you're done. I'm gonna go grab a coffee from a little place I know around the corner."

"Will do," I say without looking back at him as I close the door behind me.

I wait for Gabe's truck to pass me and exit the drive before I approach the timber, brick, and weatherboard double-storey house.

Standing on the steps in front of the double entryway doors, I look out at the sweeping views across Port Phillip Bay over to The You Yang's.

"Lauren, how are you?" I turn to see Karen standing in the doorway, looking as immaculate as ever.

"Thanks for driving up here at such short notice, come in, come in."

I follow her into a huge entryway. An exposed beamed vaulted ceiling is above me, a timber staircase to my right.

I take a deep breath in through my nose and close my eyes. A calmness settles over me as the scent of the house fills my senses. I don't get this with a new build, but with the older places I've worked on, as insane as it sounds, the house talks to me, kind of telling me what it'd like me to do.

"We only picked up the keys yesterday, and it's been empty for a while, so I apologise if it smells a little musty," Karen interrupts my moment and explains.

"It's fine, just breathing it in and getting a feel for the place."

She stares at me for a few long moments.

"How have you been, Lauren? It's been what, two years since you last worked on a project for us? Looks like you've lost some weight since last I saw you?"

I take her in as she talks, noting that she's her usual perfectly made-up self. Big dark hair, heavy makeup, designer clothes covering her curvy body.

She's in her mid-fifties and has obviously had a little work done, but it's subtle and she looks as beautiful as ever.

She's not someone you'd ever describe as cute or even pretty. She's beautiful in that Andi MacDowell, or Sandra Bullock kind of way.

Married to an Australian radio and television personality since forever, she can afford the best of everything, including property, clothes, and plastic surgeons, but nothing is ever overdone with Karen. From the properties I've styled to the clothes she wears, to the work she's had done to herself.

She screams 'I'm wealthy' in that way monied people often do, but it's not in your face, and it's always done with class.

"Yeah, I recently went through a marriage breakup, and there's nothing like the divorce diet to help drop a few kilos," I tell her honestly.

"Really? I'm so sorry, Lauren. I always thought you and Jason were so good together."

Jay's team had carried out the renovations on a number of Karen's properties in the past, and we'd had dinner with her and her husband Nick a couple of times.

I move across to the windows, take in the sun's position and estimate the amount of natural light the space would get as I work on my response.

"We were, and then we weren't, and now we're no longer together. Shit happens," I tell her with a shrug, but not telling her how recent all of this is or the reason it happened.

I like Karen. I wouldn't describe her as a friend, more a close acquaintance, but we'd shared stories and complained about our partners and kids when working together over the years, but I wasn't about to spill my guts any more than I had.

"That's a shame. I was actually going to ask you if Jason would be interested in the construction work we'll need doing to bring this place up to spec, but if it's going to make things awkward, we can use someone else?"

My role meant that I would occasionally cross paths and have to liaise with the tradies on a job, and as much as I would like to put the work Ryder's way, I did not want to run the risk of bumping into Jay at any time, but most definitely *not* on a job.

"I would really appreciate it if you used somebody else," I say. My eyes still taking in the view from the window. A thought occurs to me, and I turn around to face her. "Actually, there is another company I can recommend. I'll get them up here to give you a quote if you'd like?"

"That would be fantastic. I'm happy to work with anyone you recommend, but do you think they'd be able to fit us in? As I mentioned, we'd really like to be able to use this place by the summer."

"Well, why don't we have a walk around? I'll give my thoughts on exactly what I think needs doing, and then I'll make a call to my builder and see what we can work out?"

I'm not going to let her know just yet, that my 'builder' is Gabe, the man I'm living with, the man I moved in with on the same day I left my husband.

* * *

We walk through the property, I give her my ideas, show her the virtual mood board, and we discuss the order she'd like the rooms completed, the kitchen, family, and master bed and bath being priorities.

She gives me her thoughts on the colours and styles I've chosen, we make some changes, and I make lots of notes as I wander through, trying to get a feel for the place first before making any firm decisions, which is the way I've always worked.

When I'm close to being done, I go out to the pool area and call Gabe. He picks up on the first ring.

"Ren. You done?"

"Almost. Listen, my client needs a builder. It's not as big as your other jobs right now, but she's pretty high profile, and most of her reno's end up in Better Homes magazine, so could be lucrative."

"I'm on my way," he says without hesitation.

Wandering back inside, I find Karen on the phone in her

kitchen, so I head out to the front of the house and wait for Gabe.

My belly puts on an Olympic gold medal winning acrobatic floor show as I watch him climb out of his truck.

He's still wearing his suit trousers and shirt from this morning, but the sleeves are now rolled up to his elbows, forearms on show, stubble covering his jaw. He's undone an extra button at his neck, and dark hairs are visible at the base of his throat.

A triple salto is added to my insides' handsprings and backflips as he moves confidently towards me.

"How'd ya go?" he asks quietly, kissing my cheek and taking my hand.

"Good," I respond. "There's a lot of work, it's a big place, and some rooms haven't been touched since it was built in the seventies. I'd really like to keep some of that vibe. Kind of hippy, boho, meets log cabin type of feel," I talk as I pull him into the entryway.

We stop, and both stare up at the ceiling. Gabe whistles between his teeth.

"Sorry, Lauren. I had to take that. . ."

Silence.

"Karen, sorry. Gabe's the builder I was telling you about. He's local and was able to come straight up to take a look around."

Her eyes are on Gabe but slice to where our hands are joined. My fingers twitch as, for a split second, I think about letting go, but Gabe's grip is now so tight, I wouldn't be able to do that without making a scene.

I look from Karen to Gabe, confused for a moment as to why he's not introducing himself. Why the silence?

"Gabe," I almost whisper his name. "This is. . ."

"Gabe?" Karen interrupts my introduction.

They know each other?

Gabe turns his head towards me, and when his eyes meet

mine, he shakes it. It's so slow, so subtle, but it changes everything, making my own head spin.

"Karen, how are you?"

From where Gabe and I stand just inside the front door, I look to where she's still standing in the middle of the room. She's so still for so long, I start to think she didn't hear him.

My scalp begins to prickle, and my mouth has gone completely dry as realisation washes over me. I wonder if Karen's mouth has done the same as I watch her lick her lips, nod her head slightly and let out a short, sharp breath. In a heartbeat, it's gone. She pulls herself together and gives us both a perfectly composed smile.

But it's fake. It doesn't look fake. But I know, I *just know* it's fake.

"I'm good. Very good. I didn't realise you knew Lauren." Her eyes flash to where Gabe's still holding my hand before darting between me and him, then turning her back on us.

"Well, let's have a walk through the place, I'll tell you my thoughts, and you can tell me if it's doable," she calls out as she walks away from us.

I attempt to pull my hand from his, but Gabe's grip tightens as he leans in and whispers into my ear.

"Don't."

* * *

ALMOST TWO TORTUROUS HOURS LATER, we pull out of Karen's drive.

"We need. . ."

"You need to drive," I interrupt whatever he's going to say.

I've spent the last couple of hours going over in my head what I would say to him. I had it clear and concise, and now it's just a jumbled mess.

I can accept that he's had a past. He's thirty-five, he's been married, has a child, none of that is an issue for me. I can accept that he's only been interested in casual hook ups for most of his adult life. I've been confused but becoming convinced it was the truth as to why that's all changed, and he now wants to start something permanent with me.

But what I'm struggling with is if my suspicions are right, he has a past that involves Karen McAlister, and my brain is about to burst as I attempt to work out how and when that could've happened at a time Karen wasn't married.

"I was eighteen. . ."

"Just drive the fucking car, Gabe," I again interrupt him, not ready to hear what he has to say while I'm in such a confined space, one that puts me in such close proximity to him.

Adele's 'Someone Like You' plays quietly over the sound system, and I don't want to listen to that right now either. Leaning forward, I turn it off.

It's almost dark, and I stare out of the passenger window and out across the bay to where the city of Melbourne is just visible as it lights itself up for the evening.

Closing my eyes, I take in a few deep breaths and attempt to calm myself. I don't want to do what I usually do. I threw a tantrum just yesterday because he wouldn't talk to me, now he's trying to do exactly that, and I keep shutting him down.

"When we get back to yours, we'll talk," I tell him. "But right now, for the drive home, can we just be quiet? Can you give me that?"

"I don't want to, but I can."

"Good. Thank you."

We drive the rest of the way back to Gabe's in silence.

CHAPTER 29

Gabe

WE DON'T STAND A CHANCE.

I'm not a believer in fate, karma, or the universe conspiring, but if I did, I would have to assume that every fucking one of those was in action this afternoon. Coming together to put the nail in the coffin of any kind of hope I ever had of a future with Lauren.

Never when I walked in the front door of that fucking house did I think I would come face to face with a woman I fucked one hot summer seventeen years ago.

I don't know what the look on my face said as my eyes hit Karen's, realisation dawned, and bile filled my gut, probably the same expression of horror I saw painted on hers.

Lauren knew. Before either of us said a single word, I could hear the wheels and cogs turning in Lauren's head as she began working it out.

The drive home has been torture. She didn't want to hear me out, and I'm grateful for that. I'd rather be focused on Lauren and give her all of my attention as I explain not only Karen, but all of my other past fuck ups and indiscretions because what Lauren doesn't yet know is that Karen McAllister isn't the worst of it, not by a long fucking shot.

* * *

FORGETTING that Lauren still has my front door key, I watch as she's out of the car and letting herself in before I've even cut the engine.

I sit in my truck for a while, staring at the open front door and into my house—our house. At least it has been for a while, but now, fucked if I know.

Resolved to doing what I need to do, I let go of a sigh, I step outside, then into what might turn out to be the worst night of my life.

Lauren's in the bathroom when I get upstairs, so I give her the privacy she obviously needs, grab a beer from the fridge, and then take my cigarettes from where I hide them on the top of my fridge.

I don't smoke often these days, not since Ava was born, but every now and then, especially when I'm stressed, I'll smoke. And things don't get much more stressful than tonight's situation.

Heart crashing against my chest with each beat, I take my beer and cigarettes out onto the deck, lean up against the rail, and await my fate.

I don't have to wait long. Lauren comes and stands beside me. She's changed into a hoodie and a pair of leggings and has her own beer in her hand. She takes a swig from her bottle and joins me in staring out into the dark.

"We grew up with a certain level of wealth," I start, pausing to look at Lauren and work out if she's now willing to listen to what I have to say. She tips her bottle to her mouth, takes another large pull from it, but says nothing when she sets it down.

"You know how it is down here, it's a wealthy area and life is pretty sweet. We all had a good education, all went through private school, we went on overseas holidays; we had a lot of material things but no Mum."

I take a long chug on my beer and light up a cigarette.

"I was ten when she got sick, eleven when she died. I knew she was dying, but I was eleven for fuck's sake. I had no concept of the finality of death; I didn't get what forever meant."

Lauren shifts beside me, and I watch as she takes a cigarette from the box and lights it up. I've never seen her smoke, but the way she pulls on the toxic stick of nicotine and chemicals, she's obviously done it before.

"It was harder on my brothers. They were older, they got it and knew she was gone for good. To help my dad cope, they kept their heads down at school, got on with things, and worked for him on the weekends and during school holidays at the construction company he'd inherited from my Pops, my mum's dad."

I pause again, giving her a chance to ask questions but get nothing.

"Dad had worked for my Pop and married the boss's daughter. Nonna and Pop had no sons, so my dad took over running things. When Mum died, he just threw himself into work, wanting to make the business more successful, in her honour I suppose. To do that, he expected us to help. At first, I was just left at home to look after Dani, but he eventually put her into day care, and when I turned thirteen, he started letting me help out on site."

I put my cigarette out in the butt box and finish my beer.

"My brothers were doing the same but had already decided

by then that they didn't want a trade, they preferred to be in the office. Cooper's an architect but helps Dani with managing contracts and accounts. Zac's a draughtsman and doubles as a quantity surveyor, I prefer to be out on-site, so I project manage all of our Melbourne jobs."

"A real family business," she says. My head snapping towards her because she's finally said something.

"It is. I love it. We're all close, so that helps. But yeah, I love working with my brothers and Dan."

"That's nice. I'm glad that you've got that."

Relief almost knocks the wind out of me. She doesn't sound pissed off, so maybe I might stand a fucking chance here.

"Anyway, while we're still at school, college or uni, we were all expected to pull our weight and labour for the tradies during the holidays and weekends. Dad wanted us to know what hard work was all about and to be grateful for the dollars we earned. When I was eighteen, I was labouring for one of the bricklaying contractors that worked for us. They were renovating an old place in Glen Ira for some television personality."

"Nick McAlister," she states as she puts out her cigarette.

"Yeah. I'm gonna get another beer, you want one?"

"No, could you get me a bottle of water please."

"Of course."

I walk in and out of the house with my heart beating steadier and hope singing through my veins as I move.

Handing over Lauren's water, I continue.

"So, yeah. The couple are living in the house, we're putting a big extension on it for them, it's dry, and it's hot, and this particular day, we'd been cutting bricks, and I was orange. Hot, sweaty, and covered in brick dust."

I pause and turn and look at her. "I know it's no excuse, Ren, but at the time, there were a lot of rumours about McAlister having an affair with an intern at the television studio, and they'd paid her off or something, I can't remember all the facts, but I remember he was never home, and she was always there by herself. Anyway, the boss knocked off at two and left me to tidy up. About twenty minutes later, Karen comes out and asks if I want a cold drink, sees the state of me, asks if I wanted a shower."

I drain my second bottle of beer.

"You wanna hear the rest of this," I turn to Lauren and ask.

"Total honesty," she says without looking at me.

"I had a clean pair of boardies in my truck, so I went and got them, had a shower, put them on, walked out into the kitchen and she just came at me. Kissed me, hands straight inside my shorts."

"Did you fuck her?"

"Yeah, I fucked her. I was eighteen, Ren. She offered herself to me on a plate, so of course I fucked her."

"Once? More than once?"

My neck feels strange, the blood pumping through my veins there so hard and fast it feels like it's throbbing.

"We had a seven-month affair," I tell her.

"Gabe," she whispers as her hands come up and cover her face.

"It was sex, Lauren. There was zero emotional connection. I was eighteen and happy to be getting my dick wet on the regular, and she was just using me to get back at her husband. We'd meet up, we'd fuck, we'd leave. Sometimes we didn't even speak."

"But it was wrong, she was married."

"Yeah, *she* was married. I was eighteen and didn't give a fuck. I had nothing to feel guilty about."

"You didn't feel bad for her husband?"

"No, I fucking never. He'd been caught banging a twenty-one-year-old intern, and apparently it wasn't the first time."

I watch as she shakes her head, but still doesn't look at me.

"You want something stronger than water now, coz I fucking do?"

"No," is all I get as I head back in and pour myself a large bourbon.

Taking the bottle back outside, Lauren has turned and is watching my approach.

"How'd it end?" she asks.

I shake my head. I will tell her; I just don't want to. I pull a chair out from the table and sit in it, beckoning Lauren over to sit on my knee as I do. She rolls her eyes."It got weird," I admit. "I started at college, lost interest, and just didn't turn up at the motel we used to meet at anymore. She then started showing up outside my college. She didn't approach me, just sat there in her car watching me, following me home. Then she started leaving notes on my car. I ignored them. I walked out of the pub with a girl one night, and she was there, my truck keyed all down each side, her leaning against it. She took one look at the girl I was with and flew at her."

I watch as Lauren's eyes widen, and she opens her mouth to speak a couple of times but changes her mind.

"I had to make threats," I tell her with a shrug. "Told her if she didn't leave me alone, I'd not only tell my dad, but I'd also tell her husband. Aside from on the telly or in newspapers, online, or wherever, today's the first time I've seen her since."

Lauren lets out a long slow breath, I refill my glass, enjoying the buzz from the beer and the bourbon.

Pulling the scrunchy out of her hair, I watch as it falls around her shoulders and she massages her scalp with her fingertips.

"Come and sit with me," I hold my hand out and ask.

"No, don't do that. Don't tell me all of that, then get me to sit on your lap so you can say all the right things instead of answering my questions."

"What questions have you got? I'll answer all of them."

"I don't know. You had an affair with an older woman, a married older woman. I'm not your first. Is there a pattern? Are there others?"

My eyes meet hers over the top of my glass, and I couldn't hate myself anymore in that moment.

"No," she whispers, and I jerk as her legs start to buckle. Her hand shoots out to stop me moving to her, and I relax back in my chair. Only I'm not relaxed, I'm anything but relaxed.

Her shoulders start to shake, but I remain in my seat. She lets out a sob, but I don't go to her. Her hand comes up to cover her mouth and tears roll down her cheeks and all I do is watch her break.

"I'm not special. I'm just stupid. I—I thought—I'd started to believe—to think that I meant something."

"You mean everything," I whisper. "Out of all of them, you're the only one that has meant anything, and *that* anything is everything."

"Liar!" she leans forward and grits through her teeth. "You're a fucking liar. How can I believe anything that comes out of your mouth?"

"What did I lie about, Ren? You asked, I told you. Total honesty, remember?"

"You said you'd never hurt me," she whispers.

"My past is ugly. I can't give you the honesty without giving you the hurt, babe. You want me to lie to save you from that, then I am more than fucking happy to oblige. But I can't change the past and make it into something it wasn't, something pretty, something that won't hurt you. If I could, it'd already be done."

She closes her eyes, wraps her arms around her middle, and looks as broken as she did the first night I brought her here.

"How many?" she asks, eyes still closed.

"How many what?"

"Others?" she opens her eyes and pierces with a stare.

I have to close mine against the ugliness of what I'm about to share.

"Just one," I admit.

"Older? Married? Both?"

"Ren. . ."

"Total. Fucking. Honesty. Gabe," she leans in again and shouts.

I empty the contents of my glass, and I give her all the honesty she'll ever likely be able to handle.

"You want it, here it fucking is. When I was fifteen, the woman my dad is now married to used to sneak into my bedroom and suck my dick. How's that, Ren? How's that for honesty? While I cried, she'd stroke me until I got hard, and I tried, believe me, Ren, I fucking tried not to let that happen."

"Gabe," she whispers my name and steps towards me, but now it's me that doesn't want to be touched.

"No." Pushing back from the chair, I stand up and point at her. "No, you wanted this, and now you're gonna listen. She fucked me up, Ren. Told me she'd tell my dad I'd made a pass at her. He was happy, for the first time since my mum died, he was happy. *So I said nothing.*"

I pace as I talk, attempting to fight off the need to vomit that accompanies this topic. No one outside my brothers, their wives, and my counsellor know about this. It happened twenty years ago, and it still does this to me.

"I let it happen. I got hard. I tried not to, but I was fifteen."

"Gabe," Lauren sobs out my name, looking and sounding more defeated now than I've ever seen her. She holds her arms out, and I move so fast, I crash into her.

"I tried not to come, I tried everything, but I couldn't stop it, and I felt so ashamed, I still feel ashamed. . ."

Her hands come to either side of my face, and she pulls it down into hers. My eyes dance across her features as I try to take in what she's feeling.

"No," she says fiercely. "Do not ever tell me you feel ashamed. You were a child. What she did was wrong. Far out. This is what you wouldn't tell me yesterday. This is why you got so angry."

I nod.

"I didn't know how you'd react," I admit. "I wasn't ready to lose you if you hated me."

"No." Her face contorts as she says the word and sobs. "No, Gabe, no."

She lets go of my face and puts her hands on top of her head and takes in a few deep breaths.

Feeling drained and relieved, I sit back down in the chair and watch Lauren pace the deck.

"I need to process this. I'm so fucking angry. I can't even. . . Gabe, just think for a minute, it's a horrible thought, but imagine a man doing that to Ava when she's fifteen, would you blame *her*? Would you think for even a second that it was *her* fault?"

"Fuck no."

"So why is it any different? Is that as far as it went? Did she do anything else?"

"She made me put my fingers inside her. I knew what I was doing, I'd done it to a couple of girls before. . ."

"Was it consensual?" she leans towards me and asks.

"Of course it fucking was."

"Exactly. Doing that was *their* choice, *your* choice, plus those girls were probably *your* age. She's a peodophile. There's no other word for it. She sexually abused a child. I'm not judging you in any way, but does your dad know now?"

"No," I admit.

"He had a heart attack just before I turned sixteen, so they decided to get married. I was going to say something then, but I was scared he'd have another heart attack, by the time I'd told anyone, they were married, and he'd had his second heart attack."

"I'm so sorry." She walks towards me as she speaks, curling herself into my lap, she wraps her arms around my neck and holds on.

"Who did you tell?" she asks into my chest.

"My brothers and their wives. They went fucking insane. Zac lost his mind; he still struggles with it now. I moved in with Cooper straight after. Like me, they were scared of saying anything to Dad because of his heart, but they threatened Jackie. They let her know that they knew."

"I can't believe the front of the woman, that she did that to you and then stayed around and married your dad."

"She's a cold-hearted bitch, she's there for the money and won't let anything get in the way of that."

"Great, can't wait to meet her."

I slide my hand up the back of her hoodie and brush my fingertips across her bare skin. Contentment and calmness settle over me, and so much fucking relief I can barely breathe. I pull her in tight and hold her there.

We sit for a while in silence, and I wait for the questions she'll no doubt have.

"How do you get on with your dad? I mean, I can't even imagine how. . . sorry, do you mind talking about this?" she eventually asks.

"I hate talking about it," I tell her honestly. "But if you've got questions, I'll answer them."

"Do you feel better now you've told me?" she ducks her head so she can look right into my eyes as she asks. I won't lie to her. I want her to know the truth.

"I wouldn't say I feel better that you know. Going back to your first question, I love my dad. He's a good man and I don't want you to judge him because of the woman he ended up married to."

"I'd never do that. That'd be like people judging me for Jay's behaviour."

I get the weirdest sensation in my gut as she speaks.

"I'm relieved. That's how I feel about you knowing. I don't feel better, but I'm relieved I'm not keeping it from you, relieved at your reaction, and relieved that you get what I mean about not judging my dad. When you meet Jackie, you'll understand why he fell for her. She's a chameleon. For him, she's the perfect wife, to me and my brother's, she's. . ."

"An abuser," Lauren cuts me off.

"Pretty much, yeah."

"There's no *pretty much,* Gabe. There's no grey area with this. How old is she?"

"About fifty-five, I think."

"So she was around thirty-five when it happened, your age. That's like you putting your hands on one of Ava's mates."

I close my eyes. I don't even know how to process that.

"Yeah," I say quietly. "It's because I'm a bloke, I just always assume that people won't see it that way," I admit.

"Who cares what people think? We know the truth; your brothers and their wives know the truth. Does your sister know?"

"No, Dani was only five when it happened. We've never told her."

"Your sister's ten years younger than you?"

I nod before broaching another topic I rarely discus. "Yeah. My mum miscarried twins when I was about five, the doctors told her no more babies, but she desperately wanted a girl. They tried for a couple of years, nothing happened, then when they'd given up, she fell pregnant."

"That's so sad. She waited all that time for a girl, and never got to see her grow up, to see any of you grow up."

"Yeah," is all I manage to squeeze out around the ball of emotion in my throat.

"This is a lot, Gabe. Not just what Jackie did, but losing your mum so young. Have you had counselling?"

"Yeah, my brothers arranged it, well, Jess, my sister-in-law did."

"Did it help?"

I let out a sigh as I consider my answer. I never talk about any of this to anyone, but Lauren makes it easy. I want her to know the truth. Like she's said, If I expect total honesty from her, I need to give her my own. And now she knows the worst, I want her to know it all.

"It did a bit. I think the thing I've never come to terms with, is how disappointed I think my mum would be in me."

"Gabe, no." Lauren's hand cups the side of my face as she holds it in place. Eyes on me, she shakes her head as she talks. "I know it's not a word you want to hear, and I know it's a word I've said I hate, but you were a victim, Gabe. . ."

"It's not just what happened with Jackie, it's the way I've lived the rest of my life. My marriage, the one-night stands."

"But that's all been influenced by what she did to you. If that hadn't happened, you might've worked things out with Lena, or maybe just never been in the position of getting her pregnant in the first place."

My eyes trail a path over every inch of Lauren's face. This fucking woman. She has me talking about things I never discuss and feeling things I've never felt. And I'm not sure what those feelings are. What I do know is, they terrify me.

I nod because I don't know what else to do. And then I kiss her.

"You took your boots off," I say against her mouth. Deciding that we need to move things along and away from all the heavy shit, I trail a path of kisses to her ear.

She lets out a long slow breath, I think it's because she's enjoying my kisses, but then she says, "Well, I was either going to end up throwing one at you, or kicking you in the nuts while wearing them, so I thought it better to take them off."

"Maybe now you're calmer and not acting like a crazy redheaded Essex bird, you might wanna put them back on?"

"Maybe later, I'm actually starving. I've not eaten all day."

"I could eat. Whadya fancy?" I ask.

"I really fancy fish and chips," she says against my neck, her hot breath breathing life back into my dick which had shrivelled up and been hiding for most of the afternoon.

"I've had too much to drink, Ren, I can't drive, and I don't know anywhere that delivers."

"I'll go," she adjusts her position, looks up at me, and says.

"You're gonna drive my truck?" I question.

"I can drive a truck, babe. Can drive anything. You were eight when I got my license remember, so don't even go there with that crap."

"Ooooh, and the Essex is back." That earns me an eye roll.

"Gimme your keys." She holds out her hand. "Whadya fancy?"

"You," I tell her as I slide my hand around and find her naked tit.

She wriggles out of my lap but continues to hold out her hand.

"They're in there on the bench." I gesture with my head. "Just get me fish and chips."

She leans in, I open my legs and wrap my arms around her waist, bringing her down and flush against me.

"These last two days have been a shit show," I look directly into her eyes and say. "But now you know it all."

She nods.

"Everyone has a past, Gabe, and now I know what's happened in *your* past, it'll hopefully help me better understand you in the future. I've still got things to process and overthink, that's just the way I am, but thank you for sharing it all with me, I know none of that could've been easy to talk about."

I shrug.

"I'd like to say you're welcome, but I hated every fucking minute of it," I admit.

"Well, you hated doing that about as much as I hate doing what I'm about to do."

Not knowing what she's about to say, I feel myself tense and my gut pulls up tight.

"What?" I question.

"I don't have any money to buy fish and chips with."

I close my eyes and shake my head.

"Fuck, woman, I thought you were gonna. . . never mind. Get your arse up, my wallets inside with my keys, just take the black card. Pin's 1204. Drive carefully, I'm gonna jump in the shower while you're gone."

I smack her arse as she walks away.

"You've got the best arse," I call out, mimicking her words from this morning. She flips me her middle finger without looking back, and I head inside chuckling all the way to the shower.

* * *

TEN MINUTES LATER, I grab a bottle of water from the fridge and head back outside to wait for Lauren. Opening the water, I drink half the contents. As I'm screwing on the lid, I realise my truck is still on the drive.

"Ren?" I call out in confusion.

Turning around so fast, I catch my leg on the table.

"Fuck," I hiss out as I move through the family room and down the stairs. My front door's wide open, and laying on the floor in front of it, is Ren.

CHAPTER 30

Lauren

I STEP out of Gabe's front door and move towards his truck. Pain explodes in the side of my head, then again at my jaw—the second blow causing my legs to give way. I hit the floor, but before I can get out a scream or any other kind of sound, another blow is delivered to my belly, knocking the wind entirely out of me.

Like a boxer in a ring, I fight it. The pain, the nausea, the inability to breathe, and the black spots dancing in front of my eyes. I fight them all and keep trying to get up. A boot stamps down hard on my fingers, and that's when I vomit. I'm not sure if I'm pushed or kicked to my back, but a bright light shines down on me, my vision so blurred I'm not sure if it's the moon or a streetlight.

There's a whooshing sound rushing through my ears, pain

radiates throughout my entire body from a place I can't quite pinpoint, and I still can't get a breath in.

I hear a scuff of boots beside my head and hope with everything in me, Gabe has heard the commotion and come down to investigate.

Jay's face comes into focus, and I whimper as that hope is lost.

He spits in my face, and without even bothering to wipe at it, I attempt to curl away from him. Grabbing my hair and my shoulder, he pulls me back toward him and holds me in place.

"Who the fuck do you think you are?"

His grip on my hair tightens, and he jerks my head back so he can get right up in my face. Pressing his forehead against mine, he lets go of the back of my head and forces it into the stone step I'm lying on.

"You're a cunt. A dirty, dried up, washed up, useless, fat cunt."

This time it's his hand that comes up and squeezes my cheeks so hard, my teeth cut into them.

"And see him upstairs? He likes cunts. The dirtier, the filthier, the better. Didn't know he was into old cunt, but he's probably running out of options to stick his cock in around here."

He backhands me and blood explodes out of my nose, spraying both of us. I see stars again.

"Look at you? Why the fuck did I stay around so long? I should've left years ago, but I'm done now, fucking done. Just stay away from my house, you hear me? Next time you think you and that prick can just waltz in and take what you like, think on, coz I will hunt you down, and I will kill the fucking pair of you."

He backhands the opposite side of my face, twice as hard as the first time and I start to feel myself drifting. Instinct again takes over, I roll onto my belly, but before I can start to crawl away, another blow comes to the back of my head, and again I curl onto my side and into the foetal position as I try to protect myself.

"Go, Lauren," he hisses. "Crawl back up there to him." He grabs me by my hair and drags me forward.

"Fucking crawl, cunt."

As best I can, I start to drag myself back towards the front door.

"Gabe," I call out on a wheeze.

"Gabe," Jason mimics. "Fucking Gabe. That prick needs a reminder of who you fucking belong to."

Right before the blow comes to my temple, he pisses all over me.

END OF PART ONE

PRE ORDER BOOK TWO
LOVING WILD
HERE:
https://books2read.com/u/m2lzak

READ THE PROLOGUE HERE:

Gabe.

Turning off my wipers, I watch the rain trail a path down my windscreen. It's falling so hard my view is instantly blurred. Despite the downpour, I climb out of my truck and walk to the edge of the viewing platform. The usual view of Port Philip Bay hidden by the low cloud. Up this high, I'm amongst them. Grey and heavy, I feel those clouds right down to my very soul.
The wind whips the cold rain against my face as I tilt it towards the sky. Raising my arms, I lace my fingers and place them on top of my head, opening myself up to the icy lashes. I'm not wearing a jacket, and my long-sleeved T-shirt is instantly soaked.

"What do I do, Mum?" I ask the clouds. "He came to our house, to our home. I was there, but I didn't protect her."

Thunder rumbles, the sound echoing across the bay, the rain falling harder as the storm grows closer.

"When she told me what he'd done to her, I ran. Instead of being a fucking man, I ran, and I fucked it all up. . . Sorry for swearing. I'm sorry."

Wiping the rain from my face with the back of my hand, I stare out at the grey nothing.

This hurts. The ache in my chest and gut a physical reminder of how badly I've fucked up.

"I didn't lie, but I didn't tell her the truth either. Then I lost my temper, and now she's gone, and I don't know what to do. What do I do?"

Lacing my fingers together, I press my hands into the top of my head and tilt it towards the clouds.

The driving rain stings my skin as lightning forks across the sky, the crack of thunder sounding instantly now that the storm is directly above us . . . but from my mum, nothing.

Silence.

24 HOUR DOMESTIC VIOLENCE HELP LINES:

Aus: 1800 737 732
UK: 0808 2000 247
US: 1 800 799 7233 / 1 800 787 3224
CAN: 1 855 242 3310

FOR OTHER BOOKS BY LESLEY JONES

. . .

GO TO HER WEBSITE: lesleyjoneswrites.com

KEEP UP TO DATE HERE: NEWS LETTER SIGN UP

SOCIALS:
FB READER GROUP: LESLEY JONES BOOKBAR

INSTA: Lesley Jones Writes

TIK TOK: Lesley Jones Writes

CARNAGE BOOK ONE THE STORY OF US

I was swinging upside down by my knees on the monkey bars in our back garden the first time I met him. My best friend, Jimmie, and I were hanging facing each other, eating pop rocks, and singing what we thought was a stellar rendition of "Liza Radley" by The Jam, at the top of our voices. We'd heard my big brother, Bailey, listening to the B side of the twelve-inch version of the single "Start" the week before. He said that he liked it better than the A side, and he'd been playing it nonstop for the last few days, so we'd been listening to it and had learnt the words.

Jimmie was in love with each and every one of my three big brothers. She was convinced that if she knew the words to their favourite songs, they'd notice her. I couldn't say I blamed her. They were all very good looking. Jimmie just hadn't decided which of the three she was going to marry yet. Lennon probably wasn't really an option as he was already sixteen, and we were, after all, only eleven. Bailey, my eldest brother, was eighteen, so that pretty much ruled him out, too. So as far as I was concerned, it had to be Marley. The brother closest in age to me

that she was going to marry, and I was pretty sure, it was his legs I could see approaching us from the back of our house.
"George, I can see your knickers. Get the fuck up, will ya?"
Yep, that was Marls. I had no idea why he was moaning though. He usually loved seeing Jimmie's knickers. In fact, I'd heard him *beg* to look at her knickers in the past. Then I saw them, the other pair of legs following Marley up the garden path towards us.
Monkey Boots?
Whoever was approaching was wearing Monkey Boots. I loved Monkey Boots! They were already on my Christmas list for that year, despite the fact that it was only August.
A very loud wolf whistle interrupted my thoughts. I'd heard boys do this before. My dad and my brothers did it to me when they knew I was all dressed up for a special occasion, and my dad did it to my mum every time she came down the stairs dressed and ready for the day—it always made me so happy that he did. But this whistle did something to me I didn't quite understand. It sent feelings through me that landed in places I'd only just realised I had. That sound woke something in my body I never even knew was sleeping.
Jimmie and I swung up at the same time, grabbed the bars by our hands, and dropped to the floor. I was pretty sure we were in complete synchronisation and looked like a pair of Olympic gymnasts. We turned to Marley, took a bow, and then collapsed into each other, giggling like the pair of preteen girls we were. I looked back towards Marls who wasn't laughing. He was, in fact, glaring at the pair of us. I tipped my head back and emptied what was left of my packet of pop rocks in my mouth, letting the tiny, orange shards explode all over my tongue.
I looked back towards my brother, waiting for the popping to stop in my mouth so I could give him some attitude about the shitty look on his face when my world suddenly stopped turning. It stuttered for a few seconds and then restarted, erratically,

matching the rhythm of the candy exploding inside my mouth. But when I swallowed, the explosions didn't stop. They went down into my chest and on into my stomach, settling uncomfortably low down in my belly. And for some strange reason, the sensation caused my brain to cease its connection to my mouth, leaving me devoid of speech.

I was eleven years old, but I knew without a shadow of a doubt I was staring into the eyes of the boy I was going to love forever. Big, brown eyes locked onto mine from over Marley's shoulder. He stared at me for a little too long, and then his eyes moved down my body and locked onto my chest. Yeah, I was eleven at the time, but two years before I'd started to develop boobs and was already wearing a size B cup. Most of my friends were jealous of me, but I hated it. Everything began to change when my boobs grew. The boys treated me differently. They knocked on my bedroom door instead of just barging in, and they never came into the bathroom anymore for long chats like the ones we used to have while I soaked in an overly full bubble bath. They never pinned me down and tickle tortured me anymore either.

Then, the year before, I had gotten my first period, and things got worse. We lived in a nice house on a nice street in a nice area. I'd always been allowed to play out late because my brothers were always around to look out for me. We were a large group of about twenty kids. Both boys and girls, varying from age ten to about fifteen. It was harmless, innocent, and sexless fun. We would hang out on the bench at the corner, at the park across the road, or down at the little row of shops a street away. Up until I had gotten my period, nobody asked whom, in particular, I was going out with or who else would be there, because as long as one of my brothers were around, I was fine to go where I liked and with whom I liked.

But getting my period changed everything. I felt interrogated with questions. Where are you going? Who's going to be there?

Will there be boys? That was all they seemed to want to know—whether there'd be boys involved in anything that I was doing outside of our house. At the time, I didn't get it. It never occurred to me that at such a young age I could potentially get pregnant.

My dad wasn't home much, so it was my brothers who dished out the discipline. My mum was around, but she left it to the boys to tell me off if I'd gotten home late or couldn't be found at one of my usual hangouts when they came looking for me. This was usually Bailey or Lennon, as I gave Marley too much shit. I didn't understand why he should be the one telling me what to do. He was only thirteen himself and not yet an adult. Funnily enough, Marley was the strictest of all my brothers.

I stood, staring at the boy with my brother, and the new love of my life. Forget Adam Ant, he had nothing on the boy who stood in front of me, the boy, who was so very obviously looking at my boobs.

"Sean, this is my sister George and her mate, Jimmie," Marley introduced us.

Sean laughed before speaking, "I thought I was gonna meet some more brothers when you said, 'Let's go and see George and Jimmie,' not a pair of girls with red and pink knickers on."

"My name's Jamie and hers is Georgia, but everyone calls us Jimmie and George," Jimmie stated confidently to the new kid, my future husband.

I folded my arms across my chest, which was entirely the wrong move as it just made my boobs look bigger and it drew Sean's eyes straight back to them.

"Show us your tits." He gestured with his chin towards me.

It's a wonder I didn't disappear in a puff of smoke.

Poof! Gone! I was so embarrassed. Even my hair felt like it was blushing.

"Fuck off, Maca. She's my little sister, and she's only eleven."

I wanted to punch Marley at that moment. It might have been

true, I *was* only eleven, but as far as my naive, immature self was concerned, I knew it all. In my head, I was, in fact, already a woman. I had boobs and I had periods. I'd yet to develop curves or any kind of an arse, but that would come. So basically, yeah, as far as I was concerned, I had enough going on to qualify as 'a woman'.

But the truth was, I was eleven, and oh how little did I understand just how much growing up I still had to do.

THANK YOU'S . . .

What a year!

Thank you everyone for sticking with me after the delay in getting this book published.

For those of you that don't know, after coming out of a very long lockdown in Melbourne, I stupidly fell and broke my wrist, nose, toe and teeth! A major life lesson was learned and I will never again run in slides!

So for those of you who had your preorder cancelled, after I missed my publication date, thank you for having enough faith in either preordering again, or simply buying the book on release, I will do my utmost to *not* break anything that will result in the delay of Book Two in this series.

To all of you in the Book Bar, thank you for keeping me inspired and allowing me to vent at my frustrations. I love our random conversations, which are rarely about books, you are appreciated by me more than you will ever know.

Special thanks to all of my admin team who keep things ticking over when I'm not around, to Lisa my editor, Tiff my cover designer and Wander for the fantastic image, all of whom it's been a pleasure to work with.

Stay safe out there everyone, and see you soon for Book Two.

Printed in Great Britain
by Amazon

58511499R10195